Nebula Award Stories Sixteen

NEBULA
AWARD STORIES
SIXTEEN

Edited by Jerry Pournelle

Associate Editor John F. Carr

c.1

HOLT, RINEHART AND WINSTON   NEW YORK

S
NEBULA

Introduction by Jerry E. Pournelle. Copyright © 1982 by Jerry E.
Pournelle. Published by permission of the author and the author's agent,
Blassingame, McCauley & Wood.
Published by Holt, Rinehart and Winston, 383 Madison Avenue,
New York, New York 10017.
Published simultaneously in Canada by Holt, Rinehart and Winston of
Canada, Limited.

ISSN 0731-6690
ISBN 0-03-059787-0

FIRST EDITION

Designer: *Lucy Castelluccio*
Printed in the United States of America
10 9 8 7 6 5 4 3 2 1

"Grotto of the Dancing Deer" by Clifford D. Simak. Appeared in
Analog Science Fiction/Science Fact, April 1980. Copyright © 1980 by
Condé Nast Publications, Inc. Reprinted by permission of the author.
"Why Is There So Little Science in Literature?" by Gregory Benford.
Copyright © 1981 by Gregory Benford. Printed by special
arrangement with the author.
"Ginungagap" by Michael Swanwick. Copyright © 1980 by *TriQuarterly*.
From *TriQuarterly 49*, Fall of 1980. Reprinted by permission
of the author and his agent, Virginia Kidd.
"The Unicorn Tapestry" by Suzy McKee Charnas. Copyright © 1980
by Suzy McKee Charnas. First published in *New Dimensions 11*.
Reprinted by permission of the author and
the author's agent, Virginia Kidd.
"1980: Whatever Weirdness Lingers" by Michael Glyer. Copyright ©
1981 by Michael Glyer. Published by arrangement with the author.
"Rautavaara's Case" by Philip K. Dick. Copyright © 1980 by
Omni Publications International. Reprinted by permission of the
author and his agents, Scott Meredith Literary Agency, Inc.,
845 Third Avenue, New York, New York 10022.
"1980: The Year in Fantastic Films" by Bill Warren. Copyright © 1981
by Bill Warren. Printed here by arrangement with the author.
"The Ugly Chickens" by Howard Waldrop. Copyright © by Terry Carr.
First appeared in *Universe 10*, Doubleday & Co., 1980.
Used by permission of the author.
"What Did 1980 Mean?" by Algis Budrys. Copyright © 1981 by
Algis Budrys. Published by special arrangement with the author.
"Secrets of the Heart" by Charles L. Grant. Copyright © 1980
by Charles L. Grant. First published in the March 1980 issue
of *The Magazine of Fantasy and Science Fiction*.
Reprinted by permission of the author.

For John W. Campbell, Jr.
who created us—

Contents

NEBULA AWARD STORIES SIXTEEN

Introduction

Jerry Pournelle

The paperback racks are full of science fiction, which has displaced a good part of the other categories. Once found only in specialty bookstores (or very large paperback stores), science fiction is now ubiquitous: in drugstores and airports, and even right up near the checkout stand in supermarkets.

Recently there were four science fiction works on the *Publishers Weekly* best-seller lists.

Commercially, we've arrived.

As I sat down to do this introduction, I got a phone call asking me to participate on a panel at the 1981 World Convention. The panel isn't unique; it's one of the "where are we going from here?" discussions among several editors and writers, the kind of thing we do (quite literally) in our sleep, but it got me to thinking, because the call was from an editor of a science fiction magazine.

We have just gone through the greatest boom in SF history. When I first started in this business, *everyone* in it was starving. Well, nearly everyone. Mr. Heinlein made a comfortable income, and there were one or two others who didn't do badly; but most full-time science fiction writers ate split-pea soup and their wives made their own clothing. Then came the boom years of the seventies, and they really did boom; and so did some careers. It wasn't predictable: some writers hit it lucky and some didn't, and there didn't seem to be any pattern to who won and who lost. Mainly, though, all of us won.

Except—when the seventies ended, the SF magazines had about the same circulation as when they began, and with the exception of the slick science fact/fiction *Omni*, that doesn't look likely to change—worse, the prestigious magazines *Galaxy* and *If*, as well as some promising newcomers, have vanished.

Why is this? What happened that kept them from cashing in on the big boom?

When John W. Campbell, Jr., was editor of *Astounding Science Fiction* during the first golden age, he cultivated writers. He gave them story ideas. He read their stories and pointed out flaws. More: he'd read a story, and think about it, and suggest that the writer scrap most of the story and concentrate on some interesting little detail that only John saw the value of. . . .

And he groomed newcomers. I know; I was John Campbell's last discovery. When he died, the *Analog* files were full of my stories—so many that when his assistant, Miss Tarrant, began putting *Analog* out from John's inventory (she never did buy anything on her own initiative), they had to run some of my best work under a pseudonym to avoid having my name repeated too often.

It took me *years* to sell a story to John Campbell. The interesting part is that I kept trying. I kept sending him stories, because he encouraged me to. He didn't like what I wrote; but he thought he would, someday, if only I kept it up. When he returned my stories, he sent long letters with them: letters filled with advice and fulminations and ideas and concepts. Then one day I didn't get back a letter, only a check. It was almost a disappointment. . . .

Campbell groomed a lot of writers, with the result that

they learned their craft before leaping off to write books. Of course, John helped his magazine that way. He had to. The magazines depended on a steady supply of incoming talent, because their rates were very low. Science fiction magazines evolved from pulps, not from slicks.

My late friend Stuart Cloete (*Rags of Glory, Turning Wheels,* etc.) told me that in 1948 *The Saturday Evening Post* paid him $4,200 for a single short story. Those were times when a good secretary earned thirty dollars a week; $4,200 was wealth indeed, equivalent to considerably more than many publishing houses pay young writers for a novel nowadays. The *Post* could afford to do that, back then.

By 1970, there were few "mainstream" short-story markets; but the SF markets were intact, largely due to the work of editors like John Campbell and Horace Gold—men who knew they *had* to groom the beginning writers, find and encourage talent, work and plead and wheedle and . . .

It was traditional; you read science fiction (particularly the magazines, which I discovered in high school) and you thought about it, and one day you said to yourself, "I can write a story as good as *that,*" and maybe one day you tried it. For most, that was as far as it got, but some did send in their stories, and a few of those got encouraging letters, and kept trying; and one day they sold one. Many quit then; it was all they'd ever wanted to do. But others found the experience stimulating and tried again and again; and if they kept at it, and were any good, they sold to the magazines, and moved from the back pages to the covers, and after that they tried a novel.

It was a traditional route, and it worked; but it depended, more than we knew, on editors like Campbell and Gold.

But now it's 1981, and Mr. Campbell is dead, and Horace Gold has retired (well, almost; last weekend he told me of a new project he's working on!); and no one has come forward to replace them. Maybe no one can. John Campbell loved this field, and worked for an insultingly small salary rather than leave his post at *Analog. But for whatever reason, there are few magazine editors working closely with new writers.*

One exception to that rule is my editorial associate, John Carr. We have done five or six anthologies together. One of John's duties is to read unsolicited submissions. He doesn't get to work with very many new writers, because we don't buy many original stories; but more than once we've received stories that aren't good enough to publish—one was plain awful—but which show unmistakable signs of talent. They must be rejected, of course, but I've watched John Carr write nine-page encouraging letters. . . .

One result of John's editorial work was that a writer got a cover illustration for his first published story. I wish that could happen more often; but we can't do it, and not many others seem to be interested in trying.

And that, I think, is what happened to the magazines: the editors who made them are no longer with us, and there have been few replacements. The magazines have a problem in boom years: as fast as SF writers become known, they're offered book contracts, and books are more lucrative than short fiction. Campbell could keep authors because they felt personal loyalty to their mentor; but that relationship doesn't exist so much now.

Moreover, just as writers can't afford to do much short fiction, editors generally can't afford to stay with the kind of magazines that buy unsolicited stories. One of the best of the new editors, Jim Baen, talked his book publishing house into starting a magazine just so that he would have new authors to work with; but that folded when Jim left to go to another publisher.

Yet without the magazines and their editors, where are the newcomers to learn their craft: to learn how to sell their work, to learn that academic acclaim is all very well, but it doesn't always put roast beef on the table. . . .

I'm fortunate. I got into this field at the right time, having served an apprenticeship under its greatest editor. I can only wish others luck that good. But I'm not sure how to arrange it.

This is a strange field. I'm editing the Nebula Awards volume, and there's almost no chance that I'll ever win a Nebula. There's a fair chance that when I'm old and gray they'll vote me a Grand Master, but I doubt I'll ever write a story that wins. (I'm not alone; Grand Master Robert Heinlein has never received a story Nebula either.)

It's traditional for the Nebula editor to write about science fiction as literature, but I can't do that. I don't know much about literature. True, I've got academic degrees, but except for four compulsory "core courses" in humanities in my freshman year, I've had nothing to do with academic literature or creative writing.

In fact, I worry about science fiction as literature.

Some years ago, when I was president of Science Fiction Writers of America (I was elected president the year I joined, because they needed someone with business and management experience), I attended an awards ceremony at an academic institution. As part of the afternoon there was a literary seminar, held in a big hall with the kind of blackboard that pulls down from the ceiling like a window shade. In the middle of the discussion, someone activated the mechanism to lower the blackboard, and there, for all to see, was written in great block letters:

GET SCIENCE FICTION OUT OF THE CLASSROOM
AND BACK IN THE GUTTER WHERE IT BELONGS.

Harry Harrison had arranged that, but it's my sentiment exactly. I was fortunate to take "Masterpieces of English Literature" from a man named Carstairs, who had the right idea about how to teach *Hamlet*. He had the good sense to tell us that in Act One the King is going to go drink beer and shoot cannon—and not to worry about symbolism. I have also been unfortunate enough to hear an academician analyze my psyche through examining my choice of character names—which is hilarious, since I get the names of minor characters by glancing up at my bookshelves and using combinations of authors' names. . . .

I don't worry a lot about critics. I do worry about my readers. Especially those in airports and dentists' waiting rooms. Robert Heinlein once said that writers are professional gamblers. He also said that we write for "Joe's beer money—and old Joe likes his beer." That remark can be misinterpreted, but I take it to mean that no one *has* to buy science fiction any more than one *has* to buy beer; we're competing for entertainment money, not the food budget. And that, of course, is the reason for my fear of academia's embrace: not much entertains when it's being *studied.*

This doesn't mean that science fiction writers shouldn't try to change people's lives. We can, we should, and we do. I go to most of the big space events, such as the gatherings at the Jet Propulsion Labs during the *Voyager* encounters with Jupiter and Saturn, and I'm often struck by just how many of the scientists were guided into their career choices by science fiction—indeed, if you eliminated all those who studied high school algebra because of Robert Heinlein's novels, we might not have a space program!

We do more than recruit. We warn, through dark visions of what may happen if certain trends continue; and we prepare our readers for the future. Science fiction, through books and films, made the public aware that space travel was possible; thus John Kennedy's announcement of a moon landing by 1970 was greeted as bold leadership, not dementia praecox.

For some of us, that's the bottom line. Whatever our place in literature, we have a place in history; for we are preparing the way to the stars. As my friend and partner Larry Niven once put it, we save civilization and make a little money.

It's no small vision.

The Science Fiction Writers of America sprang from the genuine needs of SF writers. SFWA was originally intended to be something less than a labor union, but considerably more than a social club; and its principal concerns were contracts and royalty rates and other such tiresome matters of vital interest to authors.

Another objective was somehow to raise the prestige of science fiction: to gain acceptance by critics and persuade influential papers and magazines to publish serious reviews of the best SF. To that end were the Nebula Awards born. This was to be the science fiction that the writers themselves recognized as the best of the year. Given that head start, perhaps others would also pay attention.

Alas, it didn't take long for the awards to become "controversial." There were accusations of lobbying and vote-swapping. Writers were accused of voting without reading all the contenders; other writers were castigated because they never voted at all. Each year's Nebula Awards Ceremony saw one or another writer walk out in disagreement with the rules. Each year's annual meeting saw introduced a resolution abolishing the awards.

But each year, SFWA voted to keep the awards while tinkering with the rules to make them more fair. And despite all the controversy, it became obvious that the Nebula Awards were valuable: that for the most part they really did go to stories that were very good indeed; and that critics and reviewers for the most part did indeed take them seriously. The Nebulae, it seemed, more than served their intended purpose.

The Nebula winners volumes, by tradition, contain the winning short story, novelette, and novella—and whatever else the current editor wants to include. There have always been additional stories, sometimes chosen to be representative of the year, sometimes chosen purely because the editor liked them. In addition, there is usually a critical essay on the year in science fiction.

This volume continues the older traditions, and adds some new ones: a survey of SF films, a commentary by a leading fan writer, an essay by the novel award winner. John Carr and I have enjoyed working on it.

Grotto of the Dancing Deer

Clifford D. Simak

*Cliff Simak has long been acknowledged a master of short
stories. He was elected the third Grand Master by the Science
Fiction Writers of America.*

*He's also a good man to know. I never met anyone who
knows Cliff Simak and doesn't like him; I think this story will
tell why.*

*The late Richard McKenna once described a meeting of sci-
ence fiction writers as a trappers' reunion. Only those who have
shared the experience of The Great Alone can be part of the
brotherhood; and conversely, no matter how much they may
disagree, those who have worked the trap lines are members of
the order, and thus entitled to certain privileges.*

*The analogy isn't perfect, but it has its points. That was
made clear to me some years ago when I first met Cliff Simak.
The occasion was a meeting of the Science Fiction Research
Association (SFRA) in State College, Pennsylvania. SFRA is
an organization of academics: of those who teach science fiction or otherwise have professional academic dealings with the
stuff. Their meetings are relatively formal, with presentations
of papers; at least this one was.*

I was there representing the Science Fiction Writers of America (SFWA; SFRA was formed after SFWA), with an unpleasant message to deliver concerning royalties, namely that, unlike academics, we writers were not so eager to be published as to forgo our portion of the revenue from textbooks in which our works would appear, and we wanted the same pro rata *shares from academic works as we got from trade books. It wasn't a popular message.*

Most of the papers at that meeting were given by critics and scholars. There were academics who also write: I recall Dr. James Gunn, Dr. Phil Klass who writes as William Tenn, and Dr. Jack Williamson. And there were quite a few non-doctored writers: Gordon R. Dickson, John Brunner, Ben Bova, Theodore Sturgeon, and Cliff Simak come to mind. There was also a Famous Literary Critic, who boasted, during his speech, (1) that he was writing a science fiction novel, and (2) of his friendship with "Chuck" Delany. . . .

There was nothing for it but to throw a party for the writers and their friends. Not many of us had special friends, so most of the writers came alone; but there was present at the conference one very lovely young lady who had caught Gordy Dickson's eye. He wanted to meet her, but was unaccountably unable to introduce himself and invite her to the party; so I ended up bringing her (my wife and I had known her for several years).

Unfortunately, although uninvited, the Famous Literary Critic also showed up. He immediately enthroned himself in the most conspicuous part of the room, so that the rest of us, seated mostly on the floor, seemed to do him homage; and from the throne he proceeded to deliver pontifical statements about science fiction, while consuming everything alcoholic that came within two meters of his chair.

In consequence, the party broke into two pieces: the writers, who went to another room; and the academics, who remained to hang on every word of the Famous Critic. It was a delightful party. Our host was a young Ph.D. candidate from Jamaica,

who had ample quantities of a rum punch with secret ingre-
dients; Ted Sturgeon, a onetime merchant seaman who had
plied the Islands and was thus considered an expert on rum
drinks, pronounced it excellent. And all would have ended
peacefully, except that as we were saying our farewells to the
host, the Famous Critic, now thoroughly lubricated, decided to
pinch the young lady who had captivated Gordy Dickson.

There was an instant crisis. This creature really was a Famous Critic; he actually had published reviews of science fiction in really important publications, and this in a time when
all of the mainstream review sections seemed to have conspired
to ignore SF entirely. He was grossly overweight, helplessly
drunk, a thorough boor in imminent danger of having Gordy's
ample fist in his eye.

Now Gordy had plenty of provocation, and his strike would
have been just, but it would have been a disaster for the SF
profession; we really needed those reviews. . . .

I could restrain Gordon—for a moment—but how could we
distract the Famous Critic?

To the rescue came Cliff Simak. As I took Gordy's arm, Cliff
came smoothly between them and engaged the Famous Critic
in some inane discussion about Freudianism in Ted Sturgeon's
writings. I hustled Gordy and the lady out the door to repair to
a nearby watering hole for a nightcap. Cliff joined us a few
moments later, having packed the Famous Critic, completely
unaware of how near he had come to disaster, into a taxi. And
lo, in the morning, the Famous Critic sported a hangover
worthy of preservation in bronze; so justice was served. . . .

And thus did Simak prove that he knows real people, not just
those of his own creation (real as they are). . . .

Cliff Simak has been a full-time newspaper reporter and editor
for forty years. You'd think he wouldn't have time to write
fiction, but in fact he has a larger body of work than most full-
time writers.

He has explained that. He once said that you can write

whole novels, even if you have only ten or fifteen minutes a day to write. Just use the time you have. Every page written gets you closer to publication. And so, one page at a time, Cliff has accumulated an impressive bibliography and a large collection of awards, including a well-deserved Nebula for "Grotto of the Dancing Deer," a timeless story that would have been welcome in any year.

Luis was playing his pipe when Boyd climbed the steep path that led up to the cave. There was no need to visit the cave again; all the work was done, mapping, measuring, photographing, extracting all possible information from the site. Not only the paintings, although the paintings were the important part of it. Also there had been the animal bones, charred, and the still remaining charcoal of the fire in which they had been charred; the small store of natural earths from which the pigments used by the painters had been compounded—a cache of valuable components, perhaps hidden by an artist who, for some reason that could not now be guessed, had been unable to use them; the atrophied human hand, severed at the wrist (why had it been severed and, once severed, left there to be found by men thirty millennia removed?); the lamp formed out of a chunk of sandstone, hollowed to accommodate a wad of moss, the hollow filled with fat, the moss serving as a wick to give light to those who painted. All these and many other things, Boyd thought with some satisfaction; Gavarnie had turned out to be, possibly because of the sophisticated scientific methods of investigation that had been brought to bear, the most significant cave painting site ever studied—perhaps not as spectacular, in some ways, as Lascaux, but far more productive in the data obtained.

No need to visit the cave again, and yet there was a reason—the nagging feeling that he had passed something up, that in the rush and his concentration on the other work, he had forgotten something. It had made small impression on him at the time, but now, thinking back on it, he was becoming more and more inclined to believe it might have importance. The whole thing probably was a product of his imagination, he told himself. Once he saw it again (if, indeed, he could find it again, if it were not a product of retrospective worry), it might prove to be nothing at all, simply an impression that had popped up to nag him.

So here he was again, climbing the steep path, geologist's hammer swinging at his belt, large flashlight clutched in hand, listening to the piping of Luis who perched on a small terrace, just below the mouth of the cave, a post he had occupied through all the time the work was going on. Luis had camped there in his tent through all kinds of weather, cooking on a camper's stove, serving as self-appointed watchdog, on alert against intruders, although there had been few intruders other than the occasional curious tourist who had heard of the project and tramped miles out of the way to see it. The villagers in the valley below had been no trouble; they couldn't have cared less about what was happening on the slope above them.

Luis was no stranger to Boyd; ten years before, he had shown up at the rock shelter project some fifty miles distant and there had stayed through two seasons of digging. The rock shelter had not proved as productive as Boyd initially had hoped, although it had shed some new light on the Azilian culture, the tag-end of the great Western European prehistoric groups. Taken on as a common laborer, Luis had proved an apt pupil and as the work went on had been given greater responsibility. A week after the work had started at Gavarnie, he had shown up again.

"I heard you were here," he'd said. "What do you have for me?"

As he came around a sharp bend in the trail, Boyd saw him, sitting crosslegged in front of the weatherbeaten tent, holding the primitive pipe to his lips, piping away.

That was exactly what it was—piping. Whatever music came out of the pipe was primitive and elemental. Scarcely music, although Boyd would admit that he knew nothing of music. Four notes—would it be four notes? he wondered. A hollow bone with an elongated slot as a mouthpiece, two drilled holes for stops.

Once he had asked Luis about it. "I've never seen anything like it," he had said. Luis had told him, "You don't see many of them. In remote villages here and there, hidden away in the mountains."

Boyd left the path and walked across the grassy terrace, sat down beside Luis, who took down the pipe and laid it in his lap.

"I thought you were gone," Luis said. "The others left a couple of days ago."

"Back for one last look," said Boyd.

"You are reluctant to leave it?"

"Yes, I suppose I am."

Below them the valley spread out in autumn browns and tans, the small river a silver ribbon in the sunlight, the red roofs of the village a splash of color beside the river.

"It's nice up here," said Boyd. "Time and time again, I catch myself trying to imagine what it might have been like at the time the paintings were done. Not much different than it is now, perhaps. The mountains would be unchanged. There'd have been no fields in the valley, but it probably would have been natural pasture. A few trees here and there, but not too many of them. Good hunting. There'd have been grass for the grazing animals. I have even tried to figure out where the people would've camped. My guess would be where the village is now."

He looked around at Luis. The man still sat upon the grass, the pipe resting in his lap. He was smiling quietly, as if he might be smiling to himself. The small black beret sat squarely on his head, his tanned face was round and smooth, the black hair close-clipped, the blue shirt open at the throat. A young man, strong, not a wrinkle on his face.

"You love your work," said Luis.

"I'm devoted to it. So are you, Luis," Boyd said.

"It's not my work."

"Your work or not," said Boyd, "you do it well. Would you like to go with me? One last look around."

"I need to run an errand in the village."

"I thought I'd find you gone," said Boyd. "I was surprised to hear your pipe."

"I'll go soon," said Luis. "Another day or two. No reason to stay but, like you, I like this place. I have no place to go, no one needing me. Nothing's lost by staying a few more days."

"As long as you like," said Boyd. "The place is yours. Before too long, the government will be setting up a care-taker arrangement, but the government moves with due deliberation."

"Then I may not see you again," said Luis.

"I took a couple of days to drive down to Roncesvalles," said Boyd. "That's the place where the Gascons slaughtered Charlemagne's rear guard in 778."

"I've heard of the place," said Luis.

"I'd always wanted to see it. Never had the time. The Charlemagne chapel is in ruins, but I am told masses are still said in the village chapel for the dead paladins. When I returned from the trip, I couldn't resist the urge to see the cave again."

"I am glad of that," said Luis. "May I be impertinent?"

"You're never impertinent," said Boyd.

"Before you go, could we break bread once more together? Tonight, perhaps. I'll prepare an omelet."

Boyd hesitated, gagging down a suggestion that Luis dine with him. Then he said, "I'd be delighted, Luis. I'll bring a bottle of good wine."

Holding the flashlight centered on the rock wall, Boyd bent to examine the rock more closely. He had not imagined it; he had been right. Here, in this particular spot, the rock was not solid. It was broken into several pieces, but with the several pieces flush with the rest of the wall. Only by chance could the break have been spotted. Had he not been looking directly at it, watching for it as he swept the light across the wall, he would have missed it. It was strange, he thought, that someone else, during the time they had been working in the cave, had not found it. There'd not been much that they'd missed.

He held his breath, feeling a little foolish at the holding of it, for, after all, it might mean nothing. Frost cracks, perhaps, although he knew that he was wrong. It would be unusual to find frost cracks here.

He took the hammer out of his belt, and holding the flashlight in one hand, trained on the spot, he forced the chisel end of the hammer into one of the cracks. The edge went in easily. He pried gently and the crack widened. Under more pressure, the piece of rock moved out. He laid down the hammer and flash, seized the slab of rock, and pulled it free. Beneath it were two other slabs and they both came free as easily as the first. There were others as well and he also took them out. Kneeling on the floor of the cave, he directed the light into the fissure that he had uncovered.

Big enough for a man to crawl into, but at the prospect he remained for the moment undecided. Alone, he'd be taking a chance to do it. If something happened, if he should get stuck, if a fragment of rock should shift and pin him or fall upon him, there'd be no rescue. Or probably no rescue in time to save him. Luis would come back to the camp and wait for him, but should he fail to make an appearance, Luis more than likely would take it as a rebuke for impertinence, or an American's callous disregard of him. It would never occur to him that Boyd might be trapped in the cave.

Still, it was his last chance. Tomorrow he'd have to drive to Paris to catch his plane. And this whole thing was intriguing; it was not something to be ignored. The fissure must have some significance; otherwise, why should it have been walled up so carefully? Who, he wondered, would have walled it up? No one, certainly, in recent times. Anyone, finding the hidden entrance to the cave, almost immediately would have seen the paintings and would have spread the word. So the entrance to the fissure must have been blocked by one who would have been unfamiliar with the significance of the paintings or by one to whom they would have been commonplace.

It was something, he decided, that could not be passed up; he would have to go in. He secured the hammer to his belt, picked up the flashlight, and began the crawl.

The fissure ran straight and easy for a hundred feet or more. It offered barely room enough for crawling but, other than that, no great difficulties. Then, without warning, it came to an end. Boyd lay in it, directing the flash beam ahead of him, staring in consternation at the smooth wall of rock that came down to cut the fissure off.

It made no sense. Why should someone go to the trouble of walling off an empty fissure? He could have missed something on the way, but thinking of it, he was fairly sure he hadn't. His progress had been slow and he had kept the flash directed ahead of him every inch of the way. Certainly if there had been anything out of the ordinary, he would have seen it.

Then a thought came to him and slowly, with some effort, he began to turn himself around, so that his back, rather than his front, lay on the fissure floor. Directing the beam upward, he had his answer. In the roof of the fissure gaped a hole.

Cautiously he raised himself into a sitting position. Reaching up, he found handholds on the projecting rock and pulled himself erect. Swinging the flash around, he saw that the hole opened not into another fissure, but into a bubblelike cavity—small, no more than six feet in any dimension. The walls and ceiling of the cavity were smooth, as if a bubble of plastic rock had existed here for a moment at some time in the distant geologic past when the mountains had been heaving upward, leaving behind it as it drained away a bubble forever frozen into smooth and solid stone.

As he swung the flash across the bubble, he gasped in astonishment. Colorful animals capered around the entire expanse of stone. Bison played leapfrog. Horses cantered in a chorus line. Mammoths turned somersaults. All around the bottom perimeter, just above the floor, dancing deer, standing on their hind legs, joined hands and jigged, antlers swaying gracefully.

"For the love of Christ!" said Boyd.

Here was Stone Age Disney.

If it was the Stone Age. Could some jokester have crawled into the area in fairly recent times to paint the animals in this grotto? Thinking it over, he rejected the idea. So far as he had been able to ascertain, no one in the valley, nor in the entire region, for that matter, had known of the cave until a shepherd had found it several years before when a lamb had blundered into it. The entrance was small and apparently for centuries had been masked by a heavy growth of brush and bracken.

Too, the execution of the paintings had a prehistoric touch to them. Perspective played but a small part. The paintings had that curious flat look that distinguished most prehistoric art. There was no background—no horizon line, no trees, no grass or flowers, no clouds, no sense of sky. Although, he reminded himself, anyone who had any knowledge of cave painting probably would have been aware of all these factors and worked to duplicate them.

Yet, despite the noncharacteristic antics of the painted animals, the pictures did have the feeling of cave art. What ancient man, Boyd asked himself, what kind of ancient man, would have painted gamboling bison and tumbling mammoths? While the situation did not hold in all cave art, all the paintings in this particular cave were deadly serious—conservative as to form and with a forthright, honest attempt to portray the animals as the artists had seen them. There was no frivolity, not even the imprint of paint-smeared human hands, as so often happened in other caves. The men who had worked in this cave had not as yet been corrupted by the symbolism that had crept in, apparently rather late in the prehistoric painting cycle.

So who had been this clown who had crept off by himself in this hidden cavern to paint his comic animals? That he had been an accomplished painter, there could be no doubt. This artist's techniques and executions were without flaw.

Boyd hauled himself up through the hole, slid out onto the two-foot ledge that ran all around the hole, crouching, for there was no room to stand. Much of the painting, he realized, must have been done with the artist lying flat upon his back, reaching up to work on the curving ceiling.

He swept the beam of the flashlight along the ledge. Halfway around, he halted the light and jiggled it back and forth to focus upon something that was placed upon the ledge, something that undoubtedly had been left by the artist when he had finished his work and gone away.

Leaning forward, Boyd squinted to make out what it was. It looked like the shoulder blade of a deer; beside the shoulder blade lay a lump of stone.

Cautiously he edged his way around the ledge. He had been right. It was the shoulder blade of a deer. Upon the flat surface of it lay a lumpy substance. Paint? he wondered, the mixture of animal fats and mineral earths the prehistoric artists used as paints? He focused the flash closer and there was no doubt. It was paint, spread over the surface of the bone, which had served as a palette, with some of the paint lying in thicker lumps ready for use, but never used, paint dried and mummified and bearing imprints of some sort. He leaned close, bringing his face down to within a few inches of the paint, shining the light upon the surface. The imprints, he saw, were fingerprints, some of them sunk deep—the signature of that ancient, long-dead man who had worked here, crouching even as Boyd now crouched, shoulders hunched against the curving stone. He put out his hand to touch the palette, then pulled it back. Symbolic, yes, this move to touch, this reaching out to touch the man who painted—but symbolic only, a gesture with too many centuries between.

He shifted the flashlight beam to the small block of stone that lay beside the shoulder blade. A lamp—hollowed-out sandstone, a hollow to hold the fat and the chunk of moss that served as a wick. The fat and wick were long since gone, but a thin film of soot still remained around the rim of the hollow that had held them.

Finishing his work, the artist had left his tools behind him, had even left the lamp, perhaps still guttering, with the fat almost finished—had left it here and let himself down into the fissure, crawling it in darkness. To him, perhaps, there was no need of light. He could crawl the tunnel by touch and familiarity. He must have crawled the route many times, for the work upon these walls had taken long, perhaps many days.

So he had left, crawling through the fissure, using the blocks of stone to close the opening to the fissure, then had walked away, scrambling down the slope to the valley where grazing herds had lifted their heads to watch him, then had gone back to grazing.

But when had this all happened? Probably, Boyd told himself, after the cave itself had been painted, perhaps even after the paintings in the cave had lost much of whatever significance they originally would have held—one lone man coming back to paint his secret animals in his secret place. Painting them as a mockery of the pompous, magical importance of the main cave paintings? Or as a protest against the stuffy conservatism of the original paintings? Or simply as a bubbling chuckle, an exuberance of life, perhaps even a joyous rebellion against the grimness and the simplemindedness of the hunting magic? A rebel, he thought, a prehistoric rebel—an intellectual rebel? Or perhaps simply a man with a viewpoint slightly skewed from the philosophy of his time?

But this was that other man, that ancient man. Now how about himself? Having found the grotto, what did he do next? What would be the best way to handle it? Certainly he could not turn his back upon it and walk away, as the artist, leaving his palette and his lamp behind him, had walked away. For this was an important discovery. There could be no question of that. Here was a new and unsuspected approach to the prehistoric mind, a facet of ancient thinking that never had been guessed.

Leave everything as it lay, close up the fissure and make a phone call to Washington and another one to Paris, unpack his bags, and settle down for a few more weeks of work. Get back the photographers and other members of the crew—do a job of it. Yes, he told himself, that was the way to do it.

Something lying behind the lamp, almost hidden by the sandstone lamp, glinted in the light. Something white and small.

Still crouched over, Boyd shuffled forward to get a better look.

It was a piece of bone, probably a leg bone from a small grazing animal. He reached out and picked it up and, having seen what it was, hunched unmoving over it, not quite sure what to make of it.

It was a pipe, a brother to the pipe that Luis carried in his jacket pocket, had carried in his pocket since that first day he'd met him, years ago. There was the mouthpiece slot, there the two round stops. In that long-gone day when the paintings had been done, the artist had hunched here, in the flickering of the lamp, and had played softly to himself those simple piping airs that Luis had played almost every evening, after work was done.

"Merciful Jesus," Boyd said, almost prayerfully, "it simply cannot be!"

He stayed there, frozen in his crouch, the thoughts hammering in his mind while he tried to push the thoughts away.

They would not go away. He'd drive them away for just a little distance, then they'd come surging back to overwhelm him.

Finally, grimly, he broke the trance in which the thoughts had held him. He worked deliberately, forcing himself to do what he knew must be done.

He took off his windbreaker and carefully wrapped the shoulder-blade palette and the pipe inside it, leaving the lamp. He let himself down into the fissure and crawled, carefully protecting the bundle that he carried. In the cave again, he meticulously fitted the blocks of stone together to block the fissure mouth, scraped together handfuls of soil from the cave floor, and smeared it on the face of the blocks, wiping it away, but leaving a small, clinging film to mask the opening to all but the most inquiring eye.

Luis was not at his camp on the terrace below the cave mouth; he was still on his errand into the village.

When he reached his hotel, Boyd made his telephone call to Washington. He skipped the call to Paris.

The last leaves of October were blowing in the autumn wind, and a weak sun, not entirely obscured by the floating clouds, shone down on Washington.

John Roberts was waiting for him on the park bench. They nodded at one another, without speaking, and Boyd sat down beside his friend.

"You took a big chance," said Roberts. "What would have happened if the customs people . . ."

"I wasn't too worried," Boyd said. "I knew this man in Paris. For years he's been smuggling stuff into America. He's good at it and he owed me one. What have you got?"

"Maybe more than you want to hear."

"Try me."

"The fingerprints match," said Roberts.

"You were able to get a reading on the paint impressions?"

"Loud and clear."

"The FBI?"

"Yes, the FBI. It wasn't easy, but I have a friend or two."

"And the dating?"

"No problem. The bad part of the job was convincing my man this was top secret. He's still not sure it is."

"Will he keep his mouth shut?"

"I think so. Without evidence, no one would believe him. It would sound like a fairy story."

"Tell me."

"Twenty-two thousand. Plus or minus three hundred years."

"And the prints do match. The bottle prints and . . ."

"I told you they match. Now will you tell me how in hell a man who lived twenty-two thousand years ago could leave his prints on a wine bottle that was manufactured last year."

"It's a long story," said Boyd. "I don't know if I should. First, where do you have the shoulder blade?"

"Hidden," said Roberts. "Well hidden. You can have it back, and the bottle, any time you wish."

Boyd shrugged. "Not yet. Not for a while. Perhaps never."

"Never?"

"Look, John, I have to think it out."

"What a hell of a mess," said Roberts. "No one wants the stuff. No one would dare to have it. Smithsonian wouldn't touch it with a ten-foot pole. I haven't asked. They don't even know about it. But I know they wouldn't want it. There's something, isn't there, about sneaking artifacts out of a country . . ."

"Yes, there is," said Boyd.

"And now you don't want it."

"I didn't say that. I just said let it stay where it is for a time. It's safe, isn't it?"

"It's safe. And now . . ."

"I told you it is a long story. I'll try to make it short. There's this man—a Basque. He came to me ten years ago when I was doing the rock shelter . . ."

Roberts nodded. "I remember that one."

"He wanted work and I gave him work. He broke in fast, caught on to the techniques immediately. Became a valuable man. That often happens with native laborers. They seem to have the feel for their own antiquity. And then when we started work on the cave he showed up again. I was glad to see him. The two of us, as a matter of fact, are fairly good friends. On my last night at the cave he cooked a marvelous omelet—eggs, tomato, green pimientoes, onions, sausages, and home-cured ham. I brought a bottle of wine."

"*The* bottle?"

"Yes, *the* bottle."

"So go ahead."

"He played a pipe. A bone pipe. A squeaky sort of thing. Not too much music in it . . ."

"There was a pipe . . ."

"Not that pipe. Another pipe. The same kind of pipe, but not the one our man has. Two pipes the same. One in a living man's pocket, the other beside the shoulder blade. There were things about this man I'm telling you of. Nothing that hit you between the eyes. Just little things. You would notice something and then, some time later, maybe quite a bit later, there'd be something else, but by the time that happened, you'd have forgotten the first incident and not tie the two together. Mostly it was that he knew too much. Little things a man like him would not be expected to know. Even things that no one knew. Bits and pieces of knowledge that slipped out of him, maybe without his realizing it. And his eyes. I didn't realize that until later, not until I'd found the second pipe and began to think about the other things. But I was talking about his eyes. In appearance he is a young man, a never-aging man, but his eyes are old . . ."

"Tom, you said he is a Basque."

"That's right."

"Isn't there some belief that the Basques may have descended from the Cro-Magnons?"

"There is such a theory. I have thought of it."

"Could this man of yours be a Cro-Magnon?"

"I'm beginning to think he is."

"But think of it—twenty thousand years!"

"Yes, I know," said Boyd.

Boyd heard the piping when he reached the bottom of the trail that led up to the cave. The notes were ragged, torn by the wind. The Pyrenees stood up against the high blue sky.

Tucking the bottle of wine more securely underneath his arm, Boyd began the climb. Below him lay the redness of the village rooftops and the sere brown of autumn that spread across the valley. The piping continued, lifting and falling as the wind tugged at it playfully.

Luis sat crosslegged in front of the tattered tent. When he saw Boyd, he put the pipe in his lap and sat waiting.

Boyd sat down beside him, handing him the bottle. Luis took it and began working on the cork.

"I heard you were back," he said. "How went the trip?"

"It went well," said Boyd.

"So now you know," said Luis.

Boyd nodded. "I think you wanted me to know. Why should you have wanted that?"

"The years grow long," said Luis. "The burden heavy. It is lonely, all alone."

"You are not alone."

"It's lonely when no one knows you. You now are the first who has really known me."

"But the knowing will be short. A few years more and again no one will know you."

"This lifts the burden for a time," said Luis. "Once you are gone, I will be able to take it up again. And there is something . . ."

"Yes, what is it, Luis?"

"You say when you are gone there'll be no one again. Does that mean . . ."

"If what you're getting at is whether I will spread the word, no, I won't. Not unless you wish it. I have thought on what would happen to you if the world were told."

"I have certain defenses. You can't live as long as I have if you fail in your defenses."

"What kind of defenses?"

"Defenses. That is all."

"I'm sorry if I pried. There's one other thing. If you wanted me to know, you took a long chance. Why, if something had gone wrong, if I had failed to find the grotto . . ."

"I had hoped, at first, that the grotto would not be necessary. I had thought you might have guessed, on your own."

"I knew there was something wrong. But this is so outrageous I couldn't have trusted myself even had I guessed. You know it's outrageous, Luis. And if I'd not found the grotto . . . Its finding was pure chance, you know."

"If you hadn't, I would have waited. Some other time, some other year, there would have been someone else. Some other way to betray myself."

"You could have told me."

"Cold, you mean?"

"That's what I mean. I would not have believed you, of course. Not at first."

"Don't you understand? I could not have told you. The concealment now is second nature. One of the defenses I talked about. I simply could not have brought myself to tell you, or anyone."

"Why me? Why wait all these years until I came along?"

"I did not wait, Boyd. There were others, at different times. None of them worked out. I had to find, you must understand, someone who had the strength to face it. Not one who would run screaming madly. I knew you would not run screaming."

"I've had time to think it through," Boyd said. "I've come to terms with it. I can accept the fact, but not too well, only barely. Luis, do you have some explanation? How come you are so different from the rest of us?"

"No idea at all. No inkling. At one time I thought there must be others like me and I sought for them. I found none. I no longer seek."

The cork came free and he handed the bottle of wine to Boyd. "You go first," he said steadily.

Boyd lifted the bottle and drank. He handed it to Luis. He watched him as he drank. Wondering, as he watched, how he could be sitting here, talking calmly with a man who had lived, who had stayed young through twenty thousand years. His gorge rose once again against acceptance of the fact—but it had to be a fact. The shoulder blade, the small amount of organic matter still remaining in the pigment, had measured out to 22,000 years. There was no question that the prints in the paint had matched the prints upon the bottle. He had raised one question back in Washington, hoping there might be evidence of hoax. Would it have been possible, he had asked, that the ancient pigment, the paint used by the pre-historic artist, could have been reconstituted, the fingerprints impressed upon it, and then replaced in the grotto? *Impossible* was the answer. Any reconstitution of the pigment, had it been possible, would have shown up in the analysis. There had been nothing of the sort—the pigment dated to 20,000 years ago. There was no question of that.

"All right, Cro-Magnon," said Boyd, "tell me how you did it. How does a man survive as long as you have? You do not age, of course. Your body will not accept disease. But I take it you are not immune to violence or to accident. You've lived in a violent world. How does a man sidestep accident and violence for two hundred centuries?"

"There were times early," Luis said, "when I came close to not surviving. For a long time I did not realize the kind of thing I was. Sure, I lived longer, stayed younger than all the others—I would guess, however, that I didn't begin to notice this until I began to realize that all the people I had known in my early life were dead—dead for a long, long time. I knew then that I was different from the rest. About the same time, others began to notice I was different. They became suspi-

cious of me. Some of them resented me. Others thought I
was some sort of evil spirit. Finally I had to flee the tribe. I
became a skulking outcast. That was when I began to learn
the principles of survival."

"And those principles?"

"You keep a low profile. You don't stand out. You attract
no attention to yourself. You cultivate a cowardly attitude.
You are never brave. You take no risks. You let others do the
dirty work. You never volunteer. You skulk and run and
hide. You grow a skin that's thick; you don't give a damn
what others think of you. You shed all your noble attributes,
your social consciousness. You shuck your loyalty to tribe or
folk or country. You're not a patriot. You live for yourself
alone. You're an observer, never a participant. You scuttle
around the edges of things. And you become so self-centered
that you come to believe that no blame should attach to you,
that you are living in the only logical way a man can live.
You went to Roncesvalles the other day, remember?"

"Yes. I mentioned I'd been there. You said you'd
heard of it."

"Heard of it? Hell, I was there the day it happened—August 15, 778. An observer, not a participant. A cowardly little
bastard who tagged along behind that noble band of Gascons who did in Roland. Gascons, hell. That's the fancy
name for them. They were Basques, pure and simple. The
meanest crew of men who ever drew the breath of life. Some
Basques may be noble, but not this band. They weren't the
kind of warriors who'd stand up face to face with the Franks.
They hid up in the pass and rolled rocks down on all those
puissant knights. But it wasn't the knights who held their
interest. It was the wagon train. They weren't out to fight a
war or to avenge a wrong. They were out for loot. Although
little good it did them."

"Why do you say that?"

"It was this way," said Luis. "They knew the rest of the
Frankish army would return when the rear guard didn't
come up, and they had not the stomach for that. They

stripped the dead knights of their golden spurs, their armor
and fancy clothes, the money bags they carried, and loaded
all of it on the wagons and got out of there. A few miles
farther on, deep in the mountains, they holed up and hid. In
a deep canyon where they thought they would be safe. But if
they should be found, they had what amounted to a fort. A
half-mile or so below the place they camped, the canyon
narrowed and twisted sharply. A lot of boulders had fallen
down at that point, forming a barricade that could have been
held by a handful of men against any assault that could be
launched against it. By this time I was a long way off. I
smelled something wrong, I knew something most unpleasant was about to happen. That's another thing about this
survival business. You develop special senses. You get so you
can smell out trouble, well ahead of time. I heard what happened later."

He lifted the bottle and had another drink. He handed it
to Boyd.

"Don't leave me hanging," said Boyd. "Tell me what did
happen."

"In the night," said Luis, "a storm came up. One of those
sudden, brutal summer thunderstorms. This time it was a
cloudburst. My brave fellow Gascons died to the man. That's
the price of bravery."

Boyd took a drink, lowered the bottle, held it to his chest,
cuddling it.

"You know about this," he said. "No one else does. Perhaps no one had ever wondered what happened to those
Gascons who gave Charlemagne the bloody nose. You must
know of other things. Christ, man, you've lived history. You
didn't stick to this area."

"No. At times I wandered. I had an itching foot. There
were things to see. I had to keep moving along. I couldn't
stay in one place any length of time or it would be noticed
that I wasn't aging."

"You lived through the Black Death," said Boyd. "You
watched the Roman legions. You heard firsthand of Attila.

You skulked along on Crusades. You walked the streets of ancient Athens."

"Not Athens," said Luis. "Somehow Athens was never to my taste. I spent some time in Sparta. Sparta, I tell you—that was really something."

"You're an educated man," said Boyd. "Where did you go to school?"

"Paris, for a time, in the fourteenth century. Later on at Oxford. After that at other places. Under different names. Don't try tracing me through the schools that I attended."

"You could write a book," said Boyd. "It would set new sales records. You'd be a millionaire. One book and you'd be a millionaire."

"I can't afford to be a millionaire. I can't be noticed, and millionaires are noticed. I'm not in want. I've never been in want. There's always treasure for a skulker to pick up. I have caches here and there. I get along all right."

Luis was right, Boyd told himself. He couldn't be a millionaire. He couldn't write a book. In no way could he be famous, stand out in any way. In all things he must remain unremarkable, always anonymous.

The principles of survival, he had said. And this was part of it, although not all of it. He had mentioned the art of smelling trouble, the hunch ability. There would be, as well, the wisdom, the street savvy, the cynicism that a man would pick up along the way, the expertise, the ability to judge character, an insight into human reaction, some knowledge concerning the use of power, power of every sort, economic power, political power, religious power.

Was the man still human, he wondered, or had he, in 20,000 years, become something more than human? Had he advanced that one vital step that would place him beyond humankind, the kind of being that would come after man?

"One thing more," said Boyd. "Why the Disney paintings?"

"They were painted some time later than the others," Luis told him. "I painted some of the earlier stuff in the cave. The fishing bear is mine. I knew about the grotto. I found it and said nothing. No reason I should have kept it secret. Just one of those little items one hugs to himself to make himself important. I know something you don't know—silly stuff like that. Later I came back to paint the grotto. The cave art was so deadly serious. Such terribly silly magic. I told myself painting should be fun. So I came back after the tribe had moved, and painted simply for the fun of it. How did it strike you, Boyd?"

"Damn good art," said Boyd.

"I was afraid you wouldn't find the grotto and I couldn't help you. I knew you had seen the cracks in the wall; I watched you one day looking at them. I counted on your remembering them. And I counted on your seeing the finger-prints and finding the pipe. All pure serendipity, of course. I had nothing in mind when I left the paint with the finger-prints and the pipe. The pipe, of course, was the tipoff, and I was confident you'd at least be curious. But I couldn't be sure. When we ate that night, here by the campfire, you didn't mention the grotto and I was afraid you'd blown it. But when you made off with the bottle, sneaking it away, I knew I had it made. And now the big question. Will you let the world in on the grotto paintings?"

"I don't know. I'll have to think about it. What are your thoughts on the matter?"

"I'd just as soon you didn't."

"Okay," said Boyd. "Not for the time at least. Is there anything else I can do for you? Anything you want?"

"You've done the best possible," said Luis. "You know who I am, what I am. I don't know why that's so important to me, but it is. A matter of identity, I suppose. When you die, which I hope will be a long time from now, then, once again, there'll be no one who knows. But the knowledge that one man did know, and what is more important, understood, will sustain me through the centuries. A minute—I have something for you."

He rose and went into the tent, came back with a sheet of

paper, handing it to Boyd. It was a topographical survey of some sort.

"I've put a cross on it," said Luis. "To mark the spot."

"What spot?"

"Where you'll find the Charlemagne treasure of Roncesvalles. The wagons and the treasure would have been carried down the canyon in the flood. The turn in the canyon and the boulder barricade I spoke of would have blocked them. You'll find them there, probably under a deep layer of gravel and debris."

Boyd looked up questioningly from the map.

"It's worth going after," said Luis. "Also it provides another check against the validity of my story."

"I believe you," said Boyd. "I need no further evidence."

"Ah, well!" said Luis, "it wouldn't hurt. And now it's time to go."

"Time to go! We have a lot to talk about."

"Later, perhaps," said Luis. "We'll bump into one another from time to time. I'll make it a point we do. But now it's time to go."

He started down the path, and Boyd sat watching him.

After a few steps, Luis halted and half turned back to Boyd.

"It seems to me," he said in explanation, "it's always time to go."

Boyd stood and watched him move down the trail toward the village. There was about the moving figure a deep sense of loneliness—the most lonely man in all the world.

Why Is There So Little Science in Literature?

Gregory Benford

Gregory Benford is a working scientist; indeed, it's often said that Dr. Benford is the only SFWA member living who's likely to win both a Nebula and a Nobel Prize. Timescape *has brought him his second Nebula; and we understand that he's working on a new experiment. . . .*

A full professor of physics in the University of California at Irvine, Greg has gathered a prodigious academic reputation for both research and teaching, which leads naturally to the question, how has Greg found time to write science fiction? For write it he has; over the years Greg has published a number of novels and short stories, and gathered something more than his share of awards.

I don't know how Greg has managed in the past, but I may have solved some of his problems for the future. A year or so ago the Benfords came here to Chaos Manor for a party held in conjunction with the Voyager *encounter with Saturn. I introduced him to Ezekial, my friend who happens to be a Z-80 computer. Zeke is the secret of my success; not only can I write more with a computer, but the writing is a lot better,*

33

because with computers you can painlessly rewrite and polish and nitpick.

Greg watched me play about with Zeke, and it was love at first sight; within a week he called to ask how he could get one of those marvels. Had I been thinking, I would have sent him to Fly-by-Byte Computers, who'd have sold him something obsolete and unworkable, and thus I could have held down the competition; but it was early in the morning and I gave him the phone number of the consulting geniuses who built Zeke.

The other day Greg called. His system is installed and working, and now he can write twice as fast as before. Maybe, though, he'll concentrate on physics, and go get a Nobel before snarfing up another Nebula. . . .

Greg Benford's Timescape *has rightly been praised as the best work yet on what it's like to* do *science. The long hours of patient work with no progress, the sudden thrill of hypothesis, the excitement of discovery and* knowing *that you're right—this all leaps out from the book. But how can that be conveyed here?*

There's always a dilemma involved with the Nebula Awards books: What do you do about the novel winner? Obviously we can't reprint the whole novel; yet with few exceptions, novels are a seamless whole, and excerpts just don't work. That's particularly true of Timescape.

So I invented an instant tradition. Instead of trying to chop something out of Greg's novel, I'd let him *decide what to do. "You can write what you want," I said. "An essay, or a short story—old or new—or a ramble about the novel, or poetry, or anything you'd like to say."*

I'm glad I put it that way, because what we got was this readable and valuable essay.

Now and then I meet a scientist who remarks on the rarity of fiction that deals with science in a realistic fashion. This usually comes up in the course of a discussion of how scientists are portrayed in science fiction—a subject that can provoke you to laughter and tears at the same time—but the question extends over the whole of literature, I think: In this age of furious intellectual expansion, fueled by the astonishing revelations of science, driven by science's child, technology— why does literature reflect so little of these great engines of change?

It's puzzling. One's first thought is to reflect back over the successful depictions of science or scientists outside the realm of science fiction, to get away from the genre influences that might distort the answer. Alas, there is no great body of such work. Occasional novels stand out as marginal cases, such as Sinclair Lewis's *Arrowsmith*, but this is concerned with medical research, and does not delve far into medicine as science at all. (To the public, white-smocked doctors are a frequent emblem for science, but to my mind they often work as engineers of the body, using known techniques in ingenious but not deeply creative ways. It is interesting to note how often men trained as physicians become writers; Arthur Conan Doyle and Somerset Maugham come to mind. Yet they seldom portrayed scientists.) Eleazar Lipsky's *The Scientists* (1959) is an unusual and quite successful attempt to show scientific rivalry. It was quite well reviewed and widely read when it appeared, but seems to have slipped from literary memory. Other prominent writers have used scientific ideas or themes or metaphors in basically "realistic" narratives: Thomas Pynchon in *The Crying of Lot 49* (entropy), Lawrence Durrell in *The Alexandria Quartet* (relativity and quantum mechanics, rather loosely used), and Robert Coover in *The Universal Baseball Association, Inc., J. Henry Waugh Prop.* (entropy and the theory of chance).

The outstanding example of a novelist dealing with the world of a career scientist is C. P. Snow's eleven-volume series collectively called Strangers and Brothers. This long and uneven set concerns the academic and administrative career of an Englishman who begins by doing research and ends in the corridors of power, paralleling Snow's life. His first significant novel, *The Search*, was to my mind his best. It tells of the tedium and occasional excitement of research in crystallography, in Cambridge during the 1930s. It concludes with a moral question, matching personal loyalty against the scientist's implicit need to honor the standards of truth in his profession. After this book, Snow moved on to academic politics and the manner of bureaucratic man, getting further from science as an electrifying process of discovery and more into its growing role in governmental power. The series mirrors the lives of many scientists, reflecting the sobering fact that for most of us the path to higher salary and greater influence inevitably leads us away from the primary experience that got us into the scientific professions in the first place.

These are all good books, but why are there so few of them? After all, science is the big driving term in the equation of modern times. Why have literary folk (outside science fiction) so neglected the life of the scientist?

Part of it is simple ignorance. Writers are trained in humanistic departments of universities, not in labs. T. S. Eliot was quite prepared to write of the life of a bank clerk, because he had *been* a bank clerk. Nobody becomes a scientist by accident, or as a part-time job. Also, there may well be matters of style that interfere. Scientists are typically quantitative thinkers, problem-directed, and often not particularly verbally skillful. There is a natural self-selection of people into groups, according to whether they think in words or in pictures (or in mathematics, which is another kind of language).

Similarly, it's unlikely that scientists will become authors, once they are launched on their careers. Most important, there isn't *time*. Scientists pour themselves into their work, and if they have a hobby at all, it tends to be athletic or at least far removed from the glades of academe. It's also sadly true that scientists are taught to write badly from the very beginning of their careers. The standard scientific style is impersonal, methodical to the point of dullness, and remorselessly literal. Most scientific papers and reports are written in the passive voice ("The electron is directed into the chamber and made to resonate. . . .") which, after a few paragraphs, numbs the reader into a dulled acceptance. The passive voice actually hides what is doing on, who does it, and why. This has made it the preferred mode for bureaucrats. It has infiltrated scientific discourse and is a deadly block to interesting communication. Yet some scientific journals *require* it, aping the mannerisms of the administrators. This is one of the worst features of the increasing connection between government and science. For a scientist, it makes the writing of fiction a strange process, and explains the rather dull, mechanical style of C. P. Snow.

Beyond such stylistic issues, scientists are trained to revere accuracy, a constant rechecking of results, and a wariness of speculation—all quite excellent standards for finding the truth, but often unnecessary baggage when you are trying to describe personal relationships, in which there is no final "truth" to seek, and what is most interesting is the variation in points of view. I imagine the hardest thing for a scientist to do in fiction is characterization, because of his habit of making statements and ideas objective and free of bias, and couching them in a value-free style. The subtleties of real, living personality don't succumb to such descriptions. I always thought C. P. Snow's views of his characters read like the descriptions job interviewers write—an outside picture, tracing probable surface motivations and qualities, but without understanding the driving force inside.

Similarly, the nuclear physicist Leo Szilard, when he turned to fiction, produced parables. In *The Voice of the Dolphins and Other Stories* (1961) he showed a common misunderstanding of scientists: that the intellectual point of a narrative is the whole point, and the story is a kind of vehicle to carry the reader to that conclusion. Once we get the point, presumably we can dispense with the story. Szilard simply omitted characterization as unnecessary for his purposes. His short stories are worth reading, but seem a bit bloodless: fiction as freight-hauler for philosophy.

So there are good reasons why scientists as a rule should be poor dramatists, when they do find the time or inclination to write. It may be more productive for them to stick to the rather dispassionate, analytical mode of Szilard, then. Fortunately, there has been a turn in recent literature that elevates this kind of distant voice to the realm of high art. This form is yet unnamed, unless we call it *post-modernism*, my favorite example of self-decapitating academic jargon. I shall feel free to term it *irrealism*. Two well-known practitioners, Jorge Luis Borges and Stanislaw Lem, will serve to sketch in the ground I am attempting to cover. The strategy of these writers, in part, is deliberately to accent some aspect of the agreed-upon world, achieving a kind of super-realism that seems both recognizable and bizarre. Jorge Borges, with his labyrinthian library, is using a "realistic" portrayal of a mathematical abstraction. The ideas depicted are basic, underpinning much of modern mathematical thought (transfinite numbers, regression mathematics). One of the points Borges is making, I believe, is that the fundamental notions underlying our consensual reality are themselves strange, bewildering, even unhuman, when studied in the full glare of literary imagination. Behind many human ideas lurks the recurring image of the infinite, and the human imagination struggles to deal with it. Science itself has given us many of these images, and it leaves unanswered fundamental philosophical problems, to say nothing of the human quandary: how to deal with the ideas themselves. One way is through self-satire. What literary type or scientist can resist a chuckle when he begins reading the first line of Borges's "The Library of Babel"? "The universe (which others call the Library) is composed of an indefinite and perhaps infinite number of hexagonal galleries. . . ."

The shift here is not the breakdown of the consensus reality that modernism brought. It isn't the individual loss of a firm, fixed world, or a collapse into the illusions of one solitary person. Instead, it is the severe altering of an external reality for specific purposes (I would almost say it is a literary *gedanken* experiment). How better to explore what would or should or could be? The aim here is not to escape from a claustrophobic world, à la Kafka, but to embrace it, examine it in the warped mirror of possibilities. There is a continuum here, stretching from the mild dislocations of Barthelme, through the analytic fantasies of Borges and the desiccated cybernetic jokes and fables of Lem, on into the true ground of science fiction itself.

The trouble with this approach is that it's damned hard to make it *move* in the old plotting sense. You end up with rarefied fiction suited for relaxing mathematicians. We can probably expect more of this to come, because writers are generally getting more acquainted with the content of modern science. But I doubt that irrealism will be very engaging for the common reader, and although some literary scientists may contribute, I doubt that it will get across much of what the scientist himself is like. For in fact the unique facet of being a scientist is the daily confrontation with the vast landscape of the world as our intellect sees it.

The public—even the literate fraction—misses the diversity and spirit of scientists. They have been so saturated with the "white lab smock" image, and the Einstein picture, and the "cold, mechanical robot" depiction, that they fail to see scientists as real, working human beings. Once in a while a book (usually autobiography, such as Freeman Dyson's *Disturbing the Universe*) will wrench the public away from such oversimplifications. This happened with Watson's "insider's view" in *The Double Helix*. Still, few reasonably alert people see that it is perhaps less important that scientists be smart, for example, than that they be a special breed of well-organized dreamers.

The specialists in depicting scientists as dreamers—and

sometimes as fanatics—are, of course, the much-maligned science fiction writers. In the end, I think the SF authors will be seen as characteristic of our age, as poets and bards heralding a new force in human society. They were the first to notice technology, think about its effects, and see that the future would be a working out of these themes. Some SF writers are or were scientists (Asimov, Richardson, Pournelle, Hoyle, Clement, etc.). The critical fraternity still seems to feel that nobody can write about that old empty cliché, the Human Condition, and simultaneously understand how his own refrigerator works. This plainly tells us more about the origin of critics than the origin of ideas. The way science fiction emerged in America is mostly to blame for this. It was mired in the now-lost age of pulp magazine fiction, when the great demand for wordage to fill up the space between the ads led, by evolutionary momentum, to the invention of the electric typewriter, the first machine that allowed you to write faster than you could think, with results now quite obvious.

But these class origins should not—and in the long run will not—determine what we think of science fiction. It has had a long era now, existing as a well-tended private garden in which the fans loyally mistook domestic cabbages for literary roses. The confusion was usually benign. It allowed authors to say what they saw, without feeling the press of the past on their backs. Quite a few SF writers are or were engineers or scientists. As is often the case in America, engineering is confused with science; many SF works are essentially about futuristic technology, rather than the experience of the genuinely strange. This has led to many maladroit pieces of fiction, of course—the typical *Analog* yarn with its blockheaded engineers scratching their heads for six thousand words, and then slapping together the right answer to a problem, just before the boredom becomes suffocating. But often it has given us glimpses into the real conflicts of real people, men and women who rub against the vexing corners of the scien-

tific enterprise and know it by second nature. SF is a literature in which a usually silent class steps forward and sings of
its dreams, its terrors. It will, I think, be fertile ground for
study in the future. Here some distant literary archeologist
will find the underswell of a technological age, a literature
that gives glimpses of what it truly is like to do these things—
to twist reality into new forms, pushing outward the boundary of a burgeoning intellectual empire—and I suspect it will
make more interesting reading than the endless novels of
suburban adultery or corporate scandal.

I have thought of these things for quite a while, as my own
scientific career climbed, and I kept writing doggedly. Even
for a scientist, it is tempting to make your protagonist the
convenient captain of a spaceship, or some such central, ac-
tion-oriented figure. There are a multitude of established
ways of dealing with such characters, and they make it easy
to move the story along. How much harder it is to write
about science as she truly is—the tedium, the deep musings
on obscure problems, the occasional flashes of understanding. Seen from the outside, the scientist isn't much more interesting than a bank clerk. And at least the reader doesn't
have to struggle merely to understand what the bank clerk is
doing. Nevertheless, it seemed to me that SF was a bit too
easy without some sense of what science is. I tried to incorpo-
rate a good deal of science and its human dimensions in all
my work.

Still, it wasn't enough. So, starting in the late 1960s, I la-
bored at a novel that was to deal primarily with the scientific
experience. I chipped away at the problem, trying first a
short story, then a novelette, letting my subconscious do most
of the labor. (I worked only when it prompted me.) The
result was my longest book, using the backgrounds I knew
well (California, 1962, and Cambridge, England). When it
was done, I was halfway tempted to publish it as a conventional novel, not identifying it as science fiction. The American publisher was interested in this, and at first attempted

getting attention for the book among the conventional reviewing spots. They had made the fatal mistake of including the words "science fiction" in the promotional copy, however, and this naturally sank it without trace among the New York media. The British publisher, Gollancz, didn't use the SF label, and thus the novel was treated as an interesting variant on the realistic mode. This experiment taught me a good deal about preconceptions, but it has little or nothing to do with what is actually on the pages of *Timescape*. It will be interesting to see how novels of this sort—assuming there will be more of them—fare among the shoals of critical theory. By then the circumstances of birth will have faded. (The title was later purchased for use as the imprint of a whole line of paperback and hardcover books, which will undoubtedly confuse many about the whole thing.) In the long run, I don't think readers are as wedded to categories as are publishers. Otherwise we'd be thinking of *Huckleberry Finn* as a boys' adventure book, of *Moby Dick* as a fishing story, and of *The Great Gatsby* as a murder mystery.

What I'm arguing here, of course, is that the true avenue for the literary realization of what science is about lies not in the conventional novel, but in the deep roots of science fiction. Fred Hoyle understood this when he dashed off, in a month or so, a lasting piece of SF called *The Black Cloud*. As Hoyle's intelligent dust cloud enters our solar system, we see scientists dealing with the resulting problems in an analytical manner that blends with their differing personalities. As a novel it is at once exciting and awkward, moving and wooden—but it rings with truths about how scientists think.

Science fiction is not an isolated plot, but a section of a greater garden. Perhaps some lurid and grotesque varieties grow here, but their lineage is clear. They come from the fundamental phylum that is also producing, for example, what I've called irrealism. In fact, the continuity of irrealism with SF is clear in such authors as Borges and Lem, and through the connection with "alternate world" novels, such as *Bring the Jubilee, Pavane, A Transatlantic Tunnel, Hurrah!, The Man in the High Castle,* and *The Alteration.*

In the end this continuity of aim, as part of a larger pattern in which literature reacts to science, may be the most important function of SF. For my own tastes, the excesses of SF can be corrected by paying closer attention to how science is actually *done*, rather than by relying on the hoary old images of the dashing astronaut, the inevitable cranky-but-wise administrator, and the rest of the leaden cast left over from our earlier days. They can conceal more than they reveal. In particular, they obscure the fact that science is not a casebook of final answers, but rather a method of questioning. It is, like literature, a continuing dialogue among diverse and conflicting voices, no one ever wholly right or wholly wrong, a steady conversation forever provisional and personal and living.

Ginungagap

Michael Swanwick

The Nebula is a much-coveted award, given by the votes of those eligible for it. It's inevitable that the rules will be controversial, and that every new president of Science Fiction Writers of America will make changes in them.

When Nebulae were first invented, the rules were relatively simple; but then there were charges that "unworthy" stories were winning Nebulae; in one case the winning author, although accepting the award, expressed amazement that he'd won for that *story. Other winners muttered that if* that *could win, the whole award was cheapened.*

So, when I became president and was thus able to tinker with the rules, I thought to put an end to the entire controversy. I would, I thought, create a Nebula Jury, whose task it would be to review all nominated works and pronounce them worthy; any work the jury wouldn't accept couldn't be on the final list. There had also been the problem of works published in obscure places; the jury would correct that by having the right to nominate worthy works omitted in the balloting.

The rules were adopted by a vote of SFWA members and we proceeded to appoint the most prestigious jury possible.

The result was a disaster, of course. The authors chosen for the jury that year may or may not have been the most prestigious we had, but they certainly were the busiest; not one of them had time to read all the candidates for nomination, and thus all declined to vote. . . .

In the years since my reprieve from the SFWA presidency, diverse systems were tried and changed and abandoned, but every year a jury was appointed—and every year it did nothing. Then came the election of Norman Spinrad, who reminded the jury of its power to nominate works overlooked by the membership. This was a Good Thing, because "Ginungagap" was published in a more or less scholarly journal that few SFWA members had ever heard of; and lo, "Ginungagap" was nominated.

I don't know Michael Swanwick at all. He lives in Philadelphia and writes polite letters, and he wrote two stories that John Carr thought good enough to consider for this volume.

"Ginungagap" reminds me of an earlier era in science fiction. It is highly plausible action and adventure in a detailed future of marvels. I think John Campbell would have loved this one, unpronounceable title and all. I did.

Abigail checked out of Mother of Mercy and rode the translator web to Toledo Cylinder in Juno Industrial Park. Stars bloomed, dwindled, disappeared five times. It was a long trek, halfway around the sun.

Toledo was one of the older commercial cylinders, now given over almost entirely to bureaucrats, paper pushers, and free-lance professionals. It was not Abigail's favorite place to visit, but she needed work and 3M had already bought out of her contract.

The job broker had dyed his chest hairs blond and his leg hairs red. They clashed wildly with his green *cache-sexe* and turquoise jewelry. His fingers played on a keyout, bringing up an endless flow of career trivia. "Cute trick you played," he said.

Abigail flexed her new arm negligently. It was a good job, but pinker than the rest of her. And weak, of course, but exercise would correct that. "Thanks," she said. She laid the arm underneath one breast and compared the colors. It matched the nipple perfectly. Definitely too pink. "Work outlook any good?"

"Naw," the broker said. A hummingbird flew past his ear, a nearly undetectable parting of the air. "I see here that you applied for the Proxima colony."

"They were full up," Abigail said. "No openings for a gravity bum, hey?"

"I didn't say that," the broker grumbled. "I'll find— Hello! What's this?" Abigail craned her neck, couldn't get a clear look at the screen. "There's a tag on your employment record."

"What's that mean?"

"Let me read." A honeysuckle flower fell on Abigail's hair and she brushed it off impatiently. The broker had an open-air office, framed by hedges and roofed over with a trellis. Sometimes Abigail found the older Belt cylinders a little too lavish for her taste.

"Mmp." The broker looked up. "Bell-Sandia wants to hire you. Indefinite term one-shot contract." He swung the key-out around so she could see. "*Very* nice terms, but that's normal for a high-risk contract."

"High risk? From B-S, the Friendly Communications People? What kind of risk?"

The broker scrolled up new material. "There." He tapped the screen with a finger. "The language is involved, but what it boils down to is they're looking for a test passenger for a device they've got that uses black holes for interstellar travel."

"Couldn't work," Abigail said. "The tidal forces—"

"Spare me. Presumably they've found a way around that

problem. The question is, are you interested or not?"

Abigail stared up through the trellis at a stream meandering across the curved land overhead. Children were wading in it. She counted to a hundred very slowly, trying to look as if she needed to think it over.

Abigail strapped herself into the translation harness and nodded to the technician outside the chamber. The tech touched her console and a light stasis field immobilized Abigail and the air about her while the chamber wall irised open. In a fluid bit of technological sleight of hand, the translator rechanneled her inertia and gifted her with a velocity almost, but not quite, that of the speed of light.

Stars bloomed about her and the sun dwindled. She breathed in deeply and—was in the receiver device. Relativity had cheated her of all but a fraction of the transit time. She shrugged out of harness and frog-kicked her way to the lip station's tug dock.

The tug pilot grinned at her as she entered, then turned his attention to his controls. He was young and wore streaks of brown makeup across his chest and thighs—only slightly darker than his skin. His mesh vest was almost in bad taste, but he wore it well and looked roguish rather than overdressed. Abigail found herself wishing she had more than a *cache-sexe* and nail polish on—some jewelry or makeup, perhaps. She felt drab in comparison.

The star-field wraparound held two inserts routed in by synchronous cameras. Alphanumerics flickered beneath them. One showed her immediate destination, the Bell-Sandia base *Arthur C. Clarke*. It consisted of five wheels, each set inside the other and rotating at slightly differing speeds. The base was done up in red-and-orange supergraphics. Considering its distance from the Belt factories, it was respectably sized.

Abigail latched herself into the passenger seat as the engines cut in. The second insert—

Ginungagap, the only known black hole in the sun's gravity field, was discovered in 2033, a small voice murmured. *Its presence explained the long-puzzling variations in the orbits of the outer planets. The* Arthur C. Clarke *was . . .*

"Is this necessary?" Abigail asked.

"Absolutely," the pilot said. "We abandoned the tourist program a year or so ago, but somehow the rules never caught up. They're very strict about the regs here." He winked at Abigail's dismayed expression. "Hold tight a minute while—" His voice faded as he tinkered with the controls.

. . . established forty years later and communications with the Proxima colony began shortly thereafter. Ginungagap . . .

The voice cut off. She grinned thanks. "Abigail Vanderhoek."

"Cheyney," the pilot said. "You're the gravity bum, right?"

"Yeah."

"I used to be a vacuum bum myself. But I got tired of it, and grabbed the first semipermanent contract that came along."

"I kind of went the other way."

"Probably what I should have done," Cheyney said amiably. "Still, it's a rough road. I picked up three scars along the way." He pointed them out: a thick slash across his abdomen, a red splotch beside one nipple, and a white crescent half obscured by his scalp. "I could've had them cleaned up, but the way I figure, life is just a process of picking up scars and experience. So I kept 'em."

If she had thought he was trying to impress her, Abigail would have slapped him down. But it was clearly just part of an ongoing self-dramatization, possibly justified, probably not. Abigail suspected that, tour trips to Earth excepted, the *Clarke* was as far down a gravity well as Cheyney had ever been. Still he did have an irresponsible, boyish appeal. "Take me past the net?" she asked.

Cheyney looped the tug around the communications net trailing the *Clarke*. Kilometers of steel lace passed beneath them. He pointed out a small dish antenna on the edge and a cluster of antennae on the back. "The loner on the edge transmits into Ginungagap," he said. "The others relay information to and from Mother."

"Mother?"

"That's the traditional name for the *Arthur C. Clarke*." He swung the tug about with a careless sweep of one arm, and launched into a long and scurrilous story about the origin of the nickname. Abigail laughed, and Cheyney pointed a finger. "There's Ginungagap."

Abigail peered intently. "Where? I don't see a thing." She glanced at the second wraparound insert, which displayed a magnified view of the black hole. It wasn't at all impressive: a red smear against black nothingness. In the star field it was all but invisible.

"Disappointing, hey? But still dangerous. Even this far out, there's a lot of ionization from the accretion disk."

"Is that why there's a lip station?"

"Yeah. Particle concentration varies, but if the translator was right at the *Clarke*, we'd probably lose about a third of the passengers."

Cheyney dropped Abigail off at Mother's crew lock and looped the tug off and away. Abigail wondered where to go, what to do now.

"You're the gravity bum we're dumping down Ginungagap." The short, solid man was upon her before she saw him. His eyes were intense. His *cache-sexe* was a conservative orange. "I liked the stunt with the arm. It takes a lot of guts to do something like that." He pumped her arm. "I'm Paul Girard. Head of external security. In charge of your training. You play verbal Ping-Pong?"

"Why do you ask?" she countered automatically.

"Don't you know?"

"Should I?"

"Do you mean now or later?"

"Will the answer be different later?"

A smile creased Paul's solid face. "You'll do." He took her

arm, led her along a sloping corridor. "There isn't much prep
time. The dry run is scheduled in two weeks. Things will
move pretty quickly after that. You want to start your training now?"

"Do I have a choice?" Abigail asked, amused.

Paul came to a dead stop. "Listen," he said. "Rule number
one: Don't play games with *me*. You understand? Because I
always win. Not sometimes, not usually—always."

Abigail yanked her arm free. "You maneuvered me into
that," she said angrily.

"Consider it part of your training." He stared directly into
her eyes. "No matter how many gravity wells you've climbed
down, you're still the product of a near-space culture—protected, trusting, willing to take things at face value. This is a
dangerous attitude, and I want you to realize it. I want you to
learn to look behind the mask of events. I want you to grow
up. And you will."

Don't be so sure. A small smile quirked Paul's face as if he
could read her thoughts. Aloud, Abigail said, "That sounds a
little excessive for a trip to Proxima."

"Lesson number two," Paul said. "Don't make easy assumptions. You're not going to Proxima." He led her out-
ward-down the ramp to the next wheel, pausing briefly at the
juncture to acclimatize to the slower rate of revolution.
"You're going to visit spiders." He gestured. "The crew room
is this way."

The crew room was vast and cavernous, twilight gloomy.
Keyouts were set up along winding paths that wandered
aimlessly through the work space. Puddles of light fell on
each board and operator. Dark-loving foliage was set between the keyouts.

"This is the heart of the beast," Paul said. "The green
keyouts handle all Proxima communications—pretty routine
by now. But the blue . . ." His eyes glinting oddly, he
pointed. Over the keyouts hung silvery screens with harsh,

grainy images floating on their surfaces, black-and-white blobs that Abigail could not resolve into recognizable forms.

"Those," Paul said, "are the spiders. We're talking to them in real-time. Response delay is almost all due to machine translation."

In a sudden shift of perception, the blobs became arachnid forms. That mass of black fluttering across the screen was a spider leg and *that* was its thorax. Abigail felt an immediate, primal aversion, and then it was swept away by an all-encompassing wonder.

"Aliens?" she breathed.

"Aliens."

They actually looked no more like spiders than humans looked like apes. The eight legs had an extra joint each, and the mandible configuration was all wrong. But to an untrained eye they would do.

"But this is— How long have you—? Why in God's name are you keeping this a secret?" An indefinable joy arose in Abigail. This opened a universe of possibilities, as if after a lifetime of being confined in a box someone had removed the lid.

"Industrial security," Paul said. "The gadget that'll send you through Ginungagap to *their* black hole is a spider invention. We're trading optical data for it, but the law won't protect our rights until we've demonstrated its use. We don't want the other corporations cutting in." He nodded toward the nearest black-and-white screen. "As you can see, they're weak on optics."

"I'd love to talk . . ." Abigail's voice trailed off as she realized how little-girl hopeful she sounded.

"I'll arrange an introduction."

There was a rustling to Abigail's side. She turned and saw a large black tomcat with white boots and belly emerge from the bushes. "This is the esteemed head of Alien Communications," Paul said sourly.

Abigail started to laugh, then choked in embarrassment as

she realized that he was not speaking of the cat. "Julio Dominguez, section chief for translation," Paul said. "Abigail Vanderhoek, gravity specialist."

The wizened old man smiled professorially. "I assume our resident gadfly has explained how the communications net works, has he not?"

"Well—" Abigail began.

Dominguez clucked his tongue. He wore a yellow *cache-sexe* and matching bow tie, just a little too garish for a man his age. "Quite simple, actually. Escape velocity from a black hole is greater than the speed of light. Therefore, within Ginungagap the speed of light is no longer the limit to the speed of communications."

He paused just long enough for Abigail to look baffled. "Which is just a stuffy way of saying that when we aim a stream of electrons into the boundary of the stationary limit, they emerge elsewhere—out of another black hole. And if we aim them *just so*—his voice rose whimsically—"they'll emerge from the black hole of our choosing. The physics is simple. The finesse is in aiming the electrons."

The cat stalked up to Abigail, pushed its forehead against her leg, and mewed insistently. She bent over and picked it up. "But nothing can emerge from a black hole," she objected.

Dominguez chuckled. "Ah, but anything can fall in, hey? A positron can fall in. But a positron falling into Ginungagap in positive time is only an electron falling out in negative time. Which means that a positron falling into a black hole in negative time is actually an electron falling out in positive time—exactly the effect we want. Think of Ginungagap as being the physical manifestation of an equivalence sign in mathematics."

"Oh," Abigail said, feeling very firmly put in her place. White moths flittered along the path. The cat watched, fascinated, while she stroked its head.

"At any rate, the electrons do emerge, and once the data

are in, the theory has to follow along meekly."

"Tell me about the spiders," Abigail said before he could continue. The moths were darting up, sideward, down, a chance ballet in three dimensions.

"The *aliens*," Dominguez said, frowning at Paul, "are still a mystery to us. We exchange facts, descriptions, recipes for tools, but the important questions do not lend themselves to our clumsy mathematical codes. Do they know of love? Do they appreciate beauty? Do they believe in God, hey?"

"Do they want to eat us?" Paul threw in.

"Don't be ridiculous," Dominguez snapped. "Of course they don't."

The moths parted when they came to Abigail. Two went to either side; one flew over her shoulder. The cat batted at it with one paw. "The cat's name is Garble," Paul said. "The kids in Bio cloned him up."

Dominguez opened his mouth, closed it again.

Abigail scratched Garble under the chin. He arched his neck and purred all but noiselessly. "With your permission," Paul said. He stepped over to a keyout and waved its operator aside.

"Technically you're supposed to speak a convenience language, but if you keep it simple and non-idiomatic, there shouldn't be any difficulty." He touched the keyout. "Ritual greetings, spider." There was a blank pause. Then the spider moved, a hairy leg flickering across the screen.

"Hello, human."

"Introductions: Abigail Vanderhoek. She is our representative. She will ride the spinner." Another pause. More leg waving.

"Hello, Abigail Vanderhoek. Transition of vacuum garble resting garble commercial benefits garble still point in space."

"Tricky translation," Paul said. He signed to Abigail to take over.

Abigail hesitated, then said, "Will you come to visit us? The way we will visit you?"

"No, you see—" Dominguez began, but Paul waved him to silence.

"No, Abigail Vanderhoek. We are sulfur-based life."

"I do not understand."

"You can garble black hole through garble spinner because you are carbon-based life. Carbon forms chains easily but sulfur combines in lattices or rosettes. Our garble simple form garble. Sometimes sulfur forms short chains."

"We'll explain later," Paul said. "Go on, you're doing fine."

Abigail hesitated again. What do you say to a spider, anyway? Finally she asked, "Do you want to eat us?"

"Oh, Christ, get her off that thing," Dominguez said, reaching for the keyout.

Paul blocked his arm. "No," he said. "I want to hear this."

Several of the spider legs wove intricate patterns. "The question is false. Sulfur-based life derives no benefit from eating carbon-based life."

"You see," Dominguez said.

"But if it were possible," Abigail persisted. "If you *could* eat us and derive benefit. Would you?"

"Yes, Abigail Vanderhoek. With great pleasure."

Dominguez pushed her aside. "We're terribly sorry," he said to the alien. "This is a horrible, horrible misunderstanding. You!" he shouted to the operator. "Get back on and clear this mess up."

Paul was grinning wickedly. "Come," he said to Abigail. "We've accomplished enough here for one day."

As they started to walk away, Garble twisted in Abigail's arms and leaped free. He hit the floor on all fours and disappeared into the greenery. "Would they really eat us?" Abigail asked. Then amended it to, "Does that mean they're hostile?"

Paul shrugged. "Maybe they thought we'd be insulted if they *didn't* offer to eat us." He led her to her quarters. "Tomorrow we start training for real. In the meantime you might make up a list of all the ways the spiders could hurt us if we set up transportation and they *are* hostile. Then another list of all the reasons we shouldn't trust them." He paused. "I've done it myself. You'll find that the lists get rather extensive."

Abigail's quarters weren't flashy, but they fit her well. A full star field was routed to the walls, floor, and ceiling, only partially obscured by a trellis inner frame that supported fox-grape vines. Somebody had done research into her tastes.

"Hi." The cheery greeting startled her. She whirled, saw that her hammock was occupied.

Cheyney sat up, swung his legs over the edge of the hammock, causing it to rock lightly. "Come on in." He touched an invisible control and the star field blue-shifted down to a deep, erotic purple.

"Just what do you think you're doing here?" Abigail asked.

"I had a few hours free," Cheyney said, "so I thought I'd drop by and seduce you."

"Well, Cheyney, I appreciate your honesty," Abigail said. "So I won't say no."

"Thank you."

"I'll say maybe some other time. Now get lost. I'm tired."

"Okay." Cheyney hopped down, walked jauntily to the door. He paused. "You said later, right?"

"I said *maybe* later."

"Later. Gotcha." He winked and was gone.

Abigail threw herself into the hammock, red-shifted the star field until the universe was a sparse smattering of dying embers. Annoying creature! There was no hope for anything more than the most superficial of relationships with him. She closed her eyes, smiled. Fortunately, she wasn't currently in the market for a serious relationship.

She slept.

She was falling. . . .

Abigail had landed the ship an easy walk from 3M's robot laboratory. The lab's geodesic dome echoed white clouds to the north, where Nix Olympus peeked over the horizon. Otherwise all—land, sky, rocks—was standard-issue Martian orange. She had clambered to the ground and shrugged on the supply backpack.

Resupplying 3M-RL stations was a gut contract, easy but dull. So perhaps she was less cautious than usual going down the steep, rock-strewn hillside, or perhaps the rock would have turned under her no matter how carefully she placed her feet. Her ankle twisted and she lurched sideways, but the backpack had shifted her center of gravity too much for her to be able to recover.

Arms windmilling, she fell.

The rockslide carried her downhill in a panicky flurry of dust and motion, tearing her flesh and splintering her bones. But before she could feel pain, her suit shot her full of a nerve synesthetic, translating sensation into colors—reds, russets, and browns, with staccato yellow spikes when a rock smashed into her ribs. So that she fell in a whirling rainbow of glorious light.

She came to rest in a burst of orange. The rocks were settling about her. A spume of dust drifted away, out toward the distant red horizon. A large, jagged slab of stone slid by, gently shearing off her backpack. Tools, supplies, airpacks flew up and softly rained down.

A spanner as long as her arm slammed down inches from Abigail's helmet. She flinched, and suddenly events became real. She kicked her legs and sand and dust fountained up. Drawing her feet under her body—the one ankle bright gold—she started to stand.

And was jerked to the ground by a sudden tug on one arm. Even as she turned her head, she became aware of a deep purple sensation in her left hand. It was pinioned to a rock not quite large enough to stake a claim to. There was no color in the fingers.

"Cute," she muttered. She tugged at the arm, pushed at the rock. Nothing budged.

Abigail nudged the radio switch with her chin. "Grounder

to Lip Station," she said. She hesitated, feeling foolish, then said, "Mayday. Repeat, Mayday. Could you guys send a rescue party down for me?"

There was no reply. With a sick green feeling in the pit of her stomach, Abigail reached a gloved hand around the back of her helmet. She touched something jagged, a sensation of mottled rust, the broken remains of her radio.

"I think I'm in trouble." She said it aloud and listened to the sound of it. Flat, unemotional—probably true. But nothing to get panicky about.

She took quick stock of what she had to work with. One intact suit and helmet. One spanner. A worldful of rocks, many close at hand. Enough air for—she checked the helmet readout—almost an hour. Assuming the lip station ran its checks on schedule and was fast on the uptake, she had almost half the air she needed.

Most of the backpack's contents were scattered too far away to reach. One rectangular gaspack, however, had landed nearby. She reached for it but could not touch it, squinted but could not read the label on its nozzle. It was almost certainly liquid gas—either nitrogen or oxygen—for the robot lab. There was a slim chance it was the spare airpack. If it was, she might live to be rescued.

Abigail studied the landscape carefully, but there was nothing more. "Okay, then, it's an airpack." She reached as far as her tethered arm would allow. The gaspack remained a tantalizing centimeter out of reach.

For an instant she was stymied. Then, feeling like an idiot, she grabbed the spanner. She hooked it over the gaspack. Felt the gaspack more grudgingly. Slowly nudged it toward herself.

By the time Abigail could drop the spanner and draw in the gaspack, her good arm was blue with fatigue. Sweat running down her face, she juggled the gaspack to read its nozzle markings.

It was liquid oxygen—useless. She could hook it to her suit and feed in the contents, but the first breath would freeze her lungs. She released the gaspack and lay back, staring vacantly at the sky.

Up there was civilization: tens of thousands of human stations strung together by webs of communication and transportation. Messages flowed endlessly on laser cables. Translators borrowed and lent momentum, moving streams of travelers and cargo at almost (but not quite) the speed of light. A starship was being readied to carry a third load of colonists to Proxima. Up there, free from gravity's relentless clutch, people lived in luxury and ease. Here, however . . .

"I'm going to die." She said it softly and was filled with wondering awe. Because it was true. She was going to die.

Death was a black wall. It lay before her, extending to infinity in all directions, smooth and featureless and mysterious. She could almost reach out an arm and touch it. Soon she would come up against it and, if anything lay beyond, pass through. Soon, very soon, she would *know.*

She touched the seal to her helmet. It felt gray—smooth and inviting. Her fingers moved absently, tracing the seal about her neck. With sudden horror, Abigail realized that she was thinking about undoing it, releasing her air, throwing away the little time she had left. . . .

She shuddered. With sudden resolve, she reached out and unsealed the shoulder seam of her captive arm.

The seal clamped down, automatically cutting off air loss. The flesh of her damaged arm was exposed to the raw Martian atmosphere. Abigail took up the gaspack and cradled it in the pit of her good arm. Awkwardly, she opened the nozzle with the spanner.

She sprayed the exposed arm with liquid oxygen for over a minute before she was certain it had frozen solid. Then she dropped the gaspack, picked up the spanner, and swung.

Her arm shattered into a thousand fragments.

She stood up.

Abigail awoke, tense and sweaty. She blue-shifted the walls up to normal light, and sat up. After a few minutes of clearing her head, she set the walls to cycle from red to blue in a rhythm matching her normal pulse. Eventually the womb-cycle lulled her back to sleep.

"Not even close," Paul said. He ran the tape backward, froze it on a still shot of the spider twisting two legs about each other. "That's the morpheme for 'extreme disgust,' remember. It's easy to pick out, and the language kids say that any statement with this gesture should be reversed in meaning. Irony, see? So when the spider says that the strong should protect the weak, it means—"

"How long have we been doing this?"

"Practically forever," Paul said cheerfully. "You want to call it a day?"

"Only if it won't hurt my standing."

"Hah! Very good." He switched off the keyout. "Nicely thought out. You're absolutely right; it would have. However, as reward for realizing this, you can take off early *without* it being noted on your record."

"Thank you," Abigail said sourly.

Like most large installations, the *Clarke* had a dozen or so smaller structures tagging along after it in minimum-maintenance orbits. When Abigail discovered that these included a small wheel gymnasium, she had taken to putting in an hour's exercise after each training shift. Today she put in two.

The first hour she spent shadowboxing and practicing *savate* in heavy-gee to work up a sweat. The second hour she spent in the axis room, performing free-fall gymnastics. After the first workout, it made her feel light and nimble and good about her body.

She returned from the wheel gym sweaty and cheerful to find Cheyney in her hammock again. "Cheyney," she said, "this is not the first time I've had to kick you out of there. Or even the third, for that matter."

Cheyney held his palms up in mock protest. "Hey, no," he said. "Nothing like that today. I just came by to watch the raft debate with you."

Abigail felt pleasantly weary, decidedly uncerebral. "Paul said something about it, but . . ."

"Turn it on, then. You don't want to miss it." Cheyney touched her wall, and a cluster of images sprang to life at the far end of the room.

"Just what is a raft debate anyway?" Abigail asked, giving in gracefully. She hoisted herself onto the hammock, sat beside him. They rocked gently for a moment.

"There's this raft, see? It's adrift and powerless and there's only enough oxygen on board to keep one person alive until rescue. Only there are three on board—two humans and a spider."

"Do spiders breathe oxygen?"

"It doesn't matter. This is a hypothetical situation." Two-thirds of the image area were taken up by Dominguez and Paul, quietly waiting for the debate to begin. The remainder showed a flat spider image.

"Okay, what then?"

"They argue over who gets to survive. Dominguez argues that he should, since he's human and human culture is superior to spider culture. The spider argues for itself and its culture." He put an arm around her waist. "You smell nice."

"Thank you." She ignored the arm. "What does Paul argue?"

"He's the devil's advocate. He argues that no one deserves to live and they should dump the oxygen."

"Paul would enjoy that role," Abigail said. Then, "What's the point to this debate?"

"It's an entertainment. There isn't supposed to be a point."

Abigail doubted it was that simple. The debate could reveal a good deal about the spiders and how they thought, once the language types were done with it. Conversely, the spiders would doubtless be studying the human responses. *This could be interesting,* she thought. Cheyney was stroking her side now, lightly but with great authority. She postponed reaction, not sure whether she liked it or not.

Louise Chang, a vaguely high-placed administrator, blossomed in the center of the image cluster. "Welcome," she said, and explained the rules of the debate. "The winner will be decided by acclaim," she said, "with half the vote being human and half alien. Please remember not to base your vote on racial chauvinism, but on the strengths of the arguments and how well they are presented." Cheyney's hand brushed casually across her nipples; they stiffened. The hand lingered. "The debate will begin with the gentleman representing the aliens presenting his thesis."

The image flickered as the spider waved several legs. "Thank you, Ms. Chairman. I argue that I should survive. My culture is superior because of our technological advancement. Three examples. Humans have used translation travel only briefly, yet we have used it for sixteens of garble. Our black hole technology is superior. And our garble has garble for the duration of our society."

"Thank you. The gentleman representing humanity?"

"Thank you, Ms. Chairman." Dominguez adjusted an armlet. Cheyney leaned back and let Abigail rest against him. Her head fit comfortably against his shoulder. "My argument is that technology is neither the sole nor the most important measure of a culture. By these standards dolphins would be considered brute animals. The aesthetic considerations—the arts, theology, and the tradition of philosophy—are of greater import. As I shall endeavor to prove."

"He's chosen the wrong tactic," Cheyney whispered in Abigail's ear. "That must have come across as pure garble to the spiders."

"Thank you. Mr. Girard?"

Paul's image expanded. He theatrically swigged from a small flask and hoisted it high in the air. "Alcohol! There's the greatest achievement of the human race!" Abigail snorted. Cheyney laughed out loud. "But I hold that neither Mr. Dominguez nor the distinguished spider deserves to live, because of the disregard both cultures have for sentient life." Abigail looked at Cheyney, who shrugged. "As I shall endeavor to prove." His image dwindled.

Chang said, "The arguments will now proceed, beginning with the distinguished alien."

The spider and then Dominguez ran through their arguments, and to Abigail they seemed markedly lackluster. She didn't give them her full attention, because Cheyney's hands were moving most interestingly across unexpected parts of her body. He might not be too bright, but he was certainly good at some things. She nuzzled her face into his neck, gave him a small peck, returned her attention to the debate.

Paul blossomed again. He juggled something in his palm, held his hand open to reveal three ball bearings. "When I was a kid I used to short out the school module and sneak up to the axis room to play marbles." Abigail smiled, remembering similar stunts she had played. "For the sake of those of us who are spiders, I'll explain that marbles is a game played in free-fall for the purpose of developing coordination and spatial perception. You make a six-armed star of marbles in the center . . ."

One of the bearings fell from his hand, bounced noisily, and disappeared as it rolled out of camera range. "Well, obviously it can't be played here. But the point is that when you shoot the marble just right, it hits the end of one arm and its kinetic energy is transferred from marble to marble along that arm. So that the shooter stops and the marble at the far end of the arm flies away." Cheyney was stroking her absently now, engrossed in the argument.

"Now, we plan to send a courier into Ginungagap and out the spiders' black hole. At least that's what we say we're going to do.

"But what exits from a black hole is not necessarily the same as what went into its partner hole. We throw an electron into Ginungagap and another one pops out elsewhere. It's identical. It's a direct causal relationship. But it's like marbles—they're identical to each other and have the same kinetic force. It's simply not the same electron."

Cheyney's hand was still, motionless. Abigail prodded him gently, touching his inner thigh. "Anyone who's interested can see the equations. Now, when we send messages, this doesn't matter. The message is important, not the medium. However, when we send a human being in . . . what emerges from the other hole will be cell for cell, gene for gene, atom for atom identical. *But it will not be the same person."* He paused a beat, smiled.

"I submit, then, that this is murder. And further, that by conspiring to commit murder, both the spider and human races display absolute disregard for intelligent life. In short, no one on the raft deserves to live. And I rest my case."

"Mr. Girard!" Dominguez objected, even before his image was restored to full size. "The simplest mathematical proof is an identity: that A equals A. Are you trying to deny this?"

Paul held up the two ball bearings he had left. "These marbles are identical too. But they are not the same marble."

"We know the phenomenon you speak of," the spider said. "It is as if garble the black hole bulges out simultaneously. There is no violation of continuity. The two entities are the same. There is no death."

Abigail pulled Cheyney down, so that they were both lying on their sides, still able to watch the images. "So long as you happen to be the second marble and not the first," Paul said. Abigail tentatively licked Cheyney's ear.

"He's right," Cheyney murmured.

"No he's not," Abigail retorted. She bit his earlobe.

"You mean that?"

"Of course I mean that. He's confusing semantics with reality." She engrossed herself in a study of the back of his neck.

"Okay."

Abigail suddenly sensed that she was missing something. "Why do you ask?" She struggled into a sitting position. Cheyney followed.

"No particular reason." Cheyney's hands began touching her again. But Abigail was sure something had been slipped past her.

They caressed each other lightly while the debate dragged to an end. Not paying much attention, Abigail voted for Dominguez, and Cheyney voted for Paul. As a result of a nearly undivided spider vote, the spider won. "I told you Dominguez was taking the wrong approach," Cheyney said. He hopped off the hammock. "Look, I've got to see somebody about something. I'll be right back."

"You're not leaving *now*?" Abigail protested, dumbfounded. The door irised shut.

Angry and hurt, she leaped down, determined to follow him. She couldn't remember ever feeling so insulted.

Cheyney didn't try to be evasive; it apparently did not occur to him that she might follow. Abigail stalked him down a corridor, up an in-ramp, and to a door that irised open for him. She recognized that door.

Thoughtfully, she squatted on her heels behind an untrimmed boxwood and waited. A minute later, Garble wandered by, saw her, and demanded attention. "Scat!" she hissed. He butted his head against her knee. "Then be quiet, at least." She scooped him up. His expression was smug.

The door irised open and Cheyney exited, whistling. Abigail waited until he was gone, stood, went to the door, and entered. Fish darted between long fronds under a transparent floor. It was an austere room, almost featureless. Abigail looked, but did not see a hammock.

"So Cheyney's working for you now," she said coldly. Paul looked up from a corner keyout.

"As a matter of fact, I've just signed him to permanent contract in the crew room. He's bright enough. A bit green. Ought to do well."

"Then you admit that you put him up to grilling me about your puerile argument in the debate?" Garble struggled in her arms. She juggled him into a more comfortable position. "And that you staged the argument for my benefit in the first place?"

"Ah," Paul said. "I knew the training was going some-

where. You've become very wary in an extremely short
time."

"Don't evade the question."

"I needed your honest reaction," Paul said. "Not the answer you would have given me, knowing your chances of
crossing Ginungagap rode on it."

Garble made an angry noise. "You tell him, Garble!" she
said. "That goes double for me." She stepped out the door.
"You lost the debate," she snapped.

Long after the door had irised shut, she could feel Paul's
amused smile burning into her back.

Two days after she returned to kick Cheyney out of her
hammock for the final time, Abigail was called to the crew
room. "Dry run," Paul said. "Attendance is mandatory."
And cut off.

The crew room was crowded with technicians, triple the
number of keyouts. Small knots of them clustered before the
screens, watching. Paul waved her to him.

"There," he motioned to one screen. "That's Clotho—the
platform we built for the transmission device. It's a hundred
kilometers off. I wanted more, but Dominguez overruled me.
The device that'll unravel you and dump you down Ginungagap is that doohickey in the center." He tapped a keyout
and the platform zoomed up to fill the screen. It was covered
by a clear, transparent bubble. Inside, a space-suited figure
was placing something into a machine that looked like nothing so much as a giant armor-clad clamshell. Abigail looked,
blinked, looked again.

"That's Garble," she said indignantly.

"Complain to Dominguez. I wanted a baboon."

The clamshell device closed. The space-suited tech left in
his tug, and alphanumerics flickered, indicating the device
was in operation. As they watched, the spider-designed machinery immobilized Garble, transformed his molecules into
one long continuous polymer chain, and spun it out an invis-

ible opening at near light speed. The water in his body was separated out, piped away, and preserved. The electrolyte balances were recorded and simultaneously transmitted in a parallel stream of electrons. It would reach the spider receiver along with the leading end of the cat-polymer, to be used in the reconstruction.

Thirty seconds passed. Now Garble was only partially in Clotho. The polymer chain, invisible and incredibly long, was passing into Ginungagap. On the far side the spiders were beginning to knit it up.

If all was going well . . .

Ninety-two seconds after they flashed on, the alphanumerics stopped twinkling on the screen. Garble was gone from Clotho. The clamshell opened and the remote cameras showed it to be empty. A cheer arose.

Somebody boosted Dominguez atop a keyout. Intercom cameras swiveled to follow. He wavered fractionally, said, "My friends," and launched into a speech. Abigail didn't listen.

Paul's hand fell on her shoulder. It was the first time he had touched her since their initial meeting. "He's only a scientist," he said. "He had no idea how close you are to that cat."

"Look, I *asked* to go. I knew the risks. But Garble's just an animal; he wasn't given the choice."

Paul groped for words. "In a way, this is what your training has been about—the reason you're going across instead of someone like Dominguez. He projects his own reactions onto other people. If—"

Then, seeing that she wasn't listening, he said, "Anyway, you'll have a cat to play with in a few hours. They're only keeping him long enough to test out the life-support systems."

There was a festive air to the second gathering. The spiders reported that Garble had translated flawlessly. A brief visual display showed him stalking about Clotho's sister platform, irritable but apparently unharmed.

"There," somebody said. The screen indicated that the receiver net had taken in the running end of the cat's polymer chain. They waited a minute and a half and the operation was over.

It was like a conjuring trick; the clamshell closed on emptiness. Water was piped in. Then it opened and Garble floated over its center, quietly licking one paw.

Abigail smiled at the homeliness of it. "Welcome back, Garble," she said quietly. "I'll get the guys in Bio to brew up some cream for you."

Paul's eyes flicked in her direction. They lingered for no time at all, long enough to file away another datum for future use, and then his attention was elsewhere. She waited until his back was turned and stuck out her tongue at him.

The tub docked with Clotho and a technician floated in. She removed her helmet self-consciously, aware of her audience. One hand extended, she bobbed toward the cat, calling softly.

"Get that jerk on the line," Paul snapped. "I want her helmet back on. That's sloppy. That's real—"

And in that instant, Garble sprang.

Garble was a black-and-white streak that flashed past the astonished tech, through the air lock, and into the open tug. The cat pounced on the pilot panel. Its forelegs hit the controls. The hatch slammed shut, and the tug's motors burst into life.

Crew room techs grabbed wildly at their keyouts. The tech on Clotho frantically tried to fit her helmet back on. And the tug took off, blasting away half the protective dome and all the platform's air.

The screens showed a dozen different scenes, lenses shifting from close to distant and back. "Cheyney," Paul said quietly. Dominguez was frozen, looking bewildered. "Take it out."

"It's coming right at us!" somebody shouted.

Cheyney's fingers flicked: rap-tap-rap.

A bright nuclear flower blossomed.

There was silence, dead and complete, in the crew room. *I'm missing something*, Abigail thought. *We just blew up five percent of our tug fleet to kill a cat.*

"*Pull* that transmitter!" Paul strode through the crew room, scattering orders. "Nothing goes out! You, you, and you"—he yanked techs away from their keyouts—"*off* those things. I want the whole goddamned net shut *down*."

"Paul . . ." an operator said.

"Keep on receiving." He didn't bother to look. "Whatever they want to send. Dump it all in storage and don't merge any of it with our data until we've gone over it."

Alone and useless in the center of the room, Dominguez stuttered, "What—what happened?"

"You blind idiot!" Paul turned on him viciously. "Your precious aliens have just made their first hostile move. The cat that came back was nothing like the one we sent. They made changes. They retransmitted it with instructions wet-wired into its brain."

"But why would they want to steal a tug?"

"*We don't know!*" Paul roared. "Get that through your head. We don't know their motives and we don't know how they think. But we would have known a lot more about their intentions than we wanted if I hadn't rigged that tug with an abort device."

"You didn't—" Dominguez began. He thought better of the statement.

"—have the authority to rig that device," Paul finished for him. "That's right. I didn't." His voice was heavy with sarcasm.

Dominguez seemed to shrivel. He stared bleakly, blankly, about him, then turned and left, slightly hunched over. Thoroughly discredited in front of the people who worked for him.

That was cold, Abigail thought. She marveled at Paul's cruelty. Not for an instant did she believe that the anger in his voice was real, that he was capable of losing control.

Which meant that in the midst of confusion and stress, Paul had found time to make a swift play for more power. To Abigail's newly suspicious eye, it looked like a successful one, too.

For five days Paul held the net shut by sheer willpower and force of personality. Information came in but did not go out. Bell-Sandia administration was not behind him; too much time and money had been sunk into Clotho to abandon the project. But Paul had the support of the tech crew, and he knew how to use it.

"Nothing as big as Bell-Sandia runs on popularity," Paul explained. "But I've got enough sympathy from above, and enough hesitation and official cowardice to keep this place shut down long enough to get a message across."

The incoming information flow fluctuated wildly, shifting from subject to subject. Data sequences were dropped halfway through and incomplete. Nonsense came in. The spiders were shifting through strategies in search of the key that would reopen the net.

"When they start repeating themselves," Paul said, "we can assume they understand the threat."

"But we *wouldn't* shut the net down permanently," Abigail pointed out.

Paul shrugged. "So it's a bluff."

They were sharing an after-shift drink in a fifth-level bar. Small red lizards scuttled about the rock wall behind the bartender. "And if your bluff doesn't work?" Abigail asked. "If it's all for nothing—what then?"

Paul's shoulders sagged, a minute shifting of tensions. "Then we trust in the goodwill of the spiders," he said. "We let them call the shots. And they will treat us benevolently or not, depending. In either case," his voice became dark, "I'll have played a lot of games and manipulated a lot of people for no reason at all." He took her hand. "If that happens, I'd like to apologize." His grip was tight, his knuckles pale.

That night, Abigail dreamed she was falling.

Light rainbowed all about her, in a violent splintering of bone and tearing of flesh. She flung out an arm and it bounced on something warm and yielding.

"Abigail."

She twisted and tumbled and something smashed into her ribs. Bright spikes of yellow darted up.

"Abigail!" Someone was shaking her, speaking loudly into her face. The rocks and sky went gray, were overlaid by unresolved images. Her eyelids struggled apart, fell together, opened.

"Oh," she said.

Paul rocked back on his heels. Fish darted about in the water beneath him. "There now," he said. Blue-green lights shifted gently underwater, moving in long, slow arcs. "Dream over?"

Abigail shivered, clutched his arm, let go of it almost immediately. She nodded.

"Good. Tell me about it."

"I—" Abigail began. "Are you asking me as a human being or in your official capacity?"

"I don't make that distinction."

She stretched out a leg and scratched her big toe, to gain time to think. She really didn't have any appropriate thoughts. "Okay," she said, and told him the entire dream.

Paul listened intently, rubbed a thumb across his chin thoughtfully when she was done. "We hired you on the basis of that incident, you know," he said. "Coolness under stress. Weak body image. There were a lot of gravity bums to choose from. But I figured you were just a hair tougher, a little bit grittier."

"What are you trying to tell me? That I'm replaceable?"

Paul shrugged. "Everybody's replaceable. I just wanted to be sure you knew that you could back out if you want. It wouldn't wreck our project."

"I don't want to back out." Abigail chose her words carefully, spoke them slowly, to avoid giving vent to the anger she felt building up inside. "Look, I've been on the gravity circuit for ten years. I've been everywhere in the system there is to go. Did you know that there are less than two thousand people alive who've set foot on Mercury *and* Pluto? We've got a little club; we get together once a year." Seaweed shifted about her; reflections of the floor lights formed nebulous swimming shapes on the walls. "I've spent my entire life going around and around and around the sun, and never really getting anywhere. I want to travel, and there's nowhere left for me to go. So you offer me a way out and then ask if I want to back down. Like hell I do!"

"Why don't you believe that going through Ginungagap is death?" Paul asked quietly. She looked into his eyes, saw cool calculations going on behind them. It frightened her, almost. He was measuring her, passing judgment, warping events into long logical chains that did not take human factors into account. He was an alien presence.

"It's—common sense, is all. I'll be the same when I exit as when I go in. There'll be no difference, not an atom's worth, not a scintilla."

"The *substance* will be different. Every atom will be different. Not a single electron in your body will be the same one you have now."

"Well, how does that differ so much from normal life?" Abigail demanded. "All our bodies are in constant flux. Molecules come and go. Bit by bit, we're replaced. Does that make us different people from moment to moment? 'All that is body is as coursing vapors,' right?"

Paul's eyes narrowed. "Marcus Aurelius. Your quotation isn't complete, though. It goes on: 'All that is of the soul is dreams and vapors.'"

"What's that supposed to mean?"

"It means that the quotation doesn't say what you claimed it did. If you care to read it literally, it argues the opposite of what you're saying."

"Still, you can't have it both ways. Either the me that comes out of the spider black hole is the same as the one who went in, or I'm not the same person as I was an instant ago."

"I'd argue differently," Paul said. "But no matter. Let's go back to sleep."

He held out a hand, but Abigail felt no inclination to accept it. "Does this mean I've passed your test?"

Paul closed his eyes, stretched a little. "You're still reasonably afraid of dying, and you don't believe that you will," he said. "Yeah. You pass."

"Thanks a heap," Abigail said. They slept, not touching, for the rest of the night.

Three days later, Abigail woke up, and Paul was gone. She touched the wall and spoke his name. A recording appeared. "Dominguez has been called up to Administration," it said. Paul appeared slightly distracted; he had not looked directly into the recorder and his image avoided Abigail's eyes. "I'm going to reopen the net before he returns. It's best we beat him to the punch." The recording clicked off.

Abigail routed an intercom call through to the crew room. A small chime notified him of her call, and he waved a hand in combined greeting and direction to remain silent. He was hunched over a keyout. The screen above it came to life.

"Ritual greetings, spider," he said.

"Hello, human. We wish to pursue our previous inquiry: the meaning of the term 'art,' which was used by the human Dominguez six-sixteenths of the way through his major presentation."

"This is a difficult question. To understand a definition of art, you must first know the philosophy of aesthetics. This is a comprehensive field of knowledge comparable to the study of perception. In many ways it is related."

"What is the trade value of this field of knowledge?"

Dominguez appeared, looking upset. He opened his mouth, and Paul touched a finger to his own lips, nodding his head toward the screen.

"Significant. Our society considers art and science as being of roughly equal value."

"We will consider what to offer in exchange."

"Good. We also have a question for you. Please wait while we select the phrasing." He cut the translation lines, turned to Dominguez. "Looks like your raft gambit paid off. Though I'm surprised they bit at that particular piece of bait."

Dominguez looked weary. "Did they mention the incident with the cat?"

"No, nor the communications blackout."

The old man sighed. "I always felt close to the aliens," he said. "Now they seem—cold, inhuman." He attempted a chuckle. "That was almost a pun, wasn't it?"

"In a human, we'd call it a professional attitude. Don't let it spoil your accomplishment," Paul said. "This could be as big as optics." He opened the communications line again. "Our question is now phrased." Abigail noted he had not told Dominguez of her presence.

"Please go ahead."

"Why did you alter our test animal?"

Much leg waving. "We improved the ratios garble centers of perception garble wetware garble making the animal twelve-sixteenths as intelligent as a human. We thought you would be pleased."

"We were not. Why did the test animal behave in a hostile manner toward us?"

The spider's legs jerked quickly and it disappeared from the screen. Like an echo, the machine said, "Please wait."

Abigail watched Dominguez throw Paul a puzzled look. In the background, a man with a leather sack looped over one shoulder was walking slowly along the twisty access path. His hand dipped into the sack, came out, sprinkled fireflies among the greenery. Dipped in, came out again. Even in the midst of crisis, the trivia of day-to-day existence went on.

The spider reappeared, accompanied by two of its own kind. Their legs interlaced and retreated rapidly, a visual pantomime of an excited conversation. Finally one of their number addressed the screen.

"We have discussed the matter."

"So I see."

"It is our conclusion that the experience of translation through Ginungagap had a negative effect on the test animal. This was not anticipated. It is new knowledge. We know little of the psychology of carbon-based life."

"You're saying the test animal was driven mad?"

"Key word did not translate. We assume understanding. Steps must be taken to prevent a recurrence of this damage. Can you do this?"

Paul said nothing.

"Is this the reason why communications were interrupted?"

No reply.

"There is a cultural gap. Can you clarify?"

"Thank you for your cooperation," Paul said, and switched the screen off. "You can set your people to work," he told Dominguez. "No reason why they should answer the last few questions, though."

"Were they telling the truth?" Dominguez asked wonderingly.

"Probably not. But at least now they'll think twice before trying to jerk us around again." He winked at Abigail, and she switched off the intercom.

They reran the test using a baboon shipped out from the Belt Zoological Gardens. Abigail watched it arrive from the lip station, crated and snarling.

"They're a lot stronger than we are," Paul said. "Very agile. If the spiders want to try any more tricks, we couldn't offer them better bait."

The test went smooth as silk. The baboon was shot

through Ginungagap, held by the spiders for several hours, and returned. Exhaustive testing showed no tampering with the animal.

Abigail asked how accurate the tests were. Paul hooked his hands behind his back. "We're returning the baboon to the Belt. We wouldn't do that if we had any doubts. But—" He raised an eyebrow, asking Abigail to finish the thought.

"But if they're really hostile, they won't underestimate us twice. They'll wait for a human to tamper with."

Paul nodded.

The night before Abigail's sendoff they made love. It was a frenzied and desperate act, performed wordlessly and without tenderness. Afterward they lay together, Abigail idly playing with Paul's curls.

"Gail . . ." His head was hidden in her shoulder; she couldn't see his face. His voice was muffled.

"Mmmm?"

"Don't go."

She wanted to cry. Because as soon as he said it, she knew it was another test, the final one. And she also knew that Paul wanted her to fail it. That he honestly believed transversing Ginungagap would kill her, and that the woman who emerged from the spiders' black hole would not be herself.

His eyes were shut; she could tell by the creases in his forehead. He knew what her answer was. There was no way he could avoid knowing.

Abigail sensed that this was as close to a declaration of emotion as Paul was capable of. She felt how he despised himself for using his real emotions as yet another test, and how he could not even pretend to himself that there were circumstances under which he would *not* so test her. *This must be how it feels to think as he does*, she thought. *To constantly scrabble after every last implication, like eternally picking at a scab.*

"Oh, Paul," she said.

He wrenched about, turning his back to her. "Sometimes I wish"—his hands rose in front of his face like claws; they moved toward his eyes, closed into fists—"that for just ten goddamned minutes I could turn my mind off." His voice was bitter.

Abigail huddled against him, looped a hand over his side and onto his chest. "Hush," she said.

The tug backed away from Clotho, dwindling until it was one of a ring of bright sparks pacing the platform. Mother was a point source lost in the star field. Abigail shivered, pulled off her arm bands, and shoved them into a storage sack. She reached for her *cache-sexe*, hesitated.

The hell with it, she thought. *It's nothing they haven't seen before.* She shucked it off, stood naked. Gooseflesh rose on the backs of her legs. She swam to the transmittal device, feeling awkward under the distant watching eyes.

Abigail groped into the clamshell. "Go," she said.

The metal closed about her seamlessly, encasing her in darkness. She floated in a lotus position, bobbing slightly.

A light, gripping field touched her, stilling her motion. On cue, hypnotic commands took hold in her brain. Her breathing became shallow; her heart slowed. She felt her body ease into stasis. The final command took hold.

Abigail weighed fifty keys. Even though the water in her body would not be transmitted, the polymer chain she was to be transformed into would be 275 kilometers long. It would take fifteen minutes and seventeen seconds to unravel at light speed, negligibly longer at translation speed. She would still be sitting in Clotho when the spiders began knitting her up.

It was possible that Garble had gone mad from a relatively swift transit. Paul doubted it, but he wasn't taking any chances. To protect Abigail's sanity, the meds had wet-wired a travel fantasy into her brain. It would blind her to external reality while she traveled.

She was an eagle. Great feathered wings extended out from her shoulders. Clotho was gone, leaving her alone in space. Her skin was red and leathery, her breasts hard and unyielding. Feathers covered her thighs, giving way at the knees to talons.

She moved her wings, bouncing lightly against the thin solar wind swirling down into Ginungagap. The vacuum felt like absolute freedom. She screamed a predator's exultant shrill. Nothing enclosed her; she was free of restrictions forever.

Below her lay Ginungagap, the primal chasm, an invisible challenge marked by a red smudge of glowing gases. It was inchoate madness, a gibbering, impersonal force that wanted to draw her in, to crush her in its embrace. Its hunger was fierce and insatiable.

Abigail held her place briefly, effortlessly. Then she folded her wings and dove.

A rain of X-rays stung through her, the scattering of Ginungagap's accretion disk. They were molten iron passing through a ghost. Shrieking defiance, she attacked, scattering sparks in her wake.

Ginungagap grew, swelled until it swallowed up her vision. It was purest black, unseeable, unknowable, a thing of madness. It was Enemy.

A distant objective part of her knew that she was still in Clotho, the polymer chain being unraveled from her body, accelerated by a translator, passing through two black holes, and simultaneously being knit up by the spiders. It didn't matter.

She plunged into Ginungagap as effortlessly as if it were the film of a soap bubble.

In—

—And out.

It was like being reversed in a mirror, or watching an entertainment run backward. She was instantly flying out the way she came. The sky was a mottled mass of violet light.

The stars before her brightened from violet to blue. She craned her neck, looked back at Ginungagap, saw its disk-shaped nothingness recede, and screamed in frustration because it had escaped her. She spread her wings to slow her flight and—

—was sitting in a dark place. Her hand reached out, touched metal, recognized the inside of a clamshell device.

A hairline crack of light looped over her, widened. The clamshell opened.

Oceans of color bathed her face. Abigail straightened, and the act of doing so lifted her up gently. She stared through the transparent bubble at a phosphorescent foreverness of light.

My God, she thought. *The stars.*

The stars were thicker, more numerous than she was used to seeing them—large and bright and glittery rich. She was probably someplace significant, in a star cluster or the center of the galaxy; she couldn't guess. She felt irrationally happy to simply *be*; she took a deep breath, then laughed.

"Abigail Vanderhoek."

She turned to face the voice, and found that it came from a machine. Spiders crouched beside it, legs moving silently. Outside, in the hard vacuum, were more spiders.

"We regret any pain this may cause," the machine said.

Then the spiders rushed forward. She had no time to react. Sharp mandibles loomed before her, then dipped to her neck. Impossibly swift, they sliced through her throat, severed her spine. A sudden jerk and her head was separated from her body.

It happened in an instant. She felt brief pain, and the dissociation of actually *seeing* her decapitated body just beginning to react. And then she died.

A spark. A light. *I'm alive*, she thought. Consciousness returned like an ancient cathode tube warming up. Abigail stretched slowly, bobbing gently in the air, collecting her thoughts. She was in the sister-Clotho again—not in pain, her head and neck firmly on her shoulders. There were spiders in the platform, and a few floating outside.

"Abigail Vanderhoek," the machine said. "We are ready to begin negotiations."

Abigail said nothing.

After a moment the machine said, "Are you damaged? Are your thoughts impaired?" A pause, then, "Was your mind not protected during transit?"

"Is that you waving the legs there? Outside the platform?"

"Yes. It is important that you talk with the other humans. You must convey our questions. They will not communicate with us."

"I have a few questions of my own," Abigail said. "I won't cooperate until you answer them."

"We will answer any questions provided you neither garble nor garble."

"What do you take me for?" Abigail asked. "Of course I won't."

Long hours later she spoke to Paul and Dominguez. At her request the spiders had withdrawn, leaving her alone. Dominguez looked drawn and haggard. "I swear we had no idea the spiders would attack you," Dominguez said. "We saw it on the screens. I was certain you'd been killed. . . ." His voice trailed off.

"Well, I'm alive, no thanks to you guys. Just what *is* this crap about an explosive substance in my bones, anyway?"

"An explosive—I swear we know nothing of anything of the kind."

"A close relative to plastique," Paul said. "I had a small editing device attached to Clotho's translator. It altered roughly half the bone marrow in your sternum, pelvis, and femurs in transmission. I'd hoped the spiders wouldn't pick up on it so quickly."

"You actually did," Abigail marveled. "The spiders

weren't lying; they decapitated me in self-defense. What the holy hell did you think you were *doing*?"

"Just a precaution," Paul said. "We wet-wired you to trigger the stuff on command. That way we could have taken out the spider installation if they'd tried something funny."

"Um," Dominguez said, "this *is* being recorded. What I'd like to know, Ms. Vanderhoek, is how you escaped being destroyed."

"I didn't," Abigail said. "The spiders killed me. Fortunately they anticipated the situation, and recorded the transmission. It was easy for them to recreate me—after they edited out the plastique."

Dominguez gave her an odd look. "You don't—feel anything particular about this?"

"Like what?"

"Well—" He turned to Paul helplessly.

"Like the real Abigail Vanderhoek died and you're simply a very realistic copy," Paul said.

"Look, we've been through this garbage before," Abigail began angrily.

Paul smiled formally at Dominguez. It was hard to adjust to seeing the two in flat black and white. "She doesn't believe a word of it."

"If you guys can pull yourselves up out of your navels for a minute," Abigail said, "I've got a line on something the spiders have that you want. They claim they've sent probes through their black hole."

"Probes?" Paul stiffened. Abigail could sense the thoughts coursing through his skull, of defenses and military applications.

"Carbon-hydrogen-chain probes. Organic probes. Self-constructing transmitters. They've got a carbon-based secondary technology."

"Nonsense," Dominguez said. "How could they convert back to coherent matter without a receiver?"

Abigail shrugged. "They claim to have found a loophole."

"How does it work?" Paul snapped.

"They wouldn't say. They seemed to think you'd pay well for it."

"That's very true," Paul said slowly. "Oh, yes."

The conference took almost as long as her session with the spiders had. Abigail was bone weary when Dominguez finally said, "That ties up the official minutes. We now stop recording." A line tracked across the screen, was gone. "If you want to speak to anyone off the record, now's your chance. Perhaps there is someone close to you . . ."

"Close? No." Abigail almost laughed. "I'll speak to Paul alone, though."

A spider floated by outside Clotho II. It was a golden, crablike being, its body slightly opalescent. It skittered along unseen threads strung between the open platforms of the spider star-city. "I'm listening," Paul said.

"You turned me into a *bomb*, you freak."

"So?"

"I could have been killed."

"Am I supposed to care?"

"You damn well ought to, considering the liberties you've taken with my fair white body."

"Let's get one thing understood," Paul said. "The woman I slept with, the woman I cared for, is dead. I have no feelings toward or obligations to you whatsoever."

"Paul," Abigail said. *"I'm not dead.* Believe me. I'd know if I were."

"How could I possibly trust what you think or feel? It could all be attitudes the spiders wet-wired into you. We know they have the technology."

"How do you know that *your* attitudes aren't wet-wired in? For that matter, how do you know anything is real? I mean, these are the most sophomoric philosophic ideas there are. But I'm the same woman I was a few hours ago. My memories, opinions, feelings—they're all the same as they were. There's absolutely no difference between me and the woman you slept with on the *Clarke*."

"I know." Paul's eyes were cold. "That's the horror of it." He snapped off the screen.

Abigail found herself staring at the lifeless machinery. *God, that hurt,* she thought. *It shouldn't, but it hurt.* She went to her quarters.

The spiders had done a respectable job of preparing for her. There were no green plants, but otherwise the room was the same as the one she'd had on the *Clarke*. They'd even been able to spin the platform, giving her an adequate down-orientation. She sat in her hammock, determined to think pleasanter thoughts. About the offer the spiders had made, for example. The one she hadn't told Paul and Dominguez about.

Banned by their chemistry from using black holes to travel, the spiders needed a representative to see to their interests among the stars. They had offered her the job.

Or perhaps the plural would be more appropriate—they had offered her the jobs. Because there were too many places to go for one woman to handle them all. They needed a dozen—in time, perhaps, a hundred—Abigail Vanderhoeks.

In exchange for licensing rights to her personality, the right to make as many duplicates of her as were needed, they were willing to give her the rights to the self-reconstructing black hole platforms.

It would make her a rich woman—a hundred rich women—back in human space. And it would open the universe. She hadn't committed herself yet, but there was no way she was going to turn down the offer. The chance to see a thousand stars? No, she would not pass it by.

When she got old, too, they could create another Abigail from their recording, burn her new memories into it, and destroy her old body.

I'm going to see the stars, she thought. *I'm going to live forever.* She couldn't understand why she didn't feel elated, wondered at the sudden rush of melancholy that ran through her like the precursor of tears.

Garble jumped into her lap, offered his belly to be

scratched. The spiders had recorded him, too. They had been glad to restore him to his unaltered state when she made the request. She stroked his stomach and buried her face in his fur.

"Pretty little cat," she told him. "I thought you were dead."

The Unicorn Tapestry

Suzy McKee Charnas

I first became aware of Ms. Charnas's strange character Edward Weyland through a South African character: that is, I was glancing through Omni *on an airplane and somehow became aware that a certain character in one story was a lady from South Africa. Unlike most of the people who talk about that enigmatic land, I've been there. (And concluded that I don't know how to run their country. I suspect they don't either, but I know I don't know how to manage a land in which a big chunk of the population* prefers *Stone Age culture and resents any cultural aggressions by the twentieth century.) Thus I was interested . . . and found that Charnas had done an excellent job of creating someone I might well have met in my travels.*

I didn't then know her background.

Suzy McKee Charnas decided to become a writer while an undergraduate. This can be a disastrous decision; the young writer is all too often encouraged to take "writing" courses, and ends with technical skill but no experiences to write about.

Ms. Charnas chose differently. She says ". . . somewhere in college I figured out that I wanted to write, and foreseeing (so help me) that I would need to be able to create whole cultures in my head from scratch, I cobbled up a major for myself in economic history in order to have the background to do this. Graduated from Barnard College in 1961, intending to pursue my culture-building studies in the newly established African Studies program at Columbia, but that year the formation of the Peace Corps was announced, and I took the exam and got a telegram saying 'Would you be willing to teach in a West African country?' Said yes.

"Trained the summer of '61 at the Harvard Business School for Peace Corps work in Nigeria, and spent the following fall continuing training at the University of Ibadan. In 1962, I taught history (European and African), English (Great Expectations et al.), and art (drawing with pens we made for ourselves out of bamboo) at Girls' High School, Ogbomosho, W.R., Nigeria; plus library organization and acquisitions. The next year I taught introductory economic history at the brand-new University of Ife. The summer in between I spent in Liberia helping to set up a new Peace Corps program there."

From there she traveled in Europe, came home and tried to write, tried teaching, and, as she puts it, "floundered" until she went into community mental health work. In 1968 she married Stephen Charnas, an attorney. Then, she says, "In 1969 we moved to Albuquerque, and I started writing full-time. Have done so ever since, with much traveling, lecturing, and some local teaching (in the local alternative high school at the local university) mixed in. Nice life."

Edward Weyland is a vampire; but he is not human, dead or undead. He has lived a long time. In his most recent manifestation he was a professor in a small college, until he was found out by the Afrikaans lady; he fled that post after she shot him.

Fantasy doesn't often win science fiction awards. Of course, "The Unicorn Tapestry," which continues the story of Edward

Weyland and the lives he touches, may not be fantasy.
Fantasy or not, it won this year's Nebula for Best Novella.

"Hold on," Floria said. "I know what you're going to say: I agreed not to take any new clients for a while. But wait till I tell you—you're not going to believe this—first phone call, setting up an initial appointment, he comes out with what his problem is: 'I seem to have fallen victim to a delusion of being a vampire.'"

"Christ H. God!" cried Lucille delightedly. "Just like that, over the telephone?"

"When I recovered my aplomb, so to speak, I told him that I prefer to wait with the details until our first meeting, which is tomorrow."

They were sitting on the tiny terrace outside the staff room of the clinic, a converted town house on the upper West Side. Floria spent three days a week here and the remaining two in her office on Central Park South, where she saw private clients like this new one. Lucille, always gratifyingly responsive, was Floria's most valued professional friend. Clearly enchanted with Floria's news, she sat eagerly forward in her chair, eyes wide behind Coke-bottle lenses.

She said, "Do you suppose he thinks he's a revivified corpse?"

Below, down at the end of the street, Floria could see two kids skidding their skateboards near a man who wore a woolen cap and a heavy coat despite the May warmth. He was leaning against a wall. He had been there when Floria had arrived at the clinic this morning. If corpses walked, some, not nearly revivified enough, stood in plain view in New York.

"I'll have to think of a delicate way to ask," she said.

"How did he come to you, this 'vampire'?"

"He was working in an upstate college, teaching and doing research, and all of a sudden he just disappeared—vanished, literally, without a trace. A month later he turned up here in the city. The faculty dean at the school knows me and sent him to see me."

Lucille gave her a sly look. "So you thought, ahah, do a little favor for a friend, this looks classic and easy to transfer if need be: 'repressed intellectual blows stack and runs off with spacey chick,' something like that."

"You know me too well," Floria said with a rueful smile.

"Huh," grunted Lucille. She sipped ginger ale from a chipped white mug. "I don't take panicky middle-aged men anymore, they're too depressing. And you shouldn't be taking this one, intriguing as he sounds."

Here comes the lecture, Floria told herself.

Lucille got up. She was short, heavy, prone to wearing loose garments that swung about her like ceremonial robes. As she paced, her hem brushed at the flowers starting up in the planting boxes that rimmed the little terrace. "You know damn well this is just more overwork you're loading on. Don't take this guy; refer him."

Floria sighed. "I know, I know. I promised everybody I'd slow down. But you said it yourself just a minute ago—it looked like a simple favor. So what do I get? Count Dracula, for God's sake! Would you give that up?"

Fishing around in one capacious pocket, Lucille brought out a dented package of cigarettes and lit up, scowling. "You know, when you give me advice I try to take it seriously. Joking aside, Floria, what am I supposed to say? I've listened to you moaning for months now, and I thought we'd figured out that what you need is to shed some pressure, to start saying no—and here you are insisting on a new case. You know what I think; you're hiding in other people's problems from a lot of your own stuff that you should be working on.

"Okay, okay, don't glare at me. Be pigheaded. Have you gotten rid of Chubs, at least?" This was Floria's code name for a troublesome client named Kenny, whom she'd been trying to unload for some time.

Floria shook her head.

"What gives with you? It's weeks since you swore you'd dump him! Trying to do everything for everybody is wearing you out. I bet you're still dropping weight. Judging by the very unbecoming circles under your eyes, sleeping isn't going too well, either. Still no dreams you can remember?"

"Lucille, don't nag. I don't want to talk about my health."

"Well, what about his health—Dracula's? Did you suggest that he have a physical before seeing you? There might be something physiological—"

"You're not going to be able to whisk off to an M.D. and out of my hands," Floria said wryly. "He told me on the phone that he wouldn't consider either medication or hospitalization."

Involuntarily she glanced down at the end of the street. The woolen-capped man had curled up on the sidewalk at the foot of the building, sleeping or passed out or dead. The city was tottering with sickness. Compared with that wreck down there and others like him, how sick could this "vampire" be, with his cultured baritone voice, his self-possessed approach?

"And you won't consider handing him off to somebody else," Lucille said.

"Well, not until I know a little more. Come on, Luce—wouldn't you want at least to know what he looks like?"

Lucille stubbed out her cigarette against the low parapet. Down below, a policeman strolled along the street ticketing the parked cars. He didn't even look at the man lying at the corner of the building. They watched his progress without comment. Finally Lucille said, "Well, if you won't drop Dracula, keep me posted on him, will you?"

He entered the office on the dot of the hour, a gaunt but graceful figure. He was impressive. Wiry gray hair, worn short, emphasized the massiveness of his face with its long jaw, high cheekbones, and granite cheeks grooved as if by winters of hard weather. His name, typed in caps on the initial information sheet that Floria proceeded to fill out with him, was Edward Lewis Weyland.

Crisply he told her about the background of the vampire incident, describing in caustic terms his life at Cayslin College: the pressures of collegial competition, interdepartmental squabbles, student indifference, administrative bungling. History has limited use, she knew, since memory distorts; still, if he felt most comfortable establishing the setting for his illness, that was as good a way to start off as any.

At length his energy faltered. His angular body sank into a slump, his voice became flat and tired as he haltingly worked up to the crucial event: night work at the sleep lab, fantasies of blood-drinking as he watched the youthful subjects of his dream research slumbering, finally an attempt to act out the fantasy with a staff member at the college. He had been repulsed; then panic had assailed him. Word would get out, he'd be fired, blacklisted forever. He'd bolted. A nightmare period had followed—he offered no details. When he had come to his senses he'd seen that just what he feared, the ruin of his career, would come from his running away. So he'd phoned the dean, and now here he was.

Throughout this recital she watched him diminish from the dignified academic who had entered her office to a shamed and frightened man hunched in his chair, his hands pulling fitfully at each other.

"What are your hands doing?" she said gently. He looked blank. She repeated the question.

He looked down at his hands. "Struggling," he said.

"With what?"

"The worst," he muttered. "I haven't told you the worst." She had never grown hardened to this sort of transformation. His long fingers busied themselves fiddling with a button on his jacket while he explained painfully that the object of his "attack" at Cayslin had been a woman. Not young but handsome and vital, she had first caught his attention earlier in the year during an honorary seminar for a retiring professor.

A picture emerged of an awkward Weyland, lifelong bach-
elor, seeking this woman's warmth and suffering her refusal.
Floria knew she should bring him out of his past and into his
here-and-now, but he was doing so beautifully on his own
that she was loath to interrupt.

"Did I tell you there was a rapist active on the campus at
this time?" he said bitterly. "I borrowed a leaf from his book:
I tried to take from this woman, since she wouldn't give. I
tried to take some of her blood." He stared at the floor.
"What does that mean—to take someone's blood?"

"What do you think it means?"

The button, pulled and twisted by his fretful fingers, came
off. He put it into his pocket—the impulse, she guessed, of a
fastidious nature. "Her energy," he murmured, "stolen to
warm the aging scholar, the walking corpse, the vampire—
myself."

His silence, his downcast eyes, his bent shoulders, all signaled a man brought to bay by a life crisis. Perhaps he was
going to be the kind of client therapists dream of and she
needed so badly these days: a client intelligent and sensitive
enough, given the companionship of a professional listener,
to swiftly unravel his own mental tangles. Exhilarated by his
promising start, Floria restrained herself from trying to build
on it too soon. She made herself tolerate the silence, which
lasted until he said suddenly, "I notice that you make no
notes as we speak. Do you record these sessions on tape?"

A hint of paranoia, she thought; not unusual. "Not without your knowledge and consent, just as I won't send for
your personnel file from Cayslin without your knowledge
and consent. I do, however, write notes after each session as
a guide to myself and in order to have a record in case of any
confusion about anything we do or say here. I can promise
you that I won't show my notes or speak of you by name to
anyone—except Dean Sharpe at Cayslin, of course, and even
then only as much as is strictly necessary—without your written permission. Does that satisfy you?"

"I apologize for my question," he said. "The . . . incident

has left me . . . very nervous, a condition that I hope to get over with your help."

The time was up. When he had gone, she stepped outside to check with Hilda, the receptionist she shared with four other therapists here at the Central Park South office. Hilda always sized up new clients in the waiting room.

Of this one she said, "Are you sure there's anything wrong with that guy? I think I'm in love."

Waiting at the office for a group of clients to assemble Wednesday evening, Floria dashed off some notes on the "vampire."

> Client described incident, background. No history of mental illness, no previous experience of therapy. Personal history so ordinary you almost don't notice how bare it is: only child of German immigrants, schooling normal, field work in anthropology, academic posts leading to Cayslin College professorship. Health good, finances adequate, occupation satisfactory, housing pleasant (though presently installed in a N.Y. hotel); never married, no kids, no family, no religion, social life strictly job-related; leisure—says he likes to drive. Reaction to question about drinking, but no signs of alcohol problems. Physically very smooth-moving for his age (over fifty) and height; catlike, alert. Some apparent stiffness in the midsection—slight protective stoop—tightening up of middle age? Paranoic defensiveness? Voice pleasant, faint accent (German-speaking childhood at home). Entering therapy condition of consideration for return to job.

What a relief: his situation looked workable with a minimum of strain on herself. Now she could defend to Lucille her decision to do therapy with the "vampire."

After all, Lucille was right. Floria did have problems of her own that needed attention, primarily her anxiety and exhaustion since her mother's death more than a year before. The breakup of Floria's marriage had caused misery, but not this sort of endless depression. Intellectually the problem was clear: with both her parents dead, she was left exposed. No one stood any longer between herself and the inevitability of her own death. Knowing the source of her feelings didn't help; she couldn't seem to mobilize the nerve to work on them.

The Wednesday group went badly again. Lisa lived once more her experiences in the European death camps and everyone cried. Floria wanted to stop Lisa, turn her, extinguish the droning horror of her voice in illumination and release, but she couldn't see how to do it. She found nothing in herself to offer except some clever ploy out of the professional bag of tricks—dance your anger, have a dialogue with yourself of those days—useful techniques when they flowed organically as part of a living process in which the therapist participated. But thinking out responses that should have been intuitive wouldn't work. The group and its collective pain paralyzed her. She was a dancer without a choreographer, knowing all the moves but unable to match them to the music these people made.

Rather than act with mechanical clumsiness, she held back, did nothing, and suffered guilt. Oh, God, the smart, experienced people in the group must know how useless she was here.

Going home on the bus, she thought about calling up one of the therapists who shared the downtown office. He had expressed an interest in doing co-therapy with her under student observation. The Wednesday group might respond well to that. Suggest it to them next time? Having a partner might take pressure off Floria and revitalize the group, and if she felt she must withdraw, he would be available to take over. Of course, he might take over anyway and walk off with some of her clients.

Oh, boy, terrific, who's paranoid now? Wonderful way to think about a good colleague. God, she hadn't even known she was considering chucking the group.

Had the new client, running from his "vampirism," exposed her own impulse to retreat? This wouldn't be the first time that Floria had obtained help from a client while attempting to give help. Her old supervisor, Rigby, said that such mutual aid was the only true therapy—the rest was fraud. What a perfectionist, old Rigby, and what a bunch of young idealists he'd turned out, all eager to save the world.

Eager, but not necessarily able. Jane Fennerman had once lived in the world, and Floria had been incompetent to save her. Jane, an absent member of tonight's group, was back in the safety of a locked ward, hazily gliding on whatever tranquilizers they used there.

Why still mull over Jane? she asked herself severely, bracing against the bus's lurching halt. Any client was entitled to drop out of therapy and commit herself. Nor was this the first time that sort of thing had happened in the course of Floria's career. Only this time she couldn't seem to shake free of the resulting depression and guilt.

But how could she have helped Jane more? How could you offer reassurance that life was not as dreadful as Jane felt it to be, that her fears were insubstantial, that each day was not a pit of pain and danger?

She was taking time during a client's canceled hour to work on notes for the new book. The writing, an analysis of the vicissitudes of salaried versus private practice, balked her at every turn. She longed for an interruption to distract her circling mind.

Hilda put through a call from Cayslin College. It was Doug Sharpe, who had sent Dr. Weyland to her.

"Now that he's in your capable hands, I can tell people plainly that he's on what we call 'compassionate leave' and make them swallow it." Doug's voice seemed thinned by the long-distance connection. "Can you give me a preliminary opinion?"

"I need time to get a feel for the situation."

He said, "Try not to take too long. At the moment I'm holding off pressure to appoint someone in his place. His enemies up here—and a sharp-tongued bastard like him acquires plenty of those—are trying to get a search committee authorized to find someone else for the directorship of the Cayslin Center for the Study of Man."

"Of People," she corrected automatically, as she always did. "What do you mean, 'bastard'? I thought you liked him, Doug. 'Do you want me to have to throw a smart, courtly, old-school gent to Finney or MaGill?' Those were your very words." Finney was a Freudian with a mouth like a pursed-up little asshole and a mind to match, and MaGill was a primal yowler in a padded gym of an office.

She heard Doug tapping at his teeth with a pen or pencil. "Well," he said, "I have a lot of respect for him, and sometimes I could cheer him for mowing down some pompous moron up here. I can't deny, though, that he's earned a reputation for being an accomplished son of a bitch and tough to work with. Too damn cold and self-sufficient, you know?"

"Mmm," she said. "I haven't seen that yet."

He said, "You will. How about yourself? How's the rest of your life?"

"Well, offhand, what would you say if I told you I was thinking of going back to art school?"

"What would I say? I'd say bullshit, that's what I'd say. You've had fifteen years of doing something you're good at, and now you want to throw all that out and start over in an area you haven't touched since Studio 101 in college? If God had meant you to be a painter, She'd have sent you to art school in the first place."

"I did think about art school at the time."

"The point is that you're good at what you do. I've been at the receiving end of your work and I know what I'm talking about. By the way, did you see that piece in the paper about Annie Barnes, from the group I was in? That's an important appointment. I always knew she'd wind up in Washington.

What I'm trying to make clear to you is that your 'graduates' do too well for you to be talking about quitting. What's Morton say about that idea, by the way?"

Mort, a pathologist, was Floria's lover. She hadn't discussed this with him, and she told Doug so.

"You're not on the outs with Morton, are you?"

"Come on, Douglas, cut it out. There's nothing wrong with my sex life, believe me. It's everyplace else that's giving me trouble."

"Just sticking my nose into your business," he replied. "What are friends for?"

They turned to lighter matters, but when she hung up, Floria felt glum. If her friends were moved to this sort of probing and kindly advice-giving, she must be inviting help more openly and more urgently than she'd realized.

The work on the book went no better. It was as if, afraid to expose her thoughts, she must disarm criticism by meeting all possible objections beforehand. The book was well and truly stalled—like everything else. She sat sweating over it, wondering what the devil was wrong with her that she was writing mush. She had two good books to her name already. What was this bottleneck with the third?

"But what do you think?" Kenny insisted anxiously. "Does it sound like my kind of job?"

"How do you feel about it?"

"I'm all confused, I told you."

"Try speaking for me. Give me the advice I would give you."

He glowered. "That's a real cop-out, you know? One part of me talks like you, and then I have a dialogue with myself like a TV show about a split personality. It's all me that way; you just sit there while I do all the work. I want something from *you*."

She looked for the twentieth time at the clock on the file cabinet. This time it freed her. "Kenny, the hour's over."

Kenny heaved his plump, sulky body up out of his chair. "You don't care. Oh, you pretend to, but you don't really—" "Next time, Kenny."

He stumped out of the office. She imagined him towing in his wake the raft of decisions he was trying to inveigle her into making for him. Sighing, she went to the window and looked out over the park, filling her eyes and her mind with the full, fresh green of late spring. She felt dismal. In two years of treatment the situation with Kenny had remained a stalemate. He wouldn't go to someone else who might be able to help him, and she couldn't bring herself to kick him out, though she knew she must eventually. His puny tyranny couldn't conceal how soft and vulnerable he was. . . .

Dr. Weyland had the next appointment. Floria found herself pleased to see him. She could hardly have asked for a greater contrast to Kenny: tall, lean, that august head that made her want to draw him, good clothes, nice big hands—altogether a distinguished-looking man. Though he was informally dressed in slacks, light jacket, and tieless shirt, the impression he conveyed was one of impeccable leisure and reserve. He took not the padded chair preferred by most clients, but the wooden one with the cane seat.

"Good afternoon, Dr. Landauer," he said gravely. "May I ask your judgment of my case?"

"I don't regard myself as a judge," she said. She decided to try to shift their discussion onto a first-name basis if possible. Calling this old-fashioned man by his first name so soon might seem artificial, but how could they get familiar enough to do therapy while addressing each other as "Dr. Landauer" and "Dr. Weyland," like two characters out of a vaudeville sketch?

"This is what I think, Edward," she continued. "We need to find out about this vampire incident: how it tied into your feelings about yourself, good and bad, at the time; what it did for you that led you to try to 'be' a vampire even though that was bound to complicate your life terrifically. The more we know, the closer we can come to figuring out how to insure that this vampire construct won't be necessary to you again."

"Does this mean that you accept me formally as a client?" he said.

Comes right out and says what's on his mind, she noted; no problem there. "Yes."

"Good. I too have a treatment goal in mind. I will need at some point a testimonial from you that my mental health is sound enough for me to resume work at Cayslin."

Floria shook her head. "I can't guarantee that. I can commit myself to work toward it, of course, since your improved mental health is the aim of what we do here together."

"I suppose that answers the purpose for the time being," he said. "We can discuss it again later on. Frankly, I find myself eager to continue our work today. I've been feeling very much better since I spoke with you, and I thought last night about what I might tell you today."

She had the distinct feeling of being steered by him; how important was it to him, she wondered, to feel in control? She said, "Edward, my own feeling is that we started out with a good deal of very useful verbal work, and that now is a time to try something a little different."

He said nothing. He watched her. When she asked whether he remembered his dreams, he shook his head no.

She said, "I'd like you to try to do a dream for me now, a waking dream. Can you close your eyes and daydream, and tell me about it?"

He closed his eyes. Strangely, he now struck her as less vulnerable rather than more, as if strengthened by increased vigilance.

"How do you feel now?" she said.

"Uneasy." His eyelids fluttered. "I dislike closing my eyes. What I don't see can hurt me."

"Who wants to hurt you?"

"A vampire's enemies, of course—mobs of screaming peasants with torches."

Translating into what, she wondered—young Ph.D.s pouring out of the graduate schools panting for the jobs of older men like Weyland? "Peasants, these days?"

"Whatever their daily work, there is still a majority of the stupid, the violent, and the credulous, putting their feather-brained faith in astrology, in this cult or that, in various branches of psychology."

His sneer at her was unmistakable. Considering her refusal to let him fill the hour his own way, this desire to take a swipe at her was healthy. But it required immediate and straightforward handling.

"Edward, open your eyes and tell me what you see."

He obeyed. "I see a woman in her early forties," he said, "clever-looking face, dark hair showing gray; flesh too thin for her bones, indicating either vanity or illness; wearing slacks and a rather creased batik blouse—describable, I think, by the term 'peasant style'—with a food stain on the left side."

Damn! Don't blush. "Does anything besides my blouse suggest a peasant to you?"

"Nothing concrete, but with regard to me, my vampire self, a peasant with a torch is what you could easily become."

"I hear you saying that my task is to help you get rid of your delusion, though this process may be painful and frightening for you."

Something flashed in his expression—surprise, perhaps alarm, something she wanted to get in touch with before it could sink away out of reach again. Quickly she said, "How do you experience your face at this moment?"

He frowned. "As being on the front of my head. Why?"

With a rush of anger at herself, she saw that she had chosen the wrong technique for reaching that hidden feeling: she had provoked hostility instead. She said, "Your face looked to me just now like a mask for concealing what you feel rather than an instrument of expression."

He moved restlessly in the chair, his whole physical attitude tense and guarded. "I don't know what you mean."

"Will you let me touch you?" she said, rising.

His hands tightened on the arms of his chair, which protested in a sharp creak. He snapped, "I thought this was a talking cure."

Strong resistance to body work—ease up. "If you won't let me massage some of the tension out of your facial muscles, will you try to do it yourself?"

"I don't enjoy being made ridiculous," he said, standing and heading for the door, which clapped smartly to behind him.

She sagged back in her seat; she had mishandled him. Clearly her initial estimation of this as a relatively easy job had been wrong and had led her to move far too quickly with him. Certainly it was much too early to try body work. She should have developed a firmer level of trust first by letting him do more of what he did so easily and so well—talk.

The door opened. Weyland came back in and shut it quietly. He did not sit again but paced about the room, coming to rest at the window.

"Please excuse my rather childish behavior just now," he said. "Playing these games of yours brought it on."

"It's frustrating, playing games that are unfamiliar and that you can't control," she said. As he made no reply, she went on in a conciliatory tone, "I'm not trying to belittle you, Edward. I just need to get us off whatever track you were taking us down so briskly. My feeling is that you're trying hard to regain your old stability.

"But that's the goal, not the starting point. The only way to reach your goal is through the process, and you don't drive the therapy process like a train. You can only help the process happen, as though you were helping a tree grow."

"These games are part of the process?"

"Yes."

"And neither you nor I control the games?"

"That's right."

He considered. "Suppose I agree to try this process of yours; what would you want of me?"

Observing him carefully, she no longer saw the anxious scholar bravely struggling back from madness. Here was a different sort of man—armored, calculating. She didn't know just what the change signaled, but she felt her own excitement stirring, and that meant she was on the track of—something.

"I have a hunch," she said slowly, "that this vampirism extends further back into your past than you've told me, and possibly right up into the present as well. I think it's still with you. My style of therapy stresses dealing with the *now* at least as much as the *then*; if the vampirism is part of the present, dealing with it on that basis is crucial."

Silence.

"Can you talk about being a vampire—being one now?"

"You won't like knowing," he said.

"Edward, try."

He said, "I hunt."

"Where? How? What sort of—of victims?"

He folded his arms and leaned his back against the window frame. "Very well, since you insist. There are a number of possibilities here in the city in summer. Those too poor to own air conditioners sleep out on rooftops and fire escapes. But often, I've found, their blood is sour with drugs or liquor. The same is true of prostitutes. Bars are full of accessible people but also full of smoke and noise, and there too the blood is fouled. I must choose my hunting grounds carefully. Often I go to openings of galleries or evening museum shows or department stores on their late nights—places where women may be approached."

And take pleasure in it, she thought, if they're out hunting also—for acceptable male companionship. Yet he said he's never married. Explore where this is going. "Only women?"

He gave her a sardonic glance, as if she were a slightly brighter student than he had at first assumed.

"Hunting women is liable to be time-consuming and expensive. The best hunting is in the part of Central Park they call the Ramble, where homosexual men seek encounters with others of their kind. I walk there too at night."

Floria caught a faint sound of conversation and laughter from the waiting room; her next client had probably arrived, she realized, looking reluctantly at the clock. "I'm sorry, Edward, but our time seems to be—"

"Only a moment more," he said coldly. "You asked; permit me to finish my answer. In the Ramble I find someone who doesn't reek of alcohol or drugs, who seems healthy, and who is not insistent on 'hooking up' right there among the bushes. I invite such a man to my hotel. He judges me safe, at least—older, weaker than he is, unlikely to turn out to be a dangerous maniac. So he comes to my room. I feed on his blood."

"Now, I think, our time is up."

He walked out.

She sat torn between rejoicing at his admission of the delusion's persistence and dismay that his condition was so much worse than she had first thought. Her hope of having an easy time with him vanished. His initial presentation had been just that—a performance, an act. Forced to abandon it, he had dumped on her this lump of material, too much—and too strange—to take in all at once.

Her next client liked the padded chair, not the wooden one that Weyland had sat in during the first part of the hour. Floria started to move the wooden one back. The armrests came away in her hands.

She remembered him starting up in protest against her proposal of touching him. The grip of his fingers had fractured the joints, and the shafts now lay in splinters on the floor.

Floria wandered into Lucille's room at the clinic after the staff meeting. Lucille was lying on the couch with a wet cloth over her eyes.

"I thought you looked green around the gills today," Floria said. "What's wrong?"

"Big bash last night," said Lucille in sepulchral tones. "I think I feel about the way you do after a session with Chubs. You haven't gotten rid of him yet, have you?"

"No. I had him lined up to see Marty instead of me last week, but damned if he didn't show up at my door at his usual time. It's a lost cause. What I wanted to talk to you about was Dracula."

"What about him?"

"He's smarter, tougher, and sicker than I thought, and maybe I'm even less competent than I thought, too. He's already walked out on me once—I almost lost him. I never took a course in treating monsters."

Lucille groaned. "Some days they're all monsters." This from Lucille, who worked longer hours than anyone else at the clinic, to the despair of her husband. She lifted the cloth, refolded it, and placed it carefully across her forehead. "And if I had ten dollars for every client who's walked out on me . . . Tell you what: I'll trade you Madame X for him, how's that? Remember Madame X, with the jangling bracelets and the parakeet eye makeup and the phobia about dogs? Now she's phobic about things dropping on her out of the sky. Just wait—it'll turn out that one day when she was three a dog trotted by and pissed on her leg just as an over-passing pigeon shat on her head. What are we doing in this business?"

"God knows." Floria laughed. "But am I in this business these days—I mean, in the sense of practicing my so-called skills? Blocked with my group work, beating my brains out on a book that won't go, and doing something—I'm not sure it's therapy—with a vampire . . . You know, once I had this sort of natural choreographer inside myself that hardly let me put a foot wrong and always knew how to correct a mistake if I did. Now that's gone. I feel as if I'm just going through a lot of mechanical motions. Whatever I had once that made me useful as a therapist, I've lost it."

Ugh, she thought, hearing the descent of her voice into a tone of gloomy self-pity.

"Well, don't complain about Dracula," Lucille said. "You were the one who insisted on taking him on. At least he's got you concentrating on his problem instead of just wringing your hands. As long as you've started, stay with it—illumination may come. And now I'd better change the ribbon in my typewriter and get back to reviewing Silverman's latest bestseller on self-shrinking while I'm feeling mean enough to do it justice." She got up gingerly. "Stick around in case I faint and fall into the wastebasket."

"Luce, this case is what I'd like to try to write about."

"Dracula?" Lucille pawed through a desk drawer full of paper clips, pens, rubber bands, and old lipsticks.

"Dracula. A monograph . . ."

"Oh, I know that game: you scribble down everything you can and then read what you wrote to find out what's going on with the client, and with luck you end up publishing. Great! But if you are going to publish, don't piddle this away on a dinky paper. Do a book. Here's your subject, instead of those depressing statistics you've been killing yourself over. This one is really exciting—a case study to put on the shelf next to Freud's own wolf-man, have you thought of that?"

Floria liked it. "What a book that could be—fame if not fortune. Notoriety, most likely. How in the world could I convince our colleagues that it's legit? There's a lot of vampire stuff around right now—plays on Broadway and TV, books all over the place, movies. They'll say I'm just trying to ride the coattails of a fad."

"No, no, what you do is show how this guy's delusion is related to the fad. Fascinating." Lucille, having found a ribbon, prodded doubtfully at the exposed innards of her typewriter.

"Suppose I fictionalize it," Floria said, "under a pseudonym. Why not ride the popular wave and be free in what I can say?"

"Listen, you've never written a word of fiction in your life, have you?" Lucille fixed her with a bloodshot gaze. "There's no evidence that you could turn out a best-selling novel. On the other hand, by this time you have a trained memory for accurately reporting therapeutic transactions. That's a strength you'd be foolish to waste. A solid professional book would be terrific—and a feather in the cap of every woman in the field. Just make sure you get good legal advice on disguising your Dracula's identity well enough to avoid libel."

The cane-seated chair wasn't worth repairing, so she got its twin out of the bedroom to put in the office in its place. Puzzling: by his history Weyland was fifty-two, and by his appearance no muscle man. She should have asked Doug—but how, exactly? "By the way, Doug, was Weyland ever a circus strong man or a blacksmith? Does he secretly pump iron?" Ask the client himself—but not yet.

She invited some of the younger staff from the clinic over for a small party with a few of her outside friends. It was a good evening; they were not a heavy-drinking crowd, which meant the conversation stayed intelligent. The guests drifted about the long living room or stood in twos and threes at the windows looking down on West End Avenue as they talked.

Mort came, warming the room. Fresh from a session with some amateur chamber-music friends, he still glowed with the pleasure of making his cello sing. His own voice was unexpectedly light for so large a man. Sometimes Floria thought that the deep throb of the cello was his true voice.

He stood beside her, talking with some others. There was no need to lean against his comfortable bulk or to have him put his arm around her waist. Their intimacy was long standing, an effortless pleasure in each other that required neither demonstration nor concealment.

He was easily diverted from music to his next favorite topic, the strengths and skills of athletes.

"Here's a question for a paper I'm thinking of writing,"

Floria said. "Could a tall, lean man be exceptionally strong?"

Mort rambled on in his thoughtful way. His answer seemed to be no.

"But what about chimpanzees?" put in a young clinician. "I went with a guy once who was an animal handler for TV, and he said a three-month-old chimp could demolish a strong man."

"It's all physical conditioning," somebody else said. "Modern people are soft."

Mort nodded. "Human beings in general are weakly made, compared to other animals. It's a question of muscle insertions—the angles of how the muscles are attached to the bones. Some angles give better leverage than others. That's how a leopard can bring down a much bigger animal than itself. It has a muscular structure that gives it tremendous strength for its streamlined build."

Floria said, "If a man were built with muscle insertions like a leopard's, he'd look pretty odd, wouldn't he?"

"Not to an untrained eye," Mort said, sounding bemused by an inner vision. "And my God, what an athlete he'd make—can you imagine a guy in the decathlon who's as strong as a leopard?"

When everyone else had gone, Mort stayed, as he often did. Jokes about insertions, muscular and otherwise, soon led to sounds more expressive and more animal, but afterward Floria didn't feel like resting snuggled together with Mort and talking. When her body stopped racing, her mind turned to her new client. She didn't want to discuss him with Mort, so she ushered Mort out as gently as she could and sat down by herself at the kitchen table with a glass of orange juice.

How to approach the reintegration of Weyland, the eminent, gray-haired academic with the rebellious vampire-self that had smashed his life out of shape?

She thought of the broken chair, of Weyland's big hands crushing the wood. Old wood and dried-out glue, of course, or he never could have done that. He was a man, after all, not a leopard.

The day before the third session, Weyland phoned and left a message with Hilda: he would not be coming to the office tomorrow for his appointment, but if Dr. Landauer was agreeable, she would find him at their usual hour at the Central Park Zoo.

Am I going to let him move me around from here to there? she thought. I shouldn't—but why fight it? Give him some leeway, see what opens up in a different setting. Besides, it was a beautiful day, probably the last of the sweet May weather before the summer stickiness descended. She gladly cut Kenny short so that she would have time to walk over to the zoo.

There was a fair crowd there for a weekday. Well-groomed young matrons pushed clean, floppy babies in strollers. Weyland she spotted at once.

He was leaning against the railing that enclosed the seals' shelter and their murky green pool. His jacket, slung over his shoulder, draped elegantly down his long back. Floria thought him rather dashing and faintly foreign looking. Women who passed him, she noticed, tended to glance back.

He looked at everyone. She had the impression that he knew quite well that she was walking up behind him.

"Outdoors makes a nice change from the office, Edward," she said, coming to the rail beside him. "But there must be more to this than a longing for fresh air." A fat seal lay in sculptural grace on the concrete, eyes blissfully shut, fur drying in the sun to a translucent watercolor umber.

Weyland straightened from the rail. They walked. He did not look at the animals; his eyes moved continually over the crowd. He said, "Someone has been watching for me at your office building."

"Who?"

"There are several possibilities. Pah, what a stench—

though humans caged in similar circumstances smell as bad." He sidestepped a couple of shrieking children who were fighting over a balloon, and headed out of the zoo under the musical clock.

They walked the uphill path northward through the park. By extending her own stride a little, Floria found that she could comfortably keep pace with him.

"Is it peasants with torches?" she said. "Following you?"

He said, "What a childish idea."

All right, try another tack, then: "You were telling me last time about hunting in the Ramble. Can we return to that?"

"If you wish." He sounded bored—a defense? Surely—she was certain this must be the right reading—surely his problem was a transmutation into "vampire" fantasy of an unacceptable aspect of himself. For men of his generation, the confrontation with homosexual drives could be devastating.

"When you pick up someone in the Ramble, is it a paid encounter?"

"Usually."

"How do you feel about having to pay?" She expected resentment.

He gave a faint shrug. "Why not? Others work to earn their bread. I work too, very hard, in fact. Why shouldn't I use my earnings to pay for my sustenance?"

Why did he never play the expected card? Baffled, she paused to drink from a fountain. They walked on.

"Once you've got your quarry, how do you . . ." She fumbled for a word.

"Attack?" he supplied, unperturbed. "There's a place on the neck, here, where pressure can interrupt the blood flow to the brain and cause unconsciousness. Getting close enough to apply that pressure isn't difficult."

"You do this before or after any sexual activity?"

"Before, if possible," he said aridly, "and instead of." He turned aside to stalk up a slope to a granite outcrop that overlooked the path they had been following. There he settled on his haunches, looking back the way they had come.

Floria, glad she'd worn slacks today, sat down near him.

He didn't seem devastated—anything but. Press him, don't let him get by on cool. "Do you often prey on men in preference to women?"

"Certainly. I take what is easiest. Men have always been more accessible because women have been walled away like prizes or so physically impoverished by repeated childbearing as to be unhealthy prey for me. All this has begun to change recently, but gay men are still the simplest quarry." While she was recovering from her surprise at his unforeseen and weirdly skewed awareness of female history, he added suavely, "How carefully you control your expression, Dr. Landauer—no trace of disapproval."

She did disapprove, she realized. She would prefer him not to be committed sexually to men. Oh, hell.

He went on, "Yet no doubt you see me as one who victimizes the already victimized. This is the world's way. A wolf brings down the stragglers at the edges of the herd. Gay men are denied the full protection of the human herd and are at the same time emboldened to make themselves known and available.

"On the other hand, unlike the wolf I can feed without killing, and these particular victims pose no threat to me that would cause me to kill. Outcasts themselves, even if they comprehend my true purpose among them, they cannot effectively accuse me."

God, how neatly, completely, and ruthlessly he distanced the homosexual community from himself! "And how do you feel, Edward, about their purposes—their sexual expectations of you?"

"The same way I feel about the sexual expectations of women whom I choose to pursue: they don't interest me. Besides, once my hunger is active, sexual arousal is impossible. My physical unresponsiveness seems to surprise no one. Apparently impotence is expected in a gray-haired man, which suits my intention."

Some kids carrying radios swung past below, trailing a

jumble of amplified thump, wail, and jabber. Floria gazed after them unseeingly, thinking, astonished again, that she had never heard a man speak of his own impotence with such cool indifference. She had induced him to talk about his problem, all right. He was speaking as freely as he had in the first session, only this time it was no act. He was drowning her in more than she had ever expected or for that matter wanted to know about vampirism. What the hell: she was listening, she thought she understood—what was it all good for? Time for some cold reality, she thought; see how far he can carry all this incredible detail. Give the whole structure a shove.

She said, "You realize, I'm sure, that people of either sex who make themselves so easily available are also liable to be carriers of disease. When was your last medical checkup?"

"My dear Dr. Landauer, my first medical checkup will be my last. Fortunately, I have no great need of one. Most serious illnesses—hepatitis, for example—reveal themselves to me by a quality in the odor of the victim's skin. Warned, I abstain. When I do fall ill, as occasionally happens, I withdraw to some place where I can heal undisturbed. A doctor's attentions would be more dangerous to me than any disease."

Eyes on the path below, he continued calmly, "You can see by looking at me that there are no obvious clues to my unique nature. But believe me, an examination of any depth by even a half-sleeping medical practitioner would reveal some alarming deviations from the norm. I take pains to stay healthy, and I seem to be gifted with an exceptionally hardy constitution."

Fantasies of being unique and physically superior; take him to the other pole. "I'd like you to try something now. Will you put yourself into the mind of a man you contact in the Ramble and describe your encounter with him from his point of view?"

He turned toward her and for some moments regarded her

without expression. Then he resumed his surveillance of the path. "I will not. Though I do have enough empathy with my quarry to enable me to hunt efficiently, I must draw the line at erasing the necessary distance that keeps prey and predator distinct.

"And now I think our ways part for today." He stood up, descended the hillside, and walked beneath some low-canopied trees, his tall back stooped, toward the 72nd Street entrance of the park.

Floria arose more slowly, aware suddenly of her shallow breathing and the sweat on her face. Back to reality or what remained of it. She looked at her watch. She was late for her next client.

Floria couldn't sleep that night. Barefoot in her bathrobe, she paced the living room by lamplight. They had sat together on that hill as isolated as in her office—more so, because there was no Hilda and no phone. He was, she knew, very strong, and he had sat close enough to her to reach out for that paralyzing touch to the neck—

Just suppose for a minute that Weyland had been brazenly telling the truth all along, counting on her to treat it as a delusion because on the face of it the truth was inconceivable.

Jesus, she thought, if I'm thinking that way about him, this therapy is more out of control than I thought. What kind of therapist becomes an accomplice to the client's fantasy? A crazy therapist, that's what kind.

Frustrated and confused by the turmoil in her mind, she wandered into the workroom. By morning the floor was covered with sheets of newsprint, each broadly marked by her felt-tipped pen. Floria sat in the midst of them, gritty-eyed and hungry.

She often approached problems this way, harking back to art training: turn off the thinking, put hand to paper, and see what the deeper, less verbally sophisticated parts of the mind have to offer. Now that her dreams had deserted her, this was her only access to those levels.

The newsprint sheets were covered with rough representations of Weyland's face and form. Across several of them were scrawled words: *"Dear Doug, your vampire is fine, it's your ex-therapist who's off the rails. Warning: Therapy can be dangerous to your health. Especially if you are the therapist. Beautiful vampire, awaken to me. Am I really ready to take on a legendary monster? Give up—refer this one out. Do your job— work is a good doctor."*

That last one sounded pretty good, except that doing her job was precisely what she was feeling so shaky about these days.

Here was another message: *"How come this attraction to someone so scary?"* Oh-ho, she thought, is that a real feeling or an aimless reaction out of the body's early-morning hormone peak? You don't want to confuse honest libido with mere biological clockwork.

Deborah called. Babies cried in the background over the Scotch Symphony. Nick, Deb's husband, was a musicologist with fervent opinions on music and nothing else.

"We'll be in town a little later in the summer," Deborah said, "just for a few days at the end of July. Nicky has this seminar-convention thing. Of course, it won't be easy with the babies. . . . I wondered if you might sort of coordinate your vacation so you could spend a little time with them?"

Baby-sit, that meant. Damn. Cute as they were and all that, damn! Floria gritted her teeth. Visits from Deb were difficult. Floria had been so proud of her bright, hard-driving daughter, and then suddenly Deborah had dropped her studies and rushed to embrace all the dangers that Floria had warned her against: a romantic, too-young marriage, instant breeding, no preparation for self-support, the works. Well, to each her own, but it was so wearing to have Deb around playing the empty-headed hausfrau.

"Let me think, Deb. I'd love to see all of you, but I've been considering spending a couple of weeks in Maine with your Aunt Nonnie." God knows I need a real vacation, she thought, though the peace and quiet up there is hard for a city kid like me to take for long. Still, Nonnie, Floria's younger sister, was good company. "Maybe you could bring the kids up there for a couple of days. There's room in that great barn of a place, and of course Nonnie'd be happy to have you."

"Oh, no, Mom, it's so dead up there, it drives Nick crazy—don't tell Nonnie I said that. Maybe Nonnie could come down to the city instead. You could cancel a date or two and we could all go to Coney Island together, things like that."

Kid things, which would drive Nonnie crazy and Floria too, before long. "I doubt she could manage," Floria said, "but I'll ask. Look, hon, if I do go up there, you and Nick and the kids could stay here at the apartment and save some money."

"We have to be at the hotel for the seminar," Deb said shortly. No doubt she was feeling just as impatient as Floria was by now. "And the kids haven't seen you for a long time—it would be really nice if you could stay in the city just for a few days."

"We'll try to work something out." Always working something out. Concord never comes naturally—first we have to butt heads and get pissed off. Each time you call I hope it'll be different, Floria thought.

Somebody shrieked for "oly," jelly that would be, in the background—Floria felt a sudden rush of warmth for them, her grandkids for God's sake. Having been a young mother herself, she was still young enough to really enjoy them (and to fight with Deb about how to bring them up).

Deb was starting an awkward goodbye. Floria replied, put the phone down, and sat with her head back against the flowered kitchen wallpaper, thinking, Why do I feel so rotten now? Deb and I aren't close, no comfort, seldom friends, though we were once. Have I said everything wrong, made her think I don't want to see her and don't care about her family? What does she want from me that I can't seem to give her? Approval? Maybe she thinks I still hold her marriage against her. Well, I do, sort of. What right have I to be critical, me with my divorce? What terrible things would she say to me, would I say to her, that we take such care not to say anything important at all?

"I think today we might go into sex," she said.

Weyland responded dryly, "Might we indeed. Does it titillate you to wring confessions of solitary vice from men of mature years?"

Oh, no you don't, she thought. You can't sidestep so easily. "Under what circumstances do you find yourself sexually aroused?"

"Most usually upon waking from sleep," he said indifferently.

"What do you do about it?"

"The same as others do. I am not a cripple, I have hands."

"Do you have fantasies at these times?"

"No. Women, and men for that matter, appeal to me very little, either in fantasy or reality."

"Ah—what about female vampires?" she said, trying not to sound arch.

"I know of none."

Of course: the neatest out in the book. "They're not needed for reproduction, I suppose, because people who die of vampire bites become vampires themselves."

He said testily, "Nonsense. I am not a communicable disease."

So he had left an enormous hole in his construct. She headed straight for it: "Then how does your kind reproduce?"

"I have no kind, so far as I am aware," he said, "and I do not reproduce. Why should I, when I may live for centuries still, perhaps indefinitely? My sexual equipment is clearly

only detailed biological mimicry, a form of protective colora-
tion." How beautiful, how simple a solution, she thought,
full of admiration in spite of herself. "Do I occasionally detect a note of prurient interest in your questions, Dr. Landauer? Something akin to stopping at the cage to watch the
tigers mate at the zoo?"

"Probably," she said, feeling her face heat. He had a great
backhand return shot there. "How do you feel about that?"

He shrugged.

"To return to the point," she said. "Do I hear you saying
that you have no urge whatever to engage in sexual inter-
course with anyone?"

"Would you mate with your livestock?"

His matter-of-fact arrogance took her breath away. She
said weakly, "Men have reportedly done so."

"Driven men. I am not driven in that way. My sex urge is
of low frequency and is easily dealt with unaided—although I
occasionally engage in copulation out of the necessity to
keep up appearances. I am capable, but not—like humans—
obsessed."

Was he sinking into lunacy before her eyes? "I think I hear
you saying," she said, striving to keep her voice neutral,
"that you're not just a man with a unique way of life. I think
I hear you saying that you're not human at all."

"I thought that this was already clear."

"And that there are no others like you."

"None that I know of."

"Then—you see yourself as what? Some sort of mutation?"

"Perhaps. Or perhaps your kind are the mutation."

She saw disdain in the curl of his lip. "How does your
mouth feel now?"

"The corners are drawn down. The feeling is contempt."

"Can you let the contempt speak?"

He got up and went to stand at the window, positioning
himself slightly to one side as if to stay hidden from the
street below.

"Edward," she said.

He looked back at her. "Humans are my food. I draw the life out of their veins. Sometimes I kill them. I am greater than they are. Yet I must spend my time thinking about their habits and their drives, scheming to avoid the dangers they pose—I hate them."

She felt the hatred like a dry heat radiating from him. God, he really lived all this! She had tapped into a furnace of feeling. And now? The sensation of triumph wavered, and she grabbed at a next move: hit him with reality now, while he's burning.

"What about blood banks?" she said. "Your food is commercially available, so why all the complication and danger of the hunt?"

"You mean I might turn my efforts to piling up a fortune and buying blood by the case? That would certainly make for an easier, less risky life in the short run. I could fit quite comfortably into modern society if I became just another consumer.

"However, I prefer to keep the mechanics of my survival firmly in my own hands. After all, I can't afford to lose my hunting skills. In two hundred years there may be no blood banks, but I will still need my food."

Jesus, you set him a hurdle and he just flies over it. Are there no weaknesses in all this, has he no blind spots? Look at his tension—go back to that. Floria said, "What do you feel now in your body?"

"Tightness." He pressed his spread fingers to his abdomen.

"What are you doing with your hands?"

"I put my hands to my stomach."

"Can you speak for your stomach?"

"Feed me or die," he snarled.

Elated again, she closed in: "And for yourself, in answer?"

" 'Will you never be satisfied?' " He glared at her. "You shouldn't seduce me into quarreling with the terms of my own existence!"

"Your stomach is your existence," she paraphrased.

"The gut determines," he said harshly. "That first, everything else after."

"Say, 'I resent . . .' "

He held to a tense silence.

" 'I resent the power of my gut over my life,' " she said for him.

He stood with an abrupt motion and glanced at his watch, an elegant flash of slim silver on his wrist. "Enough," he said.

That night at home she began a set of notes that would never enter his file at the office, notes toward the proposed book.

> Couldn't do it, couldn't get properly into the sex thing with him. Everything shoots off in all directions. His vampire concept so thoroughly worked out, find myself half believing sometimes—my own childish fantasy-response to his powerful death-avoidance, contact-avoidance fantasy. Lose professional distance every time—is that what scares me about him? Don't really want to shatter his delusion (my life a mess, what right to tear down others' patterns?)—so see it as real? Wonder how much of "vampirism" he acts out, how far, how often. Something attractive in his purely selfish, predatory stance—the lure of the great outlaw.

> Told me today quite coolly about a man he killed recently—inadvertently—by drinking too much from him. *Is* it fantasy? Of course—the victim, he thinks, was college student. Breathes there a professor who hasn't dreamed of murdering some representative youth, retaliation for years of classroom frustration? Speaks of teaching with acerbic humor—amuses him to work at cultivating the minds of those he regards strictly as bodies, containers of his sustenance. He shows the alienness of full-blown psychopathology, poor bastard, plus clean-cut logic. Suggested he find another job (assuming his delusion at least in part related to pressures at Cayslin); his fantasy-persona, the vampire, more realistic than I about job-switching:

"For a man of my apparent age it's not so easy to make such a change in these tight times. I might have to take a position lower on the ladder of 'success' as you people assess it." Status is important to him? "Certainly. An eccentric professor is one thing; an eccentric pipe-fitter, another. And I like good cars, which are expensive to own and run." Then, thoughtful addition, "Although there are advantages to a simpler, less visible life." He refuses to discuss other "jobs" from former "lives." We are deep into the fantasy—where the hell going? Damn right I don't control the "games"—preplanned therapeutic strategies get whirled away as soon as we begin. Nerve-wracking.

Tried again to have him take the part of his enemy-victim, peasant with torch. Asked if he felt himself rejecting that point of view? Frosty reply: "Naturally. The peasant's point of view is in no way my own. I've been reading in your field, Dr. Landauer. You work from the Gestalt orientation—" Originally, yes, I corrected; eclectic now. "But you do proceed from the theory that I am projecting some aspect of my own feelings outward onto others, whom I then treat as my victims. Your purpose then must be to maneuver me into accepting as my own the projected 'victim' aspect of myself. This integration is supposed to effect the freeing of energy previously locked into maintaining the projection. All this is an interesting insight into the nature of ordinary human confusion, but I am not an ordinary human, and I am not confused. I cannot afford confusion." Felt sympathy for him— telling me he's afraid of having own internal confusions exposed in therapy, too threatening. Keep chipping away at delusion, though with what prospect? It's so complex, deepseated.

Returned to his phrase "my apparent age." He asserts he has lived many human lifetimes, all details forgotten, however, during periods of suspended animation between lives. Perhaps sensing my skepticism at such handy amnesia, grew cool and distant, claimed to know little about the hibernation process itself: "The essence of this state is that I sleep through it—hardly an ideal condition for making scientific observations."

Edward thinks his body synthesizes vitamins, minerals (as all our bodies synthesize vitamin D), even proteins. Describes unique design he deduces in himself: special intestinal microfauna plus superefficient body chemistry extracts enough energy to live on from blood. Damn good mileage per calorie, too. (Recall observable tension, first interview, at question about drinking—my note on possible alcohol problem!)

Speak for blood: " 'Lacking me, you have no life. I flow to the heart's soft drumbeat through lightless prisons of flesh. I am rich, I am nourishing, I am difficult to attain.' " Stunned to find him positively lyrical on subject of his "food." Drew attention to whispering voice of blood. " 'Yes. I am secret, hidden beneath the surface, patient, silent, steady. I work unnoticed, an unseen thread of vitality running from age to age—beautiful, efficient, self-renewing, self-cleansing, warm, filling—' " Could *see* him getting worked up. Finally he stood: "My appetite is pressing. I must leave you." And he did.

Sat and trembled for five minutes after.

New development (or new perception?): he sometimes comes across very unsophisticated about own feelings—lets me pursue subjects of extreme intensity and delicacy to him.

Asked him to daydream—a hunt. (Hands—mine—shaking now as I write. God. What a session.) He told of picking up a woman at poetry reading, 92nd Street Y—has N.Y.C. all worked out, circulates to avoid too much notice any one spot. Spoke easily, eyes shut without observable strain: chooses from audience a redhead in glasses, dress with drooping neckline (ease of access), no perfume (strong smells bother him). Approaches during intermission, encouraged to see her fanning away smoke of others' cigarettes—meaning she doesn't smoke, health sign. Agreed in not enjoying the reading, they adjourn together to coffee shop.

"She asks whether I'm a teacher," he says, eyes shut, mouth amused. "My clothes, glasses, manner all suggest this, and I emphasize the impression—it reassures. She's a copy editor for a publishing house. We talk about books. The waiter brings her a gummy-looking pastry. As a non-eater, I pay little attention to the quality of restaurants, so I must apologize to her. She waves this away—is engrossed, or pretending to be engrossed, in talk." A longish dialogue between interested woman and Edward doing shy-lonesome-scholar act—dead wife, competitive young colleagues who don't understand him, quarrels in professional journals with big shots in his field—a version of what he first told me. She's attracted (of course—lanky, rough-cut elegance plus hints of vulnerability all very alluring, as intended). He offers to take her home.

Tension in his body at this point in narrative—spine clear of chair back, hands braced on thighs. "She settles beside me in the back of the cab, talking about problems of her own career—illegible manuscripts of Biblical length, mulish editors, suicidal authors—and I make comforting comments, I lean nearer and put my arm along the back of the seat, behind her shoulders. Traffic is heavy, we move slowly. There is time to make my meal here in the taxi and avoid a tedious extension of the situation into her apartment—if I move soon."

"How do you feel?"

"Eager," he says, voice husky. "My hunger is so roused I can scarcely restrain myself. A powerful hunger, not like yours—mine compels. I embrace her shoulders lightly, make kindly-uncle remarks, treading that fine line between the game of seduction she perceives and the game of friendly interest I pretend to affect. My real purpose underlies all: what I say, how I look, every gesture is part of the stalk. There is an added excitement, and fear, because I'm doing my hunting in the presence of a third person—behind the cabbie's head."

Could scarcely breathe. Studied him—intent face, masklike with closed eyes, nostrils slightly flared; legs tensed, hands clenched on knees. Whispering: "I press the place on her neck. She starts, sighs faintly, silently drops against me. In the stale stench of the cab's interior, with the ticking of the meter in my ears and the mutter of the radio—I take hold here, at the tenderest part of her throat. Sound subsides into the background—I feel the sweet blood beating under her skin, I taste salt at the moment before I—strike. My saliva thins her blood so that it flows out, I draw the blood into my mouth swiftly, swiftly, before she can wake, before we can arrive . . ."

Trailed off, sat back loosely in chair—saw him swallow. "Ah. I feed." Heard him sigh. Managed to ask about physical sensation. His low murmur, "Warm. Heavy, here"—touches his belly—"in a pleasant way. The good taste of blood, tart and rich, in my mouth . . ."

And then? A flicker of movement beneath his closed eyelids: "In time I am aware that the cabbie has glanced back once and has taken our—embrace for just that. I can feel the cab slowing, hear him move to turn off the meter. I withdraw, I quickly wipe my mouth on my handkerchief. I take her by the shoulders and shake her gently; does she often have these attacks? I inquire, the soul of concern. She comes around, bewildered, weak, thinks she has fainted. I give the driver extra money and ask him to wait. He looks intrigued—'What was that all about,' I can see the question in his face—but as a true New Yorker he won't expose his own ignorance by asking.

"I escort the woman to her front door, supporting her as she staggers. Any suspicion of me that she may entertain, however formless and hazy, is allayed by my stern charging of the doorman to see that she reaches her apartment safely. She grows embarrassed, thinks perhaps that if not put off by her 'illness' I would spend the night with her, which moves her to press upon me, unasked, her telephone number. I bid her a solicitous good night and take the cab back to my hotel, where I sleep."

No sex? No sex.

How did he feel about the victim as a person? "She was food."

This was his "hunting" of last night, he admits afterward, not a made-up dream. No boasting in it, just telling. Telling me! Think: I can go talk to Lucille, Mort, Doug, others about most of what matters to me. Edward has only me to talk to and that for a fee—what isolation! No wonder the stone, monumental face—only those long, strong lips (his point of contact, verbal and physical-in-fantasy, with world and with "food") are truly expressive. An exciting narration; uncomfortable to find I felt not only empathy but enjoyment. Suppose he picked up and victimized—even in fantasy—Deb or Hilda, how would I feel then?

Later: truth—I also found this recital sexually stirring. Keep visualizing how he looked finishing this "dream"—he sat very still, head up, look of thoughtful pleasure on his face. Like handsome intellectual listening to music.

Kenny showed up unexpectedly at Floria's office on Monday, bursting with malevolent energy. She happened to be free, so she took him—something was definitely up. He sat on the edge of his chair.

"I know why you're trying to unload me," he accused. "It's that new one, the tall guy with the snooty look—what is he, an old actor or something? Anybody could see he's got you itching for him."

"Kenny, when was it that I first spoke to you about terminating our work together?" she said patiently.

"Don't change the subject. Let me tell you, in case you don't know it: that guy isn't really interested, Doctor, because he's a fruit. A faggot. You want to know how I know?"

Oh, Lord, she thought wearily, he's regressed to age ten. She could see that she was going to hear the rest whether she wanted to or not. What in God's name was the world like for Kenny, if he clung so fanatically to her despite her failure to help him?

"Listen, I knew right away there was something flaky about him, so I followed him from here to that hotel where he lives. I followed him the other afternoon too. He walked around like he does a lot, and then he went into one of those ritzy movie houses on Third that open early and show risqué foreign movies—you know, Japs cutting each other's things off and glop like that. This one was French, though.

"Well, there was a guy came in, a Madison Avenue type carrying his attaché case, taking a work break or something.

Your man moved over and sat down behind him and reached out and sort of stroked the guy's neck, and the guy leaned back, and your man leaned forward and started nuzzling at him, you know—kissing him.

"I saw it. They had their heads together and they stayed like that a while. It was disgusting: complete strangers, without even 'hello.' The Madison Avenue guy just sat there with his head back looking zonked, you know, just swept away, and what he was doing with his hands under his raincoat in his lap I couldn't see, but I bet you can guess.

"And then your fruity friend got up and walked out. I did too, and I hung around a little outside. After a while the Madison Avenue guy came out looking all sleepy and loose, like after you-know-what, and he wandered off on his own someplace.

"What do you think now?" he ended, on a high, triumphant note.

Her impulse was to slap his face the way she would have slapped Deb-as-a-child for tattling. But this was a client, not a kid. God give me strength, she thought.

"Kenny, you're fired."

"You can't!" he squealed. "You can't! What will I—who can I—"

She stood up, feeling weak but hardening her voice. "I'm sorry. I absolutely cannot have a client who makes it his business to spy on other clients. You already have a list of replacement therapists from me."

He gaped at her in slack-jawed dismay, his eyes swimmy with tears.

"I'm sorry, Kenny. Call this a dose of reality therapy and try to learn from it. There are some things you simply will not be allowed to do." She felt better; it was done at last.

"I hate you!" He surged out of his chair, knocking it back against the wall. Threateningly he glared at the fish tank, but contenting himself with a couple of kicks at the nearest table leg, he stamped out.

Floria buzzed Hilda: "No more appointments for Kenny, Hilda. You can close his file."

"Whoopee," Hilda said.

Poor, horrid Kenny. Impossible to tell what would happen to him, better not to speculate or she might relent, call him back. She had encouraged him, really, by listening instead of shutting him up and throwing him out before any damage was done.

Was it damaging, to know the truth? In her mind's eye she saw a cream-faced young man out of a Black Thumb Vodka ad wander from a movie theater into daylight, yawning and rubbing absently at an irritation on his neck. . . .

She didn't even look at the telephone on the table or think about whom to call, now that she believed. No; she was going to keep quiet about Dr. Edward Lewis Weyland, her vampire.

Hardly alive at staff meeting, clinic, yesterday—people asking what's the matter, fobbed them off. Settled down today. Had to, to face him.

Asked him what he felt were his strengths. He said speed, cunning, ruthlessness. Animal strengths, I said. What about imagination, or is that strictly human? He defended at once: not human only. Lion, waiting at water hole where no zebra yet drinks, thinks "Zebra—eat," therefore performs feat of imagining event yet-to-come. Self experienced as animal? Yes—reminded me that humans are also animals. Pushed for his early memories; he objected: "Gestalt is here-and-now, not history-taking." I insist, citing anomalous nature of his situation, my own refusal to be bound by any one theoretical framework. He defends tensely: "Suppose I became lost there in memory, distracted from dangers of the present, left unguarded from those dangers."

Speak for memory. He resists, but at length attempts it: " 'I am heavy with the multitudes of the past.' " Fingertips to forehead, propping up all that weight of lives, " 'So heavy, filling worlds of time laid down eon by eon, I accumulate, I persist, I demand recognition. I am as real as the life around you—more real, weightier, richer.' " His voice sinking, shoulders bowed, head in hands—I begin to feel pressure at the back of my own skull. " 'Let me in.' " Only a rough whisper now. " 'I offer beauty as well as terror. Let me in.' " Whispering also, I suggest he reply to his memory.

"Memory, you want to crush me," he groans. "You would overwhelm me with the cries of animals, the odor and jostle of bodies, old betrayals, dead joys, filth and anger from other times—I must concentrate on the danger now. Let me be." All I can take of this crazy conflict, I gabble us off onto something else. He looks up—relief?—follows my lead—where? Rest of session a blank.

No wonder sometimes no empathy at all—a species boundary! He has to be utterly self-centered just to keep balance—self-centeredness of an animal. Thought just now of our beginning, me trying to push him to produce material, trying to control him, manipulate—no way, no way; so here we are, someplace else—I feel dazed, in shock, but stick with it—it's real.

Therapy with a dinosaur, a Martian.

"You call me 'Weyland' now, not 'Edward.' " I said first name couldn't mean much to one with no memory of being called by that name as a child, silly to pretend it signifies intimacy where it can't. I think he knows now that I believe him. Without prompting, told me truth of disappearance from Cayslin. No romance; he tried to drink from a woman who worked there, she shot him, stomach and chest. Luckily for him, small-caliber pistol, and he was wearing a lined coat over three-piece suit. Even so, badly hurt. (Midsection stiffness I noted when he first came—he was still in some pain at that time.) He didn't "vanish"—fled, hid, was found by questionable types who caught on to what he was, sold him "like a chattel" to someone here in the city. He was imprisoned, fed, put on exhibition—very privately—for gain. Got away. "Do you believe any of this?" Never asked anything like that before, seems of concern to him now. I said my belief or lack of same was immaterial; remarked on hearing a lot of bitterness.

He steepled his fingers, looked brooding at me over tips: "I nearly died there. No doubt my purchaser and his diabolist friend still search for me. Mind you, I had some reason at first to be glad of the attentions of the people who kept me prisoner. I was in no condition to fend for myself. They brought me food and kept me hidden and sheltered, whatever their motives. There are always advantages. . . ."

Silence today started a short session. Hunting poor last night, Weyland still hungry. Much restless movement, watching goldfish darting in tank, scanning bookshelves. Asked him to be books. " 'I am old and full of knowledge, well made to last long. You see only the title, the substance is hidden. I am a book that stays closed. ' " Malicious twist of the mouth, not quite a smile: "This is a good game." Is he feeling threatened, too—already "opened" too much to me? Too strung out with him to dig when he's skimming surfaces that should be probed. Don't know how to *do* therapy with Weyland—just have to let things happen, hope it's good. But what's "good"? Aristotle? Rousseau? Ask Weyland what's good, he'll say "Blood."

Everything in a spin—these notes too confused, too fragmentary—worthless for a book, just a mess, like me, my life. Tried to call Deb last night, cancel visit. Nobody home, thank God. Can't tell her to stay away—but damn it—do not need complications now!

Floria went down to Broadway with Lucille to get more juice, cheese, and crackers for the clinic fridge. This week it was their turn to do the provisions, a chore that rotated among the staff. Their talk about grant proposals for the support of the clinic trailed off.

"Let's sit a minute," Floria said. They crossed to a traffic island in the middle of the avenue. It was a sunny afternoon, close enough to lunchtime so that the brigade of old people who normally occupied the benches had thinned out. Floria sat down and kicked a crumpled beer can and some greasy fast-food wrappings back under the bench.

"You look like hell but wide awake at least," Lucille commented.

"Things are still rough," Floria said. "I keep hoping to get my life under control so I'll have some energy left for Deb and Nick and the kids when they arrive, but I can't seem to do it. Group was awful last night—a member accused me afterward of having abandoned them all. I think I have, too. The professional messes and the personal are all related somehow, they run into each other. I should be keeping them apart so I can deal with them separately, but I can't. I can't concentrate, my mind is all over the place. Except with Dracula, who keeps me riveted with astonishment when he's in the office and bemused the rest of the time."

A bus roared by, shaking the pavement and the benches. Lucille waited until the noise faded. "Relax about the group. The others would have defended you if you'd been attacked during the session. They all understand, even if you don't seem to: it's the summer doldrums, people don't want to work, they expect you to do it all for them. But don't push so hard. You're not a shaman who can magic your clients back into health."

Floria tore two cans of juice out of a six-pack and handed one to her. On a street corner opposite, a violent argument broke out in typewriter-fast Spanish between two women. Floria sipped tinny juice and watched. She'd seen a guy last winter straddle another on that same corner and try to smash his brains out on the icy sidewalk. The old question again: what's crazy, what's health?

"It's a good thing you dumped Chubs, anyhow," Lucille said. "I don't know what finally brought that on, but it's definitely a move in the right direction. What about Count Dracula? You don't talk about him much anymore. I thought I diagnosed a yen for his venerable body."

Floria shifted uncomfortably on the bench and didn't answer. If only she could deflect Lucille's sharp-eyed curiosity.

"Oh," Lucille said. "I see. You really are hot—or at least warm. Has he noticed?"

"I don't think so. He's not on the lookout for that kind of response from me. He says sex with other people doesn't interest him, and I think he's telling the truth."

"Weird," Lucille said. "What about *Vampire on My Couch*? Shaping up all right?"

"It's shaky, like everything else. I'm worried that I don't know how things are going to come out. I mean, Freud's wolf-man case was a success, as therapy goes. Will my vampire case turn out successfully?"

She glanced at Lucille's puzzled face, made up her mind, and plunged ahead. "Luce, think of it this way: suppose, just suppose, that my Dracula is for real, an honest-to-God vampire—"

"Oh, *shit!*" Lucille erupted in anguished exasperation. "Damn it, Floria, enough is enough—will you stop futzing around and get some help? Coming to pieces yourself and trying to treat this poor nut with a vampire fixation—how can you do him any good? No wonder you're worried about his therapy!"

"Please, just listen, help me think this out. My purpose can't be to cure him of what he is. Suppose vampirism isn't a defense he has to learn to drop? Suppose it's the core of his identity? Then what do I do?"

Lucille rose abruptly and marched away from her through a gap between the rolling waves of cabs and trucks. Floria caught up with her on the next block.

"Listen, will you? Luce, you see the problem? I don't need to help him see who and what he is, he knows that perfectly well, and he's not crazy, far from it—"

"Maybe not," Lucille said grimly, "but you are. Don't dump this junk on me outside of office hours, Floria. I don't spend my time listening to nut-talk unless I'm getting paid."

"Just tell me if this makes psychological sense to you: he's healthier than most of us because he's always true to his identity, even when he's engaged in deceiving others. A fairly narrow, rigorous set of requirements necessary to his survival—that *is* his identity, and it commands him completely. Anything extraneous could destroy him. To go on living, he has to act solely out of his own undistorted necessity, and if that isn't authenticity, what is? So he's healthy, isn't he?" She paused, feeling a sudden lightness in herself. "And that's the best sense I've been able to make of this whole business so far."

They were in the middle of the block. Lucille, who could not on her short legs outwalk Floria, turned on her suddenly. "What the hell do you think you're doing, calling yourself a therapist? For God's sake, Floria, don't try to rope me into this kind of professional irresponsibility. You're just dipping into your client's fantasies instead of helping him to handle them. That's not therapy, it's collusion. Have some sense! Admit you're over your head in troubles of your own, retreat to firmer ground—go get treatment for yourself!"

Floria angrily shook her head. When Lucille turned away and hurried on up the block toward the clinic, Floria let her go without trying to detain her.

Thought about Lucille's advice. After my divorce, going back into therapy for a while did help, but now? Retreat again to being a client, like old days in training—so young, inadequate, defenseless then. Awful prospect. And I'd have to hand over W. to somebody else—who? I'm not up to handling him, can't cope, too anxious, yet with all that we do good therapy together somehow. I can't control, can only offer; he's free to take, refuse, use as suits, as far as he's willing to go. I serve as resource while he does own therapy—isn't that therapeutic ideal, free of "shoulds," "shouldn'ts"?

Saw ballet with Mort, lovely evening—time out from W.— talking, singing, pirouetting all the way home, feeling safe as anything in the shadow of Mort-mountain; rolled later with that humming (off-key), sun-warm body. Today W. says he saw me at Lincoln Center last night, avoided me because of Mort. W. is ballet fan! Started attending to pick up victims, now also because dance puzzles and pleases.

"When a group dances well, the meaning is easy—the dancers make a visual complement to the music, all their moves necessary, coherent, flowing. When a gifted soloist performs, the pleasure of making the moves is echoed in my own body. The soloist's absorption is total, much like my own in the actions of the hunt. But when a man and a woman dance together, something else happens. Sometimes one is hunter, one is prey, or they shift these roles between them. Yet some other level of significance exists—I suppose to do with sex—and I feel it—a tugging sensation, here"—touched his solar plexus—"but I do not understand it."

Worked with his reactions to ballet. The response he feels to pas de deux is a kind of pull, "like hunger but not hunger." Of course he's baffled—Balanchine writes that the pas de deux is always a love story between man and woman. W. isn't man, isn't woman, yet the drama connects. His hands hovering as he spoke, fingers spread toward each other. Pointed this out. Body work comes easier to him now; joined his hands, interlaced fingers, spoke for hands without prompting: " 'We are similar, we want the comfort of like closing to like.' " How would that be for him, to find—likeness, another of his kind? "Female?" Starts impatiently explaining how unlikely this is— No, forget sex and pas de deux for now; just to find your like, another vampire.

He springs up, agitated now. There are none, he insists; adds at once, "But what would it be like? What would happen? I fear it!" Sits again, hands clenched. "I long for it."

Silence. He watches goldfish, I watch him. I withhold fatuous attempt to pin down this insight, if that's what it is—what can I know about his insight? Suddenly he turns, studies me intently till I lose my nerve, react, cravenly suggest that if I make him uncomfortable he might wish to switch to another therapist—

"Certainly not." More follows, all gold: "There is value to me in what we do here, Dr. Landauer, much against my earlier expectations. Although people talk appreciatively of honest speech they generally avoid it, and I myself have found scarcely any use for it at all. Your straightforwardness with me—and the straightforwardness you require in return—this is healthy in a life so dependent on deception as mine."

Sat there, wordless, much moved, thinking of what I don't show him—my upset life, seat-of-pants course with him and attendant strain, attraction to him—I'm holding out on him while he appreciates my honesty.

Hesitation, then lower-voiced, "Also, there are limits on my methods of self-discovery, short of turning myself over to a laboratory for vivisection. I have no others like myself to look at and learn from. Any tools that may help are worth much to me, and these games of yours are—potent." Other stuff besides, not important. Important: he moves me and he draws me and he keeps on coming back. Hang in if he does.

Bad night—Kenny's aunt called: no bill from me this month, so if he's not seeing me, who's keeping an eye on him, where's he hanging out? Much implied blame for what *might* happen. Absurd, but shook me up: I did fail Kenny. Called off group this week also; too much.

No, it was a *good* night—first dream in months I can recall, contact again with own depths—but disturbing. Dreamed myself in cab with W. in place of the woman from the Y. He put his hand not on my neck but breast—I felt intense sensual response in the dream, also anger and fear so strong they woke me.

Thinking about this: anyone leans toward him sexually, to him a sign his hunting technique has maneuvered prospective victim into range, maybe arouses his appetite for blood. *I don't want that.* "She was food." I am not food, I am a person. No thrill at languishing away in his arms in a taxi while he drinks my blood—that's disfigured sex, masochism. My sex response in dream signaled to me I would be his victim—I rejected that, woke up.

Mention of *Dracula* (novel). W. dislikes: meandering, inaccurate, those absurd fangs. Says he himself has a sort of needle under his tongue, used to pierce skin. No offer to demonstrate, and no request from me. I brightly brought up historical Vlad Dracul—celebrated instance of Turkish envoys who, upon refusing to uncover to Vlad to show respect, were

killed by spiking their hats to their skulls. "Nonsense," snorts
W. "A clever ruler would use very small thumbtacks and
dismiss the envoys to moan about the streets of Varna, holding their tacked heads." First spontaneous play he's shown—
took head in hands and uttered plaintive groans, "Ow, oh,
ooh." I cracked up. W. reverted at once to usual dignified
manner: "You can see that this would serve the ruler much
more effectively as an object lesson against rash pride."

Later, same light vein: "I know why I'm a vampire; why
are you a therapist?" Off balance as usual, said things about
helping, mental health, etc. He shook his head: "And people
think of a vampire as arrogant! You want to perform cures in
a world that exhibits very little health of any kind—and it's
the same arrogance with all of you. This one wants to be
President or Class Monitor or Department Chairman or
Union Boss, another must be first to fly to the stars or to
transplant the human brain, and on and on. As for me, I wish
only to satisfy my appetite in peace."

And those of us whose appetite is for competence, for ef-
fectiveness? Thought of Green, treated eight years ago, went
on to be indicted for running a hellish "home" for aged. I had
helped him stay functional so he could destroy the helpless
for profit.

W. not my first predator, only most honest and direct.
Scared; not of attack by W., but of process we're going
through. I'm beginning to be up to it (?), but still—utterly
unpredictable, impossible to handle or manage. Occasional
stirrings of inward choreographer that used to shape my work
so surely. Have I been afraid of that, holding it down in
myself, choosing mechanical manipulation instead? Not a
choice with W.—thinking no good, strategy no good, nothing
left but instinct, clear and uncluttered responses if I can find
them. Have to be my own authority with him, as he is always
his own authority with a world in which he's unique. So work
with W. not just exhausting—exhilarating too, along with
strain, fear.

Am I growing braver? Not much choice.

Park again today (air-conditioning out at office). Avoiding
Lucille's phone calls from clinic (very reassuring that she calls

despite quarrel, but don't want to take all this up with her again). Also meeting W. in open feels saner somehow—wild creatures belong outdoors? Sailboat pond N. of 72nd, lots of kids, garbage, one beautiful tall boat drifting. We walked.

W. maintains he remembers no childhood, no parents. I told him my astonishment, confronted by someone who never had a life of the previous generation (even adopted parent) shielding him from death—how naked we stand when the last shield falls. Got caught in remembering a death dream of mine, dream it now and then—couldn't concentrate, got scared, spoke of it—a dog tumbled under a passing truck, ejected to side of the road where it lay unable to move except to lift head and shriek; couldn't help. Shaking nearly to tears—remembered Mother got into dream somehow—had blocked that at first. Didn't say it now. Tried to rescue situation, show W. how to work with a dream (sitting in vine arbor near band shell, some privacy).

He focused on my obvious shakiness: "The air vibrates constantly with the death cries of countless animals large and small. What is the death of one dog?" Leaned close, speaking quietly, instructing. "Many creatures are dying in ways too dreadful to imagine. I am part of the world; I listen to the pain. You people claim to be above all that. You deafen yourselves with your own noise and pretend there's nothing else to hear. Then these screams enter your dreams, and you have to seek therapy because you have lost the nerve to listen."

Remembered myself, said, Be a dying animal. He refused: "You are the one who dreams this." I had a horrible flash, felt I was the dog—helpless, doomed, hurting—burst into tears. The great therapist, bringing her own hangups into session with client! Enraged with self, which did not help stop bawling.

W. disconcerted, I think; didn't speak. People walked past, glanced over, ignored us. W. said finally, "What is this?" Nothing, just the fear of death. "Oh, the fear of death. That's with me all the time. One must simply get used to it." Tears into laughter. Goddamn wisdom of the ages. He got up to go, paused: "And tell that stupid little man who used to precede me at your office to stop following me around. He puts himself in danger that way."

Kenny, damn it! Aunt doesn't know where he is, no answer on his phone. Idiot!

Sketching all night—useless. W. beautiful beyond the scope of line—the beauty of singularity, cohesion, rooted in absolute devotion to demands of his specialized body. In feeding (woman in taxi), utter absorption one wants from a man in sex—no score-keeping, no fantasies, just hot urgency of appetite, of senses, the moment by itself.

His sleeves worn rolled back today to the elbows—strong, sculptural forearms, the long bones curved in slightly, suggest torque, leverage. How old?

Endurance: huge, rich cloak of time flows back from his shoulders like wings of a dark angel. All springs from, elaborates, the single, stark, primary condition: he is a predator who subsists on human blood. Harmony, strength, clarity, magnificence—all from that basic animal integrity. Of course I long for all that, here in the higgledy-piggledy hodgepodge of my life! Of course he draws me!

Wore no perfume today, deference to his keen, easily insulted sense of smell. He noticed at once, said curt thanks. Saw something bothering him, opened my mouth seeking desperately for right thing to say—up rose my inward choreographer, wide awake, and spoke plain from my heart: thinking on my floundering in some of our sessions—I am aware that you see this confusion of mine. I know you see by your occasional impatient look, sudden disengagement—yet you continue to reveal yourself to me (even shift our course yourself if it needs shifting and I don't do it). I think I know why. Because there's no place for you in world as you truly are. Because beneath your various façades your true self suffers; like all true selves, it wants, needs to be honored as real and valuable through acceptance by another. I try to be that other, but often you are beyond me.

He rose, paced to window, looked back, burning, at me. "If I seem sometimes restless or impatient, Dr. Landauer, it's not because of any professional shortcomings of yours. On the contrary—you are all too effective. The seductiveness, the distraction of our—human contact worries me. I fear for the ruthlessness that keeps me alive."

Speak for ruthlessness. He shook his head. Saw tightness in shoulders, feet braced hard against floor. Felt reflected tension in my own muscles.

Prompted him: " 'I resent . . .' "

"I resent your pretension to teach me about myself! What will this work that you do here make of me? A predator paralyzed by an unwanted empathy with his prey? A creature fit only for a cage and keeper?" He was breathing hard, jaw set. I saw suddenly the truth of his fear: his integrity is not human, but my work is specifically human, designed to make humans more human—what if it does that to him? Should have seen it before, should have seen it. No place left to go: had to ask him, in small voice, Speak for my pretension.

"No!" Eyes shut, head turned away.

Had to do it: Speak for me.

W. whispered, "As to the unicorn, out of your own legends—'Unicorn, come lay your head in my lap while the hunters close in. You are a wonder, and for love of wonder I will tame you. You are pursued, but forget your pursuers, rest under my hand till they come and destroy you.' " Looked at me like steel: "Do you see? The more you involve yourself in what I am, the more you become the peasant with the torch!"

Two days later, Doug came into town and had lunch with Floria.

He was a man of no outstanding beauty who was nevertheless attractive: he didn't have much chin and his ears were too big, but you didn't notice because of his air of confidence. His stability had been earned the hard way—as a gay man facing the straight world. Some of his strength had been attained with effort and pain in a group that Floria had run years earlier. A lasting affection had grown between herself and Doug. She was intensely glad to see him.

They ate near the clinic. "You look a little frayed around the edges," Doug said. "I heard about Jane Fennerman's relapse—too bad."

"I've only been able to bring myself to visit her once since."

"Feeling guilty?"

She hesitated, gnawing on a stale breadstick. The truth was, she hadn't thought of Jane Fennerman in weeks. Finally she said, "I guess I must be."

Sitting back with his hands in his pockets, Doug chided her gently. "It's got to be Jane's fourth or fifth time into the nuthatch, and the others happened when she was in the care of other therapists. Who are you to imagine—to demand—that her cure lay in your hands? God may be a woman, Floria, but She is not you. I thought the whole point was some recognition of individual responsibility—you for yourself, the client for himself or herself."

"That's what we're always saying," Floria agreed. She felt curiously divorced from this conversation. It had an old-fashioned flavor: before Weyland. She smiled a little.

The waiter ambled over. She ordered bluefish. The serving would be too big for her depressed appetite, but Doug wouldn't be satisfied with his customary order of salad (he never was) and could be persuaded to help out.

He worked his way around to Topic A. "When I called to set up this lunch, Hilda told me she's got a crush on Weyland. How are you and he getting along?"

"My God, Doug, now you're going to tell me this whole thing was to fix me up with an eligible suitor!" She winced at her own rather strained laughter. "How soon are you planning to ask Weyland to work at Cayslin again?"

"I don't know, but probably sooner than I thought a couple of months ago. We hear that he's been exploring an attachment to an anthropology department at a Western school, some niche where I guess he feels he can have less responsibility, less visibility, and a chance to collect himself. Naturally, this news is making people at Cayslin suddenly eager to nail him down for us. Have you a recommendation?"

"Yes," she said. "Wait."

He gave her an inquiring look. "What for?"

"Until he works more fully through certain stresses in the situation at Cayslin. Then I'll be ready to commit myself about him." The bluefish came. She pretended distraction: "Good God, that's too much fish for me. Doug, come on and help me out here."

Hilda was crouched over Floria's file drawer. She straightened up, looking grim. "Somebody's been in the office!"

What was this, had someone attacked her? The world took on a cockeyed, dangerous tilt. "Are you okay?"

"Yes, sure, I mean there are records that have been gone through. I can tell. I've started checking and so far it looks as if none of the files themselves are missing. But if any papers were taken out of them, that would be pretty hard to spot without reading through every folder in the place. Your files, Floria. I don't think anybody else's were touched."

Mere burglary; weak with relief, Floria sat down on one of the waiting-room chairs. But only her files? "Just my stuff, you're sure?"

Hilda nodded. "The clinic got hit too. I called. They see some new-looking scratches on the lock of your file drawer over there. Listen, you want me to call the cops?"

"First check as much as you can, see if anything obvious is missing."

There was no sign of upset in her office. She found a phone message on her table: Weyland had canceled his next appointment. She knew who had broken into her files.

She buzzed Hilda's desk. "Hilda, let's leave the police out of it for the moment. Keep checking." She stood in the middle of the office, looking at the chair replacing the one he had broken, looking at the window where he had so often watched.

Relax, she told herself. There was nothing for him to find here or at the clinic.

She signaled that she was ready for the first client of the afternoon.

That evening she came back to the office after having dinner with friends. She was supposed to be helping set up a work-shop for next month, and she'd been putting off even think-ing about it, let alone doing any real work. She set herself to compiling a suggested bibliography for her section.

The phone light blinked.

It was Kenny, sounding muffled and teary. "I'm sorry," he moaned. "The medicine just started to wear off. I've been trying to call you everyplace. God, I'm so scared—he was waiting in the alley."

"Who was?" she said, dry-mouthed. She knew.

Him. The tall one, the faggot—only he goes with women too, I've seen him. He grabbed me. He hurt me. I was lying there a long time. I couldn't do anything. I felt so funny—like floating away. Some kids found me. Their mother called the cops. I was so cold, so scared—"

"Kenny, where are you?"

He told her which hospital. "Listen, I think he's really crazy, you know? And I'm scared he might . . . you live alone . . . I don't know—I didn't mean to make trouble for you. I'm so scared."

God damn you, you meant exactly to make trouble for me, and now you've bloody well made it. She got him to ring for a nurse. By calling Kenny her patient and using "Dr." in front of her own name without qualifying the title, she got some information: two broken ribs, multiple contusions, a badly wrenched shoulder, and a deep cut on the scalp, which Dr. Wells thought accounted for the blood loss the patient had sustained. Picked up early today, the patient wouldn't say who had attacked him. You can check with Dr. Wells tomorrow, Dr.—?

Can Weyland think I've somehow sicked Kenny on him? No, he surely knows me better than that. Kenny must have brought this on himself.

She tried Weyland's number and then the desk at his hotel. He had closed his account and gone, providing no forwarding information other than the address of a university in New Mexico.

Then she remembered: this was the night Deb and Nick and the kids were arriving. Oh, God. Next phone call. The Americana was the hotel Deb had mentioned. Yes, Mr. and Mrs. Nicholas Redpath were registered in room whatnot. Ring, please.

Deb's voice came shakily on the line. "I've been trying to call you." Like Kenny.

"You sound upset," Floria said, steadying herself for whatever calamity had descended: illness, accident, assault in the streets of the dark, degenerate city.

Silence, then a raggedy sob. "Nick's not here. I didn't phone you earlier because I thought he still might come, but I don't think he's coming, Mom." Bitter weeping.

"Oh, Debbie. Debbie, listen, you just sit tight, I'll be right down there."

The cab ride took only a few minutes. Debbie was still crying when Floria stepped into the room.

"I don't know, I don't know," Deb wailed, shaking her head. "What did I do wrong? He went away a week ago, to do some research, he said, and I didn't hear from him, and half the bank money is gone—just half, he left me half. I kept hoping . . . they say most runaways come back in a few days or call up, they get lonely . . . I haven't told anybody—I thought since we were supposed to be here at this convention thing together, I'd better come, maybe he'd show up. But nobody's seen him, and there are no messages, not a word, nothing."

"All right, all right, poor Deb," Floria said, hugging her.

"Oh, God, I'm going to wake the kids with all this howling." Deb pulled away, making a frantic gesture toward the door of the adjoining room. "It was so hard to get them to sleep—they were expecting Daddy to be here, I kept telling them he'd be here." She rushed out into the hotel hallway.

Floria followed, propping the door open with one of her shoes since she didn't know whether Deb had a key with her or not. They stood out there together, ignoring passersby, huddling over Deb's weeping.

"What's been going on between you and Nick?" Floria said. "Have you two been sleeping together lately?"

Deb let out a squawk of agonized embarrassment, "Mo-*ther!*" and pulled away from her. Oh, hell, wrong approach.

"Come on, I'll help you pack. We'll leave word you're at my place. Let Nick come looking for you." Floria firmly squashed down the miserable inner cry, How am I going to stand this?

"Oh, no, I can't move till morning now that I've got the kids settled down. Besides, there's one night's deposit on the rooms. Oh, Mom, what did I do?"

"You didn't do anything, hon," Floria said, patting her shoulder and thinking in some part of her mind, Oh, boy, that's great, is that the best you can come up with in a crisis, with all your training and experience? Your touted professional skills are not so hot lately, but this bad? Another part answered, Shut up, stupid, only an idiot does therapy on her own family. Deb's come to her mother, not to a shrink, so go ahead and be Mommy. If only Mommy had less pressure on her right now—but that was always the way: everything at once or nothing at all.

"Look, Deb, suppose I stay the night here with you."

Deb shook the pale, damp-streaked hair out of her eyes with a determined, grown-up gesture. "No, thanks, Mom. I'm so tired I'm just going to fall out now. You'll be getting a bellyful of all this when we move in on you tomorrow anyway. I can manage tonight, and besides—"

And besides, just in case Nick showed up, Deb didn't want Floria around complicating things; of course. Or in case the tooth fairy dropped by.

Floria restrained an impulse to insist on staying; an impulse, she recognized, that came from her own need not to be alone tonight. That was not something to load on Deb's already burdened shoulders.

"Okay," Floria said. "But look, Deb, I'll expect you to call me up first thing in the morning, whatever happens." And if I'm still alive, I'll answer the phone.

All the way home in the cab she knew with growing certainty that Weyland would be waiting for her there. He can't just walk away, she thought; he has to finish things with me. So let's get it over.

In the tiled hallway she hesitated, keys in hand. What about calling the cops to go inside with her? Absurd. You don't set the cops on a unicorn.

She unlocked and opened the door to the apartment and called inside, "Weyland! Where are you?"

Nothing. Of course not—the door was still open, and he would want to be sure she was by herself. She stepped inside, shut the door, and snapped on a lamp as she walked into the living room.

He was sitting quietly on a radiator cover by the street window, his hands on his thighs. His appearance here in a new setting, her setting, this faintly lit room in her home place, was startlingly intimate. She was sharply aware of the whisper of movement—his clothing, his shoe soles against the carpet underfoot—as he shifted his posture.

"What would you have done if I'd brought somebody with me?" she said unsteadily. "Changed yourself into a bat and flown away?"

"Two things I must have from you," he said. "One is the bill of health that we spoke of when we began, though not, after all, for Cayslin College. I've made other plans. The story of my disappearance has of course filtered out along the academic grapevine so that even two thousand miles from here, people will want evidence of my mental soundness. Your evidence. I would type it myself and forge your signature, but I want your authentic tone and language.

Please prepare a letter to the desired effect, addressed to these people."

He drew something white from an inside pocket and held it out. She advanced and took the envelope from his extended hand. It was from the Western anthropology department that Doug had mentioned at lunch.

"Why not Cayslin?" she said. "They want you there."

"Have you forgotten your own suggestion that I find another job? That was a good idea after all. Your reference will serve me best out there—with a copy for my personnel file at Cayslin, naturally."

She put her purse down on the seat of a chair and crossed her arms. She felt reckless—the effect of stress and weariness, she thought, but it was an exciting feeling.

"The receptionist at the office does this sort of thing for me," she said.

He pointed. "I've been in your study. You have a typewriter there, you have stationery with your letterhead, you have carbon paper."

"What was the second thing you wanted?"

"Your notes on my case."

"Also at the—"

"You know that I've already searched both your work places, and the very circumspect jottings in your file on me are not what I mean. Others must exist: more detailed."

"What makes you think that?"

"How could you resist?" He mocked her. "You have encountered nothing like me in your entire professional life, and never shall again. Perhaps you hope to produce an article someday, even a book—a memoir of something impossible that happened to you one summer. You're an ambitious woman, Dr. Landauer."

Floria squeezed her crossed arms tighter against herself to quell her shivering. "This is all just supposition," she said.

He took folded papers from his pocket: some of her thrown-aside notes on him, salvaged from the wastebasket.

"I found these. I think there must be more. Whatever there is, give it to me, please."

"And if I refuse, what will you do? Beat me up the way you beat up Kenny?"

Weyland said calmly, "I told you he should stop following me. This is serious now. There are pursuers who intend me ill—my former captors, of whom I told you. Whom do you think I keep watch for? No records concerning me must fall into their hands. Don't bother protesting to me your devotion to confidentiality. There is a man named Alan Reese who would take what he wants and be damned to your professional ethics. So I must destroy all evidence you have about me before I leave the city."

Floria turned away and sat down by the coffee table, trying to think beyond her fear. She breathed deeply against the fright trembling in her chest.

"I see," he said dryly, "that you won't give me the notes; you don't trust me to take them and go. You see some danger."

"All right, a bargain," she said. "I'll give you whatever I have on your case if in return you promise to go straight out to your new job and keep away from Kenny and my offices and anybody connected with me—"

He was smiling slightly as he rose from the seat and stepped soft-footed toward her over the rug. "Bargains, promises, negotiations—all foolish, Dr. Landauer. I want what I came for."

She looked up at him. "But then how can I trust you at all? As soon as I give you what you want—"

"What is it that makes you afraid—that you can't render me harmless to you? What a curious concern you show suddenly for your own life and the lives of those around you! You are the one who led me to take chances in our work together—to explore the frightful risks of self-revelation. Didn't you see in the air between us the brilliant shimmer of those hazards? I thought your business was not smoothing the world over but adventuring into it, discovering its true nature, and closing valiantly with everything jagged, cruel, and deadly."

In the midst of her terror the inner choreographer awoke and stretched. Floria rose to face the vampire.

"All right, Weyland, no bargains. I'll give you freely what you want." Of course she couldn't make herself safe from him—or make Kenny or Lucille or Deb or Doug safe—any more than she could protect Jane Fennerman from the common dangers of life. Like Weyland, some dangers were too strong to bind or banish. "My notes are in the workroom—come on, I'll show you. As for the letter you need, I'll type it right now and you can take it away with you."

She sat at the typewriter arranging paper, carbon sheets, and white-out, and feeling the force of his presence. Only a few feet away, just at the margin of the light from the gooseneck lamp by which she worked, he leaned against the edge of the long table that was twin to the table in her office. Open in his large hands was the notebook she had given him from the table drawer. When he moved his head over the notebook's pages, his glasses glinted.

She typed the heading and the date. How surprising, she thought, to find that she had regained her nerve here, and now. When you dance as the inner choreographer directs, you act without thinking, not in command of events but in harmony with them. You yield control, accepting the chance that a mistake might be part of the design. The inner choreographer is always right but often dangerous: giving up control means accepting the possibility of death. What I feared I have pursued right here to this moment in this room.

A sheet of paper fell out of the notebook. Weyland stooped and caught it up, glanced at it. "You had training in art?" Must be a sketch.

"I thought once I might be an artist," she said.

"What you chose to do instead is better," he said. "This making of pictures, plays, all art, is pathetic. The world teems with creation, most of it unnoticed by your kind just as most of the deaths are unnoticed. What can be the point of adding yet another tiny gesture? Even you, these notes—for what, a moment's celebrity?"

"You tried it yourself," Floria said. "The book you edited, *Notes on a Vanished People.*" She typed: ". . . temporary dislocation resulting from a severe personal shock . . ."

"That was professional necessity, not creation," he said in the tone of a lecturer irritated by a question from the audience. With disdain he tossed the drawing on the table. "Remember, I don't share your impulse toward artistic gesture—your absurd frills—"

She looked up sharply. "The ballet, Weyland. Don't lie." She typed: ". . . exhibits a powerful drive toward inner balance and wholeness in a difficult life situation. The steadying influence of an extraordinary basic integrity . . ."

He set the notebook aside. "My feeling for ballet is clearly some sort of aberration. Do you sigh to hear a cow calling in a pasture?"

"There are those who have wept to hear whales singing in the ocean."

He was silent, his eyes averted.

"This is finished," she said. "Do you want to read it?"

He took the letter. "Good," he said at length. "Sign it, please. And type an envelope for it." He stood closer, but out of arm's reach, while she complied. "You seem less frightened."

"I'm terrified but not paralyzed," she said and laughed, but the laugh came out a gasp.

"Fear is useful. It has kept you at your best throughout our association. Have you a stamp?"

Then there was nothing to do but take a deep breath, turn off the gooseneck lamp, and follow him back into the living room. "What now, Weyland?" she said softly. "A carefully arranged suicide so that I have no chance to retract what's in that letter or to reconstruct my notes?"

At the window again, always on watch at the window, he said, "Your doorman was sleeping in the lobby. He didn't see me enter the building. Once inside, I used the stairs, of course. The suicide rate among therapists is notoriously high. I looked it up."

"You have everything all planned?"

The window was open. He reached out and touched the metal grille that guarded it. One end of the grille swung creaking outward into the night air, like a gate opening. She visualized him sitting there waiting for her to come home, his powerful fingers patiently working the bolts at that side of the grille loose from the brick-and-mortar window frame. The hair lifted on the back of her neck.

He turned toward her again. She could see the end of the letter she had given him sticking palely out of his jacket pocket.

"Floria," he said meditatively. "An unusual name—is it after the heroine of Sardou's *Tosca*? At the end, doesn't she throw herself to her death from a high castle wall? People are careless about the names they give their children. I will not drink from you—I hunted today, and I fed. Still, to leave you living . . . is too dangerous."

A fire engine tore past below, siren screaming. When it had gone, Floria said, "Listen, Weyland, you said it yourself: I can't make myself safe from you—I'm not strong enough to shove you out the window instead of being shoved out myself. Must you make yourself safe from me? Let me say this to you, without promises, demands, or pleadings: I will not go back on what I wrote in that letter. I will not try to recreate my notes. I mean it. Be content with that."

"You tempt me to it," he murmured after a moment, "to go from here with you still alive behind me for the remainder of your little life—to leave woven into Dr. Landauer's quick mind those threads of my own life that I pulled for her . . . I want to be able sometimes to think of you thinking of me. But the risk is very great."

"Sometimes it's right to let the dangers live, to give them their place," she urged. "Didn't you tell me yourself a little while ago how risk makes us more heroic?"

He looked amused. "Are you instructing me in the virtues of danger? You are brave enough to know something, perhaps, about that, but I have studied danger all my life."

"A long, long life with more to come," she said, desperate to make him understand and believe her. "Not mine to jeopardize. There's no torch-brandishing peasant here; we left that behind long ago. Remember when you spoke for me? You said, 'For love of wonder.' That was true."

He leaned to turn off the lamp near the window. She thought that he had made up his mind, and that when he straightened it would be to spring.

But instead of terror locking her limbs, from the inward choreographer came a rush of warmth and energy into her muscles and an impulse to turn toward him. Out of a harmony of desires she said swiftly, "Weyland, come to bed with me."

She saw his shoulders stiffen against the dim square of the window, his head lift in scorn. "You know I can't be bribed that way," he said contemptuously. "What are you up to? Are you one of those who come into heat at the sight of an upraised fist?"

"My life hasn't twisted me that badly, thank God," she retorted. "And if you've known all along how scared I've been, you must have sensed my attraction to you too, so you know it goes back to—very early in our work. But we're not at work now, and I've given up being 'up to' anything. My feeling is real—not a bribe, or a ploy, or a kink. No 'love me now, kill me later,' nothing like that. Understand me, Weyland: if death is your answer, then let's get right to it—come ahead and try."

Her mouth was dry as paper. He said nothing and made no move; she pressed on. "But if you can let me go, if we can simply part company here, then this is how I would like to mark the ending of our time together. This is the completion I want. Surely you feel something too—curiosity at least?"

"Granted, your emphasis on the expressiveness of the body has instructed me," he admitted, and then he added lightly, "Isn't it extremely unprofessional to proposition a client?"

"Extremely, and I never do; but this, now, feels right. For you to indulge in courtship that doesn't end in a meal would be unprofessional too, but how would it feel to indulge anyway—this once? Since we started, you've pushed me light-years beyond my profession. Now I want to travel all the way with you, Weyland. Let's be unprofessional together."

She turned and went into the bedroom, leaving the lights off. There was a reflected light, cool and diffuse, from the glowing night air of the great city. She sat down on the bed and kicked off her shoes. When she looked up, he was in the doorway.

Hesitantly, he halted a few feet from her in the dimness, then came and sat beside her. He would have lain down in his clothes, but she said quietly, "You can undress. The front door's locked and there isn't anyone here but us. You won't have to leap up and flee for your life."

He stood again and began to take off his clothes, which he draped neatly over a chair. He said, "Suppose I am fertile with you; could you conceive?"

By her own choice, any such possibility had been closed off after Deb. She said, "No," and that seemed to satisfy him.

She tossed her own clothes onto the dresser.

He sat down next to her again, his body silvery in the reflected light and smooth, lean as a whippet and as roped with muscle. His cool thigh pressed against her own fuller, warmer one as he leaned across her and carefully deposited his glasses on the bedtable. Then he turned toward her, and she could just make out two puckerings of tissue on his skin: bullet scars, she thought, shivering.

He said, "But why do I wish to do this?"

"Do you?" She had to hold herself back from touching him.

"Yes." He stared at her. "How did you grow so real? The more I spoke to you of myself, the more real you became."

"No more speaking, Weyland," she said gently. "This is body work."

He lay back on the bed.

She wasn't afraid to take the lead. At the very least she could do for him as well as he did for himself, and at the most, much better. Her own skin was darker than his, a shadowy contrast where she browsed over his body with her hands. Along the contours of his ribs she felt knotted places, hollows—old healings, the tracks of time. The tension of his muscles under her touch and the sharp sound of his breathing stirred her. She lived the fantasy of sex with an utter stranger; there was no one in the world so much a stranger as he. Yet there was no one who knew him as well as she did, either. If he was unique, so was she, and so was their confluence here.

The vividness of the moment inflamed her. His body responded. His penis stirred, warmed, and thickened in her hand. He turned on his hip so that they lay facing each other, he on his right side, she on her left. When she moved to kiss him he swiftly averted his face: of course—to him, the mouth was for feeding. She touched her fingers to his lips, signifying her comprehension.

He offered no caresses but closed his arms around her, his hands cradling the back of her head and neck. His shadowed face, deep-hollowed under brow and cheekbone, was very close to hers. From between the parted lips that she must not kiss, his quick breath came, roughened by groans of pleasure. At length he pressed his head against hers, inhaling deeply; taking her scent, she thought, from her hair and skin.

He entered her, hesitant at first, probing slowly and tentatively. She found this searching motion intensely sensuous, and clinging to him all along his sinewy length she rocked with him through two long, swelling waves of sweetness. Still half submerged, she felt him strain tight against her, she heard him gasp through his clenched teeth.

Panting, they subsided and lay loosely interlocked. His head was tilted back; his eyes were closed. She had no desire to stroke him or to speak with him, only to rest spent against his body and absorb the sounds of his breathing, her breathing.

He did not lie long to hold or be held. Without a word he disengaged his body from hers and got up. He moved quietly about the bedroom, gathering his clothing, his shoes, the drawings, the notes from the workroom. He dressed without lights. She listened in silence from the center of a deep repose.

There was no leavetaking. His tall figure passed and repassed the dark rectangle of the doorway, and then he was gone. The latch on the front door clicked shut.

Floria thought of getting up to secure the deadbolt. Instead she turned on her stomach and slept.

She woke as she remembered coming out of sleep as a youngster—peppy and clearheaded.

"Hilda, let's give the police a call about that break-in. If anything ever does come of it, I want to be on record as having reported it. You can tell them we don't have any idea who did it or why. And please make a photocopy of this letter carbon to send to Doug Sharpe up at Cayslin. Then you can put the carbon into Weyland's file and close it."

Hilda sighed. "Well, he was too old anyway."

He wasn't, my dear, but never mind.

In her office, Floria picked up the morning's mail from her table. Her glance strayed to the window where Weyland had so often stood. God, she was going to miss him; and God, how good it was to be restored to plain working days.

Only not yet. Don't let the phone ring, don't let the world push in here now. She needed to sit alone for a little and let her mind sort through the images left from . . . from the pas de deux with Weyland. It's the notorious morning after, old dear, she told herself; just where have I been dancing, anyway?

In a clearing in the enchanted forest with the unicorn, of course, but not the way the old legends have it. According to them, hunters set a virgin to attract the unicorn by her chastity so they can catch and kill him. My unicorn was the chaste one, come to think of it, and this lady meant no treachery. No, Weyland and I met hidden from the hunt, to celebrate a private mystery of our own. . . .

Your mind grappled with my mind, my dark leg over your silver one, unlike closing with unlike across whatever likeness may be found: your memory pressing on my thoughts, my words drawing out your words in which you may recognize your life, my smooth palm gliding down your smooth flank. . . .

Why, this will make me cry, she thought, blinking. And for what? Does an afternoon with the unicorn have any meaning for the ordinary days that come later? What has this passage with Weyland left me? Have I anything in my hands now besides the morning's mail?

What I have in my hands is my own strength, because I had to reach deep to find the strength to match him.

She put down the letters, noticing how on the backs of her hands the veins stood, blue shadows, under the thin skin. How can these hands be strong? Time was beginning to wear them thin and bring up the fragile inner structure in clear relief. That was the meaning of the last parent's death: that the child's remaining time has a limit of its own.

But not for Weyland. No graveyards of family dead lay behind him, no obvious and implacable ending of his own span threatened him. Time has to be different for a creature of an enchanted forest, as morality has to be different. He was a predator and a killer formed for a life of centuries, not decades; of secret singularity, not the busy hum of the herd.

Yet his strength, suited to that nonhuman life, had revived her own strength. Her hands were slim, no longer youthful, but she saw now that they were strong enough.

For what? She flexed her fingers, watching the tendons slide under the skin. Strong hands don't have to clutch. They can simply open and let go.

She dialed Lucille's extension at the clinic.

"Luce? Sorry to have missed your calls lately. Listen, I want to start making arrangements to transfer my practice for a while. You were right, I do need a break, just as all my friends have been telling me. Will you pass the word for me to the staff over there today? Good, thanks. Also, there's the workshop coming up next month. . . . Yes. Are you kidding? They'd love to have you in my place. You're not the only one who's noticed that I've been falling apart, you know. It's awfully soon—can you manage, do you think? Luce, you are a brick and a lifesaver and all that stuff that means I'm very, very grateful."

Not so terrible, she thought, but only a start. Everything else remained to be dealt with. The glow of euphoria couldn't carry her for long. Already, looking down, she noticed jelly on her blouse, just like old times, and she didn't even remember having breakfast. If you want to keep the strength you've found in all this, you're going to have to get plenty of practice being strong. Try a tough one now.

She phoned Deb. "Of course you slept late, so what? I did too, so I'm glad you didn't call and wake me up. Whenever you're ready—if you need help moving uptown from the hotel, I can cancel here and come down. . . . Well, call if you change your mind. I've left a house key for you with my doorman.

"And listen, hon, I've been thinking—how about all of us going up together to Nonnie's over the weekend? Then when you feel like it maybe you'd like to talk about what you'll do next. Yes, I've already started setting up some free time for myself. Think about it, love. Talk to you later."

Kenny's turn. "Kenny, I'll come by during visiting hours this afternoon."

"Are you okay?" he squeaked.

"I'm okay. But I'm not your mommy, Ken, and I'm not going to start trying to hold the big bad world off you again. I'll expect you to be ready to settle down seriously and choose a new therapist for yourself. We're going to get that done today once and for all. Have you got that?"

After a short silence he answered in a desolate voice, "All right."

"Kenny, nobody grown up has a mommy around to take care of things for them and keep them safe—not even me. You just have to be tough enough and brave enough yourself. See you this afternoon."

How about Jane Fennerman? No, leave it for now, we are not Wonder Woman, we can't handle that stress today as well.

Too restless to settle down to paperwork before the day's round of appointments began, she got up and fed the goldfish, then drifted to the window and looked out over the city. Same jammed-up traffic down there, same dusty summer park stretching away uptown—yet not the same city, because Weyland no longer hunted there. Nothing like him moved now in those deep, grumbling streets. She would never come upon anyone there as alien as he—and just as well. Let last night stand as the end, unique and inimitable, of their affair. She was glutted with strangeness and looked forward frankly to sharing again in Mort's ordinary human appetite.

And Weyland—how would he do in that new and distant hunting ground he had found for himself? Her own balance had been changed. Suppose his once perfect, solitary equilibrium had been altered too? Perhaps he had spoiled it by involving himself too intimately with another being—herself. And then he had left her alive—a terrible risk. Was this a sign of his corruption at her hands?

"Oh, no," she whispered fiercely, focusing her vision on

her reflection in the smudged window glass. Oh, no, I am not the temptress. I am not the deadly female out of legends whose touch defiles the hitherto unblemished being, her victim. If Weyland found some human likeness in himself, that had to be in him to begin with. Who said he was defiled anyway? Newly discovered capacities can be either strengths or weaknesses, depending on how you use them.

Very pretty and reassuring, she thought grimly; but it's pure cant. Am I going to retreat now into mechanical analysis to make myself feel better?

She heaved open the window and admitted the sticky summer breath of the city into the office. There's your enchanted forest, my dear, all nitty-gritty and not one flake of fairy dust. You've survived here, which means you can see straight when you have to. Well, you have to now.

Has he been damaged? No telling yet, and you can't stop living while you wait for the answers to come in. I don't know all that was done between us, but I do know who did it: I did it, and he did it, and neither of us withdrew until it was done. We were joined in a rich complicity—he in the wakening of some flicker of humanity in himself, I in keeping and, yes, enjoying the secret of his implacable blood hunger. What that complicity means for each of us can only be discovered by getting on with living and watching for clues from moment to moment. His business is to continue from here, and mine is to do the same, without guilt and without resentment. Doug was right: the aim is individual responsibility. From that effort, not even the lady and the unicorn are exempt.

Shaken by a fresh upwelling of tears, she thought bitterly, Moving on is easy enough for Weyland; he's used to it, he's had more practice. What about me? Yes, be selfish, woman—if you haven't learned that, you've learned damn little.

The Japanese say that in middle age you should leave the claims of family, friends, and work, and go ponder the meaning of the universe while you still have the chance.

Maybe I'll try just existing for a while, and letting grow in its own time my understanding of a universe that includes Weyland—and myself—among its possibilities.

Is that looking out for myself? Or am I simply no longer fit for living with family, friends, and work? Have *I* been damaged by *him*—by my marvelous, murderous monster?

Damn, she thought, I wish he were here, I wish we could talk about it. The light on her phone caught her eye; it was blinking the quick flashes that meant Hilda was signaling the imminent arrival of—not Weyland—the day's first client.

We're each on our own now, she thought, shutting the window and turning on the air conditioner.

But think of me sometimes, Weyland, thinking of you.

1980:
Whatever Weirdness
Lingers

Michael Glyer

From its first edition the Nebula Awards collections have in-cluded critical essays on "the year in science fiction." This is a good idea; we ought to preserve our impressions of what's going on in our profession, and the Nebula books are probably the best places to do it. The essays have usually been readable and often were valuable to our academic friends.

However, they've been incomplete; they've left out a consid-erable part of the science fiction fraternity. They've paid little or no attention to the fans.

Science fiction is unlike any other literary (print media) genre. Of course that must be so, given the subject matter; but it's true in another way. No other literary genre has a large, vocal, and organized fandom. Science fiction conventions are put on by fans, not by the writers. Fans publish "amateur mag-azines" (called fanzines or just zines), which run the gamut from four badly dittoed pages to beautifully illustrated offset print, with color cover.

There have been attempts to create a mystery-story fandom through the annual Bouchercons (conventions named after the late Tony Boucher, mystery critic for The New York Times*), but although the Bouchercons have been organized by experienced science fiction convention managers, and Boucher was himself a science fiction writer, fan, and critic, organized mystery fandom remains small and not particularly influential.*

Science fiction fandom, on the other hand, continues to grow and, indeed, through cooperation with organizations like the L-5 Society, has even gained a measure of political power. Most science fiction authors were fans at one time, and the tradition of frequent and informal interaction between writers and fans is deeply embedded in the customs of the SF community. There are writers who try to ignore science fiction fandom, some even who claim to hate it. All, however, admit SF fandom's influence.

That influence is inevitable. The Nebula Awards are supposed to be given by professional writers, and indeed many professional writers do participate in the award votes; but it is also well known that many of the writers simply haven't time to read all the eligible stories, or indeed even all those nominated. The result is that the Nebulae are given by a relatively small number of people.

Not so the Hugos. Hugos—Science Fiction Achievement Awards—are given by vote of the fans. In times long past, the Hugo Awards were also dominated by a small number of people, but no longer. Since Hugo Awards are commercially valuable to writers (as well as a great boost to the ego), it's inevitable that writers will be influenced by what the fans like. It's thus inevitable that fandom will shape a great part of written science fiction.

There are other reasons why fandom is influential. Until recently, science fiction was not respectable; even now, science fiction writers are not likely to be invited to literary teas, cocktail parties for critics, and the various civic events that are never complete without Famous Authors. This may be a bit strange—after all, many science fiction authors outsell their more famous "literary" colleagues by a factor of ten, and sci-

ence fiction works stay in print much longer than do most best-sellers or Pulitzer Prize winners. (Who won the Pulitzer in 1961? I don't know, but the Hugo winners for that year and just about all other years remain in print.) But whether or not the literati are justified in ignoring science fiction, their actions insure they will have little or no influence *over it. SF authors, snubbed at literary events, are lionized at science fiction conventions, with the result that organized fans have great influence.*

So do fan critics. A fanzine may have a circulation of no more than a few hundred copies and be very irregular in schedule, and yet have more hold over a science fiction author than would a review in the Times Literary Supplement. *After all, the* TLS *is probably going to ignore the book anyway; why worry about what they'll say? Better to worry about the fans.*

Now this inbreeding can be a bad thing. Fans, after all, read a lot of science fiction. A concept that is new and different and far out to the general public can be old-hat to the fans; and fan pressure can push an author toward ever-new, ever farther-out ideas, until SF is far out indeed, adding to our isolation and thus in turn making the fans more important—a circular process with no logical end.

Fortunately this is no longer happening. The circle of fandom is widening, but the reading public is also becoming more sophisticated. Science fiction books now regularly reach—and stay high on—the best-seller list. A few SF authors now appear on the Carson, Snyder, and Susskind shows. SF is taught in universities, and SF authors are invited to university teas (and find them deadly dull compared to science fiction conventions).

For all that, fandom will always have an important place in the SF community; and it seemed appropriate to me that fans be represented in this book.

Mike Glyer has long been one of fandom's most influential critics. He grew up in California but attended the University of Kentucky at Bowling Green, where he received his degree in popular culture. He then returned to California, where he is an officer of the LASFS—the Los Angeles Science Fantasy Society, Inc., a fifty-year-old SF club that owns its own clubhouse and presses.

I know for a fact that Glyer's writing can be influential; on one occasion, when I was president of Science Fiction Writers of America, a report in a Glyer fanzine had me making long-distance calls in the middle of the night. Another and happier time, I was so struck by his criticism of one of my stories that when I incorporated the story into a novel, I made a number of major changes to deal with Glyer's points. I can think of no one more qualified to comment on the year from the fannish view.

In 1976, when there was still some doubt that *Star Wars* would ever be released, much less become a cultural landmark, actor Mark Hamill attended the World Science Fiction Convention in Kansas City. Frustrated, Hamill reportedly said, "I'm the star of a major motion picture and nobody knows it!"

They know it now. The cinematic trend that *Star Wars* began hyped interest in science fiction even higher. And the irony that connects the events of 1976 to this report on fan activity in 1980 is, the Kansas City committee was plagued by controversy over how it planned to handle predicted record crowds: 4,000 people joined, but due to bad publicity only 2,600 showed up. However, in 1980, Boston hosted more than 5,600 attendees—more people by far than had ever shown up for the event since it began in 1939.

The year 1980 was not merely a convenient breakpoint, but was actually a watershed year for science fiction fandom in the following ways. An explosion in the size and frequency of science fiction conventions brought about new problems in fandom's self-regulation. Concrete efforts were taken to permanently preserve the two finest science fiction collections in the world. Two publishing projects, awaited by fans since 1969, finally went to press. While unusual numbers of newcomers swelled the ranks, longtime fans worked to secure their roots.

The collection and preservation of science fiction publications, perhaps the most reverent form of fan activity, seldom inspires news. But in 1980, fans tried to resolve the single critical question for major collectors: Can the collections outlive their owners? Two of the largest and most comprehensive science fiction collections in the world, one belonging to the late Ron Graham of Australia, the other to Forrest Ackerman of Los Angeles, were involved.

The future of Graham's collection *seemed* secure long before 1980. When featured on Australian television before his death in February 1979, Graham said that his will included the provision, "I give and bequeath to the University of Sydney . . . the whole of my collection of science fiction books, magazines and periodicals, and other written or printed materials concerned with science fiction. . . ."

The genre had thrived for decades before receiving serious scholarly attention, and at this late date, no academic could afford, even if he could find, the kind of archive created by a Graham or Ackerman. Graham's bequest was historic.

However, Sydney fan Jack Herman discovered and reported that "There have been two auctions of material from the Graham collection—one on 9/24/79 and the other on 12/17/79." An Australian firm, Lawson's, had circulated auction catalogues listing material from the estate, including many SF and fantasy titles which should have gone to the university under the spirit of the will.

Considerable anxiety about the fate of the collection led to correspondence, and only in early 1980 did Pauline Dickinson, of the University of Sydney's Fisher Library Selection and Collection Building Department, dispel that concern. "When Ron Graham died, his executors informed us of the will and informed us we'd get the science fiction books once the estate was settled. There was some confusion as to what 'science fiction' actually entailed, but this was irrelevant as, in the end, everything came to us from comics to detective fiction to SF. . . . I attended [the second] auction—most of the SF books were duplicates of those we already held—and I bought the one or two items we didn't appear to have." Dickinson conceded that some material had slipped through. Ironically, the best assurance that the Fisher Library got the bulk of the collection came in the form of a complaint published in *Australian Financial Review*: "James R. Lawson, Sydney, recently handled a collection of detective and other pulp material, helping prime interest in this new and developing area of collecting. Unfortunately, the best part of the library from which this came, a collection of science fiction books bequeathed by Ron Graham of East Roseville to the Fisher Library of the University of Sydney, was lost like so much of this collector's material to the market for all time."

In America, on December 7, 1979, Los Angeles Mayor Tom Bradley visited the Ackermansion, and accepted the donation of Forrest J. Ackerman's collection to the Los Angeles Public Library. Rather than expressing relief that another major collection would be kept intact, fans pointed out some facts about the LAPL. Proposition 13 cutbacks hurt the library badly. Even though Los Angeles received more federal grants than any other city during the Carter administration, the LAPL did not even have a grant-writer, according to a librarian contacted. Worse, the librarian designated to handle the Ackerman collection first learned about it from a fan who had been given her name to call.

Consequently, in 1980 Ackerman explained, "I'm not dying. I'm not selling my STF stuff for an incredible undisclosed figure. I haven't gotten tired of my collection. . . . To begin with, my guesstimate is that the Collection ain't goin' no place for several years to come . . . the christening of the Science Fiction Museum of L.A. is three to five years away. Funds have to be found first. . . . A site has to be selected. A structure has to be constructed. Seven years ago it took two thousand boxes to move my collection across town. For its move to a final resting place, who can presently say how much time it will take to get it packed up and redistributed?"

Despite the goodwill of scholars and politicians, priceless collections still have not been put safely beyond the whim of executors and budget-cutters.

Nor has the simple task of collecting been made any easier by a continued trend toward specialty publishers creating limited editions entirely aimed at collectors.

Specialty publishers, usually one or two fans with capital and an idea, are cherished in the history of science fiction as the first people to get science fiction into hardcover, and they are the people who continue to keep in print well-loved fiction that major houses have neglected.

However, the exploding popularity of science fiction, coupled with inflationary economics, has made the collecting of genre material a speculative area, despite resistance by those who only collect from an affection for SF.

One example of this conflict between preservation and speculation has been the creation of hardcover first editions barely in advance of major novel releases. For example, Philip José Farmer's *The Magic Labyrinth*, fifth in the Riverworld series, was announced for June 1980 release by Berkley. In March, Phantasia Press announced that "with the cooperation of Berkley Publishing Corporation" they would publish a five-hundred-copy "first edition" of Farmer's novel by May 1980. It so happened that the major house edition reached bookstores first (Los Angeles's Change of Hobbit Bookstore received the Berkley version on April 29, and the Phantasia version on May 15). Which, then, is the true first edition becomes a matter of debate. More important, one should ask what is the need for the creation of artificially scarce first editions of widely distributed hardcovers. But there remains no doubt about the value of hardcover editions of out-of-print works, such as Phantasia Press's own *Wall of Serpents* (part of De Camp and Pratt's Incompleat Enchanter series).

A love of science fiction, as evidenced by those who collect and maintain in print its stories, is the first requirement of a fan. Then, once fans meet, they discover that they enjoy each other's company, and have many other interests as well. This led to the formation of science fiction clubs in the 1930s, and their exchange visits were the first conventions.

An estimated two hundred fans attended the first World Science Fiction Convention (WorldCon), held in New York in 1939. The 1940 WorldCon, in Chicago, had a total budget of $145. In 1980, Boston's Noreascon II (WorldCon) reported 5,850 attendees, and a cash flow in excess of $200,000.

In the beginning, conventions were routinely undertaken as personal risks by their chairmen. The 1980 WorldCon committee incorporated as a nonprofit entity under Massachusetts law, and obtained recognition from the Internal Revenue Service as a qualified organization, to which contributions became tax-deductible.

Nevertheless, this committee continued the tradition of taking no compensation for its work. In fact, the growth of the WorldCon has been no gradual thing; only the past three drew over five thousand, and were forced to use convention centers or multiple hotels, or both. Some WorldCons of the seventies were virtually organized on the Mickey Rooney/ Judy Garland level of "My father owns a barn—we can put on a show!" Not so any longer, as the size of the event now attracts not only gadflies like fire marshals and night managers, but unions, workmen's compensation boards, and the IRS.

Despite the complexity of running this annual showcase for science fiction, WorldCons still treat as their most important programming event the ceremonial presentation of the Science Fiction Achievement Awards. These are nicknamed

Hugos, after Hugo Gernsback, editor of the first pulp devoted to the genre. They are awarded by popular vote of the WorldCon membership. Hugos are given in eleven categories, and recognize the previous calendar year's work. The following winners were selected by 1,788 voters as the best in their field in 1979, and were qualified to receive rocket-shaped trophies at the 1980 WorldCon:

BEST NOVEL: *The Fountains of Paradise* by Arthur C. Clarke

BEST NOVELETTE: "Sandkings" by George R. R. Martin

BEST NOVELLA: "Enemy Mine" by Barry Longyear

BEST SHORT STORY: "The Way of Cross and Dragon" by George R. R. Martin

BEST NONFICTION BOOK: *The Science Fiction Encyclopedia*, edited by Peter Nicholls

BEST PROFESSIONAL EDITOR: George Scithers

BEST PROFESSIONAL ARTIST: Michael Whelan

BEST DRAMATIC PRESENTATION: *Alien*

BEST FANZINE: *Locus*

BEST FAN WRITER: Bob Shaw

BEST FAN ARTIST: Alexis Gilliland

Voters also selected Barry Longyear as winner of the John W. Campbell Award for best new science fiction writer, and Ray Bradbury as winner of the Gandalf Grand Master of Fantasy Award.

Briefly it appeared as if Bradbury would also be the last winner of a Gandalf Award. Added to the number of awards administered by WorldCons, in 1974 Gandalfs were established as a memorial to the recently deceased J. R. R. Tolkien. Founder Lin Carter saw to it that Tolkien won the first, and voters in later years bestowed it on Leiber, De Camp, Norton, Anderson, and Le Guin.

In 1978, a Gandalf was also established to recognize booklength works of fantasy each year. *The Silmarillion*, by

Tolkien, ran away with the first one. Only in 1979, when Anne McCaffrey's *The White Dragon* was nominated for a Hugo and a Gandalf, did it appear that the awards duplicated one another.

At the 1980 WorldCon business meeting, there was sufficient concern about the number of awards cluttering the Hugo ballot that the Gandalf was legislatively divorced from the WorldCon.

Coincidentally, on the same day that legislation passed, the awards ceremony was scheduled. Always before, Lin Carter had taken the stage to announce the Gandalf winner. Not in 1980. Carter was absent, and no trophy was on hand. When no one associated with the award appeared, Harlan Ellison and master of ceremonies Robert Silverberg improvised some zaniness and rescued the ceremony from an awkward moment. Was Carter's absence a protest of what went on at the business meeting, fans wondered. Apparently not, as the available evidence showed no one had even manufactured Bradbury's trophy. Months later two fans associated with the Gandalf arranged to send Bradbury his award. They also reportedly plan to select the 1981 winner themselves, now that the Gandalf has been orphaned by the WorldCon.

Members of the WorldCon chose Chicago to be the site of their 1982 convention. Unlike the ABA or AMA, which decide their meeting sites years in advance, the WorldCon is chosen only two years beforehand. Much of this has to do with the difficulty of keeping an amateur, all-volunteer committee together any longer. (Information on the 1982 WorldCon in Chicago can be obtained by writing to ChiCon IV, P.O. Box A3120, Chicago Il 60690.)

Barring an energy crunch, Chicago's WorldCon is expected to set yet another attendance record. This is not surprising in an era when millions of Americans attended *Star Wars* and *The Empire Strikes Back*, flocked to see *Alien* and *Close Encounters*, and sustained "Star Trek" as a syndicated program. This broad appeal has not merely changed the size of science fiction fandom, but the composition—women, once definitely in the minority, are now nearly half of all convention attendees. And because of the media involved, a number of people of both sexes enter fandom with slight or no knowledge of its written literature. Fandom contains as diverse a variety of people as ever: space technologists, strategic weapons specialists, computer programmers, students, filmmakers, unemployed, medical doctors, tax protesters, and endless teenagers.

One of Norman Spinrad's many attacks on fandom appeared in a January 1981 *Publishers Weekly*: "In part to blame for the frivolous label attached to SF are the egregiously visible bands of fans, Spinrad believes. These are the groups done up in bizarre attire and behavior that cluster together in frequent cons. . . . [They're] largely responsible for whatever weirdness lingers around science fiction."

In American society, science fiction offers enough of the whole cloth to costume every popular myth. Nowhere is this more literally true than at a science fiction convention.

With distant echoes of Simon and Garfunkel, some fans are still looking for America, in long hair, beards, Levi's, with guitar in hand, quietly sharing grass in an upstairs room. Ironically, at the same time in another room, former Young Republicans smoke of the same leaf and echo a "Hallejulah Chorus" now that Reagan has won.

Except for the probability that Spinrad means to condemn them all, either group might agree to look askance at the costume selection of some young fans appearing at recent conventions. Stimulated by the imagery of *Star Wars*, the number of jackboot-and-leather-vest wearers has increased, in parallel with khaki-clad mercenaries with plastic mortars and aluminum copies of submachine guns. These fantasies of violence are not to be confused with those in reality who poke a shotgun out of the window of a moving Chevy and murder a rival gang member. The latter are unarguably malicious. But one can speculate that what a fifteen-to-twenty-year-old wants, either in a gang or in a paramilitary costume, is a sense of mission in the world, and recognition. At a convention, this is basically innocent.

What better place to wear fantasy gear than at a science fiction convention? There is none better, and it is a long-standing tradition. Even in the early seventies, the medieval warriors of the Society for Creative Anachronism appeared at SF cons with edged sidearms, disturbing no one; in fact, they brought a Renaissance Faire spirit into a July Fourth or Labor Day weekend. *But*—those weapons were never drawn in the hotel.

Unfortunately, each large convention of late has been good for one behavior problem involving a sword. The variety of plastic zap guns, and more lethal-looking models, has spurred hotel security into repressive measures, such as the confiscation of any prop that resembles a weapon.

Only because this article emphasizes 1980, and this issue came to a head in 1980, does it merit such attention. Conventions are beginning to announce "weapons policies" requiring the "peace-bonding" of edged weapons and the banning of realistic-appearing guns. Some fans complain that this violates the carnival atmosphere of freedom, but more are aware of cautionary tales, such as this one reported by Alexis Gilliland after Memorial Day weekend's Disclave in 1980: "Saturday evening the SWAT squad walked in. . . . An emergency vehicle, in passing, noted some people entering the back of the [convention hotel] with automatic weapons and reported it. It was fairly dark, and we had a lot of people going around in costume, including some plastic weapons of various sorts, so this is understandable. Two team members walked into the lobby with shotguns, and by the time I reached the van, the SWAT team appeared to have figured out that there were a lot of people in costume. One thing the team captain told me was a little upsetting: as the SWAT van pulled up, lights blinking, no siren, one of the costumed figures . . . pointed a (seeming) weapon at them. 'I was about one second from letting him have it,' said the Team Captain. Now it is well known that fans are Slans, but this one evidently had a knot in his tendrils." Gilliland mollified the police and they drove off.

So far the costume/weapons problem has been simply a glitch in an otherwise pleasant expansion of SF cons. Nearly ninety conventions were held throughout the world in 1980, triple the number held in 1971, and with higher average attendance.

Besides being a historic year for conventions, 1980 was marked by the completion and publication of two major projects.

The Fantasy Showcase Tarot Deck, compiled and edited by Bruce Pelz, features Tarot cards interpreted by leading professional and amateur fantasy artists. Pelz conceived the idea in 1969, when he began signing up contributors, and along the way it developed into a major undertaking of eighty-five artists. They produced seventy-eight traditional cards, a verso, two new Trumps—Separation and The Farrier—plus a Lady of each suit. Pelz was Fan Guest of Honor at the 1980 WorldCon, and with the cooperation of the committee, printed, collated, and boxed the deck in time for distribution at Noreascon II.

Contributors to the deck include longtime professionals Kelly Freas and Eddie Jones; fans who became professionals during the project's development, Alicia Austin, George Barr, Tim Kirk, Wendy Pini, Freff, Steve Stiles, and Marc Schirmeister; and other well-known pros and fans, Steve Leialoha, Helmut Pesch, C. Lee Healy, George Metzger, Don Simpson, C. Ross Chamberlain, Bill Rotsler, Randy Bathurst, Kathy Bushman Sanders, Harry Bell, Lee Hoffman, Stu Shiffman, Alexis Gilliland, ATom, Taral, Victoria Poyser, etc. The deck is in color. It costs $15, plus $2.50 postage, from Elayne Pelz, 15931 Kalisher St., Granada Hills CA 91344.

"Coming: All installments of The Harp in a single issue of Wrhn. Over 200 pages." Richard Bergeron, editor of the very popular fanzine *Warhoon*, made this announcement in the same year that Pelz started recruiting for the Fan Tarot Deck: 1969. Like Pelz, Bergeron watched an amusing idea sprout into a Grand Project.

Walter Willis, of Ireland, is acknowledged the finest writer of that brand of personal journalism and humor sought after by fanzine publishers. Most active in the fifties and sixties, Willis was such a popular essayist among fans that they twice raised funds to pay his way to American WorldCons. In *Warhoon #28*, Bergeron created a 614-page, eight-and-a-half-by-eleven hardcover, impressively preserving Willis's writing. Since those essays had only been available in rare old fanzines, Bergeron has reintroduced the best spirit of science fiction fandom to a new generation. Cost: $25, from Richard Bergeron, P.O. Box 5989, Old San Juan PR 00905. The volume has been so enthusiastically received that it is a Hugo nominee for 1981 in the Best Nonfiction Book category.

Though Willis served as the focus for two special travel funds, there exist permanent funds to provide an exchange between the fandoms of America, Europe, and Australia. Oldest is the Trans-Atlantic Fan Fund (TAFF), which selected Briton Dave Langford to travel to the 1980 WorldCon. The younger Down-Under Fan Fund (DUFF) awarded Keith Curtis a trip from Australia to the WorldCon. In each case, fans who contribute money vote on the delegates. A third fan fund, which finances travel between Australia and Europe (and vice versa), was in between trips in 1980.

In summary, fandom is full of self-contradictions, sometimes providing ammunition for those who accuse it of being a weird, fringe phenomenon, but more often persevering in its devotion to science fiction through collecting, organizing conventions, producing major projects, and promoting international contact. Though Harlan Ellison, while trying to promote the Equal Rights Amendment, accused fans of merely paying lip service to the future described in science fiction, they appear to be in the forefront of a blizzard of mail directed at the White House, trying to preserve the NASA budget against Stockman's cuts. The year 1980 seemed to prove that fans were no monolithic subculture, and represented the same variety as America itself.

The following publications, listed alphabetically, are reliable sources of news about science fiction and fandom. All have received Hugo nominations, except the last listed, and some have won the award many times (* denotes winner).

File 770, edited by Mike Glyer, 14974 Osceola St., Sylmar CA 91342. Cost: four issues for $2. Emphasizes news of SF fandom.

Locus, edited by Charles N. Brown, P.O. Box 3938, San Francisco CA 94119. Cost: $15 for twelve issues in the U.S. Monthly. Emphasizes professional SF news, but also reports news of fandom.

Science Fiction Chronicle, edited by Andrew Porter, P.O. Box 4175, New York NY 10163. Cost: $15 per year in the U.S. and Canada. Monthly. Emphasizes professional SF news.

Science Fiction Review, edited by Richard E. Geis, P.O. Box 11408, Portland OR 97211. Cost: $7 per year in the U.S. Quarterly. Articles, interviews, book reviews, and a forum among professional SF writers.

The Whole Fanzine Catalog, edited by Brian Earl Brown, 16711 Burt Rd. #207, Detroit MI 48219. Cost: four issues for $2. A regularly updated listing and review of science fiction fan publications.

Rautavaara's Case

Philip K. Dick

Philip K. Dick is a fairly private person. There was a time I'm told, when he came to science fiction conventions; but I don't remember ever seeing him at one, and certainly he doesn't come to them now. (In fact, one convention has an annual ritual: they announce that Philip K. Dick has arrived and up walks someone else, usually William Rotsler.)

I met Phil Dick only once. It was at a party in Orange County, CA, when I was president of SFWA, a few years after Phil had come out of the street-and-drug scene by way of Vancouver. He had married a very straight young lady who had just borne their son. It was an interesting party, at the home of Willis McNelly, a professor of English who tried to make science fiction academically respectable well before it became fashionable to be "into SF." (All the really hip academics know that you don't say sci-fi because if you do Harlan Ellison will berate you for hours, and better than that would be a visit by ten yentes. . . .)

I didn't know it, but Phil was starving.

*It's just as well that I didn't know it. Those were hard times;
I wasn't doing very well either. But then I didn't expect to; I
was just getting started, and I had a fairly realistic idea of how
long my savings from a previous career in aerospace would
last: long enough to get some books in print, and after that it
would be all right.* . . .

But if I'd known that the author of Do Androids Dream of
Electric Sheep *and* The Man in the High Castle *was eating
dog food (a story told in Phil's autobiographical introductory
essay to the story collection* The Golden Man*)* . . .

*Science fiction has not always done well by its leading writ-
ers. Philip K. Dick has long been recognized as one of our best
talents—perhaps the best writer in the genre. Academics, critics, fans, and other writers all concede it. So why was he starving? Ray Bradbury had long before broken out of what we used
to call "the science fiction ghetto." Kurt Vonnegut was never in
it; he wrote science fiction, then denied it with a straight face.
But within the science fiction genre itself there were, in 1971,
probably no more than ten writers who even* claimed *to make a
full-time living at it, and only two or three who made what
outsiders would consider a* good *living.*

*Well, that was ten years ago. Somewhere during the seven-
ties there was a revolution; science fiction not only became
respectable, it became lucrative. There may be as many as a
hundred writers making a living at SF, and half of those do
fairly well; and, I'm pleased to report, Phil Dick is now doing
very well indeed.* Androids *has been sold as a movie,* Blade
Runner, *by all reports for a good price; and the book will be
brought into print again, as will many of his other books. He
has sold a new novel for a respectable advance. Things seem to
be going well for him, which is no more than he deserves.*

*Salvation and messianism have long been important themes in
Philip K. Dick's writing. What will happen to religion when we
meet intelligent aliens? What will* they *make of our hopes for a
Messiah?*

The three technicians of the floating globe monitored fluctuations in interstellar magnetic fields, and they did a good job until the moment they died.

Basalt fragments, traveling at enormous velocity in relation to their globe, ruptured their barrier and abolished their air supply. The two males were slow to react and did nothing. The young female technician from Finland, Agneta Rautavaara, managed to get her emergency helmet on, but the hoses tangled; she aspirated and died: a melancholy death, strangling on her own vomit. Herewith ended the survey task of EX208, their floating globe. In another month the technicians would have been relieved and returned to Earth.

We could not get there in time to save the three Earthpersons, but we did dispatch a robot to see whether any of them could be regenerated. Earthpersons do not like us, but in this case their survey globe was operating in our vicinity. There are rules governing such emergencies that are binding on all races in the galaxy. We had no desire to help Earthpersons, but we obey the rules.

The rules called for an attempt on our part to restore life to the three dead technicians, but we allowed a robot to take on the responsibility, and perhaps there we erred. Also, the rules required us to notify the closest Earth ship of the calamity, and we chose not to. I will not defend this omission or analyze our reasoning at the time.

The robot signaled that it had found no brain function in the two males and that their neural tissue had degenerated. Regarding Agneta Rautavaara, a slight brain wave could be detected. So in Rautavaara's case the robot would begin a restoration attempt. Since it could not make a judgment decision on its own, however, it contacted us. We told it to make the attempt. The fault—the guilt, so to speak—therefore lies with us. Had we been on the scene, we would have known better. We accept the blame.

An hour later the robot signaled that it had restored significant brain function in Rautavaara by supplying her brain with oxygen-rich blood from her dead body. The oxygen, but not the nutriments, came from the robot. We instructed it to begin synthesis of nutriments by processing Rautavaara's body, using it as raw material. This is the point at which the Earth authorities later made their most profound objection. But we did not have any other source of nutriments. Since we ourselves are a plasma, we could not offer our own bodies.

They objected that we could have used the bodies of Rautavaara's dead companions. But we felt that, based on the robot's reports, the other bodies were too contaminated by radioactivity and hence were toxic to Rautavaara; nutriments derived from those sources would soon poison her brain. If you do not accept our logic, it does not matter to us; this was the situation as we construed it from our remote point. This is why I say our real error lay in sending a robot rather than going ourselves. If you wish to indict us, indict us for that.

We asked the robot to patch into Rautavaara's brain and transmit her thoughts to us so that we could assess the physical condition of her neural cells.

The impression that we received was sanguine. It was at this point that we notified the Earth authorities. We informed them of the accident that had destroyed EX208; we informed them that two of the technicians, the males, were irretrievably dead; we informed them that through swift efforts on our part we had the one female showing stable cephalic activity—which is to say, we had her brain alive.

"Her *what*?" the Earthperson radio operator said, in response to our call.

"We are supplying her nutriments derived from her body—"

"Oh, Christ," the Earthperson radio operator said. "You can't feed her brain that way. What good is just a brain?"

"It can think," we said.

"All right. We'll take over now," the Earthperson radio operator said. "But there will be an inquiry."

"Was it not right to save her brain?" we asked. "After all,

the psyche is located in the brain. The physical body is a device by which the brain relates to—"

"Give me the location of EX208," the Earthperson radio operator said. "We'll send a ship there at once. You should have notified us at once before trying your own rescue efforts. You Approximations simply do not understand somatic life forms."

It is offensive to us to hear the term *Approximations.* It is an Earth slur regarding our origin in the Proxima Centauri system. What it implies is that we are not authentic, that we merely simulate life.

This was our reward in the Rautavaara case. To be derided. And indeed there was an inquiry.

Within the depths of her damaged brain Agneta Rautavaara tasted acid vomit and recoiled in fear and aversion. All around her EX208 lay in splinters. She could see Travis and Elms; they had been torn to bloody bits, and the blood had frozen. Ice covered the interior of the globe. *Air gone, temperature gone . . . What's keeping me alive?* she wondered. She put her hands up and touched her face—or rather tried to touch her face. *My helmet,* she thought. *I got it on in time.*

The ice, which covered everything, began to melt. The severed arms and legs of her two companions rejoined their bodies. Basalt fragments, embedded in the hull of the globe, withdrew and flew away.

Time, Agneta realized, *is running backward. How strange!*

Air returned; she heard the dull tone of the indicator horn. Travis and Elms, groggily, got to their feet. They stared around them, bewildered. She felt like laughing, but it was too grim for that. Apparently the force of the impact had caused a local time perturbation.

"Both of you sit down," she said.

Travis said thickly, "I—okay; you're right." He seated himself at his console and pressed the button that strapped him securely in place. Elms, however, just stood.

"We were hit by rather large particles," Agneta said.

"Yes," Elms said.

"Large enough and with enough impact to perturb time," Agneta said. "So we've gone back to before the event."

"Well, the magnetic fields are partly responsible," Travis said. He rubbed his eyes; his hands shook. "Get your helmet off, Agneta. You don't really need it."

"But the impact is coming," she said.

Both men glanced at her.

"We'll repeat the accident," she said.

"Shit," Travis said. "I'll take the EX out of here." He pushed many keys on his console. "It'll miss us."

Agneta removed her helmet. She stepped out of her boots, picked them up . . . and then saw the figure.

The figure stood behind the three of them. It was Christ.

"Look," she said to Travis and Elms.

The figure wore a traditional white robe and sandals; his hair was long and pale with what looked like moonlight. Bearded, his face was gentle and wise. *Just like in the holoads the churches back home put out*, Agneta thought. *Robed, bearded, wise and gentle, and his arms slightly raised. Even the nimbus is there. How odd that our preconceptions were so accurate!*

"Oh, my God," Travis said. Both men stared, and she stared, too. "He's come for us."

"Well, it's fine with me," Elms said.

"Sure, it would be fine with you," Travis said bitterly. "You have no wife and children. And what about Agneta? She's only three hundred years old; she's a baby."

Christ said, "I am the vine, you are the branches. Whoever remains in me, with me in him, bears fruit in plenty; for cut off from me, you can do nothing."

"I'm getting the EX out of this vector," Travis said.

"My little children," Christ said, "I shall not be with you much longer."

"Good," Travis said. The EX was now moving at peak velocity in the direction of the Sirius axis; their star chart showed massive flux.

"Damn you, Travis," Elms said savagely. "This is a great opportunity. I mean, how many people have seen Christ? I mean, it *is* Christ. You are Christ, aren't you?" he asked the figure.

Christ said, "I am the Way, the Truth, and the Life. No one can come to the Father except through me. If you know me, you know my Father, too. From this moment you know him and have seen him."

"There," Elms said, his face showing happiness. "See? I want it known that I am very glad of this occasion, Mr.—" He broke off. "I was going to say, 'Mr. Christ.' That's stupid; that is really stupid. Christ, Mr. Christ, will you sit down? You can sit at my console or at Ms. Rautavaara's. Isn't that right, Agneta? This here is Walter Travis; he's not a Christian, but I am. I've been a Christian all my life. Well, most of my life. I'm not sure about Ms. Rautavaara. What do you say, Agneta?"

"Stop babbling, Elms," Travis said.

Elms said, "He's going to judge us."

Christ said, "If anyone hears my words and does not keep them faithfully, it is not I who shall condemn him, since I have come not to condemn the world but to save the world; he who rejects me and refuses my words has his judge already."

"There," Elms said, nodding gravely.

Frightened, Agneta said to the figure, "Go easy on us. The three of us have been through a major trauma." She wondered, suddenly, whether Travis and Elms remembered that they had been killed, that their bodies had been destroyed.

The figure smiled, as if to reassure her.

"Travis," Agneta said, bending down over him as he sat at his console, "I want you to listen to me. Neither you nor Elms survived the accident, survived the basalt particles. That's why he's here. I'm the only one who wasn't—" She hesitated.

"Killed," Elms said. "We're dead, and he has come for us." To the figure he said, "I'm ready, Lord. Take me."

"Take both of them," Travis said. "I'm sending out a radio H.E.L.P. call. And I'm telling them what's taking place here. I'm going to report it before he takes me or tries to take me."

"You're *dead*," Elms told him.

"I can still file a radio report," Travis said, but his face showed his resignation.

To the figure, Agneta said, "Give Travis a little time. He doesn't fully understand. But I guess you know that; you know everything."

The figure nodded.

We and the Earth Board of Inquiry listened to and watched this activity in Rautavaara's brain, and we realized jointly what had happened. But we did not agree on our evaluation of it. Whereas the six Earthpersons saw it as pernicious, we saw it as grand—both for Agneta Rautavaara and for us. By means of her damaged brain, restored by an ill-advised robot, we were in touch with the next world and the powers that ruled it.

The Earthpersons' view distressed us.

"She's hallucinating," the spokesperson of the Earthpeople said. "Since she has no sensory data coming in. Since her body is dead. Look what you've done to her."

We made the point that Agneta Rautavaara was happy.

"What we must do," the human spokesperson said, "is shut down her brain."

"And cut us off from the next world?" we objected. "This is a splendid opportunity to view the afterlife. Agneta Rautavaara's brain is our lens. The scientific merit outweighs the humanitarian."

This was the position we took at the inquiry. It was a position of sincerity, not of expedience.

The Earthpersons decided to keep Rautavaara's brain at full function with both video and audio transduction, which of course was recorded; meanwhile, the matter of censuring us was put in suspension.

I personally found myself fascinated by the Earth idea of the Savior. It was, for us, an antique and quaint conception—not because it was anthropomorphic but because it involved a schoolroom adjudication of the departed soul. Some kind of tote board was involved, listing good and bad acts: a transcendent report card such as one finds employed in the teaching and grading of elementary-school children.

This, to us, was a primitive conception of the Savior, and while I watched and listened—while we watched and listened as a polyencephalic entity—I wondered what Agneta Rautavaara's reaction would have been to a Savior, a Guide of the Soul, based on *our* expectations. Her brain, after all, was maintained by our equipment, by the original mechanism that our rescue robot had brought to the scene of the accident. It would have been too risky to disconnect it; too much brain damage had occurred already. The total apparatus, involving her brain, had been transferred to the site of the judicial inquiry, a neutral ark located between the Proxima Centauri system and the Sol system.

Later, in discreet discussion with my companions, I suggested that we attempt to infuse our own conception of the Afterlife Guide of the Soul into Rautavaara's artificially sustained brain. My point: It would be interesting to see how she reacted.

At once my companions pointed out to me the contradiction in my logic. I had argued at the inquiry that Rautavaara's brain was a window on the next world and, hence, justified—which exculpated us. Now I argued that what she experienced was a projection of her own mental presuppositions, nothing more.

"Both propositions are true," I said. "It is a genuine window on the next world, and it is a presentation of Rautavaara's own cultural, racial propensities."

What we had, in essence, was a model into which we could introduce carefully selected variables. We could introduce into Rautavaara's brain our own conception of the Guide of

the Soul and thereby see how our rendition differed practically from the puerile one of the Earthpersons.

This was a novel opportunity to test out our own theology.
In our opinion the Earthpersons' theology had been tested
sufficiently and had been found wanting.

We decided to perform the act, since we maintained the
gear supporting Rautavaara's brain. To us, this was a much
more interesting issue than the outcome of the inquiry.
Blame is a mere cultural matter; it does not travel across
species boundaries.

I suppose the Earthpersons could regard our intentions as
malign. I deny that; we deny that. Call it, instead, a game. It
would provide us aesthetic enjoyment to witness Rautavaara
confronted by *our* Savior, rather than hers.

To Travis, Elms, and Agneta, the figure, raising its arms, said,
"I am the resurrection. If anyone believes in me, even though
he dies, he will live, and whoever lives and believes in me
will never die. Do you believe this?"

"I sure do," Elms said heartily.

Travis said, "It's bilge."

To herself, Agneta Rautavaara thought, *I'm not sure. I just
don't know.*

"We have to decide if we're going to go with him," Elms
said. "Travis, you're done for; you're out. Sit there and rot—
that's your fate." To Agneta he said, "I hope you find for
Christ, Agneta. I want you to have eternal life like I'm going
to have. Isn't that right, Lord?" he asked the figure.

The figure nodded.

Agneta said, "Travis, I think—well, I feel you should go
along with this. I—" She did not want to press the point that
Travis was dead. But he had to understand the situation;
otherwise, as Elms said, he was doomed. "Go with us,"
she said.

"You're going, then?" Travis said, bitterly.

"Yes," she said.

Elms, gazing at the figure, said in a low voice, "Quite possibly I'm mistaken, but it seems to be changing."

She looked, but saw no change. Yet Elms seemed frightened.

The figure, in its white robe, walked slowly toward the seated Travis. The figure halted close by Travis, stood for a time, and then, bending, bit Travis's face.

Agneta screamed. Elms stared, and Travis, locked into his seat, thrashed. The figure calmly ate him.

"Now you see," the spokesperson for the Board of Inquiry said, "this brain must be shut down. The deterioration is severe; the experience is terrible for her, it must end."

I said, "No. We from the Proxima system find this turn of events highly interesting."

"But the Savior is eating Travis!" another of the Earthpersons exclaimed.

"In your religion," I said, "is it not the case that you eat the flesh of your God and drink his blood? All that has happened here is a mirror image of that Eucharist."

"I order her brain shut down!" the spokesperson for the board said; his face was pale; sweat stood out on his forehead.

"We should see more first," I said. I found it highly exciting, this enactment of our own sacrament, our highest sacrament, in which our Savior consumes us.

"Agneta," Elms whispered, "did you see that? Christ ate Travis. There's nothing left but his gloves and boots."

Oh, God, Agneta Rautavaara thought. *What is happening? I don't understand.*

She moved away from the figure, over to Elms. Instinctively.

"He is my blood," the figure said as it licked its lips. "I drink of this blood, the blood of eternal life. When I have drunk it, I will live forever. He is my body. I have no body of my own; I am only a plasma. By eating his body, I obtain everlasting life. This is the new truth that I proclaim, that I am eternal."

"He's going to eat us, too," Elms said.

Yes, Agneta Rautavaara thought. *He is.* She could see now that the figure was an Approximation. *It is a Proxima life form,* she realized. *He's right; he has no body of his own. The only way he can get a body is—*

"I'm going to kill him," Elms said. He popped the emergency laser rifle from its rack and pointed it at the figure.

The figure said, "The hour has come."

"Stay away from me," Elms said.

"Soon you will no longer see me," the figure said, "unless I drink of your blood and eat of your body. Glorify yourself that I may live." The figure moved toward Elms.

Elms fired the laser rifle. The figure staggered and bled. *It was Travis's blood,* Agneta realized. *In him. Not his own blood. This is terrible.* She put her hands to her face, terrified.

"Quick," she said to Elms. "Say, 'I am innocent of this man's blood.' Say it before it's too late."

"I am innocent of this man's blood," Elms whispered hoarsely.

The figure fell. Bleeding, it lay dying. It was no longer a bearded man. It was something else, but Agneta Rautavaara could not tell what it was. It said, "Eli, Eli, lama sabachthani?"

As she and Elms gazed down at it, the figure died.

"I killed it," Elms said. "I killed Christ." He held the laser rifle pointed at himself, gropping for the trigger.

"That wasn't Christ," Agneta said. "It was something else. The opposite of Christ." She took the gun from Elms.

Elms was weeping.

The Earthpersons on the Board of Inquiry possessed the majority vote, and they voted to abolish all activity in Rautavaara's artificially sustained brain. This disappointed us, but there was no remedy for us.

We had seen the beginning of an absolutely stunning scientific experiment: the theology of one race grafted onto that of another. Shutting down the Earthperson's brain was a scientific tragedy. For example, in terms of the basic relationship to God, the Earth race held a diametrically opposite view from us. This of course must be attributed to the fact that they are a somatic race while we are a plasma. They drink the blood of their God; they eat his flesh; that way they become immortal. To them, there is no scandal in this. They find it perfectly natural. Yet to us it is dreadful. That the worshiper should eat and drink its God? Awful to us; awful indeed. A disgrace and a shame—an abomination. The higher should always prey on the lower; the God should consume the worshiper.

We watched as the Rautavaara case was closed—closed by the shutting down of her brain so that all EEG activity ceased and the monitors indicated nothing. We felt disappointment. In addition, the Earthpersons voted out a verdict of censure of us for our handling of the rescue mission in the first place.

It is striking, the gulf that separates races developing in different star systems. We have tried to understand the Earthpersons, and we have failed. We are aware, too, that they do not understand us and are appalled in turn by some of our customs. This was demonstrated in the Rautavaara case. But were we not serving the purposes of detached scientific study? I myself was amazed at Rautavaara's reaction when the Savior ate Mr. Travis. I would have wished to see this most holy of the sacraments fulfilled with the others, with Rautavaara and Elms as well.

But we were deprived of this. And the experiment, from our standpoint, failed.

And we live now, too, under the ban of unnecessary moral blame.

1980: The Year in Fantastic Films

Bill Warren

SFWA used to award a Nebula for Best Dramatic Production.
I ought to know; I invented it. Adding that category was one of
my changes to the Nebula rules the year I was president.

A few years later SFWA, by a narrow vote, abolished the
category. Two reasons were given. The first appealed to the
cheese-paring faction: the Nebula trophy costs over a hundred
dollars, and a Best Dramatic Production trophy won't often go
to an SFWA member. Better to put that money into SFWA
parties. The second was claimed by a different group, who said
there weren't sufficient dramatic productions qualified for such
a high honor.

The award was abolished with remarkable timing: just one
year before Star Wars was released and the boom in science
fiction films began.

With any luck we'll reverse that decision. After all, most of
us aren't starving any longer, and SFWA makes fairly good
money; and there are a lot of very good science fiction
films now.

Meanwhile, given the boom in dramatic SF, it seemed wise to include something about it in this book.

Bill Warren has long been recognized as a leading authority on fantastic films. His book, Keep Watching the Skies!, *on American science fiction movies of the fifties, is destined to become a classic, and his reviews have been widely published. He was film program chairman for the 1972 World Science Fiction Convention, and has assisted at many others.*

He has given us an excellent critical review of science fiction movies: what they do right, and what could make them better.

The year 1980 was not a good one for films in general; profits were weaker and quality was way down. The movie industry tends to be run by bookkeepers, so the problem with science fiction and other fantastic movies is only a reflection of the problem with movies of all sorts. They tend to be made by cost-conscious and cowardly committees with little or no qualifications to produce art, commercial or otherwise, and movies should be at least partly motivated by artistic goals. These days, few producers will take chances. All movies, even "low-budget" movies, are expensive, and with increased costs the risk of loss climbs higher. The people in charge tend to be overly concerned with profit. And hence they want to back films with the surest chance of immediate success, regardless of considerations of quality.

In the old days, the men running the studios took bigger risks, and many of the films we recall most fondly as classics from the 1930s and 1940s, fantastic and mundane, were relatively daring experiments, and were not especially popular in their time. While few really want to see a complete return to the days when one man ruled his own studio with an iron fist in an iron glove, as long as people who are not concerned with the quality of their product are in charge of moviemaking, the chances that quality will be high are slim. Even the directors and writers have to answer to studio bosses, and projects die aborning when it looks like they may not be hits.

For instance, consider *The Final Countdown*. United Artists released this film in mid-1980, but it seems to be created by anything except *united* artists. All parts pull against each other. The story: The atomic-powered carrier *Nimitz* is swept back in time by a roving time-warp storm to December 6, 1941. The captain (Kirk Douglas) and others are presented with a dilemma: Do they try to stop the Japanese sneak attack on Pearl Harbor the next morning? They do indeed make the attempt, but that time warp comes along again, pulling everyone and everything except James Farentino back to their proper time.

Now, this premise was worked to death on "The Twilight Zone" of honored memory, but even Rod Serling's cautious scripts tended to exhibit more guts and daring. *The Final Countdown* is a mediocre movie that is hamstrung by cowardice in following through on its premise; an imaginative idea is thwarted by lack of imagination in developing it. Under Don Taylor's limp direction, the picture never comes to life and the timid ending sinks it.

The producers were afraid of raising questions that they couldn't answer. Whatever decision the captain made, it was a foregone conclusion that he would have absolutely no effect on the past. If the film had shown daring, the last words might easily have been "Now what?" which would annoy a few people in the audience, but would also have created the excitement and a sense of wonder that the flat, sealed-off ending the film did have stopped dead.

But the writers, Gerry Davis, David Ambrose, Thomas Hunter, and Peter Powell, seem to have been too afraid of disturbing people to try anything daring. A committee decided that to have the *Nimitz* change the course of history would *bother* audiences, and there's a great fear of bothering audiences even with unanswered but *intriguing* questions. No chance of "the lady or the tiger" endings in today's movies.

As a result, *The Final Countdown* (the title is misleading and meaningless) made no ripples. It probably earned back its cost and made a small profit, but it's a nothing movie.

Television productions are even more subject to this decision-by-committee that reduces everything to blandness. Although there were some daring TV shows in 1980, most were timid.

For years, Ray Bradbury's classic novel/collection *The Martian Chronicles* had been optioned again and again without a frame of film being exposed. The book presented tonal difficulties for adaptors. As far as most filmmakers are concerned, science fiction must always be presented in hard, realistic terms, so how do you express Bradbury's evocative, image-laden prose in realistic pictures? The other Bradbury film adaptations ranged from literal and therefore disastrous (*The Illustrated Man*) to semipoetic and semisuccessful (*Fahrenheit 451*). Bradbury himself had written a script for a proposed 1960s Cinerama version of *Chronicles*, and he came close to creating visual equivalents of his distinctive prose style by suggesting almost surrealistic images.

NBC television produced the mini-series of Bradbury's book; the script was written by Richard Matheson and directed by Michael Anderson. Matheson made a valiant attempt at reproducing the Bradbury style, but the relatively low budget and other compromises doomed the enterprise. The finishing touch was Anderson's pedestrian, unimaginative direction. He flattened out everything to ordinariness. The script and direction both backed away from the fantastical elements of Bradbury's book, trying to make things literal, and that should not have been done. The show worked best when the original stories were literal themselves, and failed when they were most fanciful. Rock Hudson was a peculiar choice for the leading role. He's a conscientious actor and likable, but he's somewhat inexpressive, especially when it came to fulfilling Bradbury's poetic ideas.

In addition to Bradbury's famous book, several other science fiction novels of varying degrees of fame were also adapted for television, in a period in which movies tended to stay away from published material. In fact, more recognized, modern SF novels were filmed for television in 1980 than in any one year in Hollywood history. That situation may be changing.

I am not qualified to comment on the TV adaptation of John D. MacDonald's *The Girl, the Gold Watch and Everything*. This time-control comedy was so talky in the first half that I didn't bother to watch past that point. I'm told that the second half was better, and that the adaptation was good. The show was successful enough that it has generated a sequel, to be shown sometime in 1981.

The "off-Broadway" television network in the United States is the viewer-supported Public Broadcasting System. Early in 1980 it announced a grand plan of adapting worthy science fiction novels, and began with an inexpensive but elaborate production of Ursula K. Le Guin's *The Lathe of Heaven*. The convoluted and intricate plot was a peculiar choice for a visual adaptation, especially on a small budget, as it involved the frequent complete restructuring of reality. Although the budget was low, the videotaped drama was still spectacular. The feeling of an overcrowded, bureaucratic nightmare of a future was admirably conveyed, mostly through the use of real locations, intelligent costuming, and Robbie Greenberg's imaginative photography.

It seems often that when intelligent people mostly unfamiliar with fantasy become interested in it, they are drawn to stories that fiddle with reality, so the story line of *Lathe* was probably its main attraction for the folks at PBS. But as Le Guin's novel was at least partially conceived as a juvenile (according to some sources), she never really tried to get beyond the game-playing surface of her idea—what *is* reality?—and didn't answer the questions she raised. It just wasn't her intention.

The hero (Bruce Davison in the show) has dreams that change reality, and Le Guin works amusing changes on that idea, but ultimately goes nowhere with it. Everything returns to normal at the end, even if it wasn't the "normal" we originally thought. The script was by Roger E. Swaybill and Diane English, and the videotaped show was directed by David R. Loxton and Fred Barzyk.

This brave attempt by PBS to try something new has not yet led to the intended series. In the year following its telecast, no other adaptations of SF novels have been announced by PBS.

NBC's elaborate production of Aldous Huxley's *Brave New World* was completed and ready for showing in a four-hour, two-part version in January 1979, but wasn't telecast until a year later, when an hour had been removed. This long-announced project probably should never have been filmed. The world has gone in different directions than those Huxley was warning us about, and many of his ideas are dated.

Even so, the production was not exploitative, and had a sense of fun that reflected Huxley's own playfulness in his novel. The script by Robert E. Thompson may have been too jokey, however, and it was difficult to take some of the story seriously. Keir Dullea was precisely right as the confused Director of Hatcheries, but as usual, Bud Cort was too tricky as the rebel Alpha. Burt Brinkerhoff apparently thought that satire should always be funny, and directed the film accordingly. The production design was rigid and humorless. Still, though the show was a failure, it was a respectable failure. NBC buried it behind two prime offerings on the other commercial channels, and it has not been rerun.

In motion pictures, as on television, to avoid confronting the audience with really unusual ideas is the most common way of trying to win at the box office; give them familiarity.

Director Joe Dante has pointed out that, whether you like either film or not, written science fiction is much closer to the movie of *The Man Who Fell to Earth*, which was necessarily conceived of as an art film, than to the conventional *Logan's Run*, Hollywood's idea of a viable science fiction story—and the novel had been written with that in mind.

Which brings us to sequels and imitations, other variations on the same idea of not surprising the audience. The biggest SF film of the year 1980, and ultimately one of the biggest box-office successes, was, of course, *The Empire Strikes Back*, the first sequel to *Star Wars*. Such a sequel was a sure-fire commercial idea—but people have forgotten that *Star Wars* itself almost didn't get made precisely because of this cowardice. The most popular movie of all time was thought of as a sure disaster by everyone who was approached with it, except Alan Ladd, Jr.

When *Star Wars* was made, the prospect of a sequel was only that: a prospect. George Lucas assumed that his film would make around twice its production cost, and that most of the money would come from merchandising. To the surprise of *everyone*, *Star Wars* went on to become the biggest grossing film of all time and thereby demanded a sequel. Simply because to a degree he had followed the old movie serial format, Lucas's structure for *Star Wars* easily allowed sequels, and even prequels. In time, he announced a total of three trilogies; *Star Wars* itself would be the first film in the second trilogy. Although it's unlikely that all nine films will be made, certainly the second section will be completed. *Revenge of the Jedi* started filming in the fall of 1981.

Obviously the key question about *The Empire Strikes Back* was: is it as good as *Star Wars*? It isn't. *Empire* is a good, well-paced movie, and broadens the range of approach available to the *Star Wars* story line, but it lacks the magic that infused *Star Wars*.

One reason the first film was better, other than simple novelty, is that in almost every way, George Lucas is a better director than *Empire*'s Irvin Kershner. Lucas is better at pacing, at sense of scale, at hints of wonder and beauty. And because he created it, Lucas has a better grasp on the entire sweep of his epic.

But probably thanks to Kershner, the performances in *The Empire Strikes Back* are generally better than in the first film. However, Kershner is deficient in his handling of the nonhuman characters, not helped in this regard by the otherwise good script by Lawrence Kasdan and the late Leigh Brackett. It's as if Kershner forgot that R2-D2, C-3PO, and Chewbacca actually were characters with distinctive personalities, and he treated them like animated props.

Another problem with *Empire* is that the ending is too downbeat. Luke Skywalker (Mark Hamill) has screwed up royally. He ignored the advice of Jedi master Yoda, failed to help his friends, lost a hand, and lost Princess Leia (Carrie Fisher) to the quick-frozen Han Solo (Harrison Ford). Luke even learns that the villain of the piece, Darth Vader (body of David Prowse, voice of James Earl Jones), is his own father. I understand the commercial and dramatic reasons for a cliff-hanger ending, but this was so bleak that it may have the reverse effect. In hope of avoiding another sad ending, people might be reluctant to see *Revenge of the Jedi*, the third in the series.

Of the two new characters in the film, dramatically and technically Yoda is a triumph. Yoda is, in fact, a Muppet. The voice and manipulator of Miss Piggy and Fozzie Bear, Frank Oz, also manipulates and vocalizes Yoda, and his is an Oscar-worthy performance. "Muppetry" is a term for a classical mode of rod-and-hand puppetry; the famous Punch and Judy shows are done much the same way.

The other new character, Lando Calrissian, is much less interesting. In this case, the failing was less that of the script and direction than of Billy Dee Williams, who, as Lando, is largely charmless. Whatever the real reason for casting a black actor as Lando, George Lucas and producer Gary

Kurtz could have found a more appealing performer. Sidney Poitier, Glyn Turman, James Earl Jones (in body), and Harry Belafonte are not only more appealing than Williams, but are better actors. The role of Lando called for someone with the flair and dash of Clark Gable; the main resemblance Williams has to Gable is a pencil-thin mustache. It's not that he's a bad actor; he's just not a swashbuckler, and that's what the role demanded. He'll be back in the third film.

The pacing of *Empire* is dizzyingly rapid, and for those who hadn't seen *Star Wars*, things might be confusing. Events begin at a peak of action, as the Empire blasts the surface of the snow world Hoth and the embattled Rebel warriors scramble to defend themselves. The battle is exciting, especially with the introduction of the cumbersome but awesome Walkers—huge, striding war machines manned by Empire soldiers.

The Walkers and the lizardlike Tauntauns are done in stop-frame animation by Jon Berg and Phil Tippett, respectively. The Tauntauns are lifelike and amusing, and the inclusion of a two-legged Walker tiptoeing around in the background is fun.

At the climax, Luke Skywalker fights Darth Vader in a stunningly photographed but weakly choreographed lightsaber duel. The duel is punctuated by both opponents using the Force as a telekinetic weapon, but there's no apparent structure to the fight; it doesn't rise to a climax, it just ends. Compare it with almost any swordfight featuring Errol Flynn, or with the escape from the Death Star in *Star Wars*.

The special effects in *Empire* were under the direction of Brian Johnson and Richard Edlund, and are technically more accomplished than those in *Star Wars*. They are eye-poppingly impressive at times, such as in the pursuit of Solo's ship, and deserve the cheers they get from audiences. But something about them is less exciting than similar sequences in *Star Wars*, partly because of familiarity, but also because they seem incorrectly lit, making them look more like models. The overall look of *Empire* is darker than that of *Star Wars*, and the exciting if oppressive photography by Peter Suschitzky, a fine cameraman, is in keeping with the grim story line of *Empire*.

In *2001*, Stanley Kubrick tried to create a myth for the space age, and probably did so. Black slabs floating in the void will probably always be in the minds of space travelers. But George Lucas is after something even larger than that kind of myth. In his efforts at discovering the basis of the appeal of Saturday-afternoon serials and other thrilling but juvenile entertainment that had entranced him as a kid, and in his hope of recreating that excitement for modern children, he was gradually led to the sources of the myths of the ages. (I'm told that in particular he consulted *Hero with a Thousand Faces* by Joseph Campbell.) Lucas realized that serials had tapped this timeless legend of a hero who rises from obscurity to tragic glory, and has decided to recreate that myth on an epic scale for the twentieth century.

In the past, grand myths and legends were slowly created by storytellers working over generations. Robin Hood, King Arthur, Gilgamesh, even Jesus of Nazareth, didn't spring full-blown from the mind of one person, and often had their roots in reality—but eventually took on the shape of Campbell's "monomyth." Lucas is trying to create a legend of similar proportions and weight, while at the same time producing entertaining movies. This is an astonishing chore for a soft-spoken and shy young man to embark upon. But on the basis of the broadening story of *Star Wars* as presented in *The Empire Strikes Back*, he may be able to do it. George Lucas may be the most ambitious storyteller in the history of the world.

Lucas's respect for science fiction brings me to the other big-money SF film of 1980, *Flash Gordon*. Many people assumed beforehand that Dino De Laurentiis is incapable of producing a good film; after all, his ill-advised remake of *King Kong* was a big nothing. But I recalled his earlier productions in Italy, when he worked with directors of the caliber of Federico Fellini, and I felt there was reason for hope. As it turned out, while *Flash Gordon* was better than I expected, it's still not good. At best, it's passable entertainment, which is much less than a thirty-million-dollar film should be. Director Michael Hodges employs a medium-fast but unvarying pace; you get through the film painlessly, but it never becomes exciting.

Flash Gordon was peculiarly conceived, and it's hard to grasp what market it was aimed at. It certainly isn't for children, but it's not subtle enough for adults. And it isn't exciting enough for anyone.

The script, by the reprehensible Lorenzo Semple, Jr., could only have been written by someone who has a deep contempt for comic-strip fantasy and the childlike goals of such fantasy. While the story line follows the plot of the first Buster Crabbe serial, complete with many events and plenty of cliff-hangers, the scenes added by Semple, and the tone used, are obnoxious and cynical. Semple is the man who created the "Batman" TV series, and he seems to think that the value of comic strips for filming lies only in their naive absurdity. He tries to have it both ways: to use the comic strips for their strengths—colorful characters, interesting situations—while mocking them for their weaknesses—naivete, absurdity. He clearly dislikes them. And his aloofness hurt the film.

Flash Gordon opened big, financially, but returns swiftly declined, which must have mystified De Laurentiis and Semple (they decided it was the advertising). They undoubtedly thought that they had done the same thing that Lucas had with *Star Wars,* only with more sophistication, but they were wrong. Lucas is more compassionate and observant; he knows what the weaknesses of comic-strip material are, and managed to ride over *and* use them, with a swift pace, witty dialogue, and an air of conviction. And affection. That's the most important thing: Lucas is *fond* of this kind of material, and thinks it's worth doing for its own sake. Semple thought he was superior to it, and felt it was important that audiences knew he was superior. His attitude is that of a slumming artist, and it shows. *Flash Gordon* was fueled by contempt, and that doesn't bring in audiences.

There were some good things in the film. As Ming the Merciless, Max Von Sydow is so fine that he sails over the arch lines he was given. While others in the cast read their lines as if they meant this silly drivel to be taken at face value and as if they didn't know they were being silly, Von Sydow plays Ming as if his lines are *Ming*'s jokes. He's an evil emperor who has a sense of wit as well as sense of humor; he's designed a campy world to amuse himself with. He's the best thing in the film by far.

Timothy Dalton is also good as Prince Barin. He's so intense and exciting (and is spared campy lines) that he steals every shared scene from Sam Jones's bland Flash Gordon. Ornella Muti as Princess Aura is, unexpectedly, a hot little sex kitten, and she's fine. Dale Arden is played by Melody Anderson, who looks the part, but it's hard to tell if she'd be capable of other roles.

It's unlikely that *Flash Gordon* will have a sequel; it just didn't make enough money. The backers no doubt were puzzled. They thought they were giving audiences just what they were asking for, a lampoon of space opera. But that's not what audiences want, and they recognized the calculation and the contempt; after initial interest, they stayed away. Pictures like this should thrive on repeat viewings, but it's hard to imagine what anyone would get out of seeing *Flash Gordon* repeatedly.

Another major disappointment to investors was *Saturn 3*. Stanley Donen's venture into science fiction is a failure. It's not a terrible movie, and has some virtues, but it does not do what it set out to: scare the hell out of the audience.

At a synthetic-food research base on a moon of Saturn, a large robot becomes programmed with the mind of a homicidal lunatic (Harvey Keitel), and comes after the only other two people (Kirk Douglas and Farrah Fawcett) also on the moon.

The basic problem is that there's no tension; not enough menace is generated. It takes too long to set things up. The role of the psychotic spaceman demanded a flamboyant actor. We should have the horrible feeling that if the robot ever winds up with *that* guy's mind, there'll be hell to pay. However, Harvey Keitel is a controlled actor, and his character also seems too much in control of himself. He even seems reasonable at times, and that's dead wrong. We should see the demons of madness peeping out of his eyes; instead he merely seems icily determined. He's robotlike himself from the beginning, and programming a robot with the mind of a robot seems redundant. And not scary.

Presumably we were supposed to see the scenes between Keitel and the Douglas-Fawcett pair as being laden with tension, but it just doesn't happen. Stanley Donen is usually a fine commercial director, and in the past codirected one of my favorite movies, *Singin' in the Rain*. He didn't do badly with *Seven Brides for Seven Brothers, Charade*, or *Movie Movie*, either. But he hasn't a notion of how to build gnawing tension, or even how to scare people, except with a few easily done, sudden-shock scenes.

In *Saturn 3*, the sets may be interesting and colorful, but they don't seem to have anything to do with the purpose of the base. And the blue tunnels are not at all well used for spookiness.

The script by Martin Amis (son of Kingsley) doesn't provide much for the actors to do. The dialogue does not sound like talk that ever would come out of a human mouth, and it's peppered with terms that might sound "futuristic" to the average moviegoer. There are marks on people's foreheads that seem to signify something; the same emblem is seen in the design of the spaceship. The surface of the moon is never used, even when it would seem logical. (Stills from the film show that many potentially interesting sequences were filmed but cut out.)

AFD, the distribution company, had no idea how to sell this weak film; a year later, AFD was out of business.

Like *Flash Gordon*, Ken Russell's *Altered States* sets out to knock you dead visually. There are several "psychedelic" sequences that are among the most impressive visual material ever put on the screen. The sound track is thunderous and vivid. Some of the acting is excellent, and the movie is well directed throughout. But the story line is nonsense, and all the visual and aural fun in the world can't overcome this.

Paddy Chayefsky's novel was garbage. It was opaque with technical language and fuzzy with incomplete ideas. From his fine script for *Marty*, years ago, Chayefsky turned more and more in on himself and away from the world, writing windy, empty scripts filled with stillborn ideas. It probably never occurred to him with *Altered States* that he was crossing ground heavily flattened by others who had passed before him, and he arrogantly presented his hokey story as something new. (He took his name as scripter off the credits of the film, but I don't know why; the film follows the novel closely and improves on it.)

Ken Russell seems to have understood this lack of originality in the plot more than Chayefsky could have, for he largely ignores the story, though it's still all there. He gets around the long passages of dialogue, filled with those incomprehensible technical terms, by having all his actors talk as rapidly as possible. Russell is mostly concerned with the visual aspects, and on that level the film is a triumph. Production designer Richard MacDonald and photographer Jorden Cronenweth worked together to create a richly textured and evocative look.

The story line is so simple as almost to vanish. William Hurt plays Eddie, a researcher who is desperately anxious to find the Ultimate Truth (liberal-minded Paddy flatly states that such a quest is a male trait; women accept little truths). He's been religious all his life, and while making love he approaches religious ecstasy. In his first trip sequence, all the symbolism is heavily Christian (this motif is dropped later). Eddie tries various hallucinogens in conjunction with a sensory-deprivation tank, and finally begins actually to alter his form, as some kind of memory (which the script seems to claim is on the *atomic* level) sends him further and further back in physical time.

In the best sequence in the picture, Eddie pops out of his isolation tank in the form of a fiendishly active ape man (Miguel Godreau), who scampers around Boston wreaking minor havoc, until he finally changes back into William Hurt. The agile little ape is the most interesting character in the film, and Dick Smith's makeup is excellent. If the whole film were up to the level of this sequence and the various trip scenes, it would be a masterpiece, one of the great SF films.

But it's not. It's fake and hollow. Even the suspense is bogus. The ape man clubs a guard, who doesn't die, and once we realize our hero killed no one, we know *he's* not going to die at the end, not be punished. What does happen at the end apparently embodies Chayefsky's message: There is no Ultimate Truth; we have only each other, so love is very important. This is stated early in the film by Eddie's wife (Blair Brown), and he says it himself at the end. There's a final display of pyrotechnics as somehow the wife catches the shape-shifting "disease" from her husband. It's completely unclear as to how it happened, but it's gaudy and obviously painful. Eddie overcomes his problems and restores his shape by pounding on a wall, then cures her with an embrace, and that's the end. The conclusion is banal, not worth the effort that went into the film.

A theatrical "rerun" was the release of an altered version of *Close Encounters of the Third Kind*, subtitled "special edition." Although the advertising claimed that "now there is more," in fact there was less. The restructured print was somewhat shorter than the original version. It was not, however, better.

Although there are legitimate arguments against *Close En-*

counters, it pleased most viewers on its profitable first release. Some have claimed that the movie offers simple solutions (the spacemen will help us) to complex problems, but I didn't see anyone or anything offering solutions to *any* problems in either version. Furthermore, some have complained about the apparently erratic or contradictory behavior of the aliens: bedeviling us at the beginning of the film, befriending us at the end. But that places too much human motivation on their actions. We aren't given enough clues as to why they do anything to make such judgments.

The changes between the 1977 and the 1980 versions were basically minor, and mostly took the form of deletions. The discovery of a ship that had been abandoned in a desert by the aliens, and what Roy Neary (Richard Dreyfuss) sees inside the Mother Ship at the end, were the only new sequences filmed. The other previously unseen footage had been shot for the first version but not included. Some of the old footage was removed, and some alternate scenes were added. The overall effect was a weakening of the picture's impact.

Whether one agrees with writer-director Steven Spielberg's attitudes toward UFOs, *Close Encounters* is still one of the most spectacular of the big-budget science fiction films. Douglas Trumbull's eerie and amusing UFOs are delightful. However, the "special edition" of *CE3K* did not make a stir at the box office.

Most of the other SF films of 1980 were lesser endeavors. The Italian-American *The Visitor* wasted name stars such as John Huston, Shelley Winters, and Glenn Ford in an ornately photographed but turgid and incomprehensible story involving a benign alien (Huston) here on Earth to investigate the activities of an apparently evil little girl with great ESP powers. That *may* be what the film was about. The direction and story were so confusing that the ending seemed to have no relationship to what went before. Los Angeles fan Bill Welden said it looked like Obi-Wan Kenobi and Jesus

Christ opening a school for Buddhist orphans. Could be.

Hangar 18 was a "true" story from Sunn Classic Pictures that featured some decent actors, such as Robert Vaughn, Darren McGavin, and Joseph Campanella. It was about a Watergate-like coverup of a captured UFO. Elementary, sensationalistic, and dull, the film came and went unnoticed by most.

Humanoids from the Deep was another matter. Released by Roger Corman's New World Pictures, this lurid thriller dealt with mutated fish-men who attack the Northern California coast, raping women and killing men. Although it did well at the box office, it probably would have received little notice if Barbara Peeters, the director, hadn't announced to the press that the released film bore little resemblance to the one she had made. She complained about added scenes of bare-breasted women, as well as much more violence than she filmed. It's doubtful that the film could ever have been any good, and insiders revealed that the film she shot was not even as good as the poor one that was released. The monster suits by Rob Bottin were pretty good, but the story was clumsy, the acting was hammy, and the entire film had a hangdog look. It's likely to have a sequel, however, as the highly profitable film concluded with a blatant imitation of the *Alien* chest-burster scene.

The Day Time Ended (a title that means nothing) was a silly, fast-paced thriller about a family lost in a time warp. Or something. The late Jim Davis (of "Dallas") and Oscar-winner Dorothy Malone headed the otherwise unfamiliar cast. The picture underwent many changes while being shot, and was probably too ambitious a project for the budget level. It seems primarily designed as a showcase for the numerous and mostly well-done special-effects sequences. There were gnomes and monsters, big and little spaceships, swirls of light, and other stuff. As with many other films, once the director (John "Bud" Cardos) and writers (Larry Carroll, David Schmoeller, and others) decided the film was fantastic, they must have felt they could get away with anything. Well, they can't. The movie was entertaining, but it was also very stupid.

A young writer named John Sayles improved the level of low-budget films in 1980. A non-fantasy picture he wrote, produced, directed, and acted in, *The Return of the Secaucus Seven*, was probably the best low-budget production of the year. He also worked on the script of *Alligator*, a lively, spunky monster movie about a giant alligator named Ramon that lives in the sewers beneath an unidentified city. An obvious imitation of *Jaws*, the film is also obviously better than *Jaws 2*, as was *Piranha*, an earlier film scripted by Sayles. *Alligator*'s actors, including Robert Forster, go about their chores with a verve and freshness not usually found in these inexpensive films, and Sayles's script and Lewis Teague's direction were amusing without being comic, and intelligent without being condescending. *Alligator* is bright and fresh and, oddly enough, also rather scary in places. It will be on no lists of all-time greats, but it's proof that low-budget films can still be lively fun.

As was Sayles's other 1980 SF script, *Battle Beyond the Stars*. Although the story, lifted as it was from *The Magnificent Seven*, was a little tired and the ending confusing, this Roger Corman–produced "answer" to *Star Wars* was entertaining throughout, with many amusing scenes. Sayles also incorporated some fresh ideas, which were tossed away as window dressing. The movie was even subtle here and there, and had an air of cheeky confidence. For being incredibly cheap, supposedly under a million dollars (although the Official Word claimed it was much more expensive), the picture looks astonishingly good, with imaginative if derivative special effects. It's the movie equivalent of an old Ace double novel, and as such is a good "read." It's the kind of movie many people found themselves embarrassed to enjoy. Not all SF movies are going to be blockbusters; there will always be cheap exploitation pictures, and we should be glad that ones like *Battle Beyond the Stars* are as good as they are.

Because there are worse things waiting. Things like *Without Warning*, a preposterous, boring trifle produced and directed by Greydon Clark. In this, an alien is stalking people in a rural area, killing them with things it flings at people: weapon/creatures like living, bloodthirsty Frisbees. The alien is apparently hunting only for sport, since we see a "trophy room" at one point, but this is never specified. In all fairness, that's not unreasonable; we can't always expect aliens to announce their intentions. But as with so many unimaginatively conceived pictures, *Without Warning*'s story line depends on everyone—including the alien—acting like idiots, and on improbable coincidences. In this case, the alien sometimes kills people immediately, sometimes allows them to get away. Belief in the story that survivors tell to bystanders depends entirely on what the plot requires, not on logic. It was depressing to see actors like Jack Palance, Cameron Mitchell, and Martin Landau trapped in this ugly movie.

There were some other low-budget SF films released during 1980, some of which I failed to see. These include *The Children*, in which a radioactive mist turns a busload of kids into murderous zombies. And *A Watcher in the Woods*, which was an elaborate Walt Disney SF mystery; it opened in New York to poor reviews and poorer business, and immediately closed. It is due to be rereleased in 1981 with a revised ending. (The editor of this volume was one of many writers paid to come up with a new ending.) *Supersonic Man* starred Cameron Mitchell in a parody of *Superman*, from Spain. *Mad Max* was an Australian auto-chase thriller set in the near future, which received widely mixed notices. After things fall apart, the only law and order is dispensed by implacable, motorcycle-riding policemen.

Unfortunately for most of the SF movie audience, the best science fiction film of 1980 was shown very little in the United States. I happened to see it at the Los Angeles Film Exposition, Filmex, and have had no opportunity to see it again. It was based on D. G. Compton's novel *The Unsleeping Eye* (*The Continuous Katherine Mortenhoe*), and was a French–West German coproduction shot in English in Great Britain. The title is *Death Watch*, and if you ever have a chance to see this outstanding film, take advantage of the opportunity.

The stars were Harvey Keitel, Romy Schneider, Harry Dean Stanton, and Max Von Sydow. The script was by David Rayfiel and the director, Bertrand Tavernier.

Set in the near future, the film opens after Keitel's eyes have been replaced by miniature television cameras. Although he must avoid darkness at all costs, including closing his eyes for too long, his vision is perfectly normal, while monitors back at the TV company pick up everything he sees. His alert, slimy boss is played by Stanton.

This future is one in which almost all non-accidental causes of death have been eradicated, except some rare diseases and old age. When someone does fall ill with an incurable illness, it's a matter of great curiosity and morbid interest to society. And it's exploited.

Romy Schneider, an intelligent woman trapped in a loveless second marriage, is told that she is dying, so TV executive Stanton approaches her with the idea of videotaping her last days for his TV series, "Death Watch," the most popular show on the air. At first she's reluctant, but the helplessness of her husband finally causes her to accede to Stanton's request, and he pays her an enormous amount of money.

But she skips out, leaving her husband literally holding the bag. The cameraman is assigned the task of following her, so the show can go on anyway. Keitel keeps his real purpose secret from Schneider. The story follows the two as they wend their way across England to where her first husband, Max Von Sydow, lives in isolation. Since she avoids all settlements, she never knows that her last days are being telecast, as seen through the eyes of her companion. And the show is a hit.

Predictably but believably, Keitel comes to care for her, but in a clever twist, he doesn't realize just how much he does care until he sees her on television in the shows taped from the input of his own eyes. He's such a child of the medium that he doesn't quite believe anything is real—including that which he has seen himself—until he also sees it on the tube. He comes to hate the exploitation of her tragedy, but he can't seem to stop it.

This was only the fifth film directed by Tavernier, who is going to be a top name internationally. Two of his previous films, *The Judge and the Assassin* and *The Clockmaker of St. Paul*, were very good. Here, he has created a believable future. It's not far off, but it's already beginning to crumble around the edges. We see a petitioner on behalf of "live teachers." A group of what seem to be professional protesters try to get Keitel to join them. A church is stuffed with rootless wanderers. Keitel visits a supermarket where a taped voice urges shoppers not to steal—but he's the only customer. There are virtually no children anywhere. A bazaar on the banks of the Thames is larger and more active than other shopping areas, but it seems shoddy and temporary. All of this is original for the film; there are only slight hints of this kind of subtle decay in Compton's good novel.

Death Watch is a top-notch science fiction movie. It's not flashy, it's not colorful; Pierre-William Glenn's evocative photography is resolutely low-key. It's a Real Movie, clearly a professional film made by an artist, not a big-deal exploitation picture made by a committee. It neither flaunts its genre, nor is it ashamed of being science fiction. SF is the stuff of the story, that's all. It's what SF fans often say they want: a science fiction movie that is first and foremost a good movie. (Of course, what they usually really want are flashy effects and space opera.) If you don't like *Death Watch*, it will be because you don't like the movie itself, not because you dislike its treatment of science fiction.

Because it has a downbeat ending, because it's more

slowly paced than most American films, and because the cast and the theme are not exploitable, it seems unlikely that *Death Watch* will have any wide American distribution.

Science fiction movies of 1980 can't be considered to be pointing up any real trends for the future. Aside from the obvious fact that trends in any popular art don't simply cease at the end of a decade, it's still unclear as to just what bandwagons are now being hopped on anywhere in the world. It *is* becoming clear that world moviegoing audiences love science fiction, fantasy, and horror—but that they are being fussy about what they want. *Flash Gordon* and *Saturn 3* seemed like sure-fire ideas to those who made them, but they underestimated their audiences. People want amazement, but they want it given to them honestly, not with no heart and no love. In smaller pictures like *Battle Beyond the Stars* and *Alligator*, a respect for the audience and a fondness for what was being done clearly showed, and the films were considerably better than their big-budget cousins.

If any trend from the 1980 SF film output can be seen even tentatively, perhaps it's merely Lincoln's old adage about politics now being acted out in a new arena, and those who try to fool all the people all the time are finding that it cannot be done. Moviemakers are going to have to learn to be braver and more enterprising, perhaps even to look beyond Hollywood for material.

Turning to published science fiction is only part of the solution; not all SF can be successfully filmed, including many of the classics. A winnowing process is needed, with people expert at movies *and* science fiction advising and suggesting. This is useful because although there are many filmmakers who know and love science fiction, not all do—and the most successful SF films in recent years have been made by people who know the stuff. But some SF writers act as if they *own* science fiction, and that moviemakers *must* turn to them for everything. And some moviemakers unfortunately feel that SF is a simple, lowbrow genre that anyone can do as well as those who have made a career of it. These two ideas cause alienation, bad movies, and peculiar views of science fiction films (as in the book by Frederik Pohl and his son). Mediators who understand the strengths of science fiction *and* what can be done in film are genuinely needed if science fiction movies are to continue to succeed as science fiction, art, and commerce.

The Ugly Chickens

Howard Waldrop

Howard Waldrop is another writer I've never managed to meet. He's one of a group of Texas writers, and he often works with Texan themes; in 1974 he published (with Jake Saunders) The Texas-Israeli War: 1999.

"The Ugly Chickens" is a traditional story; that is, Mr. Campbell would have been pleased to publish it in the old Astounding.

Which means that it's a good story indeed. Traditional works haven't been winning prizes lately; perhaps Waldrop has started a counter-trend, because "The Ugly Chickens" won the Nebula as the best novelette of 1980.

My car was broken, and I had a class to teach at eleven. So I took the city bus, something I rarely do.

I spent last summer crawling through the Big Thicket with cameras and tape recorder, photographing and taping two of the last ivory-billed woodpeckers on the earth. You can see the films at your local Audubon Society showroom.

This year I wanted something just as flashy but a little less taxing. Perhaps a population study on the Bermuda cahow, or the New Zealand takahe. A month or so in the warm (not hot) sun would do me a world of good. To say nothing of the advancement of science.

I was idly leafing through Greenway's *Extinct and Vanishing Birds of the World.* The city bus was winding its way through the ritzy neighborhoods of Austin, stopping to let off the chicanas, black women, and Vietnamese who tended the kitchens and gardens of the rich.

"I haven't seen any of those ugly chickens in a long time," said a voice close by.

A gray-haired lady was leaning across the aisle toward me.

I looked at her, then around. Maybe she was a shopping-bag lady. Maybe she was just talking. I looked straight at her. No doubt about it, she was talking to me. She was waiting for an answer.

"I used to live near some folks who raised them when I was a girl," she said. She pointed.

I looked down at the page my book was open to.

What I should have said was: That is quite impossible, madam. This is a drawing of an extinct bird of the island of Mauritius. It is perhaps the most famous dead bird in the world. Maybe you are mistaking this drawing for that of some rare Asiatic turkey, peafowl, or pheasant. I am sorry, but you *are* mistaken.

I should have said all that.

What she said was, "Oops, this is my stop." And got up to go.

My name is Paul Lindberl. I am twenty-six years old, a graduate student in ornithology at the University of Texas, a teaching assistant. My name is not unknown in the field. I have several vices and follies, but I don't think foolishness is one of them.

The stupid thing for me to do would have been to follow her.

She stepped off the bus.
I followed her.

I came into the departmental office, trailing scattered papers in the whirlwind behind me. "Martha! Martha!" I yelled.

She was doing something in the supply cabinet.

"Jesus, Paul! What do you want?"

"Where's Courtney?"

"At the conference in Houston. You know that. You missed your class. What's the matter?"

"Petty cash. Let me at it!"

"Payday was only a week ago. If you can't—"

"It's business! It's fame and adventure and the chance of a lifetime! It's a long sea voyage that leaves . . . a plane ticket. To either Jackson, Mississippi, or Memphis. Make it Jackson, it's closer. I'll get receipts! I'll be famous. Courtney will be famous. *You'll* even be famous! This university will make even *more* money! I'll pay you back. Give me some paper. I gotta write Courtney a note. When's the next plane out? Could you get Marie and Chuck to take over my classes Tuesday and Wednesday? I'll try to be back Thursday unless something happens. Courtney'll be back tomorrow, right? I'll call him from, well, wherever. Do you have some coffee?"

And so on and so forth. Martha looked at me like I was crazy. But she filled out the requisition anyway.

"What do I tell Kemejian when I ask him to sign these?"

"Martha, babe, sweetheart. Tell him I'll get his picture in *Scientific American*."

"He doesn't read it."

"*Nature*, then!"

"I'll see what I can do," she said.

The lady I had followed off the bus was named Jolyn (Smith) Jimson. The story she told me was so weird that it had to be true. She knew things only an expert, or someone with first-hand experience, could know. I got names from her, and addresses, and directions, and tidbits of information. Plus a year: 1927.

And a place. Northern Mississippi.

I gave her my copy of the Greenway book. I told her I'd call her as soon as I got back into town. I left her standing on the corner near the house of the lady she cleaned up for twice a week. Jolyn Jimson was in her sixties.

Think of the dodo as a baby harp seal with feathers. I know that's not even close, but it saves time.

In 1507 the Portuguese, on their way to India, found the (then unnamed) Mascarene Islands in the Indian Ocean—three of them a few hundred miles apart, all east of Madagascar.

It wasn't until 1598, when that old Dutch sea captain Cornelius van Neck bumped into them, that the islands received their names—names that changed several times through the centuries as the Dutch, French, and English changed them every war or so. They are now known as Rodriguez, Réunion, and Mauritius.

The major feature of these islands was large, flightless, stupid, ugly, bad-tasting birds. Van Neck and his men named them *dod-aarsen*, "stupid asses," or *dodars*, "silly birds," or solitaires.

There were three species: the dodo of Mauritius, the real gray-brown, hooked-beak, clumsy thing that weighed twenty kilos or more; the white, somewhat slimmer dodo of Réunion; and the solitaires of Rodriguez and Réunion, which looked like very fat, very dumb, light-colored geese.

The dodos all had thick legs, big squat bodies twice as large as a turkey's, naked faces, and big long downcurved beaks ending in a hook like a hollow linoleum knife. Long ago they had lost the ability to fly, and their wings had degenerated to flaps the size of a human hand with only three or four feathers in them. Their tails were curly and fluffy, like a child's afterthought at decoration. They had absolutely no natural enemies. They nested on the open ground. They probably hatched their eggs wherever they happened to lay them.

No natural enemies until Van Neck and his kind showed up. The Dutch, French, and Portuguese sailors who stopped at the Mascarenes to replenish stores found that, besides looking stupid, dodos *were* stupid. The men walked right up to the dodos and hit them on the head with clubs. Better yet, dodos could be herded around like sheep. Ships' logs are full of things like: "Party of ten men ashore. Drove half a hundred of the big turkeylike birds into the boat. Brought to ship, where they are given the run of the decks. Three will feed a crew of 150."

Even so, most of the dodo, except for the breast, tasted bad. One of the Dutch words for them was *walghvogel*, "disgusting bird." But on a ship three months out on a return from Goa to Lisbon, well, food was where you found it. It was said, even so, that prolonged boiling did not improve the flavor.

Even so, the dodos might have lasted, except that the Dutch, and later the French, colonized the Mascarenes. The islands became plantations and dumping places for religious refugees. Sugar cane and other exotic crops were raised there.

With the colonists came cats, dogs, hogs, and the cunning *Rattus norvegicus* and the Rhesus monkey from Ceylon. What dodos the hungry sailors left were chased down (they were dumb and stupid, but they could run when they felt like it) by dogs in the open. They were killed by cats as they sat on their nests. Their eggs were stolen and eaten by monkeys, rats, and hogs. And they competed with the pigs for all the low-growing goodies of the islands.

The last Mauritius dodo was seen in 1681, less than a hundred years after humans first saw them. The last white dodo walked off the history books around 1720. The solitaires of Rodriguez and Réunion, last of the genus as well as the species, may have lasted until 1790. Nobody knows.

Scientists suddenly looked around and found no more of the Didine birds alive, anywhere.

This part of the country was degenerate before the first Snopes ever saw it. This road hadn't been paved until the late fifties, and it was a main road between two county seats. That didn't mean it went through civilized country. I'd traveled for miles and seen nothing but dirt banks, red as Billy Carter's neck, and an occasional church. I expected to see Burma Shave signs, but realized this road had probably never had them.

I almost missed the turnoff onto the dirt and gravel road the man back at the service station had marked. It led onto the highway from nowhere, a lane out of a field. I turned down it, and a rock the size of a golf ball flew up over the hood and put a crack three inches long in the windshield of the rental car I'd gotten in Grenada.

It was a hot, muggy day for this early. The view was obscured in a cloud of dust every time the gravel thinned. About a mile down the road, the gravel gave out completely. The roadway turned into a rutted dirt pathway, just wider than the car, hemmed in on both sides by a sagging three-strand barbed-wire fence.

In some places the fence posts were missing for a few meters. The wire lay on the ground and in some places disappeared under it for long stretches.

The only life I saw was a mockingbird raising hell with something under a thornbush the barbed wire had been nailed to in place of a post. To one side now was a grassy field that had gone wild, the way everywhere will look after we blow ourselves off the face of the planet. The other was fast becoming woods—pine, oak, some black gum and wild plum, fruit not out this time of the year.

I began to ask myself what I was doing here. What if Ms. Jimson were some imaginative old crank who—but no.

Wrong, maybe, but even the wrong was worth checking. But I knew she hadn't lied to me. She had seemed incapable of lies—a good ol' girl, backbone of the South, of the earth. Not a mendacious gland in her being.

I couldn't doubt her, or my judgment either. Here I was, creeping and bouncing down a dirt path in Mississippi, after no sleep for a day, out on the thin ragged edge of a dream. I *had* to take it on faith.

The back of the car sometimes slid where the dirt had loosened and gave way to sand. The back tire stuck once, but I rocked out of it. Getting back out again would be another matter. Didn't anyone ever use this road?

The woods closed in on both sides like the forest primeval, and the fence had long since disappeared. My odometer said ten kilometers, and it had been twenty minutes since I'd turned off the highway. In the rearview mirror, I saw beads of sweat and dirt in the wrinkles of my neck. A fine patina of dust covered everything inside the car. Clots of it came through the windows.

The woods reached out and swallowed the road. Branches scraped against the windows and the top. It was like falling down a long dark leafy tunnel. It was dark and green in there. I fought back an atavistic urge to turn on the headlights. The roadbed must be made of a few centuries of leaf mulch. I kept constant pressure on the accelerator and bulled my way through.

Half a log caught and banged and clanged against the car bottom. I saw light ahead. Fearing for the oil pan, I punched the pedal and sped out.

I almost ran through a house.

It was maybe ten meters from the trees. The road ended under one of the windows. I saw somebody waving from the corner of my eye.

I slammed on the brakes.

A whole family was on the porch, looking like a Walker Evans Depression photograph, or a fever dream from the mind of a "Hee Haw" producer. The house was old. Strips of peeling paint a meter long tapped against the eaves.

"Damned good thing you stopped," said a voice. I looked up. The biggest man I had ever seen in my life leaned down into the driver-side window.

"If we'd have heard you sooner, I'd've sent one of the kids down to the end of the driveway to warn you," he said.

Driveway?

His mouth was stained brown at the corners. I figured he chewed tobacco until I saw the sweet-gum snuff brush sticking from the pencil pocket in the bib of his coveralls. His hands were the size of catchers' mitts. They looked like they'd never held anything smaller than an ax handle.

"How y'all?" he said, by way of introduction.

"Just fine," I said. I got out of the car.

"My name's Lindberl," I said, extending my hand. He took it. For an instant, I thought of bear traps, sharks' mouths, closing elevator doors. The thought went back to wherever it is they stay.

"This the Gudger place?" I asked.

He looked at me blankly with his gray eyes. He wore a diesel truck cap and had on a checked lumberjack shirt beneath the coveralls. His rubber boots were the size of the ones Karloff wore in *Frankenstein*.

"Naw. I'm Jim Bob Krait. That's my wife, Jenny, and there's Luke and Skeeno and Shirl." He pointed to the porch.

The people on the porch nodded.

"Lessee. Gudger? No Gudgers round here I know of. I'm sorta new here." I took that to mean he hadn't lived here for more than twenty years or so.

"Jennifer!" he yelled. "You know of anybody named Gudger?" To me he said, "My wife's lived around heres all her life."

His wife came down onto the second step of the porch landing. "I think they used to be the ones what lived on the Spradlin place before the Spradlins. But the Spradlins left around the Korean War. I didn't know any of the Gudgers myself. That's while we was living over to Water Valley."

"You an insurance man?" asked Mr. Krait.

"Uh . . . no," I said. I imagined the people on the porch leaning toward me, all ears. "I'm a . . . I teach college."

"Oxford?" asked Krait.

"Uh, no. University of Texas."

"Well, that's a damn long way off. You say you're looking for the Gudgers?"

"Just their house. The area. As your wife said, I understand they left. During the Depression, I believe."

"Well, they musta had money," said the gigantic Mr. Krait. "Nobody around here was rich enough to *leave* during the Depression."

"Luke!" he yelled. The oldest boy on the porch sauntered down. He looked anemic and wore a shirt in vogue with the Twist. He stood with his hands in his pockets.

"Luke, show Mr. Lindbergh—"

"Lindberl."

". . . Mr. Lindberl here the way up to the old Spradlin place. Take him as far as the old log bridge, he might get lost before then."

"Log bridge broke down, Daddy."

"When?"

"October, Daddy."

"Well, hell, somethin' else to fix! Anyway, to the creek."

He turned to me. "You want him to go along on up there, see you don't get snakebit?"

"No, I'm sure I'll be fine."

"Mind if I ask what you're going up there for?" he asked. He was looking away from me. I could see having to come right out and ask what was bothering him. Such things usually came up in the course of conversation.

"I'm a—uh, bird scientist. I study birds. We had a sighting—someone told us the old Gudger place—the area around here—I'm looking for a rare bird. It's hard to explain."

I noticed I was sweating. It was hot.

"You mean like a good God? I saw a good God about twenty-five years ago, over next to Bruce," he said.

"Well, no." (A good God was one of the names for an ivory-billed woodpecker, one of the rarest in the world. Any other time I would have dropped my jaw. Because they were thought to have died out in Mississippi by the teens, and by the fact that Krait knew they *were* rare.)

I went to lock my car up, then thought of the protocol of the situation. "My car be in your way?" I asked.

"Naw. It'll be just fine," said Jim Bob Krait. "We'll look for you back by sundown, that be all right?"

For a minute, I didn't know whether that was a command or an expression of concern.

"Just in case I get snakebit," I said. "I'll try to be careful up there."

"Good luck on findin' them rare birds," he said. He walked up to the porch with his family.

"Les go," said Luke.

Behind the Krait house were a hen house and pigsty where hogs lay after their morning slop like islands in a muddy bay, or some Zen pork sculpture. Next we passed broken farm machinery gone to rust, though there was nothing but uncultivated land as far as the eye could see. How the family made a living I don't know. I'm told you can find places just like this throughout the South.

We walked through woods and across fields, following a sort of path. I tried to memorize the turns I would have to take on my way back. Luke didn't say a word the whole twenty minutes he accompanied me, except to curse once when he stepped into a bull nettle with his tennis shoes.

We came to a creek that skirted the edge of a woodsy hill. There was a rotted log forming a small dam. Above it the water was nearly a meter deep; below it, half that much.

"See that path?" he asked.

"Yes."

"Follow it up around the hill, then across the next field.

Then you cross the creek again on the rocks, and over the hill. Take the left-hand path. What's left of the house is about three-quarters the way up the next hill. If you come to a big bare rock cliff, you've gone too far. You got that?"

I nodded.

He turned and left.

The house had once been a dog-run cabin, as Ms. Jimson had said. Now it was fallen in on one side, what they call sigoglin. (Or was it anti-sigoglin?) I once heard a hymn on the radio called "The Land Where No Cabins Fall." This was the country songs like that were written in.

Weeds grew everywhere. There were signs of fences, a flattened pile of wood that had once been a barn. Farther behind the house were the outhouse remains. Half a rusted pump stood in the backyard. A flatter spot showed where the vegetable garden had been; in it a single wild tomato, pecked by birds, lay rotting. I passed it. There was lumber from three outbuildings, mostly rotten and green with algae and moss. One had been a smokehouse-and-woodshed combination. Two had been chicken roosts. One was larger than the other. It was there I started to poke around and dig.

Where? Where? I wish I'd been on more archeological digs, knew the places to look. Refuse piles, midden heaps, kitchen-scrap piles, compost boxes. Why hadn't I been born on a farm so I'd know instinctively where to search?

I prodded around the grounds. I moved back and forth like a setter casting for the scent of quail. I wanted more, more. I still wasn't satisfied.

Dusk. Dark, in fact. I trudged into the Kraits' front yard. The tote sack I carried was full to bulging. I was hot, tired, streaked with fifty years of chicken shit. The Kraits were on their porch. Jim Bob lumbered down like a friendly mountain.

I asked him a few questions, gave them a Xerox copy of

one of the dodo pictures, left them addresses and phone numbers where they could reach me.

Then into the rental car. Off to Water Valley, acting on information Jennifer Krait gave me. I went to the postmaster's house at Water Valley. She was getting ready for bed. I asked questions. She got on the phone. I bothered people until one in the morning. Then back into the trusty rental car.

On to Memphis as the moon came up on my right. Interstate 55 was a glass ribbon before me. WLS from Chicago was on the radio.

I hummed along with it, I sang at the top of my voice.

The sack full of dodo bones, beaks, feet, and eggshell fragments kept me company on the front seat.

Did you know a museum once traded an entire blue whale skeleton for one of a dodo?

Driving, driving.

The Dance of the Dodos

I used to have a vision sometimes—I had it long before this madness came up. I can close my eyes and see it by thinking hard. But it comes to me most often, most vividly, when I am reading and listening to classical music, especially Pachelbel's *Canon in D*.

It is near dusk in The Hague, and the light is that of Frans Hals, of Rembrandt. The Dutch royal family and their guests eat and talk quietly in the great dining hall. Guards with halberds and pikes stand in the corners of the room. The family is arranged around the table: the King, Queen, some princesses, a prince, a couple of other children, an invited noble or two. Servants come out with plates and cups, but they do not intrude.

On a raised platform at one end of the room an orchestra plays dinner music—a harpsichord, viola, cello, three violins, and woodwinds. One of the royal dwarfs sits on the edge of the platform, his foot slowly rubbing the back of one of the dogs sleeping near him.

As the music of Pachelbel's *Canon in D* swells and rolls through the hall, one of the dodos walks in clumsily, stops, .tilts its head, its eyes bright as a pool of tar. It sways a little, lifts its foot tentatively, one, then another, rocks back and forth in time to the cello.

The violins swirl. The dodo begins to dance, its great ungainly body now graceful. It is joined by the other two dodos who come into the hall, all three turning in a sort of circle.

The harpsichord begins its counterpoint. The fourth dodo, the white one from Réunion, comes from its place under the table and joins the circle with the others.

It is most graceful of all, making complete turns where the others only sway and dip on the edge of the circle they have formed.

The music rises in volume; the first violinist sees the dodos and nods to the King. But he and the others at the table have already seen. They are silent, transfixed—even the servants stand still, bowls, pots, and kettles in their hands, forgotten.

Around the dodos dance with bobs and weaves of their ugly heads. The white dodo dips, takes a half step, pirouettes on one foot, circles again.

Without a word the King of Holland takes the hand of the Queen, and they come around the table, children before the spectacle. They join in the dance, waltzing (anachronism) among the dodos while the family, the guests, the soldiers watch and nod in time with the music.

Then the vision fades, and the afterimage of a flickering fireplace and a dodo remains.

The dodo and its kindred came by ships to the ports of Europe. The first we have record of is that of Captain van Neck, who brought back two in 1599—one for the ruler of Holland, and one that found its way through Cologne to the menagerie of Emperor Rudolf II.

This royal aviary was at Schloss Negebau, near Vienna. It was here that the first paintings of the dumb old birds were done by Georg and his son Jacob Hoefnagel, between 1602 and 1610. They painted it among more than ninety species of birds that kept the Emperor amused.

Another Dutch artist named Roelandt Savery, as someone said, "made a career out of the dodo." He drew and painted the birds many times, and was no doubt personally fascinated by them. Obsessed, even. Early on, the paintings are consistent; the later ones have inaccuracies. This implies he worked from life first, then from memory as his model went to that place soon to be reserved for all its species. One of his drawings has two of the Raphidae scrambling for some goody on the ground. His works are not without charm.

Another Dutch artist (they seemed to sprout up like mushrooms after a spring rain) named Peter Withoos also stuck dodos in his paintings, sometimes in odd and exciting places—wandering around during their owner's music lessons, or stuck with Adam and Eve in some Edenic idyll.

The most accurate representation, we are assured, comes from half a world away from the religious and political turmoil of the seafaring Europeans. There is an Indian miniature painting of the dodo that now rests in a museum in Russia. The dodo could have been brought by the Dutch or Portuguese in their travels to Goa and the coasts of the Indian subcontinent. Or it could have been brought centuries before by the Arabs who plied the Indian Ocean in their triangular-sailed craft, and who may have discovered the Mascarenes before the Europeans cranked themselves up for the First Crusade.

At one time early in my bird-fascination days (after I stopped killing them with BB guns but before I began to work for a scholarship) I once sat down and figured out where all the dodos had been.

Two with Van Neck in 1599, one to Holland, one to Austria. Another was in Count Solms's park in 1600. An account speaks of "one in Italy, one in Germany, several to England, eight or nine to Holland." William Boentekoe van Hoorn knew of "one shipped to Europe in 1640, another in 1685," which he said was "also painted by Dutch artists." Two were mentioned as "being kept in Surrat House in India as pets," perhaps one of which is the one in the painting. Being charitable, and considering "several" to mean at least three, that means twenty dodos in all.

There had to be more, when boatloads had been gathered at the time.

What do we know of the Didine birds? A few ships' logs, some accounts left by travelers and colonists. The English were fascinated by them. Sir Hamon Lestrange, a contemporary of Pepys, saw exhibited "a Dodar from the Island of Mauritius . . . it is not able to flie, being so bigge." One was stuffed when it died, and was put in the Museum Tradescantum in South Lambeth. It eventually found its way into the Ashmolean Museum. It grew ratty and was burned, all but a leg and the head, in 1750. By then there were no more dodos, but nobody had realized that yet.

Francis Willughby got to describe it before its incineration. Earlier, old Carolus Clusius in Holland studied the one in Count Solms's park. He collected everything known about the Raphidae, describing a dodo leg Pieter Pauw kept in his natural-history cabinet, in *Exoticarium libri decem* in 1605, seven years after their discovery.

François Leguat, a Huguenot who lived on Réunion for some years, published an account of his travels in which he mentioned the dodos. It was published in 1690 (after the Mauritius dodo was extinct) and included the information that "some of the males weigh forty-five pound. . . . One egg, much bigger than that of a goos is laid by the female, and takes seven weeks hatching time."

The Abbé Pingré visited the Mascarenes in 1761. He saw the last of the Rodriguez solitaires and collected what information he could about the dead Mauritius and Réunion members of the genus.

After that, only memories of the colonists, and some scientific debate as to *where* the Raphidae belonged in the great taxonomic scheme of things—some said pigeons, some said rails—were left. Even this nitpicking ended. The dodo was forgotten.

When Lewis Carroll wrote *Alice in Wonderland* in 1865, most people thought he had invented the dodo.

The service station I called from in Memphis was busier than a one-legged man in an ass-kicking contest. Between bings and dings of the bell, I finally realized the call had gone through.

The guy who answered was named Selvedge. I got nowhere with him. He mistook me for a real-estate agent, then a lawyer. Now he was beginning to think I was some sort of a con man. I wasn't doing too well, either. I hadn't slept in two days. I must have sounded like a speed freak. My only progress was that I found that Ms. Annie Mae Gudger (childhood playmate of Jolyn Jimson) was now, and had been, the respected Ms. Annie Mae Radwin. This guy Selvedge must have been a secretary or toady or something.

We were having a conversation comparable to that between a shrieking macaw and a pile of mammoth bones. Then there was another click on the line.

"Young man?" said the other voice, an old woman's voice, Southern, very refined but with a hint of the hills in it.

"Yes? Hello! Hello!"

"Young man, you say you talked to a Jolyn somebody? Do you mean Jolyn Smith?"

"Hello! Yes! Ms. Radwin, Ms. Annie Mae Radwin who used to be Gudger? She lives in Austin now. Texas. She used to live near Water Valley, Mississippi. Austin's where I'm from. I—"

"Young man," asked the voice again, "are you sure you haven't been put up to this by my hateful sister Alma?"

"Who? No, ma'am. I met a woman named Jolyn—"

"I'd like to talk to you, young man," said the voice. Then, offhandedly, "Give him directions to get here, Selvedge."

Click.

I cleaned out my mouth as best as I could in the service station rest room, tried to shave with an old clogged Gillette disposable in my knapsack, and succeeded in gapping up my jawline. I changed into a clean pair of jeans and the only other shirt I had with me, and combed my hair. I stood in front of the mirror.

I still looked like the dog's lunch.

The house reminded me of Presley's mansion, which was somewhere in the neighborhood. From a shack on the side of a Mississippi hill to this, in forty years. There are all sorts of ways of making it. I wondered what Annie Mae Gudger's had been. Luck? Predation? Divine intervention? Hard work? Trover and replevin?

Selvedge led me toward the sun room. I felt like Philip Marlowe going to meet a rich client. The house was filled with that furniture built sometime between the turn of the century and the 1950s—the ageless kind. It never looks great, it never looks ratty, and every chair is comfortable.

I think I was expecting some formidable woman with sleeve blotters and a green eyeshade hunched over a rolltop desk with piles of paper whose acceptance or rejection meant life or death for thousands.

Who I met was a charming lady in a green pantsuit. She was in her sixties, her hair still a straw-wheat color. It didn't looked dyed. Her eyes were blue as my first-grade teacher's had been. She was wiry and looked as if the word *fat* was not in her vocabulary.

"Good morning, Mr. Lindberl." She shook my hand. "Would you like some coffee? You look as if you could use it."

"Yes, thank you."

"Please sit down." She indicated a white wicker chair at a glass table. A serving tray with coffeepot, cups, tea bags, croissants, napkins, and plates lay on the tabletop.

After I swallowed half a cup of coffee at a gulp, she said, "What you wanted to see me about must be important."

"Sorry about my manners," I said. "I know I don't look it, but I'm a biology assistant at the University of Texas. An ornithologist. Working on my master's. I met Ms. Jolyn Jimson two days ago—"

"How is Jolyn? I haven't seen her in, oh, Lord, it must be on to fifty years. The time gets away."

"She seemed to be fine. I only talked to her half an hour or so. That was—"

"And you've come to see me about . . . ?"

"Uh. The . . . about some of the poultry your family used to raise, when they lived near Water Valley."

She looked at me a moment. Then she began to smile.

"Oh, you mean the ugly chickens?" she said.

I smiled. I almost laughed. I knew what Oedipus must have gone through.

It is now four-thirty in the afternoon. I am sitting in the downtown Motel 6 in Memphis. I have to make a phone call and get some sleep and catch a plane.

Annie Mae Gudger Radwin talked for four hours, answering my questions, setting me straight on family history, having Selvedge hold all her calls.

The main problem was that Annie Mae ran off in 1928, the year *before* her father got his big break. She went to Yazoo City, and by degrees and stages worked her way northward to Memphis and her destiny as the widow of a rich mercantile broker.

But I get ahead of myself.

Grandfather Gudger used to be the overseer for Colonel Crisby on the main plantation near McComb, Mississippi. There was a long story behind that. Bear with me.

Colonel Crisby himself was the scion of a seafaring family with interests in both the cedars of Lebanon (almost all cut down for masts for His Majesty's and others' navies) and Egyptian cotton. Also teas, spices, and any other salable commodity that came its way.

When Colonel Crisby's grandfather reached his majority in 1802, he waved goodbye to the Atlantic Ocean at Charleston, S.C., and stepped westward into the forest. When he stopped, he was in the middle of the Chickasaw Nation, where he opened a trading post and introduced slaves to the Indians.

And he prospered, and begat Colonel Crisby's father, who sent back to South Carolina for everything his father owned. Everything—slaves, wagons, horses, cattle, guinea fowl, peacocks, and dodos, which everybody thought of as atrociously ugly poultry of some kind, one of the seafaring uncles having bought them off a French merchant in 1721. (I surmised these were white dodos from Réunion, unless they had been from even earlier stock. The dodo of Mauritius was already extinct by then.)

All this stuff was herded out west to the trading post in the midst of the Chickasaw Nation. (The tribes around there were of the confederation of the Dancing Rabbits.)

And Colonel Crisby's father prospered, and so did the guinea fowl and the dodos. Then Andrew Jackson came along and marched the Dancing Rabbits off up the Trail of Tears to the heaven of Oklahoma. And Colonel Crisby's father begat Colonel Crisby, and put the trading post in the hands of others, and moved his plantation westward still to McComb.

Everything prospered but Colonel Crisby's father, who died. And the dodos, with occasional losses to the avengin' weasel and the egg-sucking dog, reproduced themselves also.

Then along came Granddaddy Gudger, a Simon Legree role model, who took care of the plantation while Colonel Crisby raised ten companies of men and marched off to fight the War for Southern Independence.

Colonel Crisby came back to the McComb plantation earlier than most, he having stopped much of the same volley of Minié balls that caught his commander, General Beauregard Hanlon, on a promontory bluff during the Siege of Vicksburg.

He wasn't dead, but death hung around the place like a gentlemanly bill collector for a month. The Colonel languished, went slapdab crazy, and freed all his slaves the week before he died (the war lasted another two years after that). Not now having any slaves, he didn't need an overseer.

Then comes the Faulkner part of the tale, straight out of *As I Lay Dying*, with the Gudger family returning to the area of Water Valley (before there was a Water Valley), moving through the demoralized and tattered displaced persons of the South, driving their dodos before them. For Colonel Crisby had given them to his former overseer for his faithful service. Also followed the story of the bloody murder of Granddaddy Gudger at the hands of the Freedman's militia during the rising of the first Klan, and of the trials and tribulations of Daddy Gudger in the years between 1880 and 1910, when he was between the ages of four and thirty-four.

Alma and Annie Mae were the second and fifth of Daddy Gudger's brood, born three years apart. They seem to have hated each other from the very first time Alma looked into little Annie Mae's crib. They were kids by Daddy Gudger's second wife (his desperation had killed the first) and their father was already on his sixth career. He had been a lumberman, a stump preacher, a plowman-for-hire (until his mules broke out in farcy buds and died of the glanders), a freight hauler (until his horses died of overwork and the hardware store repossessed the wagon), a politician's roadie (until the politician lost the election). When Alma and Annie Mae were born, he was failing as a sharecropper. Somehow Gudger had made it through the Depression of 1898 as a boy, and was too poor after that to notice more about economics than the price of Beech-Nut tobacco at the store.

Alma and Annie Mae fought, and it helped none at all that Alma, being the oldest daughter, was both her mother's and her father's darling. Annie Mae's life was the usual un-wanted-poor-white-trash-child's hell. She vowed early to run away, and recognized her ambition at thirteen.

All this I learned this morning. Jolyn (Smith) Jimson was Annie Mae's only friend in those days—from a family even poorer than the Gudgers. But somehow there was food, and an occasional odd job. And the dodos.

"My father hated those old birds," said the cultured Annie Mae Radwin, née Gudger, in the solarium. "He always swore he was going to get rid of them someday, but just never seemed to get around to it. I think there was more to it than that. But they were so much *trouble*. We always had to keep them penned up at night, and go check for their eggs. They wandered off to lay them, and forgot where they were. Sometimes no new ones were born at all in a year.

"And they got so *ugly*. Once a year. I mean, terrible-look-ing, like they were going to die. All their feathers fell off, and they looked like they had mange or something. Then the whole front of their beaks fell off, or worse, hung halfway on for a week or two. They looked like big old naked pigeons. After that they'd lose weight, down to twenty or thirty pounds, before their new feathers grew back.

"We were always having to kill foxes that got after them in the turkey house. That's what we called their roost, the tur-key house. And we found their eggs all sucked out by cats and dogs. They were so stupid we had to drive them into their roost at night. I don't think they could have found it standing ten feet from it."

She looked at me.

"I think much as my father hated them, they meant some-thing to him. As long as he hung on to them, he knew he was as good as Granddaddy Gudger. You may not know it, but there was a certain amount of family pride about Grand-daddy Gudger. At least in my father's eyes. His rapid fall in the world had a sort of grandeur to it. He'd gone from a relatively high position in the old order, and maintained some grace and stature after the Emancipation. And though he lost everything, he managed to keep those ugly old chickens the Colonel had given him as sort of a symbol.

"And as long as he had them, too, my daddy thought himself as good as his father. He kept his dignity, even when he didn't have anything else."

I asked what happened to them. She didn't know, but told me who did and where I could find her.

That's why I'm going to make a phone call.

"Hello. Dr. Courtney. Dr. Courtney? This is Paul. Memphis. Tennessee. It's too long to go into. No, of course not, not yet. But I've got evidence. What? Okay, how do trochanters, coracoids, tarsometatarsi, and beak sheaths sound? From their hen house, where else? Where would you keep *your* dodos, then?

"Sorry. I haven't slept in a couple of days. I need some help. Yes, yes. Money. Lots of money.

"Cash. Three hundred dollars, maybe. Western Union, Memphis, Tennessee. Whichever one's closest to the airport. Airport. I need the department to set up reservations to Mauritius for me. . . .

"No. No. Not wild-goose chase, wild-*dodo* chase. Tame-dodo chase, I *know* there aren't any dodos on Mauritius! I know that. I could explain. I know it'll mean a couple of grand—if—but—

"Look, Dr. Courtney. Do you want *your* picture in *Scientific American*, or don't you?"

I am sitting in the airport café in Port Louis, Mauritius. It is now three days later, five days since that fateful morning my car wouldn't start. God bless the Sears Diehard people. I have slept sitting up in a plane seat, on and off, different planes, different seats, for twenty-four hours, Kennedy to Paris, Paris to Cairo, Cairo to Madagascar. I felt like a brand-new man when I got here.

Now I feel like an infinitely sadder and wiser brand-new man. I have just returned from the hateful sister Alma's house in the exclusive section of Port Louis, where all the French and British officials used to live.

Courtney will get his picture in *Scientific American*, all right. Me too. There'll be newspaper stories and talk shows for a few weeks for me, and I'm sure Annie Mae Gudger Radwin on one side of the world and Alma Chandler Gudger Molière on the other will come in for their share of glory.

I am putting away cup after cup of coffee. The plane back to Tananarive leaves in an hour. I plan to sleep all the way back to Cairo, to Paris, to New York, pick up my bag of bones, sleep back to Austin.

Before me on the table is a packet of documents, clippings, and photographs. I have come across half the world for this. I gaze from the package, out the window across Port Louis to the bulk of Mont Pieter Both, which overshadows the city and its famous racecourse.

Perhaps I should do something symbolic. Cancel my flight. Climb the mountain and look down on man and all his handiworks. Take a pitcher of martinis with me. Sit in the bright semitropical sunlight (it's early dry winter here). Drink the martinis slowly, toasting Snuffo, God of Extinction. Here's one for the great auk. This is for the Carolina parakeet. Mud in your eye, passenger pigeon. This one's for the heath hen. Most important, here's one each for the Mauritius dodo, the white dodo of Réunion, the Réunion solitaire, the Rodriguez solitaire. Here's to the Raphidae, great Didine birds that you were.

Maybe I'll do something just as productive, like climbing Mont Pieter Both and pissing into the wind.

How symbolic. The story of the dodo ends where it began, on this very island. Life imitates cheap art. Like the Xerox copy of the Xerox copy of a bad novel. I never expected to find dodos still alive here (this is the one place they would have been noticed). I still can't believe Alma Chandler Gudger Molière could have lived here twenty-five years and not *know* about the dodo, never set foot inside the Port Louis Museum, where they have skeletons and a stuffed replica the size of your little brother.

After Annie Mae ran off, the Gudger family found itself prospering in a time the rest of the country was going to hell. It was 1929. Gudger delved into politics again and backed a man who knew a man who worked for Theodore "Sure Two-Handed Sword of God" Bilbo, who had connections everywhere. Who introduced him to Huey "Kingfish" Long just after that gentleman lost the Louisiana governor's election one of the times. Gudger stumped around Mississippi, getting up steam for Long's Share the Wealth plan, even before it had a name.

The upshot was that the Long machine in Louisiana knew a rabble-rouser when it saw one, and invited Gudger to move to the Sportsman's Paradise, with his family, all expenses paid, and start working for the Kingfish at the unbelievable salary of $62.50 a week. Which prospect was like turning a hog loose under a persimmon tree, and before you could say Backwoods Messiah, the Gudger clan was on its way to the land of pelicans, graft, and Mardi Gras.

Almost. But I'll get to that.

Daddy Gudger prospered all out of proportion to his abilities, but many men did that during the Depression. First a little, thence to more, he rose in bureaucratic (and political) circles of the state, dying rich and well hated with his fingers in *all* the pies.

Alma Chandler Gudger became a debutante (she says Robert Penn Warren put her in his book) and met and married Jean Carl Molière, only heir to rice, indigo, and sugarcane growers. They had a happy wedded life, moving first to the West Indies, later to Mauritius, where the family sugarcane holdings were among the largest on the island. Jean Carl died in 1959. Alma was his only survivor.

So local family makes good. Poor sharecropping Mississippi people turn out to have a father dying with a smile on his face, and two daughters who between them own a large portion of the planet.

I open the envelope before me. Ms. Alma Molière had listened politely to my story (the university had called ahead and arranged an introduction through the director of the Port Louis Museum, who knew Ms. Molière socially) and told me what she could remember. Then she sent a servant out to one of the storehouses (large as a duplex) and he and two others came back with boxes of clippings, scrapbooks, and family photos.

"I haven't looked at any of this since we left St. Thomas," she said. "Let's go through it together."

Most of it was about the rise of Citizen Gudger.

"There's not many pictures of us before we came to Louisiana. We were so frightfully poor then, hardly anyone we knew had a camera. Oh, look. Here's one of Annie Mae. I thought I threw all those out after Momma died."

This is the photograph. It must have been taken about 1927. Annie Mae is wearing some unrecognizable piece of clothing that approximates a dress. She leans on a hoe, smiling a snaggle-toothed smile. She looks to be ten or eleven. Her eyes are half hidden by the shadow of the brim of a gapped straw hat she wears. The earth she is standing in barefoot has been newly turned. Behind her is one corner of the house, and the barn beyond has its upper hay windows open. Out-of-focus people are at work there.

A few feet behind her, a huge male dodo is pecking at something on the ground. The front two-thirds of it shows, back to the stupid wings and the edge of the upcurved tail feathers. One foot is in the photo, having just scratched at something, possibly an earthworm, in the new-plowed clods. Judging by its darkness, it is the gray, or Mauritius, dodo.

The photograph is not very good, one of those three-and-a-half-by-five-inch jobs box cameras used to take. Already I can see this one, and the blowup of the dodo, taking up a double-page spread in *S.A.* Alma told me that around then they were down to six or seven of the ugly chickens, two whites, the rest gray-brown.

Besides this photo, two clippings are in the package, one from the Bruce *Banner-Times*, the other from the Oxford newspaper; both are columns by the same woman dealing with "Doings in Water Valley." Both mention the Gudger family's moving from the area to seek its fortune in the swampy state to the west, and tell how they will be missed. Then there's a yellowed clipping from the front page of the Oxford paper with a small story about the Gudger Family Farewell Party in Water Valley the Sunday before (dated October 19, 1929).

There's a handbill in the package, advertising the Gudger Family Farewell Party, Sunday Oct. 15, 1929 Come One Come All. The people in Louisiana who sent expense money to move Daddy Gudger must have overestimated the costs by an exponential factor. I said as much.

"No," Alma Molière said. "There was a lot, but it wouldn't have made any difference. Daddy Gudger was like Thomas Wolfe and knew a shining golden opportunity when he saw one. Win, lose, or draw, he was never coming back *there* again. He would have thrown some kind of soiree whether there had been money for it or not. Besides, people were much more sociable then, you mustn't forget."

I asked her how many people came.

"Four or five hundred," she said. "There's some pictures here somewhere." We searched awhile, then we found them.

Another thirty minutes to my flight. I'm not worried sitting here. I'm the only passenger, and the pilot is sitting at the table next to mine talking to an RAF man. Life is much slower and nicer on these colonial islands. You mustn't forget.

I look at the other two photos in the package. One is of some men playing horseshoes and washer toss, while kids, dogs, and women look on. It was evidently taken from the east end of the house looking west. Everyone must have had to walk the last mile to the old Gudger place. Other groups of people stand talking. Some men, in shirtsleeves and suspenders, stand with their heads thrown back, a snappy story, no doubt, just told. One girl looks directly at the camera from close up, shyly, her finger in her mouth. She's about five. It looks like any snapshot of a family reunion which could have been taken anywhere, anytime. Only the clothing marks it as backwoods 1920s.

Courtney will get his money's worth. I'll write the article, make phone calls, plan the talk-show tour to coincide with publication. Then I'll get some rest. I'll be a normal person again—get a degree, spend my time wading through jungles after animals that will all be dead in another twenty years, anyway.

Who cares? The whole thing will be just another media event, just this year's Big Deal. It'll be nice getting normal again. I can read books, see movies, wash my clothes at the laundromat, listen to Jonathan Richman on the stereo. I can study and become an authority on some minor matter or other.

I can go to museums and see all the wonderful dead things there.

"That's the memory picture," said Alma. "They always took them at big things like this, back in those days. Everybody who was there would line up and pose for the camera. Only we couldn't fit everybody in. So we had two made. This is the one with us in it."

The house is dwarfed by people. All sizes, shapes, dress, and age. Kids and dogs in front, women next, then men at the back. The only exceptions are the bearded patriarchs seated toward the front with the children—men whose eyes face the camera but whose heads are still ringing with something Nathan Bedford Forrest said to them one time on a smoke-filled field. This photograph is from another age. You can recognize Daddy and Mrs. Gudger if you've seen their photographs before. Alma pointed herself out to me.

But the reason I took the photograph is in the foreground. Tables have been built out of sawhorses, with doors and boards nailed across them. They extend the entire width of the photograph. They are covered with food, more food than you can imagine.

"We started cooking three days before. So did the neighbors. Everybody brought something," said Alma.

It's like an entire Safeway had been cooked and set out to cool. Hams, quarters of beef, chickens by the tubful, quail in mounds, rabbit, butter beans by the bushel, yams, Irish potatoes, an acre of corn, eggplants, peas, turnip greens, butter in five-pound molds, cornbread and biscuits, gallon cans of molasses, red-eye gravy by the pot.

And five huge birds—twice as big as turkeys, legs capped as for Thanksgiving, drumsticks the size of Schwarzenegger's biceps, whole-roasted, lying on their backs on platters large as cocktail tables.

The people in the crowd sure look hungry.

"We ate for days," said Alma.

I already have the title for the *Scientific American* article. It's going to be called "The Dodo Is *Still* Dead."

What Did 1980 Mean?

Algis Budrys

I first met A. J. Budrys (as he was then known) in Chicago in 1962. We were on a panel together: "Politics in Science Fiction." The thrust of my pitch on that panel was that there wasn't any politics in science fiction. SF authors didn't understand politics; they peopled the universe with straw men, or angels, or constructs of some kind, who mostly did what their authors wanted them to do. Those were, after all, the days when a John W. Campbell editorial was certain to inspire half a dozen stories illustrating his point. . . .

But even then I had to make an exception for Budrys, who did seem to understand something of the nature of man. Then, when he began to speak of his experiences during the Danzig Crisis before World War II, I realized that he had considerably more political experience than do most SF writers. One point that he made: When dealing with political leaders, it is impossible to be objective.

I had also greatly liked his novel The Falling Torch; *and someone had told me that it was partly autobiographical, being based on Budrys's experiences as part of the Lithuanian government in exile.*

If you look on official U.S. government maps of Eastern Europe, you will see an interesting detail: Portions of what everyone thinks is the Soviet Union are marked off with international boundary symbols, and there is a fine-print notation that the United States does not recognize the incorporation of Latvia, Lithuania, and Estonia into the Soviet Union. If you've never noticed this, don't be surprised; few citizens know it. Certainly I didn't until one day I went to a consular reception, and met the Vice-Consul of Estonia.

"Aha," I said. "I'd heard the Baltic Republics had governments in exile. . . ." I stopped because the consul was shaking his head. "No?"

"Not precisely," he said, and proceeded to explain. There are no governments in exile—but the United States does recognize diplomats appointed by the last legal governments of Latvia, Lithuania, and Estonia, and even pays them from funds deposited in the U.S. before the Russian occupation of the Baltic Republics as part of the deal Stalin made with Hitler. (In 1938, Hitler got about half of Poland; the Soviet Union got the other half, along with the three Baltic Republics. When World War II ended, the Soviets gave back part of the Polish territory they'd taken, but continued to occupy the Republics, claiming that they were a historical part of the Soviet Union.)

The situation remains to this day: The U.S. recognizes ambassadors and consuls and other diplomatic and consular officials of the Baltic Republics, as do a few other nations. For a while the exile communities kept their hopes up through activities organized around these officers, and there were considerable political efforts to get the U.S. to recognize replacements when the original appointees died; now, though, it's almost impossible to find anyone willing to take the posts, and the Baltic ethnic communities are more and more assimilated into the U.S.

A. J. Budrys grew up during the days when there was still hope.

Algis Budrys published his first science fiction in the early fifties and quickly became one of SF's leading figures. His works are literate, compassionate, and easy to read.

Science fiction writers agree on very little, but an astonishing number of them agree that Algis Budrys is the profession's leading reviewer/critic.

Science fiction proceeds in steps, or seems to.

In hindsight, we identify a "Golden Age" of what was then called Modern Science Fiction, from roughly 1939 to 1949. Noting that John W. Campbell, Jr., its founder, assumed editorial direction of *Astounding Stories* in 1937, we can postdate a period beginning with Hugo Gernsback in 1929 in which "scientifiction" evolved, via "superscience stories," into "science fiction." In 1950 we find *Galaxy* magazine emerging; by 1951 a whole new generation of writers, prominently featuring Robert Sheckley, Philip K. Dick, William Tenn, James Blish, Cyril Kornbluth, and Frederik Pohl, is well on its way to creating what might be called Post-Modernist science fiction. The early 1960s saw the flourishing of England's "New Wave," which has since become everyone's wave, just as each previous one of these short generations still flourishes within us.

Compressed over a mere fifty-five years, the evolution from Gernsback's pioneering *Amazing Stories* leaves us with many active practitioners whose preferred mode of science fiction writing was formed generations ago. But generations do occur; they can be and are frequently pointed out.

Not only are there steps, but there seems to be some rough correlation with decades. In truth it's very rough—closer examination reveals that major new writers and new views of the field appear continuously. But subjectively there does seem to be some little something to it. There are peaks, they do come in approximately ten-year and five-year intervals, and seem to represent the culminations of major changes followed by periods of assimilation.

But are they changes in the nature of the field, or simply changes in the community consensus on what is the "best" mode for science fiction? Our field is notable for the extent and energy of its soul-searchings—this essay being today's example—and perhaps what we detect in hindsight, looking back at mileposts that were invisible while we were passing them, are fashions that we are diligently creating after the fact because they are required to sustain our current fashion. We presume, for instance, that there is progress—that science fiction is moving toward more perfect forms, and that this progression can be linked to chronological markers. Inherent in such a view is the assumption that some ultimate ideal form of science fiction is located somewhere in the future. If that assumption did not exist, we would have no basis for feeling we could detect arrival at each next higher set of standards intervening between the science fiction that is and the science fiction that will be.

All right, then each year represents some increment of progress, and each year, as if to nod to this supposition, we have our annual Science Fiction Writers of America awards ceremony at which the Nebulas are conferred. The awards culminate a year-long process of recommendation and nomination by the membership at large and, granting that no annual award is totally foolproof, and certainly not proof against the occasional jape, over the years have reflected good community judgment as borne out by immediate and then continuing popularity with readers.

Gathered in this volume are some winners and finalists of the 1980 awards. This year thus meant something in our suppositional journey toward perfection. What? Can we deduce the ultimate shape of perfection from the shape of what we can see today? Bearing in mind that we are also at the culmination of ten years leading up to the decade of 1981, there should be something particularly revelatory to see, assuming there is something to look toward. What, then, did 1980 mean? Let us try this case.

I would like to speak almost entirely in terms of novels. They are what most of the public sees most. In the days when periodicals were the preeminent science fiction medium, occasional major short stories were what could be readily seen to be revolutionizing the community view of the field. They still do, but not as obviously. Books—meaning novels, most of the time—are what carry the flag at the head of the parade. And did 1980's novels in fact reflect the last year of some evolution that can now be studied and perhaps identified as an aspect of the ideal?

We could begin quite plausibly. For one thing, 1971–1980 was the Women's Decade, with all that that implies. A majority of the important new novelists were female, representing an unprecedented situation when one considers that for many years it had been politic for women SF writers to hide behind nominally male bylines, and even so, there had not been all that many of them. More important in the long view, in which an author's sex should not automatically either disparage or recommend, what science fiction gained was a demonstration that the total range of possible protagonists and world-views had not hitherto been fully explored.

This is the sort of modal lesson that science fiction seems to be having to learn, and which does account for evolutions within it. They are literary in a technical sense, since they open additional scope to all writers in the field. But they are not necessarily signs of qualitative improvement, since they do not disable minimally proficient writers from writing just as unproficiently in the new mode.

Something else, perhaps related to the influx of hitherto suppressed orientations, seems to have culminated in 1980, perhaps as the logical outcome of an undoubted 1970s phenomenon:

Among the most frequently discussed novels of 1980 were

Thomas M. Disch's *On Wings of Song,* Joan Vinge's *The Snow Queen,* Robert Silverberg's *Lord Valentine's Castle,* Gregory Benford's *Timescape,* and Gene Wolfe's *The Shadow of the Torturer,* as well as John Varley's *Wizard* and Alfred Bester's *Golem 100.* All were very carefully created books by important writers new and old. And, diverse though they otherwise are, they have a common feature. Each has a strongly mystical bent.

This is expressed in characteristic ways. Benford, a physicist, finds wonder and majesty in the workings of a rational universe—but he finds them to an extent not seen since the days when Arthur C. Clarke, with novels such as *Childhood's End,* stood conspicuously alone in that regard. Bester, a frank entertainer, finds it a little tongue-in-cheek—but he finds it, and when he does, the laughter dies. Silverberg's protagonist is like unto an Oriental god, with a god's adventures set in the province of a goddess, for all that it contains enough pumps and valves to satisfy most mechanicians. And those are the writers one would most expect to find writing what would have been called "straight" science fiction in the 1970s. For the rest, it's Joan Vinge, oddly enough, who produced a book most reminiscent of Isaac Asimov or Frank Herbert, but even there the overtones arise from Aeschylus, not from Herodotus.

The Shadow of the Torturer would have been a notable event in any literary history of science fiction from any perspective; it's a work of uncommon textures and powers, and only the first of four in Wolfe's "Book of the New Sun" tetralogy, which has already produced an equally effective second volume. But where it seems most in place in 1980 is in its conveyance of the feeling that human lives are affected by forces that, if ultimately knowable, are not totally knowable by routes commonly thought of as "scientific." The year 1980 was also one in which even casual observers might be struck by the frequency with which any number of commentators found occasion to quote Arthur C. Clarke's remark that any sufficiently advanced technology is indistinguishable from magic. Something was definitely in the air.

It was, after all, the year in which Robert A. Heinlein—the apotheosized central figure of the Golden Age of classical science fiction—published *The Number of the Beast*, a novel whose workings are made possible by the proposition that John Carter's Barsoom and the Land of Oz, and the universes of prominent Golden Age writers, including those in earlier works by Heinlein, are as real and as attainable by technological means as any *Viking* lander site.

It was, in short, a year in which Frederik Pohl's *Beyond the Blue Event Horizon*, sequel to his recent Nebula-winning *Gateway*, stood out in terms of mode; it was the only noteworthy Post-Modernist novel, lone representative of what had until quite recently been the most frequent, most orthodox approach.

So it would seem reasonable to propose that "science fiction" had become something else—that a very long process, of which the late-1970s outburst of heroic fantasy novels had been an indication, was resulting in a reevaluation of what "science fiction" writers wanted to create and what "science fiction" readers wanted to partake of. This was the year, as we shall see, in which the term "speculative fiction" became increasingly useful as a proposed meaning for those ambiguous letters, SF; in which it was possible for critics and commentators, with myself frankly among them, to assert that there was one "speculative fiction," that its writers were drawn first to speculation and then to particular modes of speculation, and that what we had called science fiction, as distinguished from what we had called fantasy, were essentially commercial marketing labels for two coeval branches of "SF," and only coincidentally, perhaps inaccurately, descriptive terms.

Perhaps this is so. Perhaps. If it is, perhaps it will not be so forever.

But before we go on toward that, 1980 was also the year in

which *TriQuarterly*, one of the last surviving influential "little" magazines, published by Northwestern University, chose to devote an entire issue to SF—new SF, by contemporary authors, as distinguished from what we in the SF community have come to expect from academe, i.e., a freight of taxonomic and otherwise "literary" papers by academics, most of them unacquainted either with the field's commercial circumstances or with the writing of SF, or any other fiction. What distinguished *TriQuarterly* #49 was that it reprinted nothing by Wells or even Ray Bradbury or Walter M. Miller, Jr.; it compiled stories roughly representative of the field as it is—if any one issue of any magazine can do that—rather than as it was in 1975 or 1965. Furthermore, it obtained the services of longtime SF fan and editor David Hartwell to do this, thus giving the community the chance to represent itself, something academe has virtually never done before. Michael Swanwick's Nebula-nominated story, "Ginungagap," is from that issue.

I don't wish to belabor that point too far. Furthermore, there *was* an essay stating a critical and historical overview, and while it, too, was from inside the community, I wrote it. Therefore, I'm hardly qualified to appraise its worth. I can report its effect on academicians from a dozen separate places, who took it seriously and unpatronizingly, as they similarly took the issue as a whole. The important thing, I think, is that *today's* SF—or at least the SF of mid-1980—was invited to stand on its own merits in a place where such opportunities have been extremely rare in the past. And from this one might argue that some long process—which began when Hugo Gernsback created commercial pulp-magazine SF as a separate and distinct entity, and thus created a separate corpus of writers—that process had come to a point of parity at which persons normally accustomed only to "mainstream" literature were willing to give its results a fair shake.

Whether all of us would find that desirable or not is beside the point. I was interested mainly in discovering whether it was possible, and I suspect that such an attitude is the broad middle position most community members would take. The appearance of the issue represents a potential major change. Whether it represents an improvement is a separate and, at this juncture, an irrelevant question. The question I would like to continue to speak to here is whether it represents an actual change, or whether it simply emphasizes something that has always been true but not stressed.

There has been, as many are aware, a long and fruitless attempt to define "science fiction" as a descriptive term. Everyone has foundered, usually in an attempt to include the words "future" and/or "science" without adding cumbersome qualifiers to exclude contemporary novels about science and/or technology, or political or religious tracts without speculative content that set themselves in "tomorrow" in order to "prove" the *inevitability* of their dogmas.

In some circles, it's become a cocksure fashion to declare there's no need for a definition, since we all know what we mean by "science fiction," and it is whatever we are pointing to when we say those words. If we cling to that cop-out, at the very least we have no beef when our work is treated as identical with the writings of occultists and UFOlogists. Even if we simply do not commit ourselves to a search for what we are, and say nothing on the point, we have no right to the severe consequent pain some of us secretly cherish so ingeniously, for we have failed ourselves.

It may be tolerable to have it that way. But let us suppose it's not, and go on.

A definition is possible, if we shift the ground a little by first defining speculative fiction as *fiction made more relevant by social extrapolation*—by setting characters and their actions in realities not known to have existed, for all that they may have only one point of difference. Then fantasy can be defined as that form of speculative fiction in which the differences are brought about magically, and science fiction as that form in which the differences are brought about techno-logically. Between those two benchmarks, there would be room for an entire spectrum of stories combining some of both elements, as in the "science fantasies" once so beloved of C. L. Moore, Leigh Brackett, and *Planet Stories*, with spaceships bringing adventurers to exotic planets where magic was operating effectively. Similarly, in a "heroic fantasy," we would find sorcerers making systematic—i.e., "scientific"—use of their catalogue of spells and their phar-macopoeia of potions to baffle the clangorous hero's nihilis-tic assaults.

This middle ground—or some portion of this middle ground—would appear to have been inhabited by a clear ma-jority of all the Nebula-nominated novels of 1980, and by almost all the shorter-length stories. And it would be fair to say that this represents the culmination of several mutually reinforcing trends.

Those trends, to recapitulate, taken in no special order of importance, are an evolution of the field back toward "main-stream" literary techniques and concerns by newer writers heavily influenced by college literature courses not enjoyed by most of their predecessors; an evolution toward fantasy for its own sake, leading to increased contamination of those writers who would never have been much aware of it, if it were not so potent a force in the same market as science fiction; a reflection, perhaps, of a general disillusionment with "science" on the part of articulate young people making up the pool from which most new speculative fiction writers emerge; the heavy shift toward a population of female writ-ers who, by reason of cultural prejudices operating in their adolescence, were never encouraged to become sciento-philes, but were pressed to develop "intuition," with all its magical implications.

It remains to be seen—it very much remains to be seen—whether this is good or bad for what we used to call "science fiction" when we pointed to work from the "science fiction" community of commercial writers, and it remains to be seen whether this is good or bad for literature as a whole. But that's a rarefied question doomed to plague researchers of a generation hence. The fact is that it has happened and, like all the other things that happen in the arts, will be assimilated by the survivors, and will find its public. In hindsight it will appear not completely seamless, but distinctly evolutionary nevertheless.

But there will be one major difficulty, and from this nearby viewpoint I'll be blessed if I can predict how it will be rationalized in extended hindsight. Any consequent attempt to picture "science fiction"—*the* science fiction we mean when we point to it—as withering away essentially in response to a general social diminution of 1920s–1940s technological optimism, is hopelessly impaired by a set of facts in contradiction: the evolution of such bellwether media as *Analog* magazine and its spiritual sibling, *Omni*, into vehicles of continued, close concern with developments in contemporary technology. Nor is the picture clarified by the undeniable attractiveness and power of Robert L. Forward's *Dragon's Egg*, Hal Clement's *The Nitrogen Fix*, or the 1980 work of such other writers as James P. Hogan, all of whom obviously are fueled by an elan that comports badly with any assertion that the "classical" science fiction story is obsolete. If anything, although this is not much discussed among those *au courant* in the field, it is flourishing as never before.

As *never* before. John W. Campbell, Jr., in the 1950s—when the world at large became sufficiently aware of SF to begin asking what it was—was wont to claim a predictive function for science fiction, and to pretend that the bulk of what he had published was tied directly to contemporary technology. Observation discloses that throughout his editorial career, from its beginning, he published any number of stories—some of them good stories, some of them still pointed to as quintessential of the Golden Age—that were as much scientific nonsense then as they are now. Nonsense by first intention, visibly nonsense, and often stories in which any science extrapolation took a distinctly minor back seat to what Campbell and his writers did take care to include in almost all ASF work: social philosophy.

What is being done in *Astounding*'s successor, *Analog*, is to actually deliver the sort of fiction Campbell liked to say he was publishing. What is being done at *Omni*, with its enormous resources, is to produce a magazine with some fiction in it, eclectically selected, but with the bulk of its wordage reflecting factual content aimed straight at the audience for *Analog*-type fiction—that is, people who read those media for the futurological content, assigning a very weak second place to "mainstream" literary values.

The two specific individuals to credit for this are Ben Bova, successor to Campbell at *Analog*, and Stanley Schmidt, who became its editor when Bova moved on to *Omni*. The year 1980 was the one in which Bova's policies became fully operative at his magazine, and was also the year in which Schmidt could visibly be seen to be firmly guiding *Analog*. The two men are very much alike in their editorial philosophies, and very much part of a generation that, in its youth, would have formed its ideas of the right and proper from what Campbell said.

Nor would they be alone. Despite the great prestige of the two periodicals, we are long past the days when any one or two editors could even attempt to dictate the shape and nature of science fiction. But they would be able to refine and point up a trend within an audience of persons similarly inclined. Among other features of what we are seeing in the vitality of what might be called "science-science fiction" is the influence not of Campbell's editorial practices toward his writers but of his utterances to his audience in the 1950s and 1960s.

So what we have are two strong trends that might be antithetical in practice, and do produce fiction that falls, roughly,

into two distinct categories. Individual writers in our community might, since we are a breed much concerned with the
right and proper, display individual instances of violent disagreement with the practices of writers at the "opposite" end
of the spectrum. But there is no theoretical reason that this
has to be generally so. I venture a guess that what will happen is what always happens in a basically vigorous creative
form: Creators will emerge who can demonstrate an ability
to combine the most viable aspects of both forms, producing
yet another kind of SF that will become, for the space of five
or ten years, *the* SF.

Not that there is ever *an* SF. Side by side with the latest
mode we always have the vigorous and able practitioners of
older modes, and these acquire their own direct adherents
who operate without respect to current fashion. This year
saw a singular demonstration of this frequent phenomenon
in SF; 1980 produced both *Dragon's Egg*—clearly the closest
thing we have ever seen to a new writer's approaching parity
with Hal Clement on that master's home ground—and *The
Nitrogen Fix*, the best new Clement novel in years.

Theoretically there is no reason a writer might not produce
work that is both hard-edged scientophilic and yet done in a
manner most would recognize as following the best accepted
"literary" models. Examples have been occurring all along,
and in hindsight from some future generation will be praised
for their "pioneering" as well as their intrinsic merit. Benford
and Varley, to name two, are writers whose professional expertise in physics and biology, respectively, has in no way
circumscribed their impulses to produce something more
than the plain tale told plainly. Swanwick's "Ginungagap,"
too, represents a far-from-rare occurrence of the story that
assumes that science does work and will persist as a major
activity in the future, and goes into some detail on that score,
yet is essentially a very human story about a rather par-
ticularized individual, without going too far in the direction
of the sort of sentimentalized, easy romanticism that was
once frequent in the field, and was frequently brought for-

ward in naive response to outside remarks that SF was a passionless and mechanistic form.

Mind you, there is no indication that we have ever gained anything permanent by giving a damn what any outsider thought or said. Nor is there any rational reason why any given mode of SF is intrinsically more desirable than any other. A piece of craftsmanship, or a work of art—and two different observers might call the same creation one or the other, to God knows what useful end—stands or falls on what it does for its audience, not on how it matches up to some template (as Harlan Ellison once again demonstrated when his latest short-story collection, *Shatterday*, appeared in the waning days of the year; Ellison is good to bring up in connection with discussions of work that doesn't give a damn for preconceptions).

But certain constraints do operate. The writer who sees SF as primarily futurological might very well couch the didactics of his exposition in the simplest workable story—the good old yarn of overt conflict unwound in chronological progression, fraught with contentions between cardboard characters distinguished from each other only by their funny hats. And from that point of view, why not? There are plenty of readers who ask no more, and are dismayed when they get more, since it interferes with the clarity of what both they and the writer feel the story is really about.

Conversely there are obviously many writers today in SF who first want to tell a subtle and intricate story, perhaps with considerable attention to prose and style, and only then search for some passable science rationale to justify their speculations. And they, too, fiind sympathetic readers.

It does seem that nurture accounts for the existence of these two extremes. The futurologist tends to have graduated from science curricula while his contemporary across the campus was absorbing the liberal-arts literature courses and the undergraduate sessions in "creative writing." There is otherwise no class difference between the two, except that cultural pressures tended to place a higher proportion of females in the latter group. But within each group there is a great variation in basic intelligence—or at least in ability to present appearances relating to intellectual skills—and in sensitivity, emotional intensity, grammar and spelling skills, and the ability to synthesize fictions from observed data. Nature—basic inclination—may have accounted for the initial impulse to set out on one path or the other, but twenty years of schooling account for the rest. And we must never forget that they all have one common bond: a lifetime of devotion to SF, which, for all its variations, is a literature with a single fundamental difference from all other literatures.

That difference—to recast some of my earlier assertions—lies in the SF writer's and the SF reader's willingness to deal with stories in which things are as they never were and might never be—in which, when all else is stripped away, the humanity of the characters is evaluated not by how well they follow known role models but by how well they continue to express human verities in the face of circumstances never encountered by humans. I said "willingness." I should have said "determination," for the impulse toward SF is no passive thing; with few exceptions, it early segregates the SF person from all others, and there, I think, is where Nature struck soon and deeply. In comparison with that unifying bond, all our various intramural variations from each other are much less significant.

What does that mean to us when we try to evaluate the "worth" and "meaning" of some segment of SF's progression—as, for instance, the segment represented within the year 1980?

It means, among other things, that a piece of work like Larry Niven's *The Ringworld Engineers* cannot stand alone, and would not stand alone even if it were not a sequel to his highly popular *Ringworld* of ten years earlier. First of all, it's a story—an account of the adventures of a cast of sentient beings interacting with an alien artifact. But it's not, in truth, an "alien" artifact—it's an artifact of the mind of a human author, who in turn drew his mental picture of it from the work of Freeman Dyson, a human scientist.

Consider the implications here. There is an inevitable unique flavor within the reader's emotional and intellectual reaction to the sheer grandeur and the underpinning intellect of the alien engineers who built an artificial world encircling their sun. That flavor is lent by a parallel consciousness that the "futuristic" grandeur derives from the speculations of two contemporary humans; to be awed by the exotic Ring-world is to celebrate the scope of a unique feature of human thought. This unique feature, demonstrated by SF writers and impossible to writers of either historical or contemporary stories, is the confirmation that there will be *something* beyond what was or is.

Definitions that require SF to be set in the future are all failures, because observation reveals a great deal of recognizable SF that is set in the past or in some corner of the contemporary world. But a definition of SF that requires a *promise* of a future—either direct or by the implication that wonders in the past augur for wonders forever—would stand unassailable at least on that point. It is possible for the reader restricted to mundane fiction to believe that what is known is all there ever will be; that we may have reached certain limits, either self-imposed or derived from some outside cause. The comforts or fears of the SF reader are on a much larger and perhaps also qualitatively different scale. We do not know if we will ever encounter an alien Ring-world, or whether we will ever build one for ourselves. But we do know that we have already thought of it; that, among other aspects of Dyson's and Niven's concept, we have already made provision for the "unthinkably" distant day when our sun begins to wane . . . when, taking into account other provisions that have already been made, our sun*s* begin to wane.

So—as other critics, notably England's Christopher Priest,

have recently been pointing out—the predilection for SF is in some sense a reflection of a faith: a nonliterary experience, occurring concurrently with the act of reading.

If that is so, then there cannot be *an* SF, and there cannot be particular virtue in holding out craftsmanship as superior to artistry—even given the unlikely accomplishment of being able to identify those qualities objectively—and conversely there is no way in SF of establishing "art," or what outside criteria would call art, as in any way superior to "craft." Those purely literary aspects of writing become merely grace notes; even the apparent clumsiness of the most straightforward piece of didactics is, in that sense, a grace note.

It's very good for this discussion that Niven published *The Ringworld Engineers* when he did, because by outside standards he is not a deft or subtle writer, and thus has provided 1980 with the perfect example for my present purposes. He is one of the most ebullient and ingenious SF writers, an indubitable ornament to the field. Furthermore, he is uniquely qualified to be held out as a personification of other points made here, because, thanks to family inheritance, he has never been constrained to do anything at all simply for the sake of financial security. Whatever fascinates him does so for its own sake alone, and whatever he chooses to do is done entirely from inclination. He does no work from a need to pay the rent, and produces no public expressions intended in some way to modify the disapproval or approval of supervisors. He is not in search of tenure, except perhaps within SF. And the existence of this single example suffices to cast severe doubt on glib outside appraisals of his kind of writing as being a mechanistic resultant of marketplace pressures. The marketplace conditions SF, yes; this does not mean that it constrains it. By and large, SF does what it does because it wants to, which is exactly the same freedom and on exactly the same plane as those which, by outside standards, "ennoble" noncommercial work.

No sensible person would deny that over the years there

has been a great deal of SF written unfeelingly for crass motives, just as there has been in all other forms of literature. Including the noncommercial ones in which gentlemen and ladies of advanced sensitivity and of the utmost concern for art have been observed battling like harpies for the temporal rewards of prestige. But as this year's Nebula nominees and winners generally reflect, community opinion has very much shifted toward conscious approval for the more ambitious effort, as distinguished from the mere piece of proficiency.

What do I mean by "more ambitious"? Well, in the first place I mean, of course, the current community definition of "ambition," i.e., the striving toward worth. And observation discloses that for the past decade, worth has become increasingly synonymous with social concern. One might say John Campbell has been coming out of the closet.

What do I mean by "proficiency"? I mean prose skill, whether defined as general literature would define it or as defined by the overwhelmingly popular mass writers since the invention of the high-speed press and swift national sales distribution—the seamlessly expert manipulation of the classic pulp plot rather badly expressed. The latter is what some call craft, and what I have come to call an evolved ritual art.

What do I mean by the reference to John Campbell? I mean what I meant some pages ago: that the common constant in what was named "modern" science fiction in 1946 was not science but social philosophy made discussable by the introduction of suppositional technological impacts. This is what has always been the single thing truly organic to "science fiction" since 1818 and *Frankenstein*, and if we broaden "technology" the little distance required for the term to also subsume "magic" and "politics," then it is the root of all SF since the days of dynastic Egypt, at the very least. Even such "hard science" stories as *Dragon's Egg* speak most directly to the question, "What sort of society could evolve under these incredible physical conditions?"; and even James P. Hogan's *Thrice in Time* is fascinating briefly for its ingenious time-communication mechanism, but is fascinating throughout as we follow the social changes created by the successive messages from the future.

These various attributes were well represented in 1980 by Norman Spinrad's *Song from the Stars.* Consider:

(1) It was recommended for the Nebula despite the fact that by conventional standards Spinrad is more polemicist than prosaist. (This is a quality he has displayed throughout his prominent career, including the days when his work was appearing in *New Worlds*, a medium with high literary pretensions. It is an attribute he shares with Norman Mailer. Those who criticize SF for containing "crudities" might reflect on whether they are not advocating a double standard.)

(2) It is heavily freighted with suppositional technology; the entire thrust of the plot is to involve the protagonists of its post-Holocaust milieu in escalating contretemps with the struggle between Black Science and its White—that is, ecologically conformal—counterequivalent. Yet its central question, despite Spinrad's very real desire to suppose ecologically clean machines that might really be built, is not "Isn't this a fascinating approach to transportation?" It is "How will it change the world?"

(3) Despite the fact that it is not in outstandingly "good" prose, that it seems to concern itself with hardware to an extent one might think repugnant to many contemporary SF practitioners, and concerns itself with hardware that strikes jaundice into the eyes of contemporary SF practitioners with a bent for engineering, a great many members of the Science Fiction Writers of America managed to agree that it was well worth nominating for the award as the year's best SF novel.

If we suppose that the Nebula is defined as an expression of community preferences in its given year—and that is essentially what it is—then community preferences in 1980 were broad enough to include a number of nominations that ran counter to the apparent principal tenor of their time in a number of ways. If I am right in my basic assumptions, what this demonstrates is that while particular modes of writing SF may predominate at any given time, the constant underlying target of speculative fiction—the thing it is "for" in the eyes of many of its practitioners and readers—is social speculation. What may change every ten years or so, and then build up to the next change, is a detectable preference for one mode as distinguished from all others, but not to the effective exclusion of all the others. What is certainly true is that SF has once again affirmed its acceptance of broad variety. At the present time we have reached a stage in which a majority of active practitioners are heavily imbued with the standards applied to general literature in liberal-arts curricula. Certainly the signatures of what is considered best in general literature appear frequently in contemporary SF, executed fully as well as they are in general literature by contemporaneous writers. But when the SFWA membership—as distinguished from the prominent SF community articulators—is polled for its opinion on the year's best, there is a spontaneous tacit recognition that general literary standards fall short of encompassing all the excellences possible to SF. As distinguished from what the "community" can be heard saying throughout the year, a larger SF community now takes this opportunity to express another set of tenets, or rather, a set of larger tenets that subsume those most frequently expressed by those who, for one reason or another, feel enabled to report constantly on the latest and most striking. Commonly accepted literary values are recognized, to be sure, but the same persons who are capable of recognizing them are also capable of recognizing "good" qualities that are not founded on what is considered good in literature.

Leaving aside how infuriating this must be to partisans of one extreme, while offering less than total comfort to partisans of the other, it is exactly how things should be if SF is intrinsically different from all other literary forms, just as those forms have basic differences from each other, differences that occur at a level far deeper than mere genre trappings. It may be that all literatures in some way find their ultimate validation not in their prose but in the social hopes they sustain. It may be; in SF, the possibility seems more clearly visible than anywhere else.

SF is not intrinsically just another sort of Western or crime story, for all that we can point to plenty of wordage in SF media where it is difficult to find anything more than that. SF *is* a separate literature. A *separate* literature. A separate *literature*, for all that it shares with all other literatures the property of containing much that is inept, cynical, or short-fallen. The Nebula Awards and this anthology are testimony that nevertheless it is capable of unique and effective literary attainments.

And that, in a sense, is what 1980 meant. Every year means something, and perhaps in the end every year then proves to have meant the same thing. But at least once a year we are reminded of it.

Secrets of the Heart

Charles L. Grant

When Poul Anderson was president of SFWA, the job nearly killed him; and when his term was over, there were few suckers willing to take the position. Eventually I was talked into it; I accepted on the condition that we radically transform the organization. A committee of ex-presidents and other interested people was created, and thorough reforms proposed.

One needed reform was to hire an executive secretary, someone to do much of the routine work that was killing off presidents. Unfortunately, SFWA had almost no money.

"That's all right," one of the ex-presidents said. "We'll find some starving young writer and pay him enough to let him live in a garret."

And lo, the search began. We wanted someone articulate, willing to work for beans, and living in New York; and oddly enough there were quite a few candidates for the post. Unfortunately, although all were articulate and eager and willing to work for slave wages, none lived in New York City; and we really did need someone able to get to Publishers' Row and pound on desks once in a while.

Then Charles L. Grant applied. He lived in New Jersey, only an hour by bus from Manhattan. He'd been writing for several years, but his career was interrupted by military service, and he was starting over. He wanted to learn more about the writing business, and Lord knows, the SFWA post would teach him that.

So I hired him. I admit I had reservations. Charlie seemed so mild-mannered and polite that I wondered if he would be tough enough to survive in a post that a lot of young writers thought they could fill better than he could. I needn't have worried. Charles L. Grant turned out to be the best thing that ever happened to SFWA, and the organization probably wouldn't still exist if he hadn't put in his years of service.

Since that time, Charles Grant has become well known. He edits Shadows, *a series of horror-story anthologies, and has almost singlehandedly revived the quiet, understated horror story.*

"Secrets of the Heart" is typical Grant, and it's no surprise that it was nominated for a Nebula.

I'm all alone in the house now, a terrible thing to be when you're used to so many people being around all the time. But the others are gone. A few of them, of course, were able to leave when I changed my mind. A few. And some of them died. A lot of them. It wasn't my fault, though. All I did was show them. Once they understood, they all asked me and I showed them. That's when some of them started to leave, and that's when they started to die. It wasn't my fault. I didn't kill them and I didn't make them leave. They asked me. They really did. They . . . asked me.

The last time there were five of them. They came to the house late at night in the rain. The biggest man, with water all dripping down his big funny hat, smiled at me when I answered the door and he said: "Excuse me, little girl, but

would you mind if I used your mother's telephone? We had a
slight accident back there around the bend a ways, and I
have to get us a tow truck."

My mother always told me never to let strangers into the
house, and my father did too, but these people were trying so
hard to smile in the rain and shivering and wet and cold. So I
let them all in and they stood around in the foyer like little
wet puppies while I took the big man back into the kitchen
and showed him the telephone on the wall.

"My name is Miriam," I said then. "Your friends aren't
very happy."

"George Braddock," the man said, holding out his hand
after he took off his glove. We shook hands just like big
people do, and he took off his hat to show me his hair, all
white and thick, just like a big cat's. "I'm afraid they're
rather shaken, Miriam," he said then. "Our car slid off the
road into a ditch. We've been driving a long way, I got us
lost, and I wasn't really paying much attention to my driving.
Let that be a lesson to you." He reached for the phone, then
looked over at the stove. "Say, would your mother mind if
we brewed up some coffee or tea or something? We sure
don't want to catch our death at this late date."

I didn't mind at all. I put on the kettle and took a jar out of
the pantry, and while he was talking to someone at a gas
station—and he was very, very unhappy at what he was hearing, I could tell—put cups out on the table and went to the
front again.

"George says you should come into the kitchen and have
coffee or tea or something else that's warm," I said. They
didn't seem to want to move right away until a lady yanked
off her bright blue kerchief—so much hair, and so bright and
yellow!—and said, "Well, I'm not going to wait around for
pneumonia, folks. Come on. This is dumb standing around
here."

The others, another lady and two men, followed her
slowly, smiling at me as they passed and being very careful

indeed not to drip too much water on the hall carpet. When they got to the kitchen, they took off their coats and hats and sat down and waited for the water to boil.

"Of all the damn luck," George said, coming away from the phone and sitting with his friends. "The man says there must be a hundred accidents out there today. He can't possibly get out here for a couple of hours, at the earliest. Looks like we're stuck for a while."

"Beautiful," the yellow lady said. "That's just beautiful."

"Oh, come on, Helen, it isn't all that bad. We could be still sitting in the car, you know." He smiled at me standing by the stove. "And at least Miriam here is a gracious hostess. We certainly won't freeze to death."

I wanted to say something then, but I didn't. Instead I just smiled and brushed my hair away from my face. The woman called Helen shrugged and looked like she'd decided it wasn't so bad in here after all, and the other woman, who was a lot older, like George, took a pack of cigarettes from her purse and lit one. When she saw that there weren't any ash trays, she dropped her match on the saucer I gave her.

"Where's your mother, Miriam?" one of the other men said. "Don't tell me you're all alone in this big old house."

"Bill, for Pete's sake, don't start," said Helen, taking a cigarette from the older lady's pack and tapping it on the back of her hand.

"Why don't you leave him alone," the white-haired lady said. Then she turned around in her chair and looked at me. She didn't like children. "I'm Mrs. Braddock. Are you alone, dear?"

"Yes, ma'am," I said. Always be polite: that's the first rule.

"She must work," said Bill, and the other man nodded. Bill was Helen's husband. The other man was a friend. Nobody liked anybody very much. I knew that.

The kettle started to whistle then, and I picked it up and poured the water into the cups. Mrs. George said that she wanted to help me, but I said that I could do it all right; and, besides, it wouldn't be good for her arm to hold the kettle because it was heavy.

"Whatever are you talking about, child?" Mrs. George said, though her smile really wasn't very nice.

"It's the way you hold it," Bill said, pointing. "Anyone can tell your shoulder's bothering you again."

"Nonsense," she said, but she put her hand in her lap and gave me a funny look.

They talked a lot after that, and I kind of walked around the kitchen listening and not listening, and then I went out to the front where I looked through the windows at the road, waiting for the tow truck that was supposed to be coming in a couple of hours. They were very polite people, I guess, but they weren't very nice. I knew that. And I don't like people who aren't very nice.

Then I touched a finger to the windowpane—it was cold and slippery, like ice—and knew that someone was standing behind me. I turned around and it was Bill. He had a funny look on his face and he bent down to push my hair back behind my ear. It felt funny. I shook my head, and it fell back where it belonged. "You should have a barrette," he said, real soft. I stepped away from him and he followed me, grinning now and rubbing one hand over his stomach. "You're afraid of me, huh? I don't see why. I guess it's because we're strangers, right? You don't know me and I don't know you."

"I know you," I said.

He kind of blinked at me then and looked around as if there was someone standing in the corner. Then he straightened, smiled funny at me, and went back to the kitchen. Then I saw Helen standing in the doorway to the hall, just looking at me. I smiled and she turned away. Their friend, whose name was Calvin, was looking in all the cupboards for something to eat. George told him it wasn't right he should do that, but Calvin only told him to keep quiet for a change, there's only a kid around and who's going to know the difference anyway for one lousy box of crackers. A moment later he found some cookies, and I guess they weren't really that mad at him because they all drank and ate, and then George got up and came out to where I was standing and said, "Miriam, I've looked over my options here, if you know what I mean, and I think I'd better take a quick walk down the road and see if I can spot the tow truck coming. I certainly don't want to have to impose on you any longer than I have to."

I shook my head.

He frowned at me a little and went to the front door. It wouldn't open. He looked over his shoulder at me. "Why did you lock it?"

I walked away from him into the kitchen. The others weren't looking at me, though, they were looking at George, who walked past them without saying anything and tried the back door that led into the yard where I used to play. He couldn't open it.

"Well, for heaven's sake," Mrs. George said. She made a funny little laugh. "It's just like in the movies."

I didn't think so, but I didn't say a word. I just stood by the stove and watched them getting more and more nervous, though they were trying not to show it, while Mr. George went around trying to open doors and windows. Helen was getting madder and madder finally, and she was glaring at me; Calvin had finished the box of cookies and he was asleep, his head resting on his arms on the table, his mouth open and snoring. Bill wouldn't look at me.

"All right, Miriam, this has gone far enough," Mr. George said. He was standing in the doorway, his hat still in one hand. "What does your father have here, some kind of electronic lock on everything? Well, it doesn't matter. I think you ought to let us go now." He reached for the telephone.

"It doesn't work," I said.

He tried it anyway, because hardly anyone ever believes me when I tell them things. Like the time a long time back when I told my father and my mother that they were always thinking bad things about me because I was their only child and they had me while they were very young and now they were wishing they didn't have me at all. *Prancing around here like you own the goddamned place, like you were some kind of princess, like you own your mother and I lock, stock, and barrel! Well, I'm sick of it, Miriam! And by God, I'm sick as hell of you, damnit!* That's what he said; and though my mother told him to stop saying things like that in front of the child, I knew she was thinking the same thing. I knew that. So I told them that if that's the way they wanted it, then they didn't have to stay in my country anymore. That's when my father spanked me. It was the last thing he did before I decided that being a princess was fun.

That's the second rule.

When Mrs. George, who was smoking again and blowing the smoke up at the ceiling, told her husband to sit down, he did. And I could see that he was trying very hard not to yell at me the way he wanted to. "Now, Miriam," he said, very softly, with a little serious frown that made tracks across his forehead. "Miriam, I—"

"You're in my country now," I told him. "You have to do what I tell you."

That's the last rule.

"Oh, it's a game!" Helen said with a clap of her hands. It was like glass breaking.

"Great," said Bill. "So how do you keep score?"

They all laughed at that except me. I didn't like them making fun of my country, or of me. As a princess, like it says in the books in my father's study, I had to show them that I was the ruler. So I decided that Calvin should stop snoring. Nobody noticed it right away, but they did after a while, and then they pushed me out of the way like I didn't belong there and began making lots of silly noises about finding a doctor and why is his face so horrid looking, and George was yelling that the damned telephone doesn't work, and Helen was crying quietly, and Bill just stood away from them and looked at me.

I didn't like him watching me.

They put Calvin down on the floor, and George tried giving him mouth-to-mouth something, but that didn't work and he was breathing real hard when he finally sat up. Then they carried him into the living room and put him on the couch, and George put his coat over his face. Then he saw me standing in the foyer looking at them, and he said, "Do you mind, young lady? This man is dead."

I knew that.

Then George decided he wasn't going to be nice anymore. He looked out at the storm for a while—shivering once when lightning came down and lit up his face—and then told the others that it looked like they were stuck for the night, if all the options were considered. He looked around a bit and, without even asking me, said they should go upstairs and see if there were any bedrooms they could use.

"But . . . but what about the child's parents?" Mrs. George said, though I knew she wasn't as calm as she looked. "Good Lord, George, they could walk in at any moment. What would they think?" She looked at Helen, who was pale and trembling. "Don't you see, Helen? They could walk right in on us."

"No," I said, and I could see George believing me. He put his arm around his wife's shoulders and led her to the stairs. Helen followed him, and Bill came last. They went up and I waited for a while, listening to them walking around and turning on all the lights and talking in loud whispers. Pretty soon they were laughing. And pretty soon I could hear Helen making funny high noises and slapping Bill, who was laughing so hard he was nearly choking. It wasn't right, though, that they should be so silly when their friend was dead on my couch. And it wasn't right that they weren't playing the game the way they were supposed to. I guess I should have expected it because none of the others did either, but I always hope that this time is going to be the different time. So I waited until it got real quiet—except for the rain scratching at the house—and then I went to my room, which is next to the kitchen beyond the pantry, and I sat on my bed and thought for a very long time; and when I was done with all my thinking, I decided that I knew all about George and Mrs. George and Bill and Helen.

And once I decided what I knew, I decided not to change my mind.

And the next day it was still raining, though the lightning and the thunder had gone away for a while. Everybody came downstairs and went into the kitchen. I could hear George cursing a lot, but the others were very quiet. They were scared. Bill tried to get out a window in the night, but the glass wouldn't break. They were very scared. And they all almost jumped up to the ceiling when I came out of my room to watch them and see if they'd learned to play the game right.

"Miriam . . ." George started to say something else, but he looked awfully old all of a sudden and only shook his head. Mrs. George's eyes were very red. Helen hadn't combed her yellow hair. Bill, who was standing by the stove, folded his arms across his chest and said, "I've read about people like you, you know. Telepaths, telekinetics—you do all those things with your mind, right?"

I knew what he was talking about. And he was wrong. Some things not even a book can tell you about.

"Bill—"

"For heaven's sake, Eleanor, don't say 'nonsense' again. We tried everything. It may be crazy, but it's the kid."

"I'm a *princess*," I told him. I was getting very mad.

"Her folks probably ditched her," Helen said, suddenly being very brave when her husband didn't fall down after I'd glared at him.

"No," I said. "They just wouldn't play by the rules."

"Wonderful," Bill said. "So what did you do, banish them from your creepy little kingdom here?"

"No," I said. "I just looked up in one of my books about princesses and queens. Sometimes I'm a fairy princess, you know, and sometimes I'm the Queen of the May. I was the Red Queen that day," and I made a slow chopping move with my left hand.

"Oh, my God," said Mrs. George, and suddenly they were all running out of the room, and George was hammering on the door while Helen was throwing things at the windows to break them. Only Bill stayed behind, still standing there, still looking at me.

"Why?" he said. I guess he was very brave.

"Because you're not nice people," I said, walking over so that the table would be between him and me. "You do bad things to little girls like me, your wife gets into accidents all the time because she drinks, Mrs. George takes things from stores when nobody's looking, and—"

"All right, all right," he said. He was pale. His hands kept pushing into his hair. "So what are you going to do, kill us all?"

"I wouldn't do that," I said, really mad that he would think that of his princess. "When you're nice again, you can go."

There was the sound of breaking vases and chair legs snapping and Mrs. George crying loud and high.

"And what about you," Bill said then. "Are you little miss perfect all the time?"

"I'm the princess."

Someone was kicking at the door.

"Does that make killing people nice?" He looked like he was going to kneel down then, but he changed his mind. "Listen, Miriam, we all have secrets of the heart, you know. Some of them are bad, some of them aren't so bad. But like I said, nobody's perfect. Not me. And, Miriam, you aren't either, princess or not."

I frowned, trying not to listen to him, but he said it again and walked out of the room like I wasn't even there. I thought about it as fast as I could. I hurried around the table and saw him look back at me, then reach out for the door. When it opened they all ran out like they were really and truly afraid of me. I didn't mind, though. They would find their car and it would be all right, but a minute later I decided that there would be this really big truck. . . .

I shrugged and went back to my room.

I knew all those words Bill was saying about me, but there was more to it and he didn't know that. He didn't know everything I could do when I thought about it and decided it would be so. And after a while I decided that I wasn't really a princess. I never had been a princess. This house wasn't my country, and the people who came here and weren't nice and didn't leave . . . I wasn't their ruler. I had broken one of my own rules.

That's not nice.

That's my secret of the heart.

So I looked in the mirror and tried to decide how old I was. But I looked the same as I did when my mother and father didn't do what I told them. That was a long time ago. I think there weren't any cars or planes then, but I don't remember. And I'm still the same. My hair never grew and my face never got skinny and I never got tall and . . . and . . . so I went into the living room and, like George always said, I tried to review my options, which I think means choices.

I could follow my own rules, of course, and punish myself—but if I did that then I wouldn't *be* any longer, and I didn't want to be dead.

Or I could be very nice all the time and everyone who came to my house would like me after that and no one would have bad things in their heads or hearts about anyone else. That would make things very easy for me.

Or I could go outside and make the whole world my country and be nice and no one would have to worry about anything ever again because I would be . . .

I don't know if I have any more choices. But I *do* know

what I can do—Bill said it was telesomethings, and the books
on the shelves say it's magic. He knows he's wrong, of course
. . . now. He knows that a telesomebody can't make something out of the summer air, the autumn wind. I can. So I
guess it's magic.

That's nice.

And since the house is empty, I decided it was time to go
outside for a change. But when I opened the door and took a
good look at my world . . . well, magic may be a nice word
and it may be nice to have it, but all of a sudden I was very
sure of one thing—that being nice all the time can be very,
very boring.

I *know* that . . . now.

Appendixes

NEBULA AWARDS

Winners of the Nebula Award are chosen by the members of Science Fiction Writers of America. Throughout the year SFWA members nominate the best science fiction stories and novels as they are published. At the end of the year there is a final nominating ballot and then an awards ballot to determine the winners. Nebula Trophies are presented at the annual Nebula Awards Banquets, held simultaneously each spring in New York City, New Orleans, and on the West Coast.

Science Fiction Writers of America was organized in 1965, and the first Nebula Awards were made in the spring of 1966 for 1965 publications. The Nebula Trophy was designed by Judith Ann Lawrence (Mrs. James Blish) from a sketch by Kate Wilhelm (Mrs. Damon Knight). Each trophy is an individual creation, consisting of a block of lucite four inches square by nine inches high, into which a spiral nebula made of metallic glitter and a specimen of rock crystal are embedded.

The categories in which the awards are made have remained unchanged from the beginning. In the following list, the year given is the year of publication for the winning entries.

NEBULA AWARDS 1980

Novel

Winner: *Timescape* by Gregory Benford (Simon & Schuster)

Runners-up: *Beyond the Blue Event Horizon* by Frederik Pohl (Del Rey)

        The Orphan by Robert Stallman (Pocket Books)

        Mockingbird by Walter Tevis (Doubleday)

        The Snow Queen by Joan Vinge (Dial Press)

        The Shadow of the Torturer by Gene Wolfe (Simon & Schuster)

Novella

Winner: "The Unicorn Tapestry" by Suzy McKee Charnas (*New Dimensions 11*)

Runners-up: "There Beneath the Silky Trees and Whelmed in Deeper Gulphs Than Me" by Avram Davidson (*Other Worlds 2*)

        "Lost Dorsai" by Gordon R. Dickson (*Destinies*)

        "The Brave Little Toaster" by Thomas M. Disch (*The Magazine of Fantasy and Science Fiction*)

        "Dangerous Games" by Marta Randall (*The Magazine of Fantasy and Science Fiction*)

        "The Autopsy" by Michael Shea (*The Magazine of Fantasy and Science Fiction*)

Novelette

Winner: "The Ugly Chickens" by Howard Waldrop (*Universe 10*)

Runners-up: "Strata" by Edward Bryant (*The Magazine of Fantasy and Science Fiction*)

        "The Way Station" by Stephen King

(The Magazine of Fantasy and Science Fiction)
"The Feast of St. Janis" by Michael Swanwick (*New Dimensions 11*)
"Ginungagap" by Michael Swanwick (*TriQuarterly*)
"Beatnik Bayou" by John Varley (*New Voices III*)

Short Story

Winner: "Grotto of the Dancing Deer" by Clifford D. Simak (*Analog*)

Runners-up: "Secrets of the Heart" by Charles L. Grant (*The Magazine of Fantasy and Science Fiction*)
"Window" by Bob Leman (*The Magazine of Fantasy and Science Fiction*)
"War Beneath the Tree" by Gene Wolfe (*Omni*)

SIXTEEN YEARS OF NEBULA WINNERS

1965

Best Novel: *Dune* by Frank Herbert

Best Novella: "The Saliva Tree" by Brian W. Aldiss / "He Who Shapes" by Roger Zelazny } tie

Best Novelette: "The Doors of His Face, the Lamps of His Mouth" by Roger Zelazny

Best Short Story: " 'Repent, Harlequin!' Said the Ticktockman" by Harlan Ellison

1966

Best Novel: *Flowers for Algernon* by Daniel Keyes / *Babel-17* by Samuel R. Delany } tie

Best Novella: "The Last Castle" by Jack Vance

Best Novelette: "Call Him Lord" by Gordon R. Dickson

Best Short Story: "The Secret Place" by Richard Mc-
                         Kenna

1967
Best Novel: *The Einstein Intersection* by Samuel R.
                         Delany
Best Novella: "Behold the Man" by Michael Moor-
                         cock
Best Novelette: "Gonna Roll the Bones" by Fritz Leiber
Best Short Story: "Aye, and Gomorrah" by Samuel R.
                         Delany

1968
Best Novel: *Rite of Passage* by Alexei Panshin
Best Novella: "Dragonrider" by Anne McCaffrey
Best Novelette: "Mother to the World" by Richard
                         Wilson
Best Short Story: "The Planners" by Kate Wilhelm

1969
Best Novel: *The Left Hand of Darkness* by Ursula K.
                         Le Guin
Best Novella: "A Boy and His Dog" by Harlan Ellison
Best Novelette: "Time Considered as a Helix of Semi-
                         Precious Stones" by Samuel R. De-
                         lany
Best Short Story: "Passengers" by Robert Silverberg

1970
Best Novel: *Ringworld* by Larry Niven
Best Novella: "Ill Met in Lankhmar" by Fritz Leiber
Best Novelette: "Slow Sculpture" by Theodore Sturgeon
Best Short Story: No Award

1971
Best Novel: *A Time of Changes* by Robert Silverberg
Best Novella: "The Missing Man" by Katherine Mac-
                         Lean
Best Novelette: "The Queen of Air and Darkness" by
                         Poul Anderson

Best Short Story: "Good News from the Vatican" by Robert Silverberg

1972
Best Novel: *The Gods Themselves* by Isaac Asimov
Best Novella:. "A Meeting with Medusa" by Arthur C. Clarke
Best Novelette: "Goat Song" by Poul Anderson
Best Short Story: "When It Changed" by Joanna Russ

1973
Best Novel: *Rendezvous with Rama* by Arthur C. Clarke
Best Novella: "The Death of Doctor Island" by Gene Wolfe
Best Novelette: "Of Mist, and Grass, and Sand" by Vonda N. McIntyre
Best Short Story: "Love Is the Plan, the Plan Is Death" by James Tiptree, Jr.
Best Dramatic Presentation: *Soylent Green*

1974
Best Novel: *The Dispossessed* by Ursula K. Le Guin
Best Novella: "Born with the Dead" by Robert Silverberg
Best Novelette: "If the Stars Are Gods" by Gordon Eklund and Gregory Benford
Best Short Story: "The Day Before the Revolution" by Ursula K. Le Guin
Best Dramatic Presentation: *Sleeper*
Grand Master Award: Robert A. Heinlein

1975
Best Novel: *The Forever War* by Joe Haldeman
Best Novella: "Home Is the Hangman" by Roger Zelazny
Best Novelette: "San Diego Lightfoot Sue" by Tom Reamy

Best Short Story: "Catch That Zeppelin!" by Fritz Leiber
Best Dramatic Presen-
  tation: *Young Frankenstein*
Grand Master Award: Jack Williamson

1976
Best Novel: *Man Plus* by Frederik Pohl
Best Novella: "Houston, Houston, Do You Read?"
    by James Tiptree, Jr.
Best Novelette: "The Bicentennial Man" by Isaac
    Asimov
Best Short Story: "A Crowd of Shadows" by Charles L.
    Grant
Best Dramatic Presen-
  tation: No Award
Grand Master Award: Clifford D. Simak

1977
Best Novel: *Gateway* by Frederik Pohl
Best Novella: "Stardance" by Spider and Jeanne Rob-
    inson
Best Novelette: "The Screwfly Solution" by Racoona
    Sheldon
Best Short Story: "Jeffty Is Five" by Harlan Ellison
Special Award: *Star Wars*

1978
Best Novel: *Dreamsnake* by Vonda N. McIntyre
Best Novella: "The Persistence of Vision" by John
    Varley
Best Novelette: "A Glow of Candles, A Unicorn's Eye"
    by Charles L. Grant
Best Short Story: "Stone" by Edward Bryant
Grand Master Award: L. Sprague de Camp

1979
Best Novel: *The Fountains of Paradise* by Arthur C.
    Clarke
Best Novella: "Enemy Mine" by Barry Longyear
Best Novelette   "Sandkings" by George R. R. Martin
Best Short Story: "giANTS" by Edward Bryant

HUGO AWARDS

The Science Fiction Achievement Awards, a title rarely used, became known as "Hugo Awards" shortly after the first such awards were presented, in 1953. The "Hugo" is named after Hugo Gernsback, author, editor, and publisher, and one of the fathers of modern science fiction. The Hugo Awards have been made annually since 1955, and their winners are determined by popular vote. Because each year's awards have been under the administration of a different group—that year's committee in charge of the year's World Science Fiction Convention—rules and categories have fluctuated from year to year, sometimes drastically.

From their inception, the Hugo Awards have been made for amateur as well as professional achievement. Thus there are usually awards for Best Fanzine (the initiate's term for amateur magazine), Best Fan Writer, and Best Fan Artist, as well as awards for

* For the history of the awards and a detailed listing of Hugo winners and nominees in all categories, the reader is referred to *A History of the Hugo, Nebula and International Fantasy Awards*, published by Howard DeVore, 4705 Weddel Street, Dearborn, Michigan 48125. The book also contains a complete listing of Nebula Award nominees.

professional writing, for Best Professional Magazine (now Best Professional Editor), for Best Dramatic Presentation, and for Best Professional Artist. Only the more standardized awards for professional writing are listed here.* In recent years, voting on both the nominating and final ballot has been limited to those who have purchased memberships in the World Science Fiction Convention. The Hugo Trophy is a miniature rocketship poised for takeoff, though details of design and materials have varied from year to year. In the following list, the year given is the year of publication for the winning entries.

HUGO AWARDS 1980

Best Novel

Winner: *The Fountains of Paradise* by Arthur C. Clarke (Harcourt Brace Jovanovich)

Runners-up: *Harpist in the Wind* by Patricia McPhillip (Atheneum/Argo)

Jem by Frederik Pohl (St. Martin's)

On Wings of Song by Thomas M. Disch (St. Martin's)

Titan by John Varley (Berkley/Putnam)

Best Novella

Winner: "Enemy Mine" by Barry Longyear (*Isaac Asimov's Science Fiction Magazine*)

Runners-up: "The Battle of the Abaco Reefs" by Hilbert Schenck (*The Magazine of Fantasy and Science Fiction*)

"Ker-Plop" by Ted Reynolds (*Isaac Asimov's Science Fiction Magazine*)

"The Moon Goddess and the Son" by Donald Kingsbury (*Analog*)

"Songhouse" by Orson Scott Card (*Analog*)

Best Novelette

Winner: "Sandkings" by George R. R. Martin (*Omni*)

Runners-up: "Fireflood" by Vonda N. McIntyre (*The
                           Magazine of Fantasy and Science
                           Fiction*)
                           "Homecoming" by Barry Longyear
                           (*Isaac Asimov's Science Fiction Maga-
                           zine*)
                           "The Locusts" by Larry Niven and
                           Steve Barnes (*Analog*)
                           "Options" by John Varley (*Universe 9*)
                           "Palely Loitering" by Christopher Priest
                           (*The Magazine of Fantasy and Science
                           Fiction*)

Best Short Story
Winner: "The Way of Cross and Dragon" by
                           George R. R. Martin (*Omni*)
Runners-up: "Can These Bones Live?" by Ted Rey-
                           nolds (*Analog*)
                           "Daisy, in the Sun" by Connie Willis
                           (*Galileo*)
                           "giANTS" by Edward Bryant (*Analog*)
                           "Unaccompanied Sonata" by Orson
                           Scott Card (*Omni*)

Best Nonfiction Book
Winner: *The Science Fiction Encyclopedia* by Pe-
                           ter Nicholls (Doubleday)
Runners-up: *Barlowe's Guide to Extraterrestrials* by
                           Wayne D. Barlowe and Ian Summers
                           (Workman)
                           In Memory Yet Green by Isaac Asimov
                           (Doubleday)
                           The Language of the Night by Ursula K.
                           Le Guin and Susan Wood (Berkley/
                           Putnam)

TWENTY-SIX YEARS OF HUGO WINNERS
1953
Best Novel: *The Demolished Man* by Alfred Bester

1955
Best Novel: *They'd Rather Be Right* by Mark Clifton and Frank Riley

Best Novelette: "The Darfsteller" by Walter M. Miller

Best Short Story: "Allamagoosa" by Eric Frank Russell

1956
Best Novel: *Double Star* by Robert A. Heinlein

Best Novelette: "Exploration Team" by Murray Leinster

Best Short Story: "The Star" by Arthur C. Clarke

1957
Best American Professional Magazine: *Astounding*

1958
Best Novel: *The Big Time* by Fritz Leiber

Best Short Story: "Or All the Seas with Oysters" by Avram Davidson

1959
Best Novel: *A Case of Conscience* by James Blish

Best Novelette: "The Big Front Yard" by Clifford D. Simak

Best Short Story: "That Hell-Bound Train" by Robert Bloch

1960
Best Novel: *Starship Troopers* by Robert A. Heinlein

Best Short Fiction: "Flowers for Algernon" by Daniel Keyes

1961
Best Novel: *A Canticle for Leibowitz* by Walter M. Miller, Jr.

Best Short Fiction: "The Longest Voyage" by Poul Anderson

1962
Best Novel: *Stranger in a Strange Land* by Robert A. Heinlein

Best Short Fiction: "The Hothouse Series" by Brian W. Aldiss

1963
Best Novel: *The Man in the High Castle* by Philip K. Dick

Best Short Fiction: "The Dragon Masters" by Jack Vance

1964
Best Novel: *Here Gather the Stars* (*Way Station*) by Clifford D. Simak

Best Short Fiction: "No Truce with Kings" by Poul Anderson

1965
Best Novel: *The Wanderer* by Fritz Leiber

Best Short Story: "Soldier, Ask Not" by Gordon R. Dickson

1966
Best Novel: *...And Call Me Conrad* (*This Immortal*) by Roger Zelazny

Best Short Fiction: " 'Repent, Harlequin!' Said the Ticktockman" by Harlan Ellison

1967
Best Novel: *The Moon Is a Harsh Mistress* by Robert A. Heinlein

Best Novelette: "The Last Castle" by Jack Vance

Best Short Story: "Neutron Star" by Larry Niven

1968
Best Novel: *Lord of Light* by Roger Zelazny

Best Novella: "Riders of the Purple Wage" by Philip José Farmer
"Weyr Search" by Anne McCaffrey

Best Novelette: "Gonna Roll the Bones" by Fritz Leiber

Best Short Story: "I Have No Mouth and I Must Scream" by Harlan Ellison

1969

Best Novel:	*Stand on Zanzibar* by John Brunner
Best Novella:	"Nightwings" by Robert Silverberg
Best Novelette:	"The Sharing of Flesh" by Poul Anderson
Best Short Story:	"The Beast That Shouted Love at the Heart of the World" by Harlan Ellison

1970

Best Novel:	*The Left Hand of Darkness* by Ursula K. Le Guin
Best Novella:	"Ship of Shadows" by Fritz Leiber
Best Short Story:	"Time Considered as a Helix of Semi-Precious Stones" by Samuel R. Delany

1971

Best Novel:	*Ringworld* by Larry Niven
Best Novella:	"Ill Met in Lankhmar" by Fritz Leiber
Best Short Story:	"Slow Sculpture" by Theodore Sturgeon

1972

Best Novel:	*To Your Scattered Bodies Go* by Philip José Farmer
Best Novella:	"The Queen of Air and Darkness" by Poul Anderson
Best Short Story:	"Inconstant Moon" by Larry Niven

1973

Best Novel:	*The Gods Themselves* by Isaac Asimov
Best Novella:	"The Word for World is Forest" by Ursula K. Le Guin
Best Novelette:	"Goat Song" by Poul Anderson
Best Short Story:	"Eurema's Dam" by R. A. Lafferty ⎫ tie "The Meeting" by Frederik Pohl ⎭

1974

Best Novel:	*Rendezvous with Rama* by Arthur C. Clarke

Best Novella:	"The Girl Who Was Plugged In" by James Tiptree, Jr.
Best Novelette:	"The Deathbird" by Harlan Ellison
Best Short Story:	"The Ones Who Walk Away from Omelas" by Ursula K. Le Guin

1975

Best Novel:	*The Dispossessed* by Ursula K. Le Guin
Best Novella:	"A Song for Lya" by George R. R. Martin
Best Novelette:	"Adrift Just off the Islets of Langerhans: Latitude 38°54′N, Longitude 77°00′13″W" by Harlan Ellison
Best Short Story:	"The Hole Man" by Larry Niven

1976

Best Novel:	*The Forever War* by Joe Haldeman
Best Novella:	"Home Is the Hangman" by Roger Zelazny
Best Novelette:	"The Borderland of Sol" by Larry Niven
Best Short Story:	"Catch That Zeppelin!" by Fritz Leiber

1977

Best Novel:	*Where Late the Sweet Birds Sang* by Kate Wilhelm
Best Novella:	"By Any Other Name" by Spider Robinson "Houston, Houston, Do You Read?" by James Tiptree, Jr. } tie
Best Novelette:	"The Bicentennial Man" by Isaac Asimov
Best Short Story:	"Tricentennial" by Joe Haldeman

1978

Best Novel:	*Gateway* by Frederik Pohl
Best Novella:	"Stardance" by Spider and Jeanne Robinson
Best Novelette:	"Eyes of Amber" by Joan D. Vinge
Best Short Story:	"Jeffty Is Five" by Harlan Ellison

1979

Best Novel: *Dreamsnake* by Vonda N. McIntyre
Best Novella: "The Persistence of Vision" by John
                            Varley
Best Novelette: "Hunter's Moon" by Poul Anderson
Best Short Story: "Cassandra" by C. J. Cherryh